OLD GLORY SAGA

DESCENT

LOCKDOWN 2020

Book 1

by

Assaf Raz

Lockdown 2020
Book 1: Descent

Published by

Assaf Raz

Sioux Falls, South Dakota

www.TannerWashington.com

Copyright © 2023 by Assaf Raz

Artwork by Assaf Raz and Gwyneth
Graphic Design of Cover by Alyssa Noelle Coelho
Interior Design by Teagarden Designs

ALL RIGHTS RESERVED. No part of this book or its associated ancillary materials may be reproduced or transmitted in any form or by any means, electronic or mechanical, including photocopying, recording, or by any informational storage or retrieval system without permission from the publisher.

DISCLAIMER. *Lockdown 2020* is a work of fiction inspired by experiences both real and imagined. Any public institutions, events, cultures, or historical figures mentioned in the story are intended to serve as a backdrop to the characters and their actions, which are wholly imaginary. The author has made every effort to ensure the accuracy of the information within this book was correct at the time of publication. In all other respects, any resemblance to actual persons, living or dead, or actual events is entirely coincidental.

Paperback ISBN: 979-8-9894396-0-7

eBook ISBN: 979-8-9894396-1-4

Printed in the United States of America

www.TannerWashington.com

In the name of my beloved wife and children…

"Here I am."

CONTENTS

SARATOGA

We hiked up Mount Rushmore as the sun began its descent. Fighter jets screamed across the skies, far above the consistent thumping of choppers protecting one of the great architectural achievements of the twentieth century and a monument of freedom and those who have fought to establish and preserve it.

Even though Grandpa had shown me black-and-white photos from the days when they dug out the hidden vault, my heart pumped hard as I approached the opening in the rock. It was flanked by heavily-armed soldiers, who stood at attention when they saw me and my security detail arrive.

The Hall of Records had been carved into the granite rock of Mount Rushmore, just behind President Abraham Lincoln's sculpted face. I paused at the opening, extending my hand to feel the rough surface, dotted with the marks of the dynamite sticks.

As we advanced into the long tunnel, soldiers filed out, orphaning the numerous screens, computers, and other devices around the hall, left beeping and flashing.

"This way, Sir," a South Dakotan National Guard Colonel motioned me toward a desk with a red phone.

"Thank you," I replied as I circled the desk to sit on the folded chair.

The Colonel didn't leave, so I raised my eyes to meet his, granting him this moment.

"Happy Independence Day, Sir," he said.

His words struck me with brute force, sending my mind into an unexpected spin—images of the last few years nearly overwhelming my senses, evoking the broadest range of emotions. One breath was all it took to calm the waves of the immense joy of victory and the unbelievable suffering of defeat and loss.

"We've still got a few hours," I grumbled back, eyes glancing at the light blinking on the red phone.

"Yeah… we trust you to get us there," he replied with a salute before turning to walk back down the tunnel.

I watched him leave, haunted by the question that had plagued me for four years—the question that would finally be answered in the next few hours.

Where am I leading them?

Shifting my attention to the main screen, I reviewed the live map of the Black Hills surrounding the Mount. Units were marked either red or blue. Another screen showed the same situation unfolding across the nation.

The magnitude of this dangerous moment in history, and my role in it, seized my chest with an iron grip.

May God help us.

"The Second Civil War cannot start that easily..." His words echoed through my mind, ringing like an old, indestructible bell, and reminding me of my responsibility to the plan I'd developed, executed, and refined to bring us to this very moment in time.

"Or a revolution..." I whispered into the ether.

I reached for the phone and brought it up to my ear.

"Please hold for the President of the United States," stated a stern female voice.

DEAR READER

Do you recall what happened in 2020?

Where have you been?

What have you done?

Always Remember...

FINAL MOMENTS OF THE OLD WORLD

– Big Bear, CA –
Saturday, November 16, 2019

The snowballs flew hard and fast. Pressing Ari's head down below the small ice barrier we built before the fight started, I shouted, "Duck, Son!"

One struck my face with deadly precision, and I chuckled when I heard Nico's laughter echoing from behind their wall of snow. He'd always had good aim and his son, David, wasn't a bad shot either.

The white-clad battlefield stretched the length of my friend's cabin in Big Bear, where our plan for a boys' weekend away had been graced by a thick white blanket the day before we arrived.

Crouching behind our wall, I grinned at Ari's excited face and the long blond hair spilling from under his beanie. He was barely four-and-a-half years old, but the thick winter jacket made him look bigger and older.

"What do we do?" I asked him.

His mischievous green-gray eyes lit with fire as his small, gloved hands packed a tight ball of snow and quickly moved on to another.

"We fight, Dad! Just like you."

His reference drew both my smile and a subtle shudder.

"I'll jump out, and they'll throw at me. That's your chance. Got it?"

Ari nodded as I patted him on his back and then packed my ball.

"Come on!" Nico's challenge boomed.

I jumped to the right of our position to find Nico and David already standing and launching their balls. Nico's pounded my chest while David's whistled just past my ear.

"Now!" I yelled.

Ari stood up and threw his projectiles in succession as I added my own to the attack. Nico and David's cries reverberated as they got pummeled with direct hits.

When the snowball supply diminished, I motioned for Nico to join me.

"Keep playing, kids. We're taking a break."

David was Nico's youngest and the same age as Ari. He was built just like his father—small, brown, and strong.

Nico's wide grin said it all, but he had to say it anyway. "Got you good, Hermano! You're getting old on me."

"I'm only four years older than you," I muttered.

Nico laughed. "Still in my thirties, Tanner."

"For just a few more months," I admonished.

We watched the boys duke it out, both refusing to surrender. David was much faster, and Ari ducked again behind his decimated cover.

"Alfa under fire!" yelled Ari.

David giggled and Nico howled with joy, but time stopped for me as the words hit me like a semi-truck full of bad memories.

"Ari's gonna give up," smirked Nico.

As his words brought me back to focus, I noticed my son's face and the look I knew all too well.

"You know that his name means 'lion' in Hebrew."

I had barely finished my sentence when my boy roared and raced toward David. He crossed the yard, zigzagging away from at least two balls, and then launched straight into his little friend, bringing them down in a pile of puffy snow clothes and giggles.

A few hours later, our little miscreants were bathed, fed, and sound asleep. I washed the dishes and scanned the dark-forested landscape glistening in the moonlight while Nico straightened up the living room.

Everything finally clean and in place, I brought mugs of steaming black coffee to the dark wood dining table, eager to finally catch up with my friend in the homey cabin.

"It's a problem, Hermano..." Nico began venting about the state of our neighborhood. While we both resided in Venice Beach, he was a true local. One had to be born and raised there to be worthy of that title.

Suddenly, he stood up and opened the back door, "It's stuffy in here."

I didn't mention that it was probably the subject that was getting him heated.

The cold night breeze carried the refreshing scent of evergreens and pines into the space as Nico perched himself against the frame and scratched his stubbled face.

"What? Say it already." I knew he debated his words.

"You could have stopped it, Hermano. We were all for you, but you didn't do it."

Let it go, Brother!

Nico spoke of District-11's 2018 special election of Victoria Sabech, a lowly bureaucrat before her fast rise to councilwoman. This was still tricky terrain in our deep bond, but it was pointless then and now.

"I just don't get involved, Brother," I replied, keeping my unsatisfactory explanations to myself.

Nico nodded, his jaw tight and voice resigned. "I know. I know." Closing the door, he sat down across from me. "I'm going to run. I spoke with Cel and the family, and now is the time."

"What about your place?" I wondered how he would manage a campaign and their generational restaurant, Taco Libertad.

"She must be removed from office. She ain't good for the neighborhood, even if she's a local. Cel will cover for me. She can do it."

Something about his voice set me on edge. I knew Celeste was a hard-working woman. She had to be to be married to Nicolas Ramirez. But this didn't feel like something that she'd fully support.

"Vic...Victoria just doesn't do anything for us. Her ideas are not from here, and they don't work!" His tone was gruff and disappointed. "She fights with the police over any arrest, and she doesn't care that our streets are becoming one big homeless camp. I'm going to put a stop to this."

Heated again, he unbuttoned his flannel shirt just enough that it caught my attention. It was on his left chest—a cross with one lone tear in the middle. Nico had this tattoo done years back, just before he'd enlisted. I was there with him, and I would never forget his expression. He was in pain, but not because of the artist's needle.

We never spoke about it and when he felt my eyes, he buttoned up.

What's with him and Victoria?

I had always felt Nico's approach to her came from a more personal perspective and figured it had something to do with the fact that they grew up in the same place and their families knew each other. I just wished I had more details as I watched the upset crease his otherwise jovial face.

He was waiting on me to jump in and tussle, but I didn't want to. I could have told him that Venice has never been clean or safe through all my years there or that his opposition to Victoria sounded personal. But there was no point.

"Do you even care about the neighborhood?" he asked, his voice full of resentment and a small bit of hope.

Blindsided by his question and tone, I countered, "Why would you say that? My own family lives there."

"Shit, Man. You lived everywhere."

Something about his tone brought it back. Of all the places my mind could have called up, I remembered Bogotá. It wasn't an image or even a sound—just a sensation I hadn't had for a long time. *No.* I pressed hard and closed the lid.

"I get your passion, but I don't think this is good for you," I pivoted from my past.

Nico's face grew darker, and his fingers pressed against his empty coffee mug.

"I was scared that night. It was pitch black and Dmitri and I barely fit at the bottom."

Of course he would make this connection.

"We could hear the Taliban threatening the Qur-bans. I still can't believe the old man didn't give us up," he said. "Being in that hole in the desert has screwed with me. It didn't matter that you took us out of it. When I came back, I was still underground, drowning in alcohol."

I knew he still got those dreams, even if he didn't admit it.

"I remember, Brother."

"Yeah? Well, here is something that I never told you. Down in that well, I made a promise when I almost lost my sanity. I said that I'd get out and do something worth doing."

"You got a wife, kids, loving parents, and a family restaurant to lead. You helped many people to a better place, me included. You've done a lot worth doing."

Nico shook his head, visibly dissatisfied with my answer.

"I wish you'd seen it."

Still rattled by the memory, he stood and left the room.

I stared into my half-empty mug, wondering if it would ever be spoken out loud. Nico had *seen* me back in that sandy hell and, even though he had never said it, it was always in the subtext of his words.

"Almost nine years, Hermano." His voice was lighter when he re-entered the room, holding a full bottle of the finest brand of whiskey.

I got up to join him in our tradition as Nico opened the bottle, shot me a wicked smile, and began pouring the amber-colored liquid down the sink drain.

The bottle was about half empty, and I hoped we'd be onto a new subject when he chose to dig again.

"What happened to you? Why did you turn your back on the service?"

Very few people had the right to ask me such a question. Of those, only a fraction received an answer.

"Because nothing changed. No matter what I did."

It was all I could offer and Nico gave up on the interrogation. He was my best friend, after all.

The vibration was barely perceptible along the edge of my left ear. It was an upload. When I sensed the new sequence of short, strong undulations, I stood up and excused myself to make a call.

I walked out onto the back deck and closed the door tightly before initiating the security sequence on my smartphone and placing the earbud in my ear.

"How's the snow, Son?"

My father's deep voice carried so clearly, I was tempted to check around me. Instead, I looked up to the clear night sky, where I thought I saw the tiniest glittering light, and resisted the urge to wave. He didn't need the satellite to know where I was, but it gave him the picture.

"We're having fun—a boys' weekend."

"Where's Danielle and my granddaughter?" he asked.

The image of my wife drinking with her closest friend, both of them talking shit about their husbands was so vivid, it made me chuckle softly. I didn't need sophisticated spyware to know it was happening.

"She and Celeste are with the girls back home."

My father had never been keen on small talk, so I waited for him to deliver his news.

"We just had a hit on patient zero in Wuhan, China." His tone was suddenly strained. "Our friend looked over the data and confirmed that it's real."

His words both rattled my mind and registered as no surprise.

"How did you find out?"

There was a long pause before Jack answered, "We got a tip."

Something about his tone made me press again, "Verified?"

"It is now," he replied, and this time it was clear he didn't want to engage further on the topic.

"Is Zhang involved?" I asked.

"We don't know yet."

Jack didn't offer much beyond that, but I knew I had to press for more.

"What about Baker?"

"Again, we don't know," he answered.

My next question stuck in my throat as my mind raced to consider multiple future options. "Do we know who released it?"

There was a pause on the line before Jack took charge. "Our friend doesn't believe that it's us. The sample he brought was inert."

I knew my father was right, but it didn't make it any better. "Related to the elections?"

"Could be," said Jack. "It's no secret that none of them like Stone."

President Howard Stone was in the last year of his first term and wasn't known to be a friend of China or the US political establishment. I didn't follow politics much but had some general knowledge because the Republican president was openly despised in California, especially around my side of town.

"Would this be a reason to get in touch—"

"No," Jack interrupted. "We don't participate in politics. I made that mistake once, and it was enough."

I didn't know what he meant, but I also figured there was no chance of getting the details from him.

"Is that all?" I hoped he would say yes, for me and the world.

"Would you consider returning? This is a good time." It was something between a plea and a demand.

Old anger mixed with fresh fear and frustration, and I blurted, "I warned both of you! You just didn't want to listen!" His silence provoked an emotional outburst, "I'm done! I'll stay with my family."

When his tone changed, it reminded me of every time he had ever thought me to be wrong.

"Whatever you think about what happened, none of it matters now. You could regret this."

The subject dropped between us as our mutual silence lengthened uncomfortably. There was one more thing, though, that nagged at me.

"What was that last download?"

"We've been working on it for a while. It's nothing unless you come back."

When I got back in the cabin, Nico handed me a fresh mug, his eyes full of questions I couldn't answer, though my mind raced to make sense of everything my dad shared and plot my next steps.

I need to warn them, but...

"Like you said, Brother. Things are crazy out there. I guess I just want to make sure you're going to be okay..." I inquired about his restaurant's financial and operational stability, asked him about his emergency supplies, and confirmed our old arrangements in case of a crisis in LA.

Nico played along, but when his hand scratched his new beard for the third time, I knew he was holding back. And this time, I didn't ask.

"I know what I want from you for my birthday," he said.

Baffled, I failed to consider the implications.

"What?" I replied.

"I want to ask you one question, and you answer it fully."

Distracted, I gave him the best I could.

THE ROAD HOME

– LA County, CA –
Sunday, November 17, 2019

The Interstate 10 Freeway stretched west, its multiple lanes packed with endless cars, probably all headed to the beach after the recent rains.

There's always a price to pay for that much fun.

When Nico and David left early that morning to attend to family commitments, Ari had talked me into taking the sleds out one last time.

So fun.

Glancing in the rearview mirror at Ari's peaceful sleeping face, I felt the start of a smile and then a surge of anger.

His life is about to change, and there's nothing I can do about it.

As the geyser of worry flooded my mind, I looked around at the cars and the people inside them. Some were families, some just individuals—and no one had any idea what was coming.

Looking for a distraction, I turned on the radio.

A deep older voice filled the car with the trace of a British accent, or maybe it was Canadian. It took me a moment to gather that I was listening to Professor Miles Bach being interviewed by a host named Don. The topic was Bach's book, *Endarkenment*, which I'd never even heard of. Doing my best to catch up, I empathized with Don, who struggled to understand the text.

"Have you served, Don? I'm specifically asking about violence-based occupations."

Don's tone was full of surprise as he answered, "No."

"Then you would never truly understand *Endarkenment*. This is a mental reality beyond the fear of loss of life. Those who manage to access it do so during hazardous situations, expanding their options to act... unhindered by societal norms."

The host's voice was suddenly an octave higher when he challenged, "Are you saying that under extreme conditions, people can do what they want? What about morality?"

Bach's hard chuckle hovered between amusement and mockery.

"Morality of what?"

"Right and wrong. Surely you understand the difference, Professor."

The long pause made me wish I could see Bach's facial expression.

"I don't fault you, Don. You're probably a decent guy, trying your best to understand. But you don't stand a chance."

"Help me understand, Professor."

"I can't. You don't belong among those who have crossed the threshold of Good and Evil, hands bloodied in the making of human history. My book is meant for, devoted even, to them only. Like most of us, you have a sheltered life, free from making decisions that mean something beyond your immediate circle. This is a sphere outside of your perception. Be happy for that, as the price..."

My growing unease won over my curiosity, and I switched the channel before the Professor finished his sentiment. There was no time to reflect on my choice, as my interest was immediately captured by a news update.

A retired general, Jeremiah Tall, and his latest effort to clear his name was the lead story, and one I vaguely recalled first breaking around 2016. The General was supposed to be in the Stone administration but ran into trouble with the FBI. It was some jurisdiction issue over an incident with some soldiers from the base he commanded. Tall decided to stand by his troops and the FBI was eventually called in. His position in the administration no longer an option, he had retired instead and gone to war to protect his reputation, his family, and his country.

An unavoidable bump in the road stirred Ari and pulled my mind away from the radio, which I quickly turned off. In the silence, he settled back to whatever dreams a four-and-a-half-year-old enjoys.

Nothing I can do about it.

I kept looking back at him, reflecting on our very different childhood experiences. His was full of play and peace, and mine was full of discipline and violence.

"Society is a thin crust over a simmering volcano." The mantra Jack used often during my training resurfaced as I thought about the virus.

Maybe Nico was right.

US AGAINST THE WORLD

The 4th Street exit loomed ahead just as the sun was making its final descent. Ari's excitement amplified with every mile. He was clearly counting on his mom to coddle him after being "with Dad" over the weekend, and I watched in amusement.

He hasn't figured out that instead of receiving treats, he's about to be interrogated about how much sugar he had with me.

I took the overpass left toward South Santa Monica, a popular part of town filled with colorful beach homes and modern architecture. The real estate agent in me always reflected on the price differences between this city and Venice, as I crossed over into the next neighborhood.

I scanned both sides of the road as I entered Venice. Folks walked their dogs with kids in tow. Most were dressed as if it were the middle of summer, which was usual for this time of the year. Everywhere I looked, the faces expressed a carefree California vibe, quite fitting for a Sunday afternoon by the beach. In the back seat, Ari echoed the attitude as he softly sang along with one of his favorite tunes.

As the homeless camps near Rose Ave came into view, I remembered Nico's anger about the situation. Sensing a pit in my stomach, I didn't let myself dwell on it or the growing tension in my body.

The Venice Circle buzzed with activity ahead of us. It was a major thoroughfare for all traffic in the neighborhood. Just two blocks from the boardwalk, the Circle was full of well-established businesses, all catering to the fun and food demanded by an endless supply of visitors.

"Can we stop to eat at Nico's?" Ari's enthusiasm filled the car.

He asked about Taco Libertad, the Ramirez family restaurant that Nico's father, Roberto, had started decades ago when he first immigrated from Mexico.

"We were just with them, Ari. Besides, your mom would kill me if we ate out again."

I drove past the one-story building painted light blue with white awnings, its usual line of people outside its open front door, and the row of surfboards balanced on parked bikes.

Did you listen, Brother?

The pressure to protect those I love expanded and constricted my chest as I got closer to home and imagined facing my wife and all of her questions.

Our townhome was part of an eighteen-unit gated community arranged in a U-shape with an open court-yard only two blocks east of the Circle. I drove in slowly, taking in the details of the multicolored townhouses and waving to some of the neighbors out in their yards.

Danielle waited in the driveway with our three-month-old daughter, Leelee, strapped face-forward in a carrier. My wife's darker complexion and long black hair contrasted Lil's pale skin and short blond hair, but both gazed at me with the same piercing blue eyes.

Ari squirmed and struggled to get out of his car seat and Danielle intervened. I knew better than to expect or ask for attention before my son had his moment with his mamma.

As I opened the back trunk to retrieve our bags, Danielle arrived at my side, holding Ari's hand. We kissed, doing our best to avoid squishing Lil, who was squealing happily between us.

"Is everything okay?" asked Dani, her beautiful face tense with worry.

I can't hide anything from this woman.

I had known it from the moment we began dating.

"Later," I pleaded jokingly, and she played along.

Sitting between Lil's crib and Ari's bed, I closed the book and smiled at their serene faces. Overcome by my love for them and their innocence, I closed my eyes and savored the quiet moment.

When I opened them, I saw Danielle standing at the door, dressed in her workout garb, which did very little to hide her fit body. Shadows played on her face, and I could tell she somehow knew I needed that moment with the kids as she smiled and walked out of the room. It was my cue, and I followed after planting one last kiss and "I love you the most" on each of my angels.

Our three-floor townhouse was perfect for our small family. This top floor held all of the bedrooms, each with their own personality and flavor. Just down the stairs was the main level, which included the kitchen and living area. The wide open space looked and felt lived in with Ari's books and Lil's toys strewn about the modern, simple, and usually well-organized look that Dani worked hard to keep. The ground floor housed my studio, which generally served as my office.

And my last resort—

I pushed the thought away.

Reaching the end of the hallway, I saw Dani busy in the kitchen and appreciated her quick and graceful movements as I walked down the stairs.

"I missed you," I whispered as I shut off the sink and pulled her close, interrupting her tasking with a long kiss.

"Mmm... I missed you too. How was it?" she asked.

I gave her all the fun highlights while she finished the dishes, focusing on Ari and the roaring snowball fight. As I poured her a glass of red wine, her eyebrow went up—a clear sign that she knew something was up.

"He asked me to return," I offered as I handed her the glass.

She didn't look surprised. "It's been years. Why now? Something must have happened, right?"

They were valid questions, and I was debating my words when I noticed Ari quietly eavesdropping on us. He laughed and charged us when he realized he had been found out.

"I'll help mamma if you go!" he yelped as I caught him and carried him back to his room.

"You brat!" I grumbled with fake irritation.

After complimenting his ninja-like skill, I plopped him down in bed, covered him with his favorite blanket, and said goodnight.

Still undecided about what I should reveal, I joined Danielle on the balcony where she waited with her wine glass and a café-mocha for me—my favorite.

"Are you going back, Honey?" she asked, staring into the dark sky in between sips.

"No. It's not an option." I kissed her shoulder lightly.

She smiled, but something told me my response wasn't exactly what she was looking for.

"How are the dogs?" I quickly changed the subject to business.

Dani was an impressive trainer, and I enjoyed the stories about her quickly-growing clientele. When she finished, I added my drama with some of the properties I had listed. This was our usual weekly update session, and I was grateful for its triviality.

"How's Tami doing these days?"

This time, my eyebrow went up. She couldn't hide anything from me either.

She asked about my sister, who was six years younger and a Constitutional lawyer in Pierre, South Dakota. We had a solid relationship and I was always happy to speak with her, even though it wasn't often. I played along and updated her with the latest news I had about Tami's valiant efforts to balance the role of a new mom with work. Her son, Adam, was about Leelee's age. We laughed as we wondered out loud how Henry, Tami's computer engineer husband, had survived the last few months with a lawyer-turned-momma.

"And how's Chad? You spoken with him lately?"

Her eyes glinted, telling me this question was more loaded than the last. She knew about my perpetually rocky relationship with my baby brother.

"Last I checked, he was still writing for that wacko newspaper in Seattle. He's among his kind and good… for him."

"He's your brother, Tanner. He's just young and… full of ideas."

He's full of something, I agreed silently, frustration heating my skin.

My mom had always defended Chad, and that was enough for me.

"He's only nine years younger—your age—and he's still acting like an entitled toddler!"

She playfully retreated from the subject but stayed on point.

"We need to get to the Ranch again. It will be great for the kids and your parents."

A memory of Ari racing across the open green meadows made me smile. We had visited while Dani was pregnant with Lil.

"Yeah. We should go sometime when we can," I muttered.

"Don't you miss it, Baby? It's so beautiful there."

Her words were open doors I wished not to walk through—doors I never opened to discuss my lack of connection with our family's generational land. Dani was usually good at not pushing on the subject.

What are you up to, Woman?

"You know that I was just there for a moment in life." I referred to my short time on the Ranch right before I enlisted. Beyond that, there was just one other time I was there, which she knew nothing about.

She must have felt my unease, as she moved closer. With her head on my shoulder, she sighed.

"I guess I'm missing my family too... Maybe we can plan a trip to see them soon."

Fonder memories surfaced as I thought about her family's estate back in Israel, where she was born and raised.

Before I could respond, my phone buzzed. As I pulled it from my back pocket and saw the name Eli

Peled on the screen, Danielle's face betrayed she had known her father would reach out.

Ah, now I understand.

"I see you, Woman," I growled in jest before I kissed her and retreated down the stairs into my ground-level studio.

The door closed behind me before I turned on the light in the square-shaped open space I used for an office and "man cave." Surfboards on one side, rows of equipment shelves on the other, and my office at the back by the door. Sitting at my desk, I opened the phone to read Eli's message.

Once the encryption sequence ended, I found only two words, "Call me."

Unsurprised by my father-in-law's directness, I turned on the sound scrambler attached to the back of the desk and waited for the solid green light. Considering the level of encryption on both sides of the call, it was unnecessary, but old habits die hard.

He answered on the first ring and didn't waste a second. "You know why I'm calling."

"He spoke with you." We had a well-worn habit of speaking in statements that were also questions.

"Of course he did. I don't know how he got that lead, but it's correct."

"Did you verify this for him?"

Eli chuckled, which was the closest to an admission I was going to get. My father-in-law was the head of the Israeli Mossad, their CIA equivalent. He and Jack went back decades in both friendship and operational cooperation.

"How serious is it?" I knew there was a chance that Eli would be more forthcoming with me than my father had been.

"Enough that I told Dani to keep her phone handy and not on silent as she loves doing." He released a sigh. "Israelis are used to living under duress. She's strong for that. But this is different. New. Don't shelter her. She'll back you up."

I was still mulling over the implication of his words when he blindsided me with an actual question.

"How are *you* about this? You Americans have that saying about chickens coming home to roost, right?"

Eli knew about Operation Market and the fallout after, but he'd only hinted once in 2015 when he heard I was discharged and "going civilian." He didn't seem pleased back then but kept it under wrap, knowing his daughter would have torched him if he had done anything else.

"He's asking me to return, as you probably know already." I cleared my throat, Danielle's expression and questions from earlier suddenly making total sense. "Did you and Dani speak about this?"

"We did," he admitted, yet added no more.

My frustration grew, but I knew enough not to let it express indiscriminately.

He must have felt it.

"Like it or not, Tanner, your father has prepared you. What you decide to do with it is up to you." He then switched to another statement question, "You are supplied."

"Always."

"Are their documents in order?"

I briefly looked at the closed double-door closet.

"Yes, they are."

"Good."

SURF AND FORGET

– Venice Beach, CA –
Saturday, December 7, 2019

The sky was still dark when I reached for my phone to silence the upcoming alarm and then looked at Dani. Her hair sprawled from under the covers, and I smiled as I noticed her scent was still all over me.

My queen.

Resisting the urge to kiss her face, lest I wake her highness too early, I sneaked out of bed to start my day.

A quick peek at the slumbering children produced an involuntary sigh of relief. I didn't want to miss the Daddy Dawn Patrol, as waking Dani on Saturday morning was dangerous.

I kept my footsteps soft as I hustled down the two flights of stairs.

Flipping the light switch in the studio, I closed the door and turned on the news from the East Coast to listen as I prepared, since it was only 4:30 a.m. on this coast.

I chose the winter wetsuit, remembering my surfer buddies' chiding about using thick suits in Southern

California's warm water. I didn't care. I'd sworn, back in boot camp, to never be cold in water if I could help it.

My ears perked when the news anchors began speaking about the 2020 Election and their concerns about who the Democrats would run against Stone during the upcoming primaries.

I was about to pull my suit on when I caught a glimpse of myself in the wall mirror.

"You look just like him." Those who met my family always said that my dad and I looked the same. Brown hair, gray eyes, wiry 6'1" bodies, and crooked smiles. Most of them didn't know that our bodies were covered in similar scars.

A call disrupted the morbid thoughts of our shared pain, and I placed the earbud so I could continue getting dressed.

"Good morning," said Jack. "The Chinese decided to announce their first positive case."

"When?"

"We're not sure. Sometime in December."

I zipped the suit up and reached for my booties and gloves. The action helped my mind orient itself to something I knew was coming.

And did nothing to stop!

"Eli again?" I asked.

He gave a short laugh. "No. Did you say anything to Danielle?"

"Not yet. She knows something's up. It will be easier once the news breaks out."

When he didn't respond, I continued, "I just heard something about that General Tall. Didn't you know him?"

Jack's tone muted, "Yeah. He's a good guy, Tanner. It's a shame he's being treated this way." Before he ended the call, he added, "Custer would love to hear from you, Son. Enjoy the surf."

Thinking about the General, my eyes shifted to the open closet where I saw the black plastic covering hanging.

The red morning light broke above the buildings behind me as I walked to the beach.

Once on the boardwalk, I paused to take it all in. For those who only know Venice as a tourist, this grand, expansive walkway is always filled with thousands of people and colorful sights. But, for the locals, the early morning is the only time to feel like the place belongs to us too, even if most of the wandering souls seemed sketchy.

My destination still a bit north, I continued past shop owners starting to bring their wares out for another sunny day and many out-of-town wallets. The "FUCK STONE" memorabilia provoked more indignation than usual, and I decided to stop looking.

So much division. No appreciation.

A renewed faith in humanity surged in me when I saw the tall, lean, older black man on the grassy hill just across from the police beach station.

"Good morning, Brother!" I shouted.

Todd Fulton waved his hand slowly and offered a big smile with his greeting, "Surf's up."

We had met on the beach years before, and I'd developed deep respect for this homeless man who used his time and energy to educate the young. Rather than giving them his answers, he designed exciting pictures and printed material displays to provoke discussion and open their minds. My kids loved him, and so did the cops stationed nearby.

I stopped to say hello and ask about his most recent effort to spark dialogue about social media and its effect on teens and children. Impressed as always, I thanked him for his service to our community before continuing the last few steps to my destination.

I realized Holden must have gotten my text in time, as one of his cops called for him when they saw me. "Cap! Your surfer buddy is here."

Roger Holden emerged from the front door of the police station, wearing a thick jacket on top of his uniform. He was about my height, black, and built like a mean bear. He commanded the Pacific Division with a firm hand, and I knew his troops admired him. He was also a good friend.

I was elated to see him holding two cups of coffee as he walked toward me.

We met by the concrete wall next to the bike path, looking at the beach. It had been our spot for years. We embraced, and I thanked him for the coffee as we turned our eyes to the breaking waves.

"Looking nice out there," he said as I watched the breaking sets without a single surfer enjoying them. It was a gesture coming from a man who wasn't even a good swimmer, and I appreciated it.

He asked about Dani and the kids before bringing up the growing police challenges in the neighborhood.

If you only knew what's coming.

I felt guilty about my foreknowledge and grateful the news would break soon.

They all need to start preparing.

"How was it with Nico?" Holden changed the subject to our friend.

He and Nico went back decades, both having grown up in Venice from birth. I'd arrived on the scene and developed a friendship with them in our early twenties when I first moved into the neighborhood.

"He told me he's running." I wondered what Holden had to say about it.

He sighed and sipped from his coffee. It was his usual shtick when a challenging response was needed, so I waited.

"Those two... I think it's bad business," he finally grumbled. "Nico got all these noble things in his head, but this is LA."

It wasn't the complete picture, but I didn't expect him to give me the goods. For all his rough upbringing, Holden had become a "company man" through and through. Victoria was the councilwoman of his district, and he knew on which side the bread was buttered.

"Sometimes, I think politics are more dangerous than these streets," he added.

"I hope you're wrong about that." I clapped his back and stood up to walk toward one of my safest places.

Paddling into the great blue, I left the person I was on shore behind. Since my twenties, these early morning hours had healed my soul many times over. This was my fortress of solitude. And today, the sets were clean, glassy, and about three feet high.

I caught a few rides and then took a moment to relax on my board. Time stood still as I breathed the salty air and listened to the waves lap gently against the shore. As my eyes scanned the horizon, my body and mind relaxed into the vastness that always reminded me of my small place and size in the world.

What?

Sensation shattered my tranquility and my eyes darted, looking for its source. It took only a moment to locate the black-gray fin protruding from the water, slowly advancing toward me.

A wave rose, the red dawn light reflected on its curl, as the fin picked up speed. I paddled, feeling its power pushing my board forward. Popping up, I started to curve up and down the wave's hollow body and away from the unknown creature pacing me beneath the surface.

Not wanting to take any chances, I hurried back to shore.

Standing on the sand, I looked back to locate it. I didn't spot the fin, but the trepidation remained lodged in my guts. My fortress had been compromised.

STILL SELLING

The For Sale signs were stacked in the back of the SUV, and I was about to close the trunk door and head over to my new listing when the phone buzzed.

"TV. Now." Jack was always short with words, especially over text.

"Tanner! Come here!" Dani's voice was also tight and short when she called to me from the second-story window. This was no coincidence.

Strained voices echoed down the stairway as I approached the main level and found Dani holding Leelee on her chest in the middle of the living room, staring wide-eyed at the large wall TV.

Video of Chinese officials speaking to suited officials from the World Health Organization played as the American anchors reported. The chyron was bold.

"...China reports pneumonia of an unknown cause in Wuhan, China, to the WHO. According to them, there are 137 confirmed cases of this mysterious virus. Unknown how many of them have died."

Dani's eyes were glued to the TV, her hand absently patting Lil's head.

"The most recognized symptom is a red throat. Infected people also have shortness of breath, nausea, and intense headaches."

"The virus seems lethal to older people and adults with comorbidity..."

"There's no confirmation, but we hear that children are not among the dead."

Dani exhaled, and I didn't have the heart to tell her that our children would face other dangers soon.

"We're hearing reports the virus is now dubbed the 'Dragon Virus' due to the red throats phenomena..."

The Land of the Red Dragon. I wondered if and how the ancient reference for China might have contributed to the virus's name as well.

My fists clenched and released.

"President Stone has called China to restrict its international travel. Democrats blast his position as short-sighted and unfair. They vow to oppose him on all levels if he bans flights from China unilaterally."

Dani lowered the volume and turned to face me, her dark olive face paling as she connected the dots.

"That's what my dad meant," she said.

She sounds like him when she's anxious.

Amusement replaced my tension for a moment.

"Yes," I replied.

"You knew." It was a statement, not a question.

I offered the slightest of nods and pivoted away from that line of inquiry. I told her the anchors were correct—the virus wasn't lethal to healthy children and adults.

"People will figure out they need to protect the old and weather the storm." I finished my reassurances, knowing full well my wife wouldn't be satisfied with them.

She squinted her sapphire blues.

Don't ask me right now, Dani, I silently pleaded, certain she was struggling to separate what my words revealed from what I was obviously hiding.

As if she'd heard my thoughts, she exhaled again and offered a resigned smile.

"You got your open house, Baby. Good luck."

Relieved, I kissed her and hustled to the car.

The Dragon Virus will be our test, I thought as I pulled out of the driveway and focused on my next task.

To call it a house was indeed an understatement. It was more like an expansive mansion built over four lots. The architect was already a visionary back in the '60s when he was commissioned to design it for a rock star. Thirty-foot ceilings hovering over a black concrete structure created an enormous cubical space to play within. The ground level was one stark space with concrete floors. Upstairs, the second floor was all hardwood and bright white walls, made complete with a truss ceiling.

While the upper level was filled with natural light, this wasn't the case downstairs. Part of the lower level's design was an almost complete lack of natural light, for which the architect crafted an elaborated system of lights to be a part of the art itself. The rock star's family estate representative told me he had insisted on the darkness—something about being able to feel more downstairs in the dark whenever he chose to.

I'd worked hard to get the listing from the estate, and the open house went great with close to one hundred visitors, agents, and principals walking through. It was as I'd expected, several brokers checking with me about offers. As I watched them explore the home, I wondered how many of them had seen the news. If anyone had paid significant attention to the information from the East, they had yet to show it.

When the last visitor left, I secured the front door and headed upstairs to begin turning everything off. I was distracted, sending a quick text to Dani that I'd be home soon, as I descended the stairs and froze in my tracks when all the lights went out. In the pitch black, I knew I wasn't alone.

Adrenaline rushed as my body fell into a battle stance. There were two options—both painful, one deadly.

"ALFA... ALFA..." a male voice broke out.

Fast jabs from each side were the only invitations I needed.

Let's dance!

Besides the mixed martial arts sessions with the boys at the gym, I hadn't fought for years, but these guys would never have known it. I howled as I blocked a few strikes and landed a kick into one of the assailant's stomachs. He flew backward and thudded against a wall.

It was fast and silent, short of the painful grunts that occasionally filled the air. We took a break as they circled me in the darkness.

"Last round," I told them before they roared and charged.

I caught a few in my ribs and legs, and I knew it was time to cut their fun before I had too much explaining to do at home.

My next attack was vicious—a barrage of punches and grapples that knocked them to the hard floor and forced their retreat.

"We're done," I said as I walked to the wall to turn on the light and they laughed.

"Damn it, Sir. You're supposed to be retired."

The switch clicked and I turned to face the Nordic giant who'd made the comment. Huxley Jorgensen was in his early thirties with the broad shoulders and muscles you get only through intense training for battle. His mischievous blue eyes matched the wide smile under his brown-blond beard.

"Dumbass," said the second man still standing behind me.

Dex Bradly was just a bit older than Hux. Slightly shorter than me, with dark eyes and cropped hair, he was a force of nature despite looking tiny next to his partner in crime.

We all laughed and hugged. I'd trained them both from scratch—these life-and-death brothers.

"Fill me in." I knew our time was always finite.

Dex's face and tone turned serious as he updated me on the team's whereabouts and condition. I knew he'd been the commander since I'd left, and I was grateful. It allowed me to sleep well.

Realizing they were dancing around a bit, I cut to the chase, "Were you sent to convince me?"

Hux tensed.

"With all due respect, Sir, it's all over the news."

Dex coughed and Hux paused. His face was hard, but compassion filled his eyes.

"We get why you left, Brother. But, like Hux said…"

Their words cut deep, especially the ones left unsaid. I knew it would come one day.

I fucking warned them.

In the end, it didn't matter.

"I'm done, Guys. Got kids now. Say hi to everyone."

Dex nodded first and Hux took a moment to join him. After another hug, they departed like receding waves.

Trying to ignore the pain in my chest, I closed up the place and went home.

PRAYERS

I was smiling down at Ari who entertained Leelee from his favorite spot on her stroller when Dani tensed beside me. It was getting dark, and her eyes scanned the environment as we passed the tents and lived-in cars. Between them, humanity did what it always did, housed or not.

Her agitation inspired me to casually check under the handlebar and confirm that the concealed small pepper spray canister was still there. I'd installed it when Ari was born, and I realized she'd be pushing a stroller around Venice. She knew how to use it well.

Smiling at her, I tried to distract her with a kiss while pushing the stroller onward.

We were on our way to our synagogue, "Or Adonai," one of the few that still remained in the area. Located on a street corner with primarily residential traffic, it was an old property sitting on a large lot. There were two separate buildings. One was the place in which we worshipped. The other housed a preschool Ari attended.

The sight of the house of worship always brought a smile to my face. It used to be an old surf store that had closed in the '50s. Purchased and repurposed for worship, the community had kept the beachy facade with its large glass doors, bamboo awnings, and windows throughout. Inside, it had been gutted and rebuilt with a stage and rows of seats.

As we approached the street, we saw the doors were open and the light from inside beamed far enough to create a dimly-lit pathway at our feet. Crossing, we noticed Rabbi Chaim Shemtov greeting people inside.

He was chubby and short, with a thick silver beard and bald head at his seventy years. For decades, he'd been known as "The Hobbit" among the surfers in the area.

As soon as we stepped through the door, the kids were scooped up first for a hug and then Dani. Leaving me for last, his surprisingly strong arms crushed me as they always did.

"Let's get the flag together," he said, motioning for me to follow him.

Dani took the kids inside while I walked to the flagpole standing to the left of the doors. As he brought down our national flag and gathered it into the triangular fold of Old Glory, I stood at attention. He had been an Army chaplain in another life.

"Find me after the ceremony, would you?" he muttered without his trademarked smile.

We'd joined the synagogue shortly after I'd returned to the neighborhood, this time with my newlywed Israeli wife. Shemtov was an old friend, and he and the community had helped Dani feel close to her heritage. And of course, I'd made a promise during my conversion that I would at least adhere to this one thing—the Kiddush, or the Jewish way of welcoming the Sabbath.

Lil fussed on my lap while Dani kept Ari engaged. To my left and right, people repeated the blessings after Shemtov who stood on the stage regaled in his dark suit, brimmed hat, and the white Tallit, a fringed garment worn as a prayer shawl. We were about fifty strong.

My Hebrew was better than most in the crowd, Shemtov included, yet they all seemed far more connected to the ancient prayers.

Some things never change.

Right before I took the Rabbinical Court oath and became Jewish, my mom had asked me why I was converting. She figured Dani was my main reason, or maybe it had something to do with the fact that we had all lived in Israel for years during my dad's deployment to the Jewish State.

"Grandpa's war stories. The camps," I'd responded, referring to my dad's father, Ulysses Lee Washington. Her eyes were sad as she wished me good luck, revealing her deep love for my grandfather and knowledge of the horrors he had seen and done during the war against the Nazis.

Leelee pinched me just as the ceremony ended. As everyone rose to greet each other, Shemtov departed toward the back and I followed him after handing Lil off to Dani.

My queen's knowing smile warmed me. She knew I wasn't a social butterfly and never pressed me to be something I wasn't.

Shemtov's office door was always open unless he was already helping someone. It wasn't a large room, and the heavy wooden desk filled about a third of it. He was a prominent rabbi, and his life's work was displayed in the countless pictures, awards, and memorabilia that graced the walls.

Finding him seated, I closed the door behind me.

"Come, come," he beamed and gestured to the sofa chair in front of him.

As I moved to the chair, I smiled at the family pictures on the desk. He had four daughters and a lovely wife who had passed away years earlier. Right next to their faces was one faded photo from Vietnam. In a group photo with other soldiers, I saw a much younger version of him, in uniform. In all the years of friendship, he'd never offered a word about it, nor did I ask for one. But I could see his former life on him, even that first day.

We'd met in the water when I'd first picked up surfing. The Hobbit was a local legend with a few good stories known among the locals who spent time in the waves. For example, Shemtov always gave a quick prayer before paddling out for a ride.

Whether by God's grace or some other force, he rode his 9-footer longboard in flawless perfection that morning. After observing him out there for a while, I'd surprised him when we were just past the point-break. When he started his prayer and I joined him, my Hebrew opened a conversation about my time in Israel.

Now, almost two decades later, he waited for me to get comfortable in the chair before he started, "I sensed that you were distracted today—more than usual."

"Never been my thing, Rabbi."

Shemtov laughed. "God chooses interesting times for his people to feel his love. I always taught that to my baby girl."

He lovingly picked up one of the pictures. I knew her name was Rivka, but we'd never met. The photo was old as she looked to be in her teens back then—brown braids and a wide smile, genuine like her father's.

He didn't buy my deflection and pressed again about my state of mind, knowing he had earned the right to do so.

"I know that look, Tanner."

I know you do.

Back in the day, Shemtov was there when my first marriage collapsed. He knew that I'd quit service to heal my home to no avail. After the divorce, he'd kept close to me as I dove deeper and deeper into alcohol and self-destruction.

While he never fully admitted it, I knew Shemtov suspected I was different. He'd hinted about it as he'd helped me acquire the emotional tools needed to deal with the wreckage of my divorce.

"Is it about that wet market closure in China?" he wondered.

The pit in my stomach grew.

The Chinese had begun to blame the Dragon on some infection in one of their infamous exotic food bazaars. Shemtov wasn't one to ask about the obvious, but he was right.

I never lied to him, so I kept quiet, my eyes moving to his Army photo.

"How is your father doing with all of this?" he pressed with another question about the same subject.

You're not gonna let it be, are you?

Shemtov knew Jack and I'd had a tough relationship. Though much hadn't been revealed, the rabbi had put enough pieces together to realize that I'd worked for my father.

"You helped me after Jessica, Rabbi. It got me better."

"I thought I made you a better surfer," he teased, inviting me not to deflect again.

My quick smile faded. "Yes. That's also true."

After healing from the divorce, I'd enlisted again and gone abroad. Shemtov, like my wife and maybe Nico, had always suspected but never pried.

"I'm haunted, Brother," I finally admitted.

His eyes told me he had connected my response to his question and didn't like the result.

"Maybe it's your opportunity for Tikkun Olam, my friend."

Shemtov's reference to the Jewish concept of "repairing the world" with actions that can improve ourselves and those around us set the pit in my stomach on fire. The resentment had grown inside, provoked more and more of late, as people looked to me to act. But my rabbi deserved the best of me.

"It's not my job."

He nodded and smiled. It wasn't an acceptance of my words but rather the forming of a lecture. For the first time in all these years, Shemtov lifted his Vietnam picture and stared into it and I wondered if it would finally be told.

The few words he offered were those of a philosopher I knew well, "The only thing necessary for the triumph of evil is for good men to do nothing."

BREAKING BREAD

– Venice Beach, CA –
Saturday, February 1, 2020

I was enjoying the quiet in the kitchen, cleaning up after everyone while our friends chatted, Nico and Celeste included. But only a few minutes into my work, my equanimity shattered when Dani huffed into the space.

"Go sit at the table, Baby."

Her tone told me the time was now, so I cleaned my hands and followed her. We reached the long dining table in time to hear Nico addressing one of our guests, Pete, who worked in a local high-tech firm.

"He would have placed the ban, and I wish he did." Nico's tone was harsh.

"We both know he was afraid to be overruled. He's a coward," returned Pete.

They were arguing over President Stone's back-and-forth on the China travel ban and his final surrender when he realized that enough Republicans would join all the Democrats in drafting a bill to stop him.

The ban would have helped, but not in the long run, I mused uncomfortably, determined to stay out of the conversation.

According to Jack, the Chinese had locked Wuhan out of China while allowing the provincial international airport to still work for outbound flights worldwide. The implication was horrendous. Jack was calling it an "intentional mega-spreader event that no one could stop."

Nico looked at me, but I remained quiet while they argued about the growing Dragon measures, a slang term for all the new virus-related regulations and restrictions. So far, it was just about health screening checks at entry points to the country, but Nico was concerned how far they would take it.

"What's to prevent them from shutting us all down?" Nico grumbled.

He's got good instincts.

"Maybe they should, for the sake of the community," countered Pete.

"Are you out of your fucking mind, Man?! Who's gonna pay for all of this?" Nico glared in my direction again. "It would be a shitshow! The country would go crazy, small businesses would be crushed, and those in uniform would be asked to somehow keep it all together."

"Maybe that's what we need. To finally bring change. This president is a douche. Maybe this plague can even the score a bit. No change comes without some pain. Tough luck for the military and police."

Danielle's hand gently squeezed my thigh and nodded at my fists clenched on the table.

I stared at her in disbelief.

This dipshit is using collectivist propaganda at my table!

But I said nothing.

At my refusal to speak up, she intervened to cool off the atmosphere and Celeste joined in the effort to calm Nico. Unfortunately, it was too late. Pete's spewing of more academia-bred elitist crap tripped the fuse in my brother.

"Listen, you piece of Marxist shit!" Nico exploded and slammed both of his palms on the table as he stood.

Pete was about to rise in protest, but something about Nico's scowl kept him glued to his seat.

The first smart thing he's done.

Nico's voice shook with determination as he lowered himself back into his seat.

"There will always be assholes like you, full of resentment, trying to take from those who produce. But guess what, there will always be people like me, ready to stop you."

Pete smirked. "Yeah, then what happens if you're not around?"

Nico calmed down, his lips curling up a bit as he glanced at Celeste. Looking back at Pete, he measured his words, "Pray to be wrong. I'm not the only one. This will not end with me."

Pete had no comeback and we all understood that the night was over.

"You could back me up, Hermano! This is spreading!"

Nico and I sat alone in the studio while Celeste and Danielle finished cleaning up.

"What, the virus?" I asked.

"Stop playing games! The virus will spread no matter what. I'm talking about the effect on us. What will happen when this shit gets out of hand and into the population? Fucking locos! Everywhere!"

I wish I could tell him how right he is.

Exasperated with me, he looked around the studio. Though he had been in it countless times, he searched for something in a new way.

"How come you hide your service, Hermano?"

"What?" He'd caught me by surprise.

He waved his hand around. "You were a Marine, but there isn't one photo or anything to suggest you ever served."

"Where are you going with this?" I didn't like it when he tried to pull the strings I hid so carefully.

Pointing to the level above us, he continued, "During dinner, when that fucker dissed our men and women in uniform, you said nothing! Do your friends even know that you served? Does anyone in the neighborhood?"

"This place is hard Left, Brother. We both know it. I choose to hold back on my service to get along better."

Nico scratched his short beard and sighed, letting me know he didn't believe me for a second.

"We need leaders, like right now, Tanner."

"Have you prepared? I'm talking about the restaurant."

"Yes, of course. But I need to stop her. She's gonna use this virus fear to consolidate more power."

Again with Victoria?

"How well do you know her?" I asked just before Celeste and Danielle opened the door. Tipsy, Celeste smiled at me and then her husband, "It's time to go."

As he stood up to leave, he looked at me and muttered quickly, "Good enough."

We bid them farewell at the gate and walked back through the dimly-lit courtyard.

"You should've said something at dinner. He's afraid. We all are, Baby." My queen's tone was matter-of-fact.

You all should be, I thought.

Putting my arm around her shoulder, I kissed her head. It was my admission of guilt, whether I admitted it or not.

BOYS WILL BE BOYS

– Venice Beach, CA –
Monday, February 24, 2020

I enjoyed the quiet day at home, free of my regular work grind.

Real estate dried up fast. Folks were too concerned about the recently-declared Dragon pandemic, and open houses were a pointless endeavor. There were only a few casualties in America, but the panic became deadly.

The book I'd chosen wasn't that interesting, so I turned on the TV. Every channel had dumb-ass experts spouting predictions, except for one. I paused when I saw the Chinese Consul urging people to understand that they were doing whatever they could to stop the spread.

Fucking liar.

It took only a few days for the legacy media to tie the Dragon to the 2020 Election and Stone who was scrutinized for every word and action.

You signed up for this.

Dani's text interrupted my thoughts. "Honey, don't forget the meeting."

We had a parent teacher association meeting at the preschool, and she'd mentioned that Ari's obsession with toy guns might be a topic. It wasn't an issue for us, but this was California; and the attitude toward weapons was uncompromising, even if they were toy space guns apparently.

This should be fun, I mused as I clicked off the TV and grabbed my keys.

A high metal fence and a reinforced gate protected the preschool, and we used our digital key to unlock it and enter the courtyard. Once inside, it was a world of art and fun. The preschool was painted in bright colors and filled with kids' attractions of slides, towers, and boxes of toys. I knew exactly why our son loved being there every day.

We punched in the code for the door and entered a long hallway after the soft ding-dong buzz. Hearing the voices on our way to the study room, I quietly teased that we were "already late for the show."

All the parents sat in a large circle with the three teachers facing them. Dani gave me a look as we both realized that most parents wore masks.

They don't even wear it properly.

I shrugged and pointed her toward two open seats.

We quickly discovered the teachers were on the defense as some parents pushed regarding the Dragon measures for the preschool. When the teachers pointed out that there were no indications that the children were in any danger, the parents pushed back harder with accusations about why the teachers weren't masked.

My skin crawled with irritation, and Dani must have sensed it as her hand began to rub my back.

Finally, it was time for the scheduled action item. As suspected, it was about the kids playing "Cops and Robbers." I suppressed my chuckle when the great offense turned out to be children using their hands to imitate handguns. The same group who demanded masking from the teachers now called for the cessation of such play from the kids, using a term I had never heard: toxic masculinity.

One of the individuals was a psychologist and gave a speech about how men had to be reprogrammed from their innate affinity for violence. According to her, stopping the kids' pretend gun play was a great example of preemptive violence reeducation. In return, it would lead to healthier masculinity.

The teachers asked each family to voice their opinion, and Dani smiled in my direction, knowing I was about to be forced to speak up.

Nice one, Baby. I see you.

The parents were divided. Some cautiously suggested not to make a big fuss about it while the others were up in arms, demanding swift action from the teachers.

Our turn arrived and I shook my head slightly at Dani. Doing my best to smile at them all, I made eye contact with the parents and cleared my throat.

"My name is Tanner Washington. As some of you might know, our son, Ari, is big on that 'Cops and Robbers' game."

Some parents bristled.

Fuck off.

I gave my queen a look that said, *You asked for this,* and returned my attention to the parents.

"Ari has dozens of army toy games. All kinds of guns and whatever. He loves it, so we work with him. I'm teaching him the value of the guardian role."

One of the objecting parents, in a sharp business suit and manicured beard, squirmed. He looked around at his wife and compatriots.

I continued, "A soldier, cop, knight, guard. It doesn't matter. The point is that Ari is learning to help and defend like they do."

My time was almost up, so I made one last effort to defuse the conflict.

I know my son.

"Now, I get that the intentions here are good, but consider the possibility that it's productive for our boys to play roles and learn something."

The businessman barged in, his hands waving as he barked at me. "Well, I don't know where you were raised, but here in *civilization,* we teach our kids differently!"

His face was masked but his eyes conveyed malice.

I clenched my fist against the childhood memories that stormed in. Being forced to crawl through a thorny rough field, left out in the freezing rain with only pants and a knife—*the cold*—at only five years old. I could still hear Grandpa talking in my head, urging me onward, and wondered if my dad knew about his secret visits.

"How about you tell your son to stop influencing ours?" challenged the businessman. His wife nodded with the other lemmings in her band.

The sound of a mighty hammer echoed in the caverns of my mind. It called for my attention to something undefined yet eerily familiar.

What the hell?

Her hand gently touched my right arm and brought me out of the darkness.

"Are you okay?" Dani mouthed.

Finding my bearings, I noticed the guy couldn't stop playing with his mask as he relaxed back and his wife patted his lap in support.

One of the teachers leaned forward on her chair. She looked like a college student.

Pretty and maybe brave.

She focused on the angry group and said, "The kids are fine. They love playing, and we support it." Then she turned to look at me and smiled.

Brave.

The teachers and parents continued their silly duel, and Dani eventually got involved and reproached the businessman.

"Hey! You! If you don't want your baby influenced, then stop talking nonsense."

Damn, I love this woman.

As she debated and challenged enough for the both of us, I sat with one troubling thought. *We're fucked. A storm is coming, and this is the shit people fight about.*

WE FINALLY SPEAK

– Venice Beach, CA –
Wednesday, March 4, 2020

"Bye, Honey. Have a good day, doing whatever you do around here when I'm gone." Her tone was playful, but her smile told me she knew this was hard for me. My business had tanked, but when folks began to stay at home, hers took off.

They're scared to walk outside. Unbelievable.

"Bye, Love. I'll get by. Don't worry about me."

I was left alone for good portions of each day, feeling like a caged animal. Zoos were never my thing. More than the cages, there was always something so degrading about seeing great predators subdued to a shadow of their former bestial selves. With each day that passed, I found myself contemplating more and more that I was no different from them. I did my best to be productive around the house, stopping occasionally to look out the windows at streets that became emptier with each passing day.

Our state governor, Richard Knight, had just made an emergency declaration. Los Angeles County, and many others, rushed to issue their statements. Our health department reported a few infections in the county and hinted at debates about upcoming actions.

Our very own zoo. It's coming down, and I'm doing house chores.

The General crept into my thoughts. Custer and I hadn't spoken a word since this had started, and I knew he was waiting for me to reach out.

If I call, I'll have to...

I grabbed my phone to start the process. There was an extra security step to take because Custer was still in the military.

"RCC," came a female voice. We never knew the names of those who answered at the Rogue Command Center, but I did recognize the voice, as there were only a few of them.

I gave her my code and asked to be patched to General William Custer.

"Hold," said the operator, and the line went silent.

"Finally! I missed hearing you, Boy." His booming voice filled my ears and my heart.

"Thanks, Sir. It's been a bit."

After I answered his questions about the kids and Danielle, he cut to the quick, "You're wasting daylight, Tanner. What's going on?"

The General was always short with his words, so like my father that it hurt at times. But even those few remarks made me aware that he was more tense than usual.

"It's getting weird here, Sir." I remembered what was at stake and swallowed my pride. "How bad is it?"

"We lost control of it. FUBAR."

Fucked up beyond all repair? Did he just say that?

The General was a devoted Christian, so this was about as close to cursing as I'd heard in four decades.

"Will the president stand up to them?" There was no need to define *them.*

Custer sighed. "I don't know. He has in the past, but we're not getting any indication of more decisive action."

"The elections," I muttered.

"Yeah. That and the legacy media. Those clowns are swallowing up everything the Chinese tell them."

"The boys visited me."

He chuckled. "Yes, sounds like you haven't lost your touch."

I knew my next ask would probably cross the line, but I was worried for *them* even though it was my choice to leave.

"How's the team? Are they..."

"They're working," Custer replied sharply and then he softened up. "They're safe for now."

A mixture of relief and guilt rushed through my chest.

"Analyze the situation. What do you see, Soldier?" came his order.

"Do I get more details?"

"No. Give it your best."

You chose to be out of the loop, I admonished myself. *Tough luck.*

My mind raced to the encounter at the preschool and the growing unease in the streets. People were already so divided that this matter added more fuel to the fire.

"I'm concerned about our civil liberties, about what will happen in the country."

"Go on, Soldier."

"China is an untouched adversary on a good day. The election is coming and we're about to have a circus here at home."

Custer remained quiet as I felt my old training clicking in, setting my thoughts on a path.

"The virus would give the cover for infringement on our rights, and I'm worried about eventual civil unrest. The reason won't matter as much as the ripe conditions on the ground. An extended lockdown would easily provide for that."

"Lockdown?" he queried.

I couldn't tell whether he was surprised or engaged.

"Why not? If the government gets spooked, who's to say they won't revert to some of those techniques the Chinese are reportedly using?"

My words referred to some news from the East about the Chinese welding people into their homes in a forced quarantine around Wuhan.

Yet they still let them fly out! Bastards!

My resentment grew and I couldn't contain it.

"It could have been averted, Sir! We should have listened to Lee and taken it seriously. We didn't do enough."

"Really? How do you know the actual price we paid back then and since? It's so easy for you to pass judgment." Custer's tone was irritated and tense.

The unsolved riddle resurfaced.

How did we get out without the Chinese closing on us?

I felt ready to ask it finally, "Market?"

"Yes. Other Rogues died to let your team escape. More died since, fighting to keep this from happening."

His admission hit me hard, confirming my suspicions.

Nameless and loyal.

Words didn't form so easily. "Rest in peace," came out eventually.

"Amen," Custer echoed.

After an elongated silence, his anger was replaced with sadness. "Listen, Son. Jack and I made mistakes, yes. But you don't comprehend the danger we face, its roots, and related results." Custer sighed again. "You left, and your team carried on since. It is what it is."

A small part of me offered a warning. My stubbornness was not leading to a good place, but I was just too damn hurt.

And not just about Market.

"I gave everything you demanded. Did it matter in the end? No. It was time for me to live for myself for a change. And now, my family needs me here."

"We live and die by our decisions, Tanner. You remember that."

ABOUT THAT THING

"**B**aby, what's going on? Is it true that they're closing the skies?" Dani asked the minute she got to the top of the stairs.

Lil was playing on the living room floor with me, unperturbed by the rapid changing of our world, and I was doing my best to get a sweet coo out of her.

These days, Dani turned on the news as soon as she returned from work if Ari wasn't around. We had an agreement about shielding him from anything about the virus for as long as we could.

"Yes. We're not the only ones though. Every country is issuing those bans now."

Once the WHO had classified the Dragon as a pandemic, all the chips had begun to fall accordingly.

Power, hunger, and fear are great friends to any bureaucrat.

The insanity had escalated quickly as the governor and multiple counties began to shut down schools from elementary to higher education. We'd dodged a bullet on the preschool due to the age and because it was a private school.

Dani grunted at yet another disparaging report about Stone's emergency declaration, which had preceded the ones on the state level. My wife wasn't political. If anything, she resembled her liberal friends; but as she dropped the remote with frustration, I wondered how long that would last.

"Who loves you the most?" I cooed as I planted a kiss on Lil's face. "I do," I smiled at my little princess before I pushed myself off the ground. "I need to head out to Libertad. Nico wants to show me something."

"Yeah. It would be best if you went," she responded, her eyes glued to the screen.

She knows something.

My growing sense of unease swelled as I left the complex and crossed the street. In all my years in Venice, it had never been clean or safe, but this was different. It reminded me of some urban zones I'd had the "pleasure" of being deployed to worldwide. Once law-abiding folks retreated to their homes, the jackals took over.

Some young guys in hoodies and masks cased me from across the street and figured to leave me alone.

Smart.

Most businesses were already shutting down their operations and posting bizarre signage outside their doors: "We're doing our part. Stay strong." Dystopian advertising covered walls and the ground as well, hailing the virtue of masking and social distancing.

So quickly.

We'd always had an issue with graffiti and vandalism in the neighborhood, but I had never encountered so many cars with busted windows and so much tagging.

Noticing a new image painted on an off-white apartment building one block from Nico's, something stopped me and urged me to check it out.

What's this? I wondered as I came face-to-face with a disturbing Dragon Skull, painted red, menacing, and facing forward. I'd seen great horrors through life and done my share as well, but something about this turned my stomach.

"Wear a mask!" A woman yelled at me from a slow-moving vehicle, interrupting my trance.

I better hurry, I thought, suppressing the desire to make eye contact and shake my head back at the zombie wearing a mask over her face in a car with no one else inside of it.

To say that Taco Libertad appeared more festive than neighboring establishments was an understatement. A flagpole had been installed on the small patio and the United States and US Marine Corps flags waved above it. The awnings sported red, white, and blue decorations above the "Nicolas Ramirez for District 11" window decals.

When did this happen? I looked left and right across the Circle, seeing some folks pointing and others gawking. *Today?*

Nico had turned the restaurant into "take-out and delivery only" because the county and state orders had left no other option. He'd told me about it, but it was my first time seeing the operation—masked people retrieving their orders from the side window.

I knocked on the front door, and Celeste let me in. When she hugged me, it was rigid and tense—very unlike her usually warm and inviting presence. Forcing a smile, she pointed toward the dining area.

"He's back there with Holden. Waiting for you."

Taco Libertad was "home away from home" for me and so many of the locals. The dining area was divided into rows of booth-style seating with large vintage black-and-white pictures from Mexico gracing its walls.

Holden and Nico halted their heated discussion when they saw me and stood for hugs. For one precious moment, we were those three buds that hung out when I first arrived in Venice.

As we sat down, Holden swiftly shot me a look that said "glad to have you here."

"What's up with all the festivities, Brother?" I hoped my tone was light enough.

Nico looked bothered, or maybe agitated, but determined to calm down a bit.

Trying to be a politician already.

"Look here, you all know about all these emergency declarations." Nico pointed around his place. "See, look what's happening. There are barely two hundred infected cases today and already we treat it as if it's the end of the world." He cleared the emotion out of his throat. "Donnelly is a jackass. He'll play along with Knight and lock us up. There are already reports of such ideas floating around."

I resonated with his feelings about Los Angeles Mayor Nick Donnelly, but Holden shook his head in dismay.

Nico didn't care to stop.

"Victoria is egging for this as well. I heard her at the city council meeting, begging them to enact harsher measures. For our *safety*..." He spewed the last words like poison.

"And this is your answer?" interjected Holden. "Come on, Man. You're turning your family heritage into a pariah."

Nico stopped for a second and glanced at his wife, who was working with the staff in the front. Lowering his voice, he responded, "I spoke with my parents. We barely have business anyway. This would at least bring purpose to the building. Besides, I learned that the 'political campaign space' designation would protect us from being shut down." Suddenly animated again, his hands flew around as he spoke, "Imagine when all that shit is happening out there, Taco Libertad stands tall. Giving hope, Hermano."

Holden sighed and looked at me for help.

I'm fucking tired of everyone looking at me for help.

"This is my campaign. Clean and safe streets. Back the police. Fight against fear." His tone rose again, "This is America! We got rights, and we gotta fight for them."

Holden did his best to smile at one of his oldest friends.

"Okay, fine. You want to take on the system. I get it. But this is dangerous, Man. You're running as an Independent and sound like a Republican. It isn't smart." Holden looked around and lowered his tone. "I hear you about your issues, and I might even agree with some. But they *are* doing their best to protect us. They might not be the best people we've met, but I think they want to save lives. This is the time to hold ranks and fight together."

Nico sat back in his chair, shaking his head.

"This disease doesn't kill everyone the same. It's targeting the old and those with prior cases. It's not right to use the virus for such an overreach of our liberties."

Holden held his head between his hands, the way he often did when Nico exasperated him.

"You got to slow down and think it through." Holden pointed at the campaign signs. "You're in their game now. Everything will be used against you."

"Shit. Are you talking about my past? I'll deal with it," blurted Nico.

Holden was gentle with him, remaining the mentor who had once arrested Nico to get him on the straight path. "Don't make so many enemies so fast."

Nico didn't seem to take any of his words to heart. Instead, he pushed, "Well, at least admit it about Victoria. Don't I have a point here?"

"She's challenging. Like she always was," Holden agreed as he gathered his keys and phone from the table. "No good will come of it." He reached to hug Nico. "I got to go."

He shook his head at me as we embraced.

Join the line, Brother. But what did he mean about Victoria? I wondered as I watched him say goodbye to Celeste and walk out the door.

"Hey, you," said Nico as I turned back to him. "Yeah, dumbass. How come you're all quiet these days? Just watching your friends duking it out."

"So, you're doing it," I deflected.

His zeal getting the best of him, he played along and asked my opinions on his campaign.

"I think you should listen to Holden. Your values and opinions, noble as they may be, don't belong in this arena. You should know that."

He crossed his arms and tilted his head.

"I was raised this way. The Corps did the rest. How can you ask me to turn my back on it?"

"You asked for my opinion, so I gave it." My mind returned to what I'd seen across the street. "Humanity is changing in front of us. Provoked like a herd. Watch out for the stampede."

When Nico rubbed his eyes, I noticed how tired he looked.

"Yeah. It's happening fast. I can't believe it, even when I see it." He paused and looked at me for a long moment. "How come you warned me back in Big Bear? Yeah, when you started to ask about my preparedness and all?"

"Is this your early fortieth birthday question, Brother?" I didn't know whether I was ready to deliver, but it was a gamble I had to take with him.

Be careful what you wish for.

His eyes widened, and he scratched his beard. "No. No. I'm not ready to use that card."

I nodded as I rose from my seat. "Make sure to reinforce this place well. You've made yourself a target, and you've got your wife and family coming in and out. This is no game."

We walked together toward the entrance, where I bid Celeste farewell. Her eyes pleaded with me, but all I had for her was a shrug. Outside the restaurant, we watched the few stragglers who loitered around and the scant cars moving around the Circle.

"Hey, could you do me a favor and listen to some folks I've been following?"

When I nodded, he mentioned a Texan Senator named Bill Garcia, a social media journalist named Ken Lim, and a political commentator named Brett

Cohen. I knew nothing of the first two, but I had heard about Brett—that he had a popular podcast that many conservatives listened to.

Something about his expression and posture agitated me as he spoke, and I wondered out loud, "You get the urge recently?"

He looked back, maybe not wanting to be heard by Celeste, and nodded, "Yes. It's been coming back hard." Then he brightened up and pointed at all his political decorations. "But I don't need alcohol. I got a mission that keeps me focused."

ONLY ESSENTIALS

– Santa Monica Mountains, CA –
Friday, March 27, 2020

It didn't matter how many times I walked up to the home of the Ramirez family, the real estate agent in me smiled at the two large houses that made up their little estate not too far from the Circle. Roberto had the foresight to purchase two lots back when dirt was cheap, intending to have their grandkids close one day, especially since Nico was their only son. It was worth a fortune.

"Alright, Leelee, it's time to play with Tia Celeste," Dani cooed at our sweet little girl as she pulled the diaper bag off my shoulder and set off to the house on her own.

Ah, got it. Understanding this cue from my wife, I hung back so the two ladies could talk alone.

I'd been drafted to help Dani with the dogs on the trail, and Celeste was going to watch the baby. Nico and Cel had pulled their children out of the education system, effectively homeschooling David and their daughter, Odalys, who was seven. Roberto and Paulina loved to help, so it was easy to add Lil most mornings.

Dani approached the low wood fence lined with berry bushes and opened the gate as Celeste stood up to greet her. Everyone but Nico was sprawled out on the grass reading books or playing with toys.

I waved to Celeste, who moved much more slowly than usual. She returned a half-smile and focused her attention on Dani. I mused at their likeness as they spoke. About the same height, both with jet-black hair and olive complexions, and both sassy as hell—they were forces of nature.

I chuckled to myself, amused until I saw Dani hug her friend firmly, almost hiding Celeste from me.

Is she crying?

As soon as Celeste pulled Lil out of her arms, Dani was on the move.

"Okay, let's go. Our customers await..." She began talking about the dogs we had to service.

Two minutes into the walk, I interrupted her, "Babe, what was that thing with Cel?"

Dani slowed for a moment and shot a sad smile in my direction.

"She's worried about Nico. Not only is the business nearly dead, but he spends more and more money and time on his campaign." When she stopped completely to look at me, I knew what was coming. "What do you know about it?"

"Well, when I stop by, he just talks about his politics and doesn't seem to notice they barely have any customers."

"Could he get any of that government money? Those grants I heard about." Dani had heard about the federal and state support programs from a few of our entrepreneurial friends.

Gotta love how the government so quickly offered mass payouts to the business owners they shut down with heinous lockdown measures.

When the daily deaths and cases of infection rose, the governor, mayor, and county board of supervisors had issued their overlapping orders. Like a triple-stacked parking sign, the edicts had been confusing and lacking any rationale. Overnight, humanity had been divided into "essential" and "non-essential" people. The former were "free" to continue working, while the latter were ordered to "shelter in place" with newly-issued unemployment bonuses.

Fortunately, Dani's dog business was tagged as "essential," as it was considered a "care service" and enough wealthy folks needed it. It had saved us from financial ruin when my income dried up quickly.

"Yeah. He applied for that big government grant. But who knows if he'll get it?"

Fucking assholes.

As far as I could tell, Nico and countless others like him were being ruined across the nation by bureaucrats who already knew the Dragon's lethality was focused on late age and comorbidity. It didn't matter.

To keep us safe...

To the same tune of other tyrannic rhapsodies of the past, the same vultures who took everything from the people then manifested the support programs to save the ones they crushed while hailing themselves as heroes of the people.

Los Angeles County went a step further and issued its eviction moratorium to prevent all evictions due to the pandemic. They were ahead of the curve, as the Centers for Disease Control and Prevention issued a similar nationwide order just days later.

And who will pay for that? What will happen to the owners?

"I can't believe what's happening," she blurted as she increased our pace.

Our second car was the "doggie wagon"—a boxy SUV with the back seats removed. With the modifications, the space could hold ten dogs easily.

As we zigzagged through town for pickups, we cringed at the empty streets and closed businesses. The heaviness hung silently between us until we reached the Pacific Coast Highway.

It was a beautiful sunny day, and hundreds of seagulls bounced between the cliffs to our right and the dark blue ocean to our left.

When she lowered the windows and took a long, deep breath, I felt gratitude replace the growing tightness in my chest.

The world is crazy, but we can face it together.

I placed my hand on her thigh, and she dropped her hand on top of mine. We smiled, wordlessly agreeing to enjoy the moment.

Dani took six of the ten dogs, including the two more troublesome and enormous mutts. She displayed her natural talent with animals while I fought for dear life not to mix my pack's four leashes or be tripped by them.

Alfa would laugh at me.

Brown mountain ridge, desert shrubs, and a switchback road made of hard stone gravel—this was her favorite route. We climbed for more than forty minutes in comfortable silence.

"You can't tell it's a mess from up here," said Dani as we stopped for a water break.

My eyes took in the stony caps and dry creeks.

"My dad told me that Israel also began to enact some harsh Dragon measures. He's not happy about it." She paused. "God, I miss home..."

She didn't continue, and I would have noticed if my thoughts weren't in such disarray.

"You didn't listen to a word, Tanner," she said, snatching my attention back. "You have that look again."

"What? What look?" I asked, trying to play it cool.

Dani smiled, but it felt more like pity. "When you finally retired and stopped working with your dad. 2015."

Shit. Just like Shemtov.

"I thought bringing you up here, with fresh air and the dogs, would help. I was wrong. Looks like you brought *it* with you." She kissed me softly and started to collect the leashes, cuing me that it was time to start moving again.

Dani wasn't the kind to push. She knew it was futile. So, the next best thing was to drip water on my stone until it cracked and revealed something.

"Because it's all related," I finally blurted out after a few minutes.

One eyebrow rose, proving my answer had only created more questions. But she also nodded, silently thanking me for not deflecting.

"Is this also related to hiding your service from everyone?" she gently probed.

She always knows more than she says...

This time, I only offered a nod, as words would only have dug me deeper into a hole.

Recalling that she'd mentioned her homeland, I circled our conversation back to it. Dani always enjoyed filling me in about her giant family there.

But when she was finished, she deviously shifted the conversation from her family to mine. "What's up with Chad's new article? What do you think of it?"

I see you.

She was referring to Chad's recent editorial, "On the Virtue of Masking." Usually, I refrained from reading his crap, but this one was quite popular and Dani wasn't the first to ask me about it. I can't say I was surprised at the hodgepodge of pseudo-science and wishful thinking that constituted a popular article. Its basic premise was that masking yourself and your children was the most loving act toward your neighbor.

Yeah, let's give up all of our rights in the name of love, Little Brother.

I restrained the eyeroll.

"He's writing like an activist. A journalist would have taken a moment to think it through and do more than find ways to coerce people."

Dani stopped her pack and tilted her head.

"You know that I agree. But how come you are so hard on him but do nothing yourself? At least *he* acts according to his convictions."

Her tone was piercing, and her words rang my bell. We didn't fight often, but this felt like the beginning of a round.

Just as I opened my mouth, my phone rang. I pulled it out to see "Preschool" on the screen and pressed the speaker. It was Shemtov, and he was glad to have us both listening.

"I was just notified about the new Dragon measures for preschools," he grumbled.

"How bad, Rabbi?" asked Dani.

"Bad..." He told us that in its benevolent wisdom, the state had decided to enforce the strictest measures on the children. Toddlers were to be separated to play individually with their personal bucket of toys, stay masked the whole day, and be fumigated with sanitizer sprays and wipes before entering and leaving.

If she wasn't ready for a fight before the call, Dani was fuming now. When she started to curse in Arabic, Shemtov coughed like a teacher and my queen promptly got a grip on herself.

"This is ridiculous!" The tightness in my chest had returned and exploded. "No matter how many times they spin it, in the end, they'll see this virus barely threatens children."

Dani's eyes narrowed, a million questions dancing in them.

Oops.

"How come you know so much about the Dragon, my boy?" Shemtov asked one of the questions for her.

"Rabbi, please hold for a moment." I would have deflected, but I didn't need to this time. We had bigger fish to fry. I muted the call.

"What do we do?" I asked.

Her face reddened a darker shade.

"What do you mean, 'What do we do?' We get him out of there and ask Cel to add him to their sessions." She said it all in Hebrew, her go-to when she was pissed.

I was grateful that Dani had reached the same conclusion without my having to share the forbidden knowledge I held.

At least we're on the same page with this. I took a deep breath, grateful to have avoided the battle it looked like we were heading into before the call. *I hate fighting with this woman.*

"My Queen…" I smiled and her face brightened.

Caressing my cheek gently, she searched my eyes. "Tell me if I'm wrong about it—the measures, the masks, everything."

This was the closest she would get to asking for my secrets.

"You're correct and quite brave, My Love," I replied, touching the hand that had stopped on my face.

Dani cracked a smile and pointed at the phone. "Do it then."

"Yes, ma'am." I smiled back until I remembered how much I hated homeschooling. Unmuting the call, I apologized for the wait. "Rabbi, we spoke about it and decided to pull Ari out. Today will be his last day."

His voice cracked, "I'm so sorry. They're threatening to take our license for any infraction. This is so wrong!"

You have no idea just how wrong it is, my friend.

JUST IN CASE

The afternoon sun bathed my studio with light as I sat at my desk, grateful for the cool breeze coming through the patio's glass door.

Keeping up with the news these days felt like drinking out of a firehose. Part of my training had included rapid prioritization of data and shielding my psyche from a useless obsession with horrid ramifications. I was deeply concerned for all those who were locked in their homes, glued to a screen showing doom and gloom.

A herd is being created. For what? By whom?

Shortly after we'd pulled Ari out, the mayor had shut down all the preschools. The entire education system raced to create online platforms as millions of students, in Southern California alone, were sent home indefinitely.

We lucked out with the Ramirez hacienda.

As the world's infections surpassed a million, the CDC advised masking everyone, toddlers included.

It was just the ammo the mayor and many like him needed. Within hours after the federal announcement, our lockdown had been extended to May and masks had become mandatory for ages two and above. Our freedom shrunk to the walls of our homes.

Meanwhile, the federal government kept the money-printing machine working nonstop. It was the onset of another future crisis, beyond my immediate bandwidth to even consider.

The most concerning matter of the last two weeks was the formation of the WSC. The innocuous acronym stood for "Western States Coalition." California, Oregon, and Washington had joined to create an advisory board in order "to coordinate efforts to combat the Dragon pandemic." However, the political intentions of it weren't very subtle. All three states were heavily Democrat, California remaining the chief rival to the president, both on the state and congressional levels. And true to form, the legacy media did wonders to stoke the fire.

Elections, of course.

I disengaged from the screen when I heard Dani's voice, "Tanner, it would help if you came out to speak with the neighbors." Her hands were firmly on her hips, and her chin was up.

Like I have a choice.

I raised my hand for cover against the bright light and squinted at the spectacle before me. About a dozen plus of our neighbors were huddled in the middle of the courtyard. Some were masked, and others weren't, but all of them kept some distance from the others. Chelsea Roberts was the most protected with rubber gloves, long sleeves, and pants. She was also the most obnoxious—doing all the talking as we reached them.

Chelsea was in her early thirties and worked for a successful film company in an executive role. Her brown hair was tied in a tight bun; her blue eyes were hidden behind sunglasses. I despised the new "mask and shades" fashion, but it might have been a fitting improvement in Chelsea's case. She wasn't an easy neighbor on a good day.

Dani coughed loudly to get their attention and then spoke. She briefly touched on the Dragon itself, knowing how divisive it could be depending on what you read and believed, and focused instead on the fact that the lockdown had thrown the neighborhood into disarray.

"You all feel how it is to walk outside. Scary."

"Well, technically, you're not *supposed* to wander around. We should all do our part and shelter in place," interjected Chelsea.

Dani nodded quickly and talked about the need for the complex to come together during this time.

That's my girl. Let that bait go.

My wife's strong hand reached for my arm and nudged me forward as she finished her speech with, "I thought that Tanner might be able to give us some words about that."

Some faces forced a smile. The rest were frozen in one way or another.

"Our complex is in the middle of a parking lot, so we have visibility on all sides. We also have high fences around us and a controlled gate." I then identified some of the neighbors I knew to be solid. "Your units look to all sides of the complex. Let's get a text group going, and just let us know if you see anything suspicious. If it's urgent, then bang on our door."

Chelsea's mask gave away her attitude as her heavy breathing heaved it back and forth before she even spoke. "Who exactly are we fighting? We're supposed to be together with the community to do our part!"

"It's just a precaution," tried one of the neighbors.

"Words can be violence!" she barked at him.

Invigorated by his retreat, she continued, "It should be mandatory to have us *all* masked here. It may sound harsh, but it's the loving thing to do."

"Where are you taking this from?" challenged Dani, her face flushed.

"Senator Dwayne Jackson. He's closely working with the Federal Emergency Management Agency and the CDC," Chelsea sneered.

Who is this guy? He's getting so much media play, it's ridiculous.

I didn't know much about the New York US Senator, but his harsh pro-Dragon measures position was well-documented. The media featured him everywhere.

Dani went back and forth with her as I drew back, excusing myself to the studio.

I exposed too much, and Chelsea sniffed it.

"Thanks for talking there."

She meant it but also left much unsaid, and I took the temporary victory as she climbed the stairs to prepare dinner.

Back at my desk, I recalled Nico's request and turned on Brett Cohen's podcast. The host earned my respect as he addressed the WSC's earlier news. He was reasonable, analytical, and factual.

When it was over, I turned the podcast off and looked out the patio door. A lone large raven perched on the stone wall that separated the complex from the street.

I should call him.

My mind yearned to rebut and discuss my concerns with my dad, but I knew there was no point.

THIS IS BS

– Venice Beach, CA –
Saturday, May 2, 2020

"**U**p there," the woman started, pointing toward the ceiling above us, "we all tell lies about how good everything is." She was our chapter organizer and this was our last session.

About a dozen of us were in a local underground parking structure, standing in a wide circle. None of us were masked, as we had already broken the lockdown order by being present.

In the last few weeks, we had all witnessed an unprecedented intensification of draconian Dragon measures as the infection spread around the country. Houses of worship were ordered to shut down, and such was the fate of other public support programs. Any call for rational consideration was drummed out in the name of safety.

"Down here," she pointed at the hard cement floor, "we honor each other as we expose the worst in us, admitting our urges and then holding each other accountable so we don't fall again and, instead, improve the world."

How's he going to get by without these meetings? I wondered as Nico's head bobbed and his breath shortened.

When Nico returned from Afghanistan around 2005, his nightmares sent him back into the bottle. It was bad. It had taken three years for him to get on the healing path, and he hadn't strayed since. The meetings were a constant in his life, rain or shine.

"Nicolas, would you honor us and close our last gathering?" The organizer wiped a tear quickly, doing her best to hide it.

I noticed the sly smile in my direction as he walked to the front to join her and lifted his hands up like a good politician.

Stage presence.

Nico spoke of his old life in the neighborhood, the allure of the gang, and his reverence for his loving parents. I'd seen him speak before and witnessed some of his stories in person, but something set me at attention in that moment.

As he arrived at the story about Holden and the arrest, he revealed something I'd never heard before. He offered more details about his last night in the gang, how he had brandished a gun and arrived home feeling like a king.

"When I opened the door softly, I found Holden and my parents waiting for me." His smile faded. "My dad was pissed, and that's dangerous. But my mom's tears were even worse." Nico looked around the circle as he quoted his father, "He told me that if I was man enough to hold a weapon, then it was time for me to choose what came next. I'll never forget the look in their eyes as Holden cuffed me in front of them and took me to the car." He gave a quick hoot. "Well, I was in a bad place. I chose the Marines, and got my life in order. But demons can come home with you, even from across the ocean."

Nico continued, sharing the parts about his return and fall to alcohol and rehabilitation. As always, he never mentioned the nightmares because their content was deemed confidential.

I'm glad he at least told me about them.

"God works in wonderful ways. You all met Cel before. I saw her on the street as I rushed to the meeting. It was my first anniversary, and here I was being late." For one moment, his face was free of lines, and a genuine smile crossed it. Then, as suddenly as it took over, it disappeared.

Nico turned to the organizer and repeated her words, "Down here, we speak the truth." She smiled and nodded. Then he faced us all, although I felt his eyes fixate on mine. "It's crazy up there, maybe around the whole fucking world. But that doesn't give you the option to cop out." His tone raised, he exclaimed, "It's the time to act! To rise because many are afraid to do so." Nodding slowly, he finished with, "Well, I'm doing it."

They all applauded, mesmerized by his vision.

It was chilly as we walked quietly along Abbot Kinney Boulevard. On any other day, it was one of the priciest blocks in America, full of clothing stores and eateries that could drain your wallet fast on a Friday night. But today, it was just another shut-down, neglected place.

A lone car slowly passed on its way up to the street. We all gawked at the masked driver, who looked back at us with disdain.

"You surprised me tonight." I broke the silence.

Immediately, he began his rant about Holden and their conflicting visions, "I mean, just as I said, I owe him everything. But, how come he turned out to be such a party-man? How come he doesn't see?"

"I was referring to Cel and your one-year," I added, hoping to get him off that soapbox and into something more cheerful.

Nico softened immediately. "Yeah. She's my gift, Hermano." Then he changed the conversation to my upcoming ninth anniversary.

"We got some time until September," I teased.

He picked up an empty bottle from the sidewalk and dropped it into the overflowing trash can.

"I was so happy when you had your rebirth and got sober. But it sucked when you left again... for God knows where."

Nico knew I was somewhere in the Middle East during those years, but we never discussed it. This nostalgia wasn't typical for Nicolas Ramirez, and I waited to see where he was headed.

"At least you brought Dani." He was shaking his head, and it was hard to tell whether it was meant for me or just a reaction to the trash-filled streets.

He had no idea that I knew her long before that trip—that our fathers had worked together since my dad's deployment to Israel and that I'd known her since she was a young girl.

"Happy wives, happy lives," I responded and we laughed.

However, my joy didn't last as I recalled my recent admission to Shemtov—that I felt haunted by that period of my life.

"What's up with your face, Hermano? Don't you worry. I'm used to your mysterious, spooky life."

When we had to divert to the street to avoid the debris and makeshift camps, Nico's mood changed and he began to curse in Spanish.

"This! I've been seeing this more and more." I followed his gaze to an empty, neglected cottage home with the Dragon Skull graffiti, blazing red across the front. "Punk-ass kids are making a joke out of this. But maybe they're the ones seeing it right."

"What?" I was confused and conflicted.

What is it about that damn image? I wondered as I tore my eyes away from it.

"Our politicians have been using fear to get what they want. Donnelly, Victoria, they're all the same. They don't give a crap about the neighborhood, playing as our saviors while our society is falling apart and they get more power."

My heart pounded faster, or maybe it was just pressure.

"It's just graffiti, Buddy," I replied, hoping he wouldn't see my anxiety.

"Nah, nah. You just decided not to look straight, Hermano. Look here. People do see it for what it is. Control, Man. Control. You know about that anti-lockdown protest in Sacramento."

That rally had no chance. Knight had ordered the State Police to stop the protest before it became meaningful, but Nico had been invigorated by it, irrespective of its dimmed results.

"The media blackballed that whole thing from being noticed. What's the point?" I grumbled.

He halted our steps with the back of his hand on my chest. I glanced up in time to see his wide eyes and dumbfounded expression. "Really? Really?" Then, shaking his head, he resumed the walk.

Recalling Cel's worries about Nico, I decided to see if he'd open up if I went first. I shared our household's financial difficulties, and he listened carefully but didn't take the bait.

"Thanks for handling our kids, Brother. Your parents are godsent." I hoped to pivot more successfully this time.

His lips were pursed, but he eventually nodded.

"It's a shame what they're doing to the children."

It was his turn to change the conversation and ask about my family back in South Dakota. He'd met them once or twice and they'd left a good impression, but I soon realized his true agenda.

"Have you seen that post by their governor?"

"Who?" I was surprised.

"Lynn Norton-Bower, South Dakota," he replied, stopping us again. Beaming, he pulled out his phone and searched. "Look, right here."

It was a short social media clip of Lynn speaking to a group of assembled reporters, declaring that South Dakota would not infringe on its people's rights and liberties.

She really is something.

Seeing her standing proud and beautiful, warm memories of earlier times poured in. Lynn's father, Jerome, was one of Jack's best friends and she and I had spent a romantic summer at the Ranch before I enlisted.

I nodded at Nico, agreeing that her speech was admirable. But he didn't stop there. He went on to connect Lynn with other examples of people rising up to oppose the increasing tyranny. The more he talked, the more my mood soured.

TALKING WITH GRANDMA

– Venice Beach, CA –
Thursday, May 14, 2020

Thanks to my children, our living room had become a war zone of discarded toys. I'd long given up trying to bring order to the chaos and decided to dive into the mayhem with them instead.

Like Ari, Lil had crawled early and was doing her best to stand on her own at only nine months old.

"There you go, Baby. You're doing it," I encouraged as she grappled for balance and giggled happily. There was barely time for one kiss before she fell back on her bottom.

Ari had his army figurines in formation. He loved simulating large battles and took his time setting each piece carefully, which stopped him from eventually doing a quick ten-second smash-up.

"Who are we fighting today?" I crouched to inspect his setup. He had all the tanks on one side and all the soldiers arrayed on the other.

"The tanks are going into an ambush, Dad," he replied, eyes focused on the soon-to-be demolished armies.

"Good hunting, Son." I suppressed a chuckle and ruffled his hair before running to move some toys out of the way of a toppling Leelee.

Since we'd pulled Ari out of school, I moonlighted between being a father and a teacher on the days he didn't go to the Ramirez's. That morning, we'd kept the kids at home because Nico needed Celeste's help at the restaurant.

When the kids were both happily playing on their own, I looked outside the kitchen window into the barren Venice Boulevard. Our forced isolation at home looked so different from our old world, and Dani and I often spoke about how many things we had taken for granted. Gone were the days of walking to a restaurant and eating out.

Or just walking out in general without being yelled at. A weary grunt escaped me as I turned back from the window in time to see Ari's army men flying everywhere and Leelee clapping joyfully.

"Watch out, kids, here comes the police." I imitated the sound of a police siren and lunged toward them. They loved that game and did their best to avoid being arrested and tickled.

After a good tussle, I turned on the TV for them while I cleaned up and listened to Ari do his best to explain the show to Lil.

If I lose this, I lose myself.

I scanned the counters for my phone, as the ear vibration tended to preempt the ring by only a second. When I found it, I saw it was a video call.

I smiled at my mom, noticing her blue eyes were beaming more than usual and her wavy auburn hair looked freshly-tousled by one of her outdoor hikes. Ali and Jack were high school sweethearts, and she had aged far better than he had.

"Hi, Mom."

"Hi, Sweetie." The sound of her voice immediately regulated my breath and heartbeat. It had been the only source of nurture and soothing in my childhood, no matter what was happening around me. "I was hoping to see my grandkids, if possible."

Ali called to see the kids about once a week, and never took offense at the fact that they cared very little about staying in front of the phone screen. Today was no different, so I moved the camera around to show her the disaster zone, asked them both to say a quick hello, and then returned to the kitchen.

"You look tired, Honey," she said.

"How's everything at home?"

She offered a half-smile at my deflection before playing along. Starting with the harsh weather they had experienced lately, which buried them under heavy snow, she continued sharing about the house, the dogs, and her favorite subject—her greenhouse.

She loves that place so much, and I feel like a stranger to it all.

"Oh, and your sister just accepted an offer from our dear governor. Lynn told Tami that since she's so good with Constitutional law, she might consider working on the governor and state's behalf as they try to protect the rights of the people."

Ah, that's why the calls.

Tami had tried to reach me in the last few days, but we'd played phone tag. I knew how important it was for my sister to be a defender, so it was surprising to hear that she'd switched sides.

Mom read my face like a book.

"Tami wasn't keen on it until Lynn explained the severity of the situation. She told her that with the Dragon pandemic, the real danger would come from government overreach and asked her to be her torch-bearer on keeping the state open and free from civil liberties infringement."

"Wow, good for her," I said, recalling Nico's admiration for Lynn.

Right again, Brother.

Leelee yelled at Ari, and I took a moment to intervene.

"How's Chad? I haven't spoken with him lately," I admitted, eyes still on my two trouble-makers.

The neck rubbing and hair stroking told me more than her words as she shared that Chad's articles had become more contentious as he launched direct attacks on the Stone administration, specifically focused on the response to the Dragon.

"He's egging them to imitate his state's strict Dragon measures—that failure to do so would cost lives." Her voice was so strained, my heart rate picked up.

"Have he and dad...?"

Her face dropped. "Yes. We tried to have a civilized conversation with him and Chad kept attacking him and his values... our values!"

"And Dad...?"

Her brow creased and then softened.

I can't hide from her.

She sighed, "He took the punches and hopes that Chad will come around someday."

"Dad, Leelee is sleeping," called Ari quietly across the room. I excused myself for a moment and took my little land rover to her bed, tucking her gently under the covers.

"How's Danielle doing?" she asked when I finally got back in front of the screen.

I knew she didn't mean the mundane stuff.

"She's onto me, Mom. She knows enough to wonder why I'm doing nothing about what's happening."

Ali's tight-lipped smile was brief.

"Be gentle, Tanner. This is the price of your... departure. She doesn't know how much you've already paid."

Her hint did nothing to elevate my mood. Instead, I grumbled about how the Dragon and its measures spread like wildfire across America with very little opposition.

"And why is that happening, Baby?"

She tried to lead me to more constructive thinking, but all it accomplished was reminding me of my increasing emotional weight.

"How should I know? You raised me abroad pretty much until I enlisted."

She nodded, but her eyes were hard. "A decision which you took freely."

We were at an impasse, but my mom wouldn't let go. She disagreed with the morbidity of my outlook, pointing out that while many governors became tyrannical, others opposed the harsh restrictions like Lynn.

"There are only a few of them who stand tall," I muttered.

"All you need is one person to stand. You know better," she chided.

The soft snores pulled my attention back to the living room where Ari was crashed out on the sofa. I turned off the TV and covered him as well.

"You're a great dad, Tanner."

We were silent, as I didn't know how to thank her without reverting to my anguish. A nod was my only response, and she didn't venture further.

"Is anything else bugging you?" she probed.

"I had a moment recently," I answered, barely noticing my lowered tone.

"When?" she asked, not needing to confirm the subject matter.

She listened attentively as I recounted the events of the preschool PTA meeting.

"Did the nightmares return? Did you see anything new?" Her voice was gentle.

Alley rhymes with Ali. Alley rhymes with Ali.

Inexplicable resentment surged inside my heart, shaking the pillars of my mental defenses. I shook my head hastily.

"I'm fine, Mom. Saw nothing. And I better go and pick this place up before Dani gets home."

"Okay, Honey. I love you dearly."

My smile wasn't forced but it wasn't easy either.

"I love you, too."

THE MATCH

The surf report said the swell was supposed to be great—four-to-six feet and no wind—and I couldn't wait to get out there. The last two weeks had been hectic with the kids and helping Dani with the booming dog-walking business. We were lucky to have our pod with the Ramirez family. It was the only way I was able to find some solace in my favorite place.

As I grabbed my shortboard off its shelf in my studio, the black plastic cover hanging in the closet caught my eye. Paralyzed momentarily, Dani's words clamored into my mind, "Is this also related to hiding your service from everyone?"

Ugh, I need to hit the waves! I gruffly closed the closet and headed to the beach.

When I reached the sand, there was just enough light on the horizon to see that the report was correct—the waves broke perfectly. But before I could take another step, the ear vibration ended my hopes of a morning alone in the water.

"Good morning, Son." There was an apology in his tone. "At least I caught you just in time."

They always know.

I resisted the old urge to touch the ear as I walked back to the house.

"What's going on?"

"Turn on the news. Something in Chicago. We'll talk later."

The combination of his tone and brevity made me pick up my pace and resist the urge to use my phone to discover what happened.

"Are you back already?" asked Dani as she shuffled into the studio with sleepy eyes and disheveled hair.

She hugged me as I clicked on the remote and kissed her head.

"Let's see." I sighed before I even saw what was coming.

It was on every single channel—a high-speed chase had turned into a horrible traffic incident in Chicago. The motorist had died at the hands of the police who stopped him while many onlookers watched and recorded.

Oh my God.

Dani began to cry as the motorist exhaled his last breath and my stomach turned. I hugged her and held my disgust back until she left the room.

Images of the suffering of the deceased motorist burdened my mind and my step as I walked back to the beach.

Why this one?

"Got change?" A shabby-looking woman pulled my attention back. I looked down at my wetsuit and shook my head, and she smiled.

The homeless camps had multiplied during the pandemic, sprawling both residential and commercial streets where shop owners had shuttered their businesses by order. When the city had decided to stop enforcing the removal of temporary habitats in front of our homes, the neighborhood had begun to feel more like a rat maze.

Except here, I thought as I wiggled my toes deep into the cold sand and hurried toward the water, my enthusiasm returning at the mere sight of it.

But the waves were merciless, most of them crashing and shoving me to the sandbar underneath.

Ready for a break, I sat on my board, past point-break, grateful to see only a few surfers and no rookies. It was peaceful as the sun rose and covered the rough water in its orange hue. The waves broke hard and tall behind me, sending white spray upward.

Why this?

Every word and action of Jack's had at least two, if not many, purposes. They were calculated, with no mercy, preparing for some future chess move on the board he'd been playing long before I was born.

Why would he insist I see it?

When an image of Dani and the kids quickly floated in and out of my awareness, I shouted, "Never!" loud enough to startle a random pelican looking for breakfast nearby.

The last wave turned out to be a great ride, and I was all smiles as I left my fortress. As I wrapped my leash on the board, I noticed some movement at the police station and then some noise from the nearby hill.

Todd was a man of peace, so it was no surprise to find him trying to end a heated argument taking place right by his display. I wasn't clear on the reason for the argument, but one thing was certain—one side was masked and the other wasn't.

Todd managed to defuse it just before I arrived.

"Doing the holy work, aren't you, Brother?" It was my best preacher impersonation.

"Tanner, my friend." He embraced me. "It's so good that you still go surfing. I wish I could be away from this noise for a moment."

I laughed. "I don't buy it. You were meant for this."

Todd was in his mid-seventies and his signature white robes made him look like a modern-day prophet, but there was a sadness in his smile today.

"Maybe so. Maybe so." He looked toward the board-walk, his brow deeply furrowed with old lines. "What do you think it was about?"

"I don't know. Masks?" I guessed.

He turned to look at me, his dark face paling, and shook his head. "It was about that thing from Chicago," he pointed to the station, "and the cops."

People are already fighting about this?

Todd turned toward his display, and we spent a moment reading the material and looking at the picture focused on the importance of proper nutrition for kids. Scratching his white beard, he wrinkled up his nose the way he did when in deep thought.

"I need to rethink my display. More help is needed," he said cryptically as he clapped my back.

"Good for you, Brother. I'll keep checking on you when I can."

Dani met me at the door, her eyes wide. "Chicago's on fire. It's spreading to other places too!" She ran upstairs and I followed close behind.

With the kids still asleep, we kept the volume low as we watched thousands riot in the streets.

"Baby…" she blurted as the newscast diverted to a helicopter's view of the riots and showed the widespread looting and fires.

Why?

"I'm going downstairs. Keep the kids home today."

"No shower first?" Her eyes narrowed as she looked between the TV and me.

Don't ask, Baby. I have no answers for you right now.

★ ★ ★

"How did you know, Dad?" I asked, even though I knew I didn't want to hear the answer.

"There was a huge spike in online chatter about it."

I didn't know whether to be grateful or upset about the deflection.

"Anyone in particular?"

"Mostly centered in far-left and anarchist groups..." After a moment of apparent deliberation, he went on to share about two groups in particular: Comrades and Ryse. While the former was mainly centered around social justice and soft Marxism, the latter was a more secretive organization specializing in civil disorder and known to operate in small, decentralized cells across the country.

"These two are already activated both online and on the street. And there are other players," he hinted.

Unsurprisingly, the WSC and its three governors came out against the police and voiced support for the "peaceful demonstrations" in Chicago.

Farce.

What I had just watched with Dani was anything but peaceful.

"The elections."

"Yes. Big time. And the media outlets are already on it," he agreed.

Jack added that Chicago was already a tinderbox with the harsh Dragon measures enacted by both their mayor and governor.

"We're being distracted," I grumbled, thinking of the fight I'd seen Todd break up.

"Yes, and the Chinese are taking advantage of that..." He filled me in on an evolving situation in Hong Kong, as China, against all the signed treaties, started to move its military into the island to consolidate its rule. "You should consider carrying again," he said matter-of-factly.

"Listen, Dad. I'll review all the supplies and ensure we're ready, but I'm done carrying weapons outside."

"Well, be careful, Son. The world didn't get a memo on your decision."

The sudden constriction in my throat prevented me from responding, and he ended the call with a frustrated grunt.

I know! I'm disappointing everyone right now!

I came downstairs after a refreshing shower and found the kids with Dani. She'd decided to stay home that morning too, so I took the opportunity to get prepared just in case.

Checking the gear was about an hour-long ordeal, including oiling and cleaning the weapons, and it couldn't have been a coincidence that Custer texted while I did it, adding his own words of caution.

Staring at the handgun, my mind raced for the answers.

How did he know? Why this?

COME AND TALK WITH HIM

Ari wasn't keen on ball games, but he had insisted we turn the courtyard into a soccer field that morning.

"Yes!" Ari howled and danced around after kicking the small ball into my makeshift goalpost. I never made it easy when we played, as I wanted him to learn to fight for his victories. But after the twentieth kick, "Goalie Dad" had missed and the ball got through.

I gave him a big high-five, his happy celebration inspiring me to join in.

"Babe." Dani called me from our balcony, and I squinted up against the morning sun to see her holding Lil in one arm. "Cel is on the phone for you. She's at the restaurant and sounds concerned."

"Man!" Ari was upset when he realized we had to finish the game and I was sending him back upstairs to his mom.

"Sorry, Buddy. Sounds like your Tia needs me." I tousled his hair as I handed him the ball and walked back to the house with him.

★ ★ ★

Dani was right. Cel's tone was hurried and scared as she explained Nico was holed up at Libertad, refusing to come home, even with the news of the riots breaking out in LA. To make things worse, she had to take the phone into the restroom and speak quietly so he wouldn't hear her.

"He's loco, Tanner! He talks nonsense about what's right and wrong, and I'm losing my mind here!" she nearly shrieked. "I'm afraid for him... for us... He has kids!"

Shit.

I turned on the TV, muted it, and watched the live helicopter coverage from Downtown as she continued. The looting, the fires, the crowds demanding social justice, and the violent assaults on the police.

Just like Chicago. What are the chances?

"He's not thinking right. This is too dangerous."

She worried about all the flags and patriotic decorations Nico had all over Libertad, knowing it would attract severe reactions from protesters if they arrived in our area.

"You gotta come here and force him to close. You're his best friend. Please, Tanner. Help me get him home to his family." Her tone was pleading, caught somewhere between tears and rage. "I called Holden too."

"I'm on my way, Cel. I'll do what I can."

★ ★ ★

Something's different! my mind yelled as I crossed out of the complex into the empty streets. Since the lockdown began, people had left their doors and windows open to breathe some freedom into their cloistered experience. But today, everything was shuttered.

I couldn't shake the "pre-combat" sensation that those who have fought know well.

About a block from the Circle, I noticed small bands of masked folks heading north toward Santa Monica, carrying signs and other items I couldn't decipher on the fly.

Where are they going?

Some assholes on bicycles gravitated toward me and then started shouting, "Mask up or eat up!"

Noticing the sticks in their hands, I stopped, positioning my back against the nearby fence as they kept on with their curses.

Beat a man in the name of safety? Really?

The standoff broke when their leader saw something on his phone and ushered them north.

Where are they headed?

Glancing back toward the fence, I saw a fresh red Dragon Skull painted on the wall, and the heaviness grew in my chest. For the first time in years, my hand reached to the small of my back to find nothing waiting for me.

"Well, be careful, Son. The world didn't get a memo on your decision."

An aggravated snort escaped at my dad's warning as I ran to help my friend.

Besides the random hooting and hollering of those who passed by on their way up the street, the Circle and restaurant's pickup window was empty.

When I looked up and saw the flags waving, something old stirred in me.

Don't go there.

Celeste opened the front door, eyes red, and gave me a desperate hug. "Thank you," she whispered before leading me to the dining room, where Nico and Holden stood arguing.

"Nico, this is no joke! You need to close this place down and head home!"

"Are you going to make me, Officer?" barked Nico, squaring off with his chest forward.

"Guys..." I called out, hoping to disarm them.

They stopped when I entered the room.

Holden turned to me, bags under his eyes and no smile. Looking back at Nico, he told me that the riot was growing, and there seemed to be a mass movement of people joining. "They're marching west along Santa Monica Boulevard. They could arrive any day now."

This is insane.

I almost admonished Holden for allowing this march to creep forward but decided against it, guessing the decision came from city hall.

"I'm not going to abandon Taco Libertad!" Nico spewed several stories of plunder and looting per Brett Cohen and Ken Lim's reports while Holden and I stared back at him in disbelief.

"Tell him what you did for your defense, Nico!" challenged Holden.

"I installed some secret cameras inside the shop," responded Nico proudly.

Celeste began cursing and praying in Spanish simultaneously, an amusing combination if not for the emergency at hand.

"For what?" I finally added my own words.

"So that I have it recorded!" he exploded.

"But you can't use it! Damn it, Man! These cameras record audio as well. It's not admissible in court!" Holden's tired face flushed red as he yelled back at his friend.

"Well, maybe if you finally get police into the area, I won't have to use them," blurted Nico.

Holden stubbed Nico's chest with his finger hard.

"This is not a game. My officers are doing what they can, and we're stretched thin and handcuffed!"

"Handcuffed?" I wondered.

Holden tilted his head toward me.

"Where have you been, Tanner? It's like the entire world has decided that all police are bad. We're... under new restrictions," he grumbled without clarifying any further.

"Well, the cameras are hidden and the feed is stored locally, behind my grandpa's picture in the back. Nobody will find it," Nico added as his eyes lingered on mine for the briefest moment.

What?

"Mi Amor, at least take the flags down," pleaded Celeste.

Holden nodded emphatically as she hugged Nico.

Nico's face softened for a moment as he kissed her forehead, but then he shook his head as he turned to face Holden.

"This will *not* happen! We hung those flags back in the sandbox. We fought for these flags across the world!" He stood more regal. "This is Taco Libertad, my family's home away from home. This is where I'm running my campaign. And I will not back down for some assholes."

Celeste's eyes were full of tears when she looked directly at me. "Tanner, please tell him to take them down."

Holden added the pressure with a scowl, but Nico remained hopeful for another reaction.

When we locked eyes, I gave it to him. "I can't. Not on that. I'm sorry."

He smiled at me, and we were on the same page for one brief moment before he doubled-down on his position.

"Knight, Donnelly, and Victoria are supporting the rioters. They preach their bullshit 'peaceful protests' crap while we're all under lockdown, and they have the streets..." He went on about how the local government was only making things worse, placing emphasis on Victoria and how she got Donnelly to back down from using the police.

While Nico was talking, Celeste started to fidget and looked relieved when a lone customer called out from the window and diverted her attention.

Was that about Victoria? I wondered as I watched her depart.

Holden begged him to stop aiming at the whole world.

"Don't make more heated mistakes. You know they cost too much." Holden didn't mince his words, and Nico seemed to be listening. He sighed and looked down at the floor. Then raised his eyes to mine.

"What about you, Hermano? You also telling me to back down?"

Jack's warnings and my tribulations collided inside as time slowed to give space for my speech to either mean something or nothing.

"You should go home, Brother."

He looked deflated as he scratched his beard.

"I gotta bail out," Holden insisted, looking at his phone. He silently thanked me with a tired nod before leaving.

"Where is the man who killed everyone to bring us back home? You know that evil is coming. Why are you silent about it?"

"Do you really want to know?" I folded my arms, trying to contain the war that waged within.

It took him a moment to nod slowly, as if he had realized that he'd ventured beyond his own intentions.

"That man isn't here anymore. His fight is over." The flatness in my tone surprised even me.

I felt someone's presence behind me and turned. Thinking it was Celeste, I was surprised to see Dani and shuddered when I saw her expression.

She heard me.

Gone was the moment when Nico feigned a smile as he hugged her and we all played along until Dani, and I left.

She held my hand as we walked and talked. Dani thought Nico was careless with his actions, but she also made it clear that she supported his spirit. Stopping us on an empty street corner, she faced me.

"Nico might be making bad decisions, but how come you don't see any value in what he's standing for?"

Her question winded me with its brutal honesty, and I inhaled to catch my breath when I realized she wasn't done.

"You know he suspects your true occupation—your past. Maybe that's why he believes you're meant to do more, especially now."

I shrugged and implored her to start walking again. "It's not safe out here, Baby."

Dani didn't move as her eyes searched mine, waiting for my answer.

Shit. She's not talking about Nico. This is about her.

FAMILY MATTERS

– Venice Beach, CA –
Thursday, May 28, 2020

"Hi! I'm so glad you're all here!" My mom had always loved technology. She became a computer whiz when they were invented, and she hadn't stopped since. Once video communication was a thing, Ali coordinated digital get-togethers, particularly for her two sons who lived so far away from the Ranch.

This was our first video chat since the pandemic broke out, and I wasn't excited about it.

A family of secrets.

She started the conversation on a high note while my dad tapped his fingers silently. I always found it fascinating how my commander's energy shrank back when she held the baton.

The elephant in the room was the growing nation-wide riots and the fact that both of her sons lived in cities that were currently under siege.

"I, for one, am worried about both of you," Tami chimed in.

A younger version of our mom, my sister's auburn hair was pulled back in a professional bun and her pale blue eyes glistened with concern. Both women were small in physical stature but giant in inner power. I smiled, noticing that her look, her posture, and her words exuded this strength—the energy she needed for her new position at the South Dakota Attorney General's office.

My sister wasn't shy as she spoke against the growing call to "defund the police" and the new trend that lumped all officers together as "tools of oppression" and other distasteful idioms being attributed to the men and women who had devoted their lives to protecting communities.

"I thought you were hired to handle Dragon issues," snickered Chad. His short black hair was always properly combed, but his gray-blue eyes betrayed the disorder within.

"You're such a jackass." She didn't take the bait and expanded on that as well, detailing how her office was entrusted with ensuring the governor's "open state" policy remained in effect and was not misconstrued by localities around the state.

"Lynn will have blood on her hands," murmured Chad.

This time, Tami's face flushed red. But before she could up the ante on the sibling rivalry, Ali intervened, "How about you, Chad?" She invited her youngest child to speak his mind, and everyone else on the call visibly tensed.

"The fact is that law enforcement is one of many systems of oppression..." He smiled in mock deference to my mom before he went on to attack law enforcement and the "systems of oppression," which the cops have served while killing those who didn't obey. I wasn't well-versed in police-involved fatalities, but his words didn't match the 2019 research I'd read at length. "The cops behave like the 'Ten Commandments' are the law of the land," Chad finally blurted, mixing religious undertones with his political convictions.

What the hell happened to him? How did he come out of a family like ours?

"Tanner, do you have something to add?" Ali asked.

It wasn't ideal, asking me to speak right after Chad's rubbish. But refusing my mom wasn't an option.

"I get it. That Chicago incident was horrendous and shouldn't have happened. There will be a trial and justice will be served. But, to lump all the good men and women in uniform is just a witch hunt, and it *will* end badly. We need them to protect us..." Putting forth my best effort to remain factual, I shared some of the 2019 research data points about policing in America.

Chad's mouth twisted and his eyes narrowed while I spoke until he couldn't contain himself.

"Men and women in uniform, you say? Right!" His mockery slid out into the open. "You still love Dad's war stories, Brother? He poisoned our minds, just like Grandpa did to him."

My fist slammed my desk. Jack had his faults—many of them—but this open disrespect was unacceptable.

"You're way out of line."

"I'm not one of your soldiers!" he barked back at me.

"That's for sure! You never served anything but your own selfish needs!" I growled, feeling the urge to punch him for his disrespect.

"Enough." My dad said it quietly, but his one word reverberated like thunder, and we all quieted immediately.

When Ali laid her hand on his shoulder, I was struck by how her touch softened his gaze.

Just like Dani.

"You know that my whole life has been focused on defending the freedom of speech and all of the other liberties this country holds dear. All of you were raised with a voice in our home and invited to speak your mind freely." He paused before he addressed Chad. "As for you, Son. Those were tough words that you used. I hope you'll never learn their real meaning as your grandpa and I did."

"Alright..." Ali intervened again to bring us back together.

We all knew to play along, and we ended the chat peacefully.

I waited by my desk when the family chat ended, expecting his call.

"Well, that was fun," was all he said about the family meeting, and I wondered what he was holding back as he changed directions. "Have you heard Rod Grayson's speech about the 2020 election?"

"No." I vaguely recalled that Grayson had been the Defense Secretary during the Charlton administration, which preceded Stone's.

"He threw his hat in the ring for the Democratic presidential primaries. He's going against Stone."

"Why are we talking about this, Dad?" His topic puzzled me as he had trained me to stay out of politics in the mission's name.

"Because Grayson is very much in favor of strict Dragon measures. He also came out against the police as soon as the Chicago incident happened."

I was frustrated with the data breadcrumbs he'd been giving me as of late—riddles and hints for me to follow like a mouse chasing cheese in a maze.

He knows I'm looking.

"Can you give me clearance for RCC data?" I asked.

There was a long pause.

"You want to know? Do what I trained you to do," Jack replied, dashing my hope. "You did well to save Lee, but your other actions are one big growing mistake. I get it, though. You wanted to live for yourself, and you do."

"Custer?"

"Yes, your words definitely reached me," Jack muttered.

There was no point in escalating the situation, so I remained quiet.

"Listen, Son." He'd warmed his tone. "It wasn't easy for me to realize that I enabled evil either. The hardest part comes after the realization."

Enabled evil?

The outright rebuke of my decision to leave hurt, and his admission only increased my unease about whatever my father was holding back.

He's haunted too.

"We'll talk soon, Dad."

"Stay frosty," he replied.

REALLY

– Venice Beach, CA –
Friday, May 29, 2020

Maybe this was a bad idea.
I pushed the stroller on the street to avoid the sidewalks littered with human feces, debris, and those who didn't mind the filth.

Dani had returned to work that morning as the riots seemed to stall just west of Downtown LA. The kids were going stir-crazy in the complex, so I agreed to take them out.

With the lockdown in full force, people had to have a good reason to be out, like buying food or medical supplies. The few who ventured into the streets were masked and kept their distance, so we stood out like a sore thumb.

Against my better judgment, I gravitated toward the Circle and stopped as soon as Taco Libertad came into view. The restaurant's patriotic decorations, including the flags that waved with the light ocean breeze, inspired a surge of pride.

How come I don't tell him that?

"Daddy, take us to Nico!" demanded Ari. Lil turned around in her front seat to smile as if she might have understood her brother's wish.

I was about to cross the road when a masked group emerged from a side street between the restaurant and us and an oversized man hung around one of the other guys.

What's going on?

Stomach turning, my grip on the stroller tightened as I watched them out the side of my eyes, not wanting to draw attention.

"Daddy, wake up!" Ari called again.

I patted his head, silently asking him to be patient for a moment while I watched the group meander toward the restaurant with their backs to us.

I can't help.

"Well, be careful, Son. The world didn't get a memo on your decision." I clenched my fists tighter as Jack's words echoed.

"Dad, let's go to Nico." Ari was agitated and losing patience.

"Quiet." He rarely heard that tone of my voice, and it stunned and silenced him immediately.

I pulled out my phone, eyes on the group, and called him instead.

"What's up, Hermano?" He sounded busy, even though he'd answered on the first ring.

"Nothing, just checking on you. You good?"

"Coast's clear. Just working on the campaign and tacos."

One of the guys from the group looked back at us, and I shifted my attention to the kids to dissuade any connection between them and my call.

"I'm glad to hear. Been missing seeing you."

"Well, you could come and help me, you know. I'm always here." His tone was irritated. Or maybe it was…

Hurt?

Before I could pursue the thought, a well-dressed woman with oversized shades and a designer mask emerged from another side street, and one of the group approached her for a chat. They seemed to have a good conversation, which made me relax and release my concern.

Maybe it has nothing to do with him.

"I'll catch you another time. Gotta get the kids home for lunch."

"Whatever, Man. Peace." His words didn't match the resignation in his voice.

One last look at Libertad and I turned the stroller back to head home. Ari was obviously pissed, but he kept it mostly to himself.

"Are you keeping an eye on his restaurant?" I asked.

When we got home, the kids wanted to watch their show, which gave me time to reach out to Holden.

"As much as I can, Tanner." Holden sounded weary. "Why? Is there something I need to know?"

"No," I eventually replied, deciding not to mention the suspicious group I'd seen earlier.

Holden sighed, "Give me a moment." I listened as he navigated to a better spot to talk in private and then muted his tone before speaking, "We can't do jack shit. They told us to stand down unless someone is about to die…" He mentioned the protests in Chicago, New York, Atlanta, and even the one in DC, which reportedly got the White House on a temporary security lockdown. "How do you fight when your superiors doubt your ability to handle your tasks? At least the Los Angeles protest is not moving westward… yet."

I debated myself while he spoke, *I can't be dragged back in, but I gotta know…*

"Have you been briefed about Ryse and Comrades? Did you see them among the rioters?" I asked, inwardly bracing myself for the answer.

There was a moment of silence. "We were just told about them. Not a lot is known about their organizations. How have you heard about them?"

Luckily, there were some viral online posts about them, which Jack had forwarded to me. So, I mentioned them to Holden, who seemed to accept the explanation, at least on the surface.

"What about your brother, Man? Nico sent those articles to me. Man, he's so blind. He should be careful with his rhetoric up there in Seattle. You never know the kind of attention that you'll attract."

"I agree, but Chad isn't the only blind person these days," I murmured.

"What are you saying, Tanner? Don't play games with me."

"The politicians who lock us in our homes for our safety are the same ones who are now against the police. See the connection?"

Holden scoffed and shut it down, "Cut the crap, Man. Two separate subjects."

I could hear the fatigue increasing in my friend.

I don't want to fight, especially with my friend, I thought, noticing the heaviness returning to my chest.

"Hey, Brother, I don't want to get into it now. Let's talk again soon..."

CLOUDS GATHERING

– Venice Beach, CA –
Saturday, May 30, 2020

I needed that, I thought as I gave myself one more minute to stare at the ocean.

The swell was good that morning, but only the locals enjoyed it. Everyone else missed out, even though the police were allegedly not enforcing the lockdown.

Surprise, surprise. I shook my head and started walking home.

My body bristled at the sound of several agitated voices as I entered the complex and paused to look through the gate. Noticing that Chelsea was one of the neighbors gathered in the courtyard, I wished myself invisible or at least for night cover to sneak by them all.

No such luck. They all fell silent and turned when they heard the pedestrian side gate open.

"Hi, guys," I mumbled and returned my eyes to the asphalt, hoping to avoid further interaction.

"Tanner, join us!" called one of the neighbors.

Damn it.

The cold morning air on my soaked wetsuit made it even less fun to listen to their heated conversation about the rise in Dragon infections and fatalities.

"What do you think? Should we all decide to mask up in the courtyard?" an anxious neighbor asked the group.

As I waited for others to answer, I noticed Chelsea was not only the one masked person in this group, but her mask had the Comrade symbol embossed on it.

Breathe, I commanded myself, my blood boiling at the soviet-like hammer and sickle on top of an image of the earth.

Focusing on the neighbor who'd asked the question, I did my best to remind them that the data suggested that we were past the winter infections and fatalities peak, and the virus fundamentals hadn't changed.

"Listen, this thing hurts the old and those with comorbidities. If you don't belong to these groups, you can probably relax and do your best to live normally." I looked at them all, avoiding eye contact with Chelsea, who fidgeted and rocked in place. "Our residents, to my knowledge, aren't in great danger. So, let's keep it like this, and if you want to mask..." I glanced at Chelsea for a quick moment, "then mask, and that's it."

When the neighbors nodded, I turned and walked away.

"What about your civic duty?" Chelsea screeched in my direction.

I stopped and looked back at her.

After a cautionary breath, I asked, "For?"

She heaved her hands up and shrieked, "For? For all of us, for the common good, Tanner!"

It took careful attention to keep the bubbling ire from rolling over.

"Decided by whom?" I challenged and turned toward home, refusing to give her the opportunity to continue this dangerous debate with me.

After a scalding hot shower and a breakfast burrito, I settled into my studio to scan the news and updates.

Cities across the nation were on fire, Chicago being the most devastating pyre. The violence didn't spread out evenly, of course. Democratic-governed cities and states experienced the lion's share of destruction because their governors and mayors had kept their law enforcement and National Guard from protecting their residents.

Disgraceful.

My phone chirped and I glanced down to see a text from Holden. "Downtown LA protest begins moving westward. LAPD is asking the mayor to stop the march. I'll talk to Nico. Get your family inside for the next day or so."

Dani and the kids were already at the Ramirez compound, so I texted her to come home immediately and kept browsing. Digging past the legacy media's "news," which seemed more like a steady stream of endorsements of looters as "social justice warriors," I had to look for other sources for information.

Where have the good journalists gone? I wondered until I found a report by Brett Cohen, who had covered a story about a restaurant owner in the Midwest.

Comrade goons had walked into his establishment and begun harassing his customers, demanding the patrons mask up and raise their fists to support their cause. When the owner, an Army veteran, objected, he was beaten. But when he pulled his gun, they finally retreated. The DA pressed charges against the owner for "attempted murder," which triggered a cascading reaction and led the owner to take his own life when the police came to arrest him. He blew his brains out when they broke down his door to get inside.

What?!? I slammed the desk as I stood up and began to pace.

Another chirp from my phone. This time, it was Dex. "Watch your six, Sir."

"Thanks," I wrote back without even looking at the screen.

My mind remained focused on the Midwest veteran.

What happened to self-defense? The Second Amendment? What about our rights? Why can't I stop thinking about this shit?

The third text was from Jack. I looked down to see a live satellite feed showing the protest marching westward on Santa Monica Blvd.

Thousands...

My anger was replaced by terror when it sounded like they were outside.

Oh shit. Dani!

It took me only four seconds to reach the gate and hear my wife's roar, "You bitch!"

The scene in front of me would have been amusing if not for the subject matter. Dani faced Chelsea, fists clenched and eyes blazing. Her back to the gate and stroller to her side, I could see the kids were visibly puzzled by their mom's rage, as were the other neighbors gathering in the courtyard.

"You're not putting this on the gate!" yelled Dani.

Looking more closely at Chelsea, I noticed a giant flag in her hand which she opened and held up for Dani to see. The Comrade symbol, prominent and red, unleashed a wave of acidic rage and turned my stomach.

"This would send the right message of support—of unity. We should be clear about our support for the movement," insisted Chelsea, her tone leveled and dripping with passive-aggressiveness.

"What the fuck?" barked Dani. Her accent thickened with her rage. "You put this on *your* home. They are burning and looting, you stupid bitch!"

I stepped between the two.

"Alright, let's cool it, ladies."

But my own heat increased when I saw the masked guys in black clothing stopping to look at us from the boulevard.

Shit.

"Chelsea, you know all the complex rules and regulations are clear on not placing any banners or advertisements outside the units."

She narrowed her eyes before she gave up and stomped back to her unit.

Dani kept quiet as she trudged home and I kept pace behind her with the kids in tow. When we brought them upstairs and she only addressed the children, I knew I was in trouble.

"What?" I asked once the kids were in the tub playing.

"What? What? You didn't give me any support there," she growled, eyes flashing and hands on her hips.

How long can I do this? I thought about the guys I'd seen on my way to Taco Libertad.

"Exactly. Stay quiet in your thoughts and secrets," she hissed in a low tone before she walked into the bathroom and slammed the door behind her.

Jack's text interrupted my first step toward the door and intention to barge in after her.

"Knight is about to declare an emergency and activate the National Guard."

I snorted and shook my head.

Finally, and fucking too late.

THE ALAMO

– Venice Beach, CA –
Sunday, May 31, 2020

The full moonlight bounced from the jagged
surface of the lone mountain covered with
charcoal-black tree trunks, some with
twisted branches, like arms crying
out to heaven in great suffering.
There was a gap of blackness
between the rocks, and I…

My eyes opened to the sensation of my body coiled and fists clenched across my chest. The only sounds in the pitch dark were Dani's light snores. I looked to my right, where the soft blue digits said, "5:31 a.m. May 31st" and my eyes stayed on the clock until the minute turned.

Knowing my pounding heart and racing mind would not let sleep return, I rose and looked out on the still-slumbering neighborhood. Windows were shuttered and no cars or people moved along the empty streets. It wasn't typical in this part of town that usually bustled with activity at all hours of the day and night, beginning with the surfers' meditative movement toward the ocean in the early mornings.

People are afraid.

Dani's movement drew my attention from the window, and the pressure in my chest expanded as I watched her turn a few times and search my side of the bed with her hand. Kissing her head gently, I went to check on the little ones who were still sound asleep.

Seeing my loved ones safe and at rest should have been relaxing, yet shivers traveled my spine as I stood paralyzed in their doorway.

I can't lose this. I can't.

My eyes scanned the updates flashing across my computer screen. The riots had begun to morph into direct attacks on institutions and their symbols. Monuments were toppled across the country, whether they belonged to those with troubling pasts or heroic achievements. The rioters didn't care. All were symbols of oppression to them. Police officers were attacked in numerous places, and one cop was murdered the previous evening in a nearby city.

It seemed as if there was a nightly truce during the hours of the wolf—3 a.m. and 5 a.m.—and the pressure crept to my throat when I noticed the clock turning 6 a.m.

Something's happening. My mind raced to try to find it but was interrupted by the sound of footfalls on the hardwood floor above me.

I smiled when I found Dani nursing Lil on the sofa, an innocent and sacred act that always placed me in a relaxed state of mind.

Unfortunately, my wife didn't let the relaxation last long.

"What's going on?"

I was searching for a way to ease her mind when her phone rang.

"Hi Cel, wha…" Dani stopped to listen and my spine quivered again at the pitch and pace of our friend's voice coming through the line. I didn't need to hear the words to know something was terribly wrong.

"He did what?!?" Dani exclaimed, provoking a panicked squeal from Leelee. Instinctively, my queen soothed Lil with her soft touch, but kept her eyes locked onto mine. "Yeah. Yeah. Come over. I'll tell him."

Her head shook in disbelief as she put the phone down.

"Nico left to open the restaurant. They're all coming here for the day. They want your help with him."

It was already 7 a.m. when the Ramirez tribe arrived, and Paulina and Dani quickly marshaled the kids when Nico's father and Celeste asked to speak in private.

"He wouldn't listen, Tanner. I tried and cried, and nothing. He's so... obstinado!" Celeste exploded once my studio door was closed behind us.

Roberto hugged her, his stern face showing new lines of worry. He looked at me over her shoulder.

"Mi hijo is stubborn, but he's doing what he thinks is right. I told him, 'Nicolas, it's just a restaurant,' but it only got him mad." His breath and voice were tight. "I wanted to join him, but he stopped me. He said that this was his time to protect the familia."

Cel's eyes were red as she turned to me and pled. "Please, Tanner. Talk to him. Tell him to shut down and take down the flags. Just for today. The restaurant isn't worth him getting hurt. Please."

Resisting the urge to avert my gaze from her pain, I offered what I could, "I'll do my best, Cel. You know Nico. Once he gets on a track..." I hugged her to offer some comfort. "I'll call him now. Why don't you two go upstairs and grab some coffee while I talk to him?"

Just as they closed the door behind them, my phone buzzed. A text from Jack indicated that crowds were beginning to gather again on Santa Monica Blvd, just around the 405 Freeway.

I have time.

I turned the news on mute while I waited for him to pick up.

"Tanner. They there?"

"Yes, Brother. They're all here."

On my screen, I saw a feed from some network's chopper. Hundreds of people had already amassed with countless signs and flags, indiscernible from that high.

Don't have to see them to know what's on them.

"You should be here with us. Seems like the protest on Santa Monica Blvd is starting again."

He snorted, "Bunch of assholes. Who gives a shit?"

"Definitely assholes. But Nico, your family is quite worried about you. Come stay with us."

"Enough with this, Hermano." His dead serious tone had dismissed all affection. "This is where I make my stand. How can I be a leader if I abandon campaign headquarters at such a time?"

"You're taking needless risks. Somebody could get hurt." I measured my words and tone against the anxiety beginning to crackle in my chest as I watched the crowds swarm in his direction.

"It's just me, Tanner. I told my staff not to come."

Seeing some of the flags the protesters carried, I thought of the two that waved proudly above Taco Libertad and cringed.

Those will make him a target.

But I knew it would have been pointless to mention the possibility of pulling them down, both for him and me.

Some things don't change, even in retirement.

"Listen, Hermano. This is my moment. I stand tall now and Victoria will have no chance against me. I'll be able to turn this place around."

"What is it about her, Nico?"

He paused and sounded distant when he finally replied, "She's off the reservation, Hermano. She doesn't understand what she's doing and supporting."

"Nico, you can fight her without being out in the streets." I gave up trying to understand for the moment and focused on his safety.

"No. No. You don't get it. Being in the street is everything. Vic would know it too, even if she forgot her roots." Nico took a breath. "Listen, I won't be threatened to close. My campaign will never survive that."

What the hell is he talking about?

"Don't be a fucking pussy, Tanner. I had to tell Dmitri the same thing. I got this. Gotta go. Talk later."

He even bucked Dmitri? Fuck, I thought as I made the next call.

Holden answered on the fifth ring, his voice nearly drowned by all the sounds in the background. "Santa Monica Police is preparing to create a blockade around the pier."

"The pier? Why not sooner? It's a straight shot down to Venice if they get there."

"First Amendment, Tanner. It would be best if you understood that." He didn't try to hide his irritation.

Indignation exploded in my chest. "Damn it, Holden. The First Amendment protects the right to assemble *peacefully*, not to riot."

"Well, they're not rioting now. Just marching. Let's talk later. I'll keep Nico updated. I promise."

They all looked up when I emerged from the studio into the courtyard, where they played with the kids. As soon as I told them Nico refused to reason, Cel rushed back into the house to call him again, her mother-in-law, Paulina, on her heels. Only a few minutes later, they returned with worry etched more deeply into their faces.

As the day progressed, we watched the protest grow to tens of thousands as they reached the border of Santa Monica, most of them unmasked.

Hypocrites. What kind of health officials claim that social justice is more important than Dragon measures?

Nico refused all of his family's efforts and grew more irritable with each call.

I should go to him. I debated again and again, but each time found a different reason to stay back. *What am I afraid of?* I wondered as I watched my loved ones wring their hands and rub their faces as the mob got closer to our home.

By noon, the protest had reached the Santa Monica Pier area, where the police were spread out to block them from going any further south.

Oh my God!

The kids were upstairs watching a show and we were all seated in the studio when the news broke that the protest had turned into a full-scale riot. We watched with horror as the entire Santa Monica Downtown area was ransacked. Jack provided me with some satellite imagery and it confirmed the live feed from the choppers.

Where are the cops? I clenched my fists at the sight of needless destruction.

Glancing over to see Celeste and Paulina visibly shaken and holding each other, the shudder returned when I noticed Roberto's hard eyes on the screen and how still his body stayed.

He's used to violence.

I recalled bits and pieces from Nico's stories about his dad's younger years in Mexico.

City officials blathered on and on to news anchors, explaining that these protests were "mostly peaceful" and that we must exercise patience with the justified rage over the Chicago incident. The next moment, we understood the meaning of the bureaucrats' empty words as they ordered the police to allow the herd to continue south.

My grip threatened the chair's destruction as we watched the Santa Monica Police open their ranks and allow thousands of people to pass through them, my blood boiling over at the sight of the Comrade flags waving alongside a new one. The Ryse flag's white lightning over a black background was simple but clear in its intention.

They want to burn it all to the ground.

Celeste was calling Nico again when angry voices outside yanked my attention away from the screen.

Shit. Dani. I was out of my chair and at the door in seconds, only to find my queen already walking toward me.

"It was Chelsea again. She was frightening the neighbors, so I took care of it."

Damn, Woman.

I hugged her as she walked inside and corralled everyone upstairs for lunch, leaving me to suppress a chuckle at the sight of a slumped Chelsea stomping out of the empty courtyard.

Back in the studio, I texted Jack to ask if there was any chance we could get the Eye tasked to our area. He responded quickly that the satellite was occupied elsewhere.

He must have pulled favors to get me those images he'd sent.

I kept the news on mute as I watched the rioters barreling south, their speed slowing down enough to loot the shuttered stores along the way.

I called Holden, who picked up faster than before. "Did you get Nico?"

"Not for a while now. His family has been trying as well."

"Shit," he grumbled. "Listen, this clusterfuck is still within South Santa Monica, so we don't have any jurisdiction."

"Are you getting ready along Rose Avenue if they come that way?" I asked, noticing the pressure mounting up my chest and into my head.

"Wait a moment." I could hear him telling some people that he'd be right back. When the noise behind him had died down a bit, he continued, "Listen, Tanner. They're not letting us enter Venice. We even had to evac our beach station."

Coldness spread through my veins. "Who ordered this?"

Holden cursed quietly. "Victoria is running the shots on behalf of Donnelly. She convinced him to let the demonstrators release their steam without giving them a reason to agitate further."

"Are you kid...?"

"Gotta go, Man. Later." Holden cut the line.

My eyes caught the news chyron about riots growing in other cities.

Is this coordinated?

My eyes glazed at the screen while the phone kept chirping and buzzing with texts from all who cared and worried. But none were from Nico.

I should go. What am I afraid of?

A growl escaped my gritted teeth.

*There was a gap of blackness,
and I knew it was the forbidden place.*

The phone rang and I clicked to receive the call, returning from the depths.

"They entered Venice and headed south. Did you get Nico? He's not answering." Holden's frantic demeanor added more concern. The guy was usually good at keeping his cool in an emergency.

Before I could answer, Dani barged into the studio, "Baby, they're coming down Main St. Are you seeing this?"

I placed my palms on my desk, unable to stop the disorienting swirl collecting at the edges of my vision. So many things happened at once. Dani, the agitated voices from the main floor above me, Holden on the line, the war waging inside me.

*I looked further into the abyss
between the stumps and rocks.
There was something familiar about it...*

Pulling myself back from the precipice, I replied, "Yes, I'm with Holden on the line. Give me a moment."

"Oh my God, the Circle," said Holden.

We both watched our screens as thousands of people converged on the Circle from other directions ahead of the central mass along Main St.

They knew where to converge.

"It's their gathering point," I replied, more to myself than to him.

The line went dead and I heard excited voices from above me.

They got Nico on the phone.

When I reached the main level seconds later, I saw Paulina holding the phone and crying. Spanish was one of the first few languages I'd learned, so it was easy to follow as Nico's mom begged him to come home. Roberto held his wife as she pled with their son, and Dani consoled Celeste on the sofa.

Thank God the kids are upstairs!

The TV screen showed a chopper view over Venice where countless people roamed, small fires burned in dozens of locations, and no police could be seen.

In the middle of it all, Taco Libertad still stood with its flags waving.

When Paulina collapsed into deep anguish, Roberto took the phone and listened with a dark grimace and then handed the phone to Celeste.

She rose from the sofa and held the phone with trembling hands. Crying, she pleaded, "No... No, mi amor. No." Beginning to shake, she tried to stay calm, "Yes, they are safe upstairs. No, they're not watching. I love you, Baby. I love you."

Dani rose and hugged Cel as she held the phone out to me.

"He wants to talk with you."

★ ★ ★

"Get away from them, Hermano," he said as soon as I got the phone to my ear.

"Okay," I replied and turned to the stairs, feeling all of their eyes following me.

Walking downstairs felt like crossing a carefully-guarded boundary between two lives. The cries above me quieted as the door closed behind me.

"It's just me, Brother. What's going on?"

"Guess what I'm doing now?"

Hearing the tenor of his voice and the hiss of the bubbles, my stomach dropped.

My TV was left on, and the live chopper feed above the restaurant was all over my wall.

"How many have you had already?" I asked, feeling my anxiety over my brother increasing.

I was projected forward.
The gap turned out to be a cave mouth.
It was huge and growing in size as I got closer...

"Enough," he replied and hiccupped, which made him snicker for a moment. Then his tone turned serious. "Hermano, you remember about the secret camera, right?"

On the screen, people began to scream outside of Libertad, and I could hear their voices muffled in his background. He yelled back, primarily with Spanish profanities, and even laughed as he did it.

"Nico, why are we talking about your camera? Can you get out of there?" I had no time to even consider the implications of him drinking again.

He laughed, and I knew the futility of my question as I scanned my screen and watched people begin banging on the restaurant alley door.

"It's okay," he said. "The windows have metal screens, and I barricaded them further with tables. It will take them some time to get in. You remember the camera, right, Ese?"

"Yes. Behind your grandpa's picture," I answered, my heartbeat quickening.

My fear of the cave was immense,
recalled somehow…

"Wait, wait, I'm calling dibs on my fortieth birthday question, Hermano." Jest returned to his voice.

"This wasn't the deal, Nico. You still have a few months," I half-jested back, eyes glued to the mayhem expanding in the Circle and the streets around it.

"Well, shit. Now's the time, please."

Relying on one of the earliest lessons in my training, I focused my mind, shutting everything down until all that remained was Nico's voice.

"Okay, Brother. Shoot."

"Back there when you guys saved us. Your team, you, and what you all did… that wasn't any military? Right?"

I knew it.

"No, Nico. It wasn't," I admitted, tilting my head to release some of the mounting pressure.

"Then, what *are* you?" he asked.

"Those are two questions, Nico."

"Damn it, Man. Related! What *are* you? I've been thinking and thinking ever since getting back here. Sometimes, my nightmares are less about the Taliban and more about what I saw you and your people..."

I should go.

An old calm spread through my body.

"I don't know what you thought of me, but I'm worse than that." It was the best and most honest reply I could offer my dearest friend.

"Fuck me," was all he said.

The background sounds became more violent with the increasing efforts to break into the restaurant.

"Listen, Hermano. I got to go. If something happens..." He paused. "Please watch over my family and remember one thing... This United States Marine Corporal Nicolas Ramirez did what he believed was right." Before I could respond, he laughed and hissed, "You should try it again."

The line went dead at the same moment they all rushed into the studio. They all spoke at once, but it was the voice of someone not in the room that was the loudest: "This is a mental reality beyond the fear of loss of life. Those who access it do so during hazardous situations, expanding their options to act, unhindered by societal norms."

He's a free man, I mused as Bach's words reverberated through me.

"Tanner." Danielle's voice wrenched me out of my trance.

I looked past her to the closet, where the hanging black plastic covering stared back at me. My safe was right there, but the memory of the veteran who took his life dissuaded me from going that route.

"I'm going," I told Dani as I looked at all of their worried faces. "Alone."

The street outside our complex gate teemed with people —mostly a younger crowd—shouting, laughing, and generally heading in the direction of the Circle.

Head covered with a black beanie and face masked, I opened the side gate and walked out into the road.

Invisibility.

My body mimicked those around me, melding and drifting like a fake zombie among a herd of the undead, becoming invisible in plain sight.

Turning on the *Sense*, I emptied my mind so I could discern everything. Without looking around, I captured the numerous conversations and intentions of those who walked by me, screaming for social change.

The general mood was one of victory as the rioters cheered in the streets without any authority in sight. Flowing with them toward the Circle, I held back a tidal wave of dark emotions.

*I grabbed a rock,
holding it to prevent myself from
being tempted into the cave...*

About two blocks from the target, the crowds began to howl and curse. Then the sounds of machines reached me. It was a convoy of large police vehicles, sirens blaring as the hordes opened in front of them. The cops passed my position, and I drifted forward with the rest.

★　★　★

By the time I arrived, all sides of the wide roundabout were barricaded with police trucks and angry cops in full riot gear, preventing us all from stepping inside.

Taco Libertad was the closest to my location, but it was obscured completely, except for the flagpole. Raising my eyes toward the symbols of freedom, my heart sank.

NOOOOO! Focus. Focus! I tore my eyes from the Comrades and Ryse banners that flew in their place.

*My hand released the grip on the rock.
I stepped toward the cavemouth.
There was something in the dirt...*

The dismayed shouts around me rose to new octaves as the police held the line firmly and I scanned the crowds and faces.

"Holden!" Pulling my mask down with my gloved hand, I yelled a few times when I saw him shouting and giving orders.

He didn't hear me, but someone else did—the slender black female officer next to him. When she turned to look in my direction, I doubled the effort.

The officer spoke into Holden's ear, and he flipped around and locked eyes with me. Excusing himself, he double-marched my way with the young officer at his side.

"Let him in. That one. With the black beanie," commanded Holden when he arrived behind the blockade of cops.

Breaking free of the pushing and grabbing of the mob around me, I squeezed into the opening created for me between the large riot shields.

I gave a silent thankful nod to the officer, and she offered a shy smile.

Who is she?

The thought evaporated as Holden's low voice commanded, "Stay on me. Don't make a scene," before he led us back to the throng of police assembled in front of Taco Libertad. I pulled my mask up and followed him.

The cops held control of the Circle's inside perimeter, but it didn't help much. The restaurant was already encircled by at least two hundred rioters, creating a human shield made of signs.

As I got closer, I noticed the Dragon Skull graffiti painted on the wall by the door.

"They beat us here. We now know there was much coordination on social media," Holden said quietly. "We received frantic calls about a lone man facing a crowd that fought to break inside. We didn't get here in time."

Only one part of my mind was dedicated to Holden and his report while the rest scanned and assessed. The cops surrounded the restaurant, effectively cutting it off from the outside masses raging beyond the Circle boundaries.

At least there's that.

"Victoria is talking with the occupiers. Donnelly has tasked her with full authority here," he continued.

My fists clenched at the sound of her name and again when her voice came over a megaphone. Following it, I saw Victoria walking from among the cops in the front to call the rioters.

"What are they saying?" I asked, straining to hear Victoria without success.

Holden snorted angrily. "They blame Nico, saying he was the first to attack them, and they subdued him inside. They're making shit demands—defund the police and all the rest."

No time.

Adrenaline rushed to all of my limbs.

"Why aren't you breaching already? These are your cops. Your jurisdiction."

Holden's face contorted as he motioned with his head toward Victoria.

"We can't. She wants to deal with this peacefully."

I'm unarmed.

My blood boiled as I thought of the veteran who took his life.

"This is madness! He could be hurt in there!"

The marks in the dirt turned out to be small footprints. They were faced outward from the cavemouth. Someone was here before... a kid?

An officer rushed toward us, telling Holden that Victoria was calling for him.

"Don't do anything stupid, Man," he grumbled and followed the cop. The young female officer gave me one last concerned look and turned to follow her partner.

I drifted after Holden, seeing the fast conversation with Victoria as he shook his open hand and head and then sighed in apparent resignation. Victoria stepped toward the restaurant, megaphone in hand, and called out to the rioters, "I'm ready to speak with your leader."

Libertad's front entrance—the door my family had walked through countless times before—opened up and two men emerged. Both clad in black attire, gloves, and high combat boots. One of them was large and his face was covered with an Arabic-styled shemagh, a headcloth that obscured his face. The other guy was closer to my size and moved like an agile predator.

A fighter.

He wore a helmet, designed as a Demon face, red and menacing, and with barred sharp teeth opening where his mouth was. His eyes looked through the holes and he took in the surroundings with a slow head motion.

He's not afraid. Fuck.

The Demon guy roared, "Remember Chicago!" and all of their human shield rioters chanted back, hooting and hollering.

In return, Victoria asked for the place to be vacated and the owner to be released. She added that everything would be okay and that the city understood their anguish and looked to support social change and reform within the police department.

Fucking bitch. The cops are here—listening.

Holden turned to look at me. As if hearing my thoughts, he shook his head slowly, giving me a silent warning.

The Demon said something to the big fellow, who ordered the human shield to open up. Victoria stepped forward, and she and the Demon spoke quietly to each other after she prevented Holden from joining her.

When they finished talking, and Victoria reached Holden, I watched my friend's body droop forward as she spoke. The Demon, on the other hand, turned to face his people and yelled, "We're going! Now!"

Holden clicked on the mic on his shirt and I heard his command from all the police radios around me. "Stand down. Let them all leave the Circle."

The cold shiver returned.

This can't be happening.

Victoria and Holden rushed back to join us as the cops opened their line and the rioters bunched into a tight formation and ran out, howling with joy.

Time stopped.

"If you step in, I step out," came the guttural growl within my mind.

I entered the cave.

"Now," commanded the bestial voice.

The word that Jack had whispered to wake me up in the dead of night resounded inwardly. And just as I was once expected to jump up and act, digesting my surroundings on the bounce, I bolted forward, zigzagging from two cops who tried to stop me.

"Tanner! No!" I heard Holden's voice booming.

The rioters weren't ready for my move, and I waded into them as they all did their best to move away.

A kick to my ribs shot searing pain through my body. It might have been the Demon guy, but all that mattered was getting through the open door.

I was in the cave,
pitch darkness...

"You got seconds, Soldier!"

I rushed to the dining room where I saw him, or at least the old khaki pants that he loved so much.

Shit.

Nico was splayed on the floor, hands stretched to the sides in a cross, the US and USMC flags covering most of his torso and head.

No!

As I lifted Old Glory off his face, the stench of urine reached my nostrils.

My best friend's lifeless face told the dark tale of malevolence. His jubilant expression was gone from the crushed and battered remains.

"*Seconds, Soldier!*" thundered the alien voice.

They were just outside the door and Holden was calling my name.

I reached the area at the back of the restaurant, immediately assessing that all the standard camera equipment was either smashed or gone. But Grandpa's picture was still on the wall high above, undisturbed.

"Tanner, where the fuck are you?" Holden yelled from somewhere behind me.

The secret hard drive was untouched and, in one quick motion, I removed the small memory card, shoved it in my underwear, and threw the picture and the rest of the device among the smashed equipment.

We met back in the dining room. Holden stood over what remained of our friend, frozen and unmoving. There were other cops behind him, but they gave us a moment.

As my eyes adjusted to the darkness,
I could see a barrier ahead of me.
It ran across the entire width and height of the cave.
Bang! Something massive hit it from the other side.

Holden lifted his head and looked at me, tears streaming down his face.

"He's gone..." He barely got the words out.

Bang... Bang... Boom.
I ran back as I heard the barrier falling apart.
Something powerful rushed through
and pushed me aside as it passed me,
clanking on the rocky floor.

Using the *Sense* to focus and calm my body, I pointed at the flags, "We'll need them back quickly."

I rose from the ground, hearing a faint roar.
Something had escaped...

The young female officer touched Holden's arm, pulling him gently back to his role. He nodded at her softly and then looked up at me and nodded as well.

"As soon as we get them examined. I'll rush it."

A shrill cry erupted behind Holden as Victoria rushed toward us. She lamented frantically in Spanish while Holden used his remaining strength to hold her back from touching Nico.

"What's he doing here?" she asked, her silk-embroidered mask down and eyes blazing in my direction.

Holden motioned toward the young officer. "He's leaving now."

Blood pounding through every inch of my body, nearly deafening my eardrums, I kept my posture and countenance relaxed as I looked one last time at my best friend and walked past Victoria and Holden.

"Are you…? Can I…?" asked the young officer, whose name tag identified her as "Dee Hopkins."

Words barely formed in my mouth, "I'm going home, Officer."

The time-stop dropped as I entered the Circle full of police, fire department, and medical personnel. Gone were the crowds.

I looked at Libertad quietly for a few moments, sensing a disturbing attraction to the Dragon Skull graffiti before I turned to walk home. Once outside the roundabout, I reached into my underpants and pulled out the small black memory card.

"*Watch it,*" the bestial voice commanded.

I resisted the urge to check my surroundings for its origin, and It laughed and then faded. I finally looked around to confirm that nobody was around me in the empty and desolate street before the pain surged and doubled me over.

Oh God… What have I done?

FOR YOUR EYES ONLY

– Venice Beach, CA –
Sunday, May 31, 2020

My phone chirped and buzzed the whole way home, and the pressure in my chest mounted with every notification. Once inside the complex, I replied only to my father, more as a matter of duty than anything else.

I can't…

Throughout my military career, I'd visited many homes of the fallen, bearing the worst of news. Now, it was my door, and my hand refused to reach for the knob to open it. Anguished cries drowned out the TV sounds and threatened to split me in two.

It's my fault.

"Daddy!"

I lifted my head toward his bedroom window, smiling sadly at my innocent boy's worried face.

Your daddy fucked up.

A second later, the door opened and Dani stood in front of me. Without a word, she crossed the threshold I couldn't and wrapped her arms around me.

She's the only one.

"My brother…" my voice cracked and shattered into millions of pieces of pure anguish.

My face buried in her chest, I could barely hear Cel and Paulina's sobs over my own. Dani held me close until mine began to subside.

When I finally looked up into her watery blue eyes, she wiped some of my tears away and whispered, "We know. I'll bring them downstairs in two minutes."

They were seated in front of me, except for Dani. She stood behind me, her hands on my shoulders.

She's the only one.

Cel and Paulina's faces were swollen with tears, hands gripping Roberto's, who sat between them. His face was contorted in pain and something else. Maybe it was the impossible responsibility of being strong for these two women. Maybe not.

The TV screen was black for the first time in days.

They had to hear about his death from those who egged the mob.

Realizing I could barely gaze in their direction without guilt hammering me to pieces, I used the *Sense* to center myself. I had to tell them what I'd seen. The details came out factually as though it was an after-mission debrief, devoid of the emotion that lurked beneath the surface. All that remained unsaid was the detail of the memory card, which felt like smoldering charcoal in my pocket.

I'm not ready. Not yet.

Dani's nails gently dug into my flesh as her silent tears fell on my neck. Cel and Paulina started to wail, and Roberto pulled them both closer. His eyes remained fixed on me, unmoving like the rest of his face.

Yes, he knows violence.

Our intercom buzzed, and Dani left the room to see who was by the gate.

Roberto looked ready to ask me something when the studio door opened and Dani walked back in with Holden on her heels.

After he hugged each member of the Ramirez family, he grabbed a chair and sat with us.

My friend struggled to keep his own composure as he spoke. His lip quivered a few times, though he was no stranger to this conversation either.

Holden told them everything he knew and saw, promising to do whatever he could to bring justice to those who killed Nico. My body remained paralyzed, breaths moving in and out in solid, mechanical rhythm.

When he finished, Roberto asked the question on everyone's mind, "Roger, do you know how Nicolas died?"

Holden allowed a faint smile. Not many people called him by his first name.

"We don't know yet. We're gathering evidence." His eyes briefly found mine.

You won't see anything, Brother.

Cel wiped her tears, face flushed. "Was anyone arrested, at least?"

Holden bowed his head momentarily and shook it again. "It would have been beyond complicated to try arresting a crowd of hundreds..."

Cel bolted out of her chair, cursing in Spanish. "Really? Really?"

But the rage was quickly replaced by grief, and she collapsed into tears, Dani catching her on her way to the ground.

Holden stood, moving as though his weight had doubled.

"I'm sorry for your loss. I promise I'll do what I can."

As he turned to leave, he motioned for me to follow him.

"Walk me to the car." It sounded more like an order than a request.

We silently crossed the empty courtyard and reached the street where his police SUV was parked. Officer Dee was at the wheel and answered my nod with a sad smile.

When he turned to face me, his eyes were narrow and bloodshot. "Did you take the memory card?"

I'm still in the cave.
My eyes see nothing through the pitch darkness.
The gruff laughter echoes over the stony walls.

"No. Did they find the hiding spot?" The words rolled out effortlessly as my old life trickled back without me paying attention.

Eyebrows raised in concern, Holden answered, "Yes. Both the secret and his regular camera systems were destroyed. Nico stored everything locally, and we couldn't find the hard drives." He paused, his face softening a bit. "I warned you, and you still charged in. Why did you do that? You almost got in serious trouble."

I allowed the *Sense* to recede enough for my emotions to show.

"Fucking amazing if I need to explain to you my reasoning, Holden."

His eyes widened for a moment and then flashed.

"Stay out of this, Tanner. We'll handle it. We're on the same side."

My lip curled. "Right. Of course. One team…"

Holden leaned toward me, his clenched jaw hardening his countenance again. "Look in the mirror before criticizing me."

The truth gripped my chest and threatened to eliminate my breath altogether.

I fucked up.

"Thought so," said Holden, turning to get into the car.

Dee looked at me one last time before pulling away.

Paralyzed by regret, I watched their car disappear onto a side street. Finally alone, my fingers touched the memory card in my pocket.

I didn't listen to you when I had the chance.

The kids' howls broke my heart. Both David and Odalys were on the sofa, with everyone around them. Ari had wrapped his arm firmly around David.

I'm so sorry.

Dani's eyes gently met mine as she leaned in to console the Ramirez kids.

My head down, I turned and left for my sanctuary below. I had a decision to make.

Seated by my desk, I could barely stomach the garbage narratives spewing from my TV about the "unfortunate incident in Venice." Some anchors even went as far as to suggest that Nico might have been the aggressor in the entire sad affair. Hours passed, as I listened and stared at the small memory card on the desk in front of me.

Why didn't I go to him?

"Want to know?" the guttural voice whispered.

Time stopped as my hand clicked the TV off. I nodded into the empty air, eyes closing.

Back in the cave,
I'm trying to retrace my way back to
the cavemouth without success.

*There is something ancient below me,
down beyond the broken barrier.*

"*Bogotá...*" the merciless, inhuman voice reverberated and then turned into laughter.

When I opened my eyes, the memory card was in the palm of my right hand. I debated whether to see it first alone and then decided otherwise.

They deserve to know if they choose to.

When the grief-stricken children were all asleep upstairs, we gathered in my studio again.

I held the memory card up for them to see.

"I took this from the restaurant. It's the memory card for Nico's secret camera... his last moments." Various expressions looked back at me. "This is an illegal recording. It was a felony for me to take it, so it must not leave this room. However, it's your right to see it now if you choose to. Stay or leave. The decision is yours." I sat down quietly to give them time.

A silent minute passed, and no one left. Dani looked at me, resolved to remain, as though she sensed my desire for her to go.

"He was our only child. Show us, Tanner." Roberto's voice was final and solid.

"Very well." I inserted the card into my laptop and broadcasted it to the TV screen.

★ ★ ★

The wide camera angle captured the entire dining room up to the front door and Nico standing in the middle of the space, holding his phone to his ear.

His voice boomed from the TV speakers.

"Listen, Hermano. I got to go. If something happens… Please watch over my family, and remember one thing… This United States Marine Corporal Nicolas Ramirez did what he believed was right. You should try it again."

My heart squeezed, recalling these final words. The *Sense* returned, calming my body and mind, so I could stay in my seat.

I need to see this.

Nico hung up and took his SIM card out. After smashing it and the phone, he threw the remains away.

Rioters screamed at him from outside, demanding to get inside. He laughed and yelled back as the front door began to buckle. Nico rushed to put his weight against it, his eyes looking straight at the camera, his sly smile barely holding up.

A shiver coursed through me as I watched him walk away from the buckling door into the main dining room where he looked at the camera again and professed his love to his parents, Celeste, and the kids.

"I choose this, Hermano," was his final sentence before the front door exploded open.

The large, brown-skinned man with thick muscles burgeoning through his black tank top and a shemagh covering his face was the first to enter the shop. A dozen other rioters flooded in behind him.

"Don't touch him!" roared the giant.

They began to destroy the place while Nico stood, facing the large man. The next one to enter was the Demon guy, flanked by a dozen or so similarly black-clad masked men.

Paulina cried out and Cel began to sob.

The Demon spoke and his men pushed all the other rioters outside.

They work like a unit. Are they Ryse? The large man flanked the Demon as they advanced toward Nico. *Is that the same big fucker I saw that day with the kids?*

Nico laughed and pointed at the Demon. "You again? I already told you my answer."

He'd seen him before?

"Create the shield, destroy the cameras, and get the hard drive," the Demon ordered his men, and they rushed to comply as he focused on Nico.

Another rioter entered the restaurant laughing, holding the US and USMC flags. He handed them to one of the Demon's men, who passed them to their leader.

Nico bristled but kept quiet, observing the intruders surrounding him and the blades they held.

"Oh, Dios!" yelped Paulina, and Roberto comforted her quietly, eyes entranced on the nightmare unfolding on the screen.

Dani's eyes found mine and my heart ached with despair.

She will never be the same.

The Demon threw the flags in front of Nico, and he and his men began to close the circle.

"Kneel on your sacred flags," commanded the Demon.

"Never!" roared Nico, his body crouching to a battle stance.

"Me alone," grumbled the Demon as he moved toward Nico, fists up.

Nico knew how to brawl and even throw good punches at a bag, but this wasn't a street fight. The Demon thwarted every move and then rained kicks and punches, getting around all of Nico's efforts to block him.

A professional fighter.

When Nico hit the ground, the Demon took a break and nodded at his giant friend, who entered the circle to take his turn.

"Not so tough after all, soldier boy," taunted the Demon after his friend knocked Nico to the floor again.

Motioning for the giant to stand down, he stood over Nico.

Blood oozing from the dozens of gashes and slices on his face, Nico tried to roll over and stand but could only get to his knees. A lone fist on the ground prevented him from falling.

The Demon bent a knee just a few feet from him. "Just kneel, and we'll be done."

Nico spat blood. He turned his head toward the camera for the briefest of moments and back to the Demon.

"Listen," whispered the voice.

"Kneel," demanded the Demon.

My best friend picked himself up slowly, took a deep breath, and yelled, "Semper Fidelis!" as he charged the Demon. Quickly batting aside Nico's feeble attempt to hit him, he knocked him down with a massive right hook to the face.

Screams erupted in my studio, but I didn't turn to see who it was. I couldn't.

Nico was on his back, his shirt torn open and chest visible. Using his boot, the Demon moved the shirt remains aside, exposing the "cross and tear tattoo."

He chided, "Was that Latin you used? Do you pray?" Still laughing, he challenged, "Where's your Christian God now?"

Nico used his last bit of strength to grab the boot and surprised the Demon by twisting his leg and dropping him to the ground. He tried to rise, to use his momentum, but the giant rushed in and kicked him straight in the head. Nico was crumpled to the floor again, unmoving.

The Demon bounced up and angrily ordered his minions to hold Nico spread like a cross and stretch the USMC flag over his face.

"Waterboarding time, soldier boy," said the Demon, inspiring an eruption of laughter from his men.

I barely registered any of the pain filling the studio as the Demon ordered his men to piss on Nico's face. Only he and the giant refrained.

No DNA trace.

My dearest brother gasped for air as they drowned him in their urine. But he was still alive when they finished and removed the flag from his face.

"Night night, Bitch!"

The Demon roared again and smashed Nico's face under his heavy boot.

More screams resounded through the studio and somewhere deep within.

*I screamed into the nothingness
of the tunnel.*

"Now you know..." growled the voice at my suffering.

"Cover him with the flags," commanded the Demon as Nico's broken skull bled on the floor.

Someone came from the outside and spoke to the large man, "The councilwoman is out calling for you."

Both the giant and Demon went outside as their men took positions.

They know what they're doing.

Eventually, the men rushed out. And seconds later, I barged in, stopped by Nico, and went to the back before the feed cut.

Soft sobs were the only sounds in the studio for minutes as we all struggled to digest what we'd just witnessed.

Eventually, I turned from the screen to the rest of them. Paulina and Cel sobbed while Roberto and Dani did their best to console them.

A river of tears stormed inside, but the *Sense* kept me together.

"Not for long. Not for long."

Dani's head snapped toward me, her face wet with tears but no cries.

Did she hear the voice?

Cel bolted off the couch, refusing to let anyone stop her. Fixing her eyes on me, she shrieked, "It always pained him that you hid your service. He hung those flags for *you* so that *you* would wake the fuck up! It's not too late. He died viewing you as a hero. Are you? Are you?"

Her words seared my soul even more deeply than her blazing eyes, and I could find no words. Finally resigning to my silence, she walked slowly toward the studio door and Paulina followed. Dani was the next to leave, giving me one last vacant stare.

Roberto remained. There were no tears on his hard old face either. He just nodded before he left.

Crack.
Alone in the tunnel, hands searching
franticly for the wall for solace,
for something to hold beyond the
impenetrable darkness.

"This is the second time, Tanner. Find me. You know where." The voice came from everywhere and nowhere.

I sat on the floor, against the wall, heart thundering with terror, right hand trembling to hold my weight as I repeated, "Alley rhymes with Ali... Alley rhymes with Ali," trying to stave off the truth.

The last echo faded,
leaving me alone in the abyss.

I FUCKED UP

I squinted at the dawn's light entering the studio, surprised by the invasion of the sun. It was a sleepless night, which I'd spent emotionally-shackled to my desk, watching him die again and again, remembering all we had shared, from our early days in Venice, his enlistment, Afghanistan, how we supported each other out of the alcohol hellscape, and then back to the good days.

A popup on my computer screen confirmed the upload was complete, and it didn't take long for my dad to reach out.

"Morning, Son," Jack said, his voice warmer than usual.

"Hi, Dad," I replied, gathering myself with a deep breath.

"I got your files." He paused and cleared his throat. "No Soldier should die like this. I'm sorry, Son."

The words lodged in my throat threatened to crack me wide open.

After a few moments of silence, he continued, "We'll review and analyze for any details, but why did you send the Dragon Skull graffiti photo with the film?"

When I told him I had seen it a few times before, and inside the restaurant on the day of the attack, Jack confirmed it had been seen in other riots' hotbeds. It seemed to be used by both Ryse and Comrades.

"Have you noticed the soviet likeness of their messaging and symbols?" he asked.

"Yes, Sir." His question kept my mind away from the pain.

"Communism and collectivism couldn't beat us openly, so they subverted us. No bullets were needed while they slowly corrupted our democratic soul." His indignance reverberated.

Closing my eyes, I could see Grandpa's wrinkle-lined hard face.

"He warned us about that."

Jack sighed loudly. He rarely opened up about his father, Ulysses Lee Washington.

He must miss him.

I caught my breath, feeling the stabbing pain of loss return to my chest.

"Yes, like in his stories," was all he replied, though his haunted tone said much more.

We both took a moment to remember the great man who'd left us and the mission nearly two decades earlier.

"I'm glad your blood pressure is decreasing a bit."

They always know. I resisted the urge to touch my ear and remained quiet.

"Speak, Son."

My anger crackled, and harsh words formed at the tip of my tongue.

"If it helps, consider this an order." His tone was unrelenting.

Retired or not, he's my commander.

I relaxed back into my chair.

"I missed it all, Dad. From the beginning to the end." The words shredded me on their way out of my mouth.

"The end?"

Fuck! I'm always in training.

Fury erupted again. "Yes. The end! Nico's dead! He survived the Taliban, and now he's dead. Tortured in his own place!" My voice trembled as more guilt poured out of me.

"Enough!" Jack commanded. "Use the *Sense*. Honor your friend and tell me what's next!"

It wasn't easy, but the *Sense* returned at the first deep breath.

"First, I need to deal with the funeral." My words were empty of emotion as I slipped into soldier mode.

"Agreed. Corporal Nicolas Ramirez will be honored. Just tell us how we can help." His timber was warm again.

After a few moments of silence, Jack kept me in soldier mode by pivoting the conversation to Chad in Seattle and bringing me up to speed on the escalating situation over there. There had been nightly riots in various locations.

Bitterness managed to sneak by the *Sense,* or maybe I allowed it.

"His beloved oppressed."

Jack didn't like my response and snapped me out of it. "No matter what he believes in, he's your brother. Sometimes it takes some pain to wake up. You should know."

His words stung, but there was no way for me to rebut them, and we found ourselves at a familiar impasse.

My mom saved us when she took over the conversation.

"Drop the *Sense,* Baby. It's just us," were her first words to me.

Ali had been involved in everything since my birth, and rare were the moments in which she had invoked her motherly rights over my father's training.

She managed to get a bit more from me, primarily due to her questions about all the others, starting with Nico's family and then Dani and the kids.

There was a growing temptation building inside me to tell her about the cave, the darkness, the voice, and what *It* told me.

I'm not ready, even if I use her old mantra to hold it together.

"Mom, I should go. I hear everyone waking up."

She might have believed me or maybe not, but she let me go anyway.

"Okay, give them all a hug from me. I love you, Son. You remember that, no matter what."

My phone collected messages and voicemails while I raged in the isolation of my cave, lit only by the light from the computer screen where the scene played on repeat. I ignored all of them, except Shemtov's text. During the "Venice riot" on Sunday, he'd barricaded himself inside the synagogue.

My awareness suddenly expanded beyond my four walls, I quickly checked the Venice Beach camera and was relieved to see Todd on his hill, safe and sound, with a few US flags out with him.

This is his response.

My bandwidth wasn't free enough to also debate this new worry.

The studio door opened and Dani shuffled in, still sleepy. Back in the world before Sunday, she always entered with that naughty smile—it was just her signature. This morning, however, her pretty face was swollen from crying, her tired eyes haunted.

I rose from my chair and met her at the door. We said nothing and everything as we embraced, frozen in time, embarking on a new reality not of our choosing.

When she pulled her head back and kissed me, something rattled inside and my body started to shake. My legs buckled under me.

She's the only one.

On my knees, head buried in her belly, no sound emerged.

Her hands stroked my hair gently until my body quaked.

"I fucked up! I fucked up!" It spewed out of me like a torrent breaking through a dam wall.

Still holding my head, she whispered, "It's not too late, Sweetie. It's not too late."

Torn between searing pain and cold white rage, I trembled uncontrollably and Dani held me tighter.

No, Baby. It's too late for him. But not for what I'm about to do.

"*Yes…*" whispered the voice.

FACE IT

"**A**lley rhymes with Ali. Alley rhymes with Ali. Alley..."

My eyes opened, my mouth still mumbling my mantra into the dark nothingness that choked me in my sleep.

The sun was up, and I was alone in bed. Sounds of children talking and delicious smells from the kitchen wafted up from below. When I grabbed my phone from the nightstand and looked at the screen, it all hit me again.

Another day in hell. I growled into the thin air and willed myself into the master bathroom to shower and then made my way to the top of the stairs.

The Ramirez kids and ours were playing on the main level while Dani and Cel were prepping breakfast quietly in the kitchen. The TV was off.

Thank God.

"Daddy's awake!" Ari ran toward me as I descended the stairs and Lil followed behind him, squealing incoherently. There was no way I was getting out of our morning rituals, and I didn't want to. I needed it as much as they did.

Odalys had always been shy, and now it was nearly impossible to get anything besides a muted hello from Nico's sweet daughter. David was younger and didn't fully comprehend his loss, so he cracked a smile that warmed my heart when I greeted him.

Once they all had their morning hugs, they scampered back to their play and I approached the ladies in the kitchen. Dani handed me a plate with scrambled eggs and salad and kissed me softly on the cheek.

"Thanks, Baby." I paused to pull her close. "I'll eat it downstairs."

She nodded, a sad smile on her face.

I turned toward Cel who only looked at me, her usual warmth lost behind anger.

With me.

"We have our appointment at the morgue today. Can we take the van?" I asked gently. The large gray Taco Libertad van had been Nico's pride and joy—two seats in the front, open space in the back, and tinted windows.

Privacy is important now.

"Yes, I'll be ready," she mumbled as she turned back to wash the dishes.

When I looked back to Dani, she shrugged sadly and returned to help her friend.

I ate slowly while the TV and the computer caught me up on the madness outside our front door.

The mayor had decided to make the lockdown even harder by adding a mandatory curfew from 6 p.m. until 6 a.m.

Unless you're a peaceful protester, right? I snarled silently.

The media was building their false narrative about Taco Libertad. Somehow, they connected the "awful incident in Venice" with Chicago, and the LAPD was criticized for how they handled the entire affair, while implications of Nico's responsibility floated between the lines.

I'm so glad they're not watching this shit.

The worst was Victoria's speech in front of the ransacked restaurant. I resisted the urge to throw my plate against the wall as she publicly mourned Nico, admitting to knowing the family and usurping the moment to talk about her roots in Venice.

"This was a generational restaurant that served us all. I ate here since childhood…" But Victoria didn't stop there. She referred to the murder as an "unintended consequence" of violence, stemming from the people's understandable rage about Chicago and Nico's misunderstanding of it all. "His flags offended them, causing unnecessary pain among the protesters."

His flags? You fucking bitch! I pushed the rage down. *Not now.*

When the phone rang and I saw Tami's name, I inhaled deeply and answered.

"Hi, Big Brother, been trying to reach you."

Her baby, Adam, cooed in the background.

"Hi, Sis. Sorry. It's awful here…"

I didn't have much to give, so she filled in the gap with her frustration over how the law wasn't being enforced in so many places across the country.

"Those district attorneys just refused to press charges. It's unbelievable. That nonsense isn't tolerated here in South Dakota under Lynn's leadership. It barely exists."

"I'm glad to hear you and Lynn are doing good work," I offered and wrapped up the call as quickly and with as much kindness as I could muster.

As soon as I set the phone down, it rang again.

Ugh, this could be a disaster, I thought as I picked up Chad's call.

Fortunately, it was one of our better conversations. His rarely witnessed compassionate self shared his deepest condolences for Nico's death.

"A man's love for another man is underrated," he said before hanging up.

I reached to turn the volume back up on my TV and froze when I saw my mom's name pop up on my phone. I hesitated, wondering if it was a good idea after how I'd woken up.

It'll probably be fine.

Ali always called when the times were rough, even when it wasn't being blasted on the news. More than once, her insider knowledge and maternal instinct had found me at just the right moment at the end of a black-op operation in some distant foreign land.

"Hi, Sweetie. How are you this morning?"

"The nightmare returned last night," I admitted, getting straight to it.

The same long pause that always met these admissions didn't surprise me.

"It's been so many years since the last time. Have you used the mantra?" She didn't dig or ask for further details, nor would I have provided them.

But why doesn't she?

"Yes, Mom. It's okay. I just wanted to let you know."

The walk to the Ramirez compound was uneventful. The streets were mostly empty, as if even they were ashamed of what had taken place within them the last few days.

Roberto met me outside with the keys to the van parked on their lot. As I took them, I noticed the exhaustion around his eyes and the days-old stubble.

"I'll meet you at the morgue," I said, opening the driver's side door to get in.

He nodded while stroking his unshaved chin, and I held the door open and waited.

Just like Nico. He's got something to say.

"See you there, Tanner."

Huh. Another time, I guess.

I relaxed into the thick leather chair and recalled how Nico had his buddy install it for his achy back on those long days of finding the best produce for his clientele. The US Marines' globe and anchor sticker on the dashboard was worn but not faded.

He's gone. The ache that never went away tightened its grip.

Cel was waiting for me outside our complex gate. When I opened the door for her to come in, I got a faint nod in return.

"Drive by the restaurant," she instructed, her voice distant and detached.

I was grasping the wheel harder, bracing myself against the internal rumble, when I saw the yellow tape protecting the crime scene and the new door that had been installed. Nico's friends had taken care of that with Holden's permission.

Stopping near the front, not too far from the Dragon Skull on the wall, I sat entranced by the grotesque skull-like image until Cel's voice wrested me back.

"That's enough," she said. "Let's go."

I pulled into traffic, expecting silence until she blindsided me.

"Tell me about Afghanistan."

"What do you know about it?" I asked, fortifying myself with a deep breath.

"Not much. He never spoke. All I have is what I understood from his screams at night through the years."

"Which is?" I coaxed, a bit relieved.

She shifted in her seat, measuring me for a moment. "I think he was in a hole—maybe underground or something?"

The nightmare scene flashed before me, and I hastened the *Sense* to close any gaps and help me respond.

"I'll tell you what I can. Agreed?" I glanced at her pale and puffy face.

Cel nodded, still watching my face closely as I navigated the side streets of Venice.

I told her the official story, which was classified on its own. Nico's platoon got off-course on a patrol and wandered into a dangerous Taliban zone by the Pakistani border where they were ambushed. Only Nico and one other soldier survived.

"Dmitri. Right?"

"Yes, they sought refuge in an Afghani village, and the local chief hid them in a deep well where they stayed until their rescue arrived."

"Was that it?" asked Cel, her eyes locked onto mine, taking advantage of the fact that we were stopped at a red light.

"That's all that you can know." It was the honest response she was owed.

The light changed to green, and she remained quiet for a while, clearly working to connect the dots.

"There was this thing he used to say in the nightmares. 'I'm sorry... I'm sorry.' Do you know what that was about?"

"I don't." It was the truth but not all of it. Nico was repeating those words when we pulled them out of the well, and it had taken him a few minutes to regain his composure. Once focused, he deflected when asked what it was about. I always knew something haunted Nico even before the enlistment and considered asking her about the "cross and tear" tattoo, but decided it wasn't the right time.

"This is it," I said, pointing at the giant building in the middle of a large parking lot, hesitating for a moment as I caught sight of a lone biker by the tree up the slope.

Roberto, Paulina, and some friends of Nico's were already huddled inside the cold, sterile lobby when we walked through the morgue's double glass doors.

Dmitri was around Nico's age, maybe a year older. He had the frame of a bodybuilder, a bald head, and a full dark beard, but his usually bright eyes were dull and gray today. He gave a silent grunt, and I nodded in return as I followed Cel.

He and I had not spoken since Afghanistan, but it didn't matter. When we saved them, the deadly Russian had done his part and more.

I know you, and you know me.

I'd barely acknowledged Roberto and Paulina when the glass doors opened again and Holden and Officer Dee stepped through, holding the folded flags.

Pride and sadness competed within me, but the soldier won and I stood taller at the sight of Old Glory.

Some of Nico's buddies squirmed, likely because they didn't exactly operate within the law. But that didn't matter in this building. They were all Nicolas Ramirez's friends from the same neighborhood, and they all embraced Holden accordingly.

As Dee approached Celeste with the flags, Holden gestured to his partner and said, "She has worked hard cleaning and folding them properly."

The sight of the young officer made me wonder about Holden. I'd known him for decades, but I'd never seen him interact with this officer, and I'd definitely never seen such tenderness in his expression.

Who is she?

Dee's smile disappeared as she bowed slightly to Cel and handed her the flags.

"I'm sorry for your loss."

When she turned, we exchanged appreciation before she took her spot just behind Holden who thanked her again.

Like a daughter. Huh.

Holden knew we were eager for an update.

"Unfortunately, urine samples aren't a good source to authenticate DNA and we got no match on any database."

"What about the cameras?" asked Roberto. Though depleted, he stood erect and alert.

Holden grimaced. "They were all masked and they broke the cameras in the restaurant. Nobody has been ID'd yet."

Everyone bristled.

Those fuckers aren't in the database.

Cel's eyes fired up as she stepped forward and raised her voice. "Are you really doing everything you can, Holden?"

He turned back to look at Dee briefly.

He's ashamed too.

My fingers began their tap on my thigh, and then stopped as my friend's eyes gravitated toward me.

"Ever since Chicago," he stopped and looked around, voice lowered, "it's just not the same. We're facing difficulties obtaining warrants unless we have a smoking gun."

A dissatisfied murmur ripped through the group and only Dmitri and Roberto stayed quiet, keeping their eyes trained on me.

I know. I fucked up. I'm here now.

Seeing Cel's face contorting at something behind me, I turned to see a large black SUV with a police escort parking in front of the building. The back passenger door opened and Victoria emerged with three of her staff, all masked with thin face diapers embroidered with the city's logo. One of them had his phone up as soon as his feet touched the asphalt.

She's recording!

I quickly stepped back and away from the camera.

A young staffer opened the door for Victoria, who marched in with more authority than she possessed. She offered condolences in Spanish to Roberto, Paulina, and Celeste, and then repeated a shorter version in English while looking at the phone of her staffer.

The tranquility was broken quickly as Emmanuel Perez, one of Nico's best friends, lashed out.

"No competition left, Vic?" he challenged.

He was wiry, with a goatee beard and a white tank top, showing off the many tattoos on his brown tanned skin.

A ripple of concern crossed her face, but she didn't take the bait.

"It's uncalled for, Emmanuel. I mourn the loss, just like you," she replied, touching her eye as if to wipe away an invisible tear.

"You betrayed the neighborhood," hackled one of the other guys.

She knows them all?

"Enough!" commanded Roberto as he stepped forward and placed himself between Victoria and the rest. He hugged her and Paulina did the same. Celeste stayed behind, eyes narrow and full of fury.

The *Sense* registered every detail as my hands relaxed.

A masked doctor in a white lab coat shuffled toward us from down the hall, his tired eyes conveying nothing. All he needed was someone to identify the body.

I forced my fingers to stay still.

"I'll do this," offered Roberto, kissing Paulina on her head, who then reached for Cel and sobbed as he walked away.

We all kept quiet during the few minutes it took Roberto to return with the doctor, his eyes haunted by what he'd just seen.

I'm sorry, Roberto.

"Due to the Dragon measures, only one immediate family member is allowed to attend the funeral," the doctor said, his tone empty and robotic.

Celeste exploded, berating the doctor while a murmur rumbled through the rest.

Holden stepped forward. "Calm down. He's just doing his job."

"Fuck that, Holden!" Cel shrieked with rage. "Those killers can riot freely in the street, and we cannot attend his funeral? Suddenly you care about the virus? Is that what you're telling me?"

I sighed, keeping myself quiet and away from the camera, wishing I could just disappear as Victoria marched forward and demanded a better answer from the doctor.

"Well, tell that to your boss. Those are *his* rules," the doctor said matter-of-factly. "I'm sorry. It is awful," he admitted to Celeste before he turned and left.

★　★　★

Victoria said goodbye and left with her crew and the police escort, and nobody spoke as we all dragged ourselves out of the building.

"Go home and I'll be there in a few hours. I need to sort a few things first," I told the Ramirez family.

"We'll see you there." Roberto put his arms around Cel and Paulina and held my gaze.

Yes, Sir. We can talk then.

Dmitri was the last one, hanging back and looking composed behind his large silver shades while he waited for everyone else to leave.

"How many of your old battalion could be mustered up and brought to town?" I asked.

"How long we got?"

"Twenty-four hours."

My answer provoked laughter that cracked like a shipwreck in the empty parking lot.

"For Nico, enough will come." His face was dead serious again.

"Get them ready. Dress uniforms," I instructed.

"I remember this voice. Good." He nodded and a wicked smirk played at the edge of his lips.

Definitely a killer.

"*Like you*," the voice whispered.

Dmitri tilted his large head toward the lone tree on the hill where the biker still waited before he said goodbye in Russian and left.

Did he see him?

I walked back into the morgue and began my search for a back exit.

Ten minutes later, the biker turned toward me as I allowed my shoes to make a sound on the asphalt. He wore dark jeans and a heavy black biker jacket and his helmet rested on his dark sport bike.

"Damn! You got out of the back! I lost $100 now." Danberry Moss's broad smile revealed perfectly a mouth full of white teeth and a childish personality. His dark chocolate skin and mischievous smile made him look even younger than his early thirties.

He moved to greet me with a firm hug.

"Sorry for your loss, Alfa-leader," he offered in a more subdued tone.

"Are the others around?" I asked when I released him from a tight embrace.

Moss nodded. "They're all here or on their way." He reached into his pocket and pulled out a sleek black cube, flipping it open to reveal a phone.

"Been told to give this to you. It's all ready for activation." His voice sounded hopeful.

As I reached for it, a wave of fear tore through me.

I can't lose them.

"Sir?" Moss broke my trance.

I took a deep breath and began the sync with the new phone, which included calling the RCC for voice activation. It all felt like wading into a parallel reality, and my body and mind silently screamed their countless objections.

Immediately, the radar app showed the pings of the team, and Moss nodded in approval.

"We're here for you, Sir."

"The big Russian might have just made you, Moss. I need you all invisible."

Moss laughed. "I remember him. I'll be better."

We hugged one last time, and I turned toward Nico's van.

"Does this mean you're back?" he called after me.

That tone again.

His words made me stop, but only to turn my head slightly and allow one slow nod.

Yes. May God have mercy.

NEED YOUR HELP

The van door closed, taking the daylight with it.

I'm a fan of the privacy too, Brother.

I sighed and pulled out the Rogue-issued smartphone, looking at it.

Rogues. Nameless and Loyal.

One text later, I turned on the engine and drove off the lot.

Seeing the traffic ahead, I turned on Brett Cohen's podcast, figuring I would make the most of my time. Though a lot was going on around the country, Brett focused on Nico's death and the lackluster response by the local government to the horrific murder.

Thank you.

I smiled again when he highlighted the depravity of celebrities who donated money to post bail for violent rioters who had pillaged Chicago's Magnificent Mile area. When he mentioned Senator Dwayne Jackson and his recent talk in defense of the "mostly peaceful protests," I grunted at the recollection of Chelsea's insufferable words about the New York politician.

Suddenly his tyrannical Dragon measures can be placed on hold. All in the name of social justice.

My whole body tensed as I took in the dark reality of what had become my town. Streets were either empty or roamed by those you didn't want to meet. Comrades and Ryse anti-police and socialist slogans abounded. Shattered glass and boarded-up businesses, an alarming number of them sprayed with messages supporting the rioters.

Fucking cowards. Writing "Remember Chicago" on your store won't save you.

The chip vibrated in my ear as the Rogue phone rang.

"I'm sorry, Son. What do you need?" It was Custer responding to my text.

When I told him about the challenges with a funeral related to the Dragon measures and local government edicts, he asked, "What's your plan, Soldier?"

"I'm requesting a military funeral at the Los Angeles Military Cemetery. He would have wanted it, and it will also solve this predicament."

Custer grunted. "Nice workaround." His long pause told me he was looking for the best way to address the elephant in the room. "That's a high price, Tanner. You know the locals will lose it over this stunt. Are you willing to pay?"

My fists clenched on the wheel. "Yes, Sir. Just let me do this one thing right..."

"Very well. I'll talk to Jack and make some other calls. In the meantime, see if you can arrange a Chaplin."

"Would a retired one do the job?" I didn't try to hide the smirk.

He released a short laugh. "Yes. Talk soon."

Shemtov was outside the synagogue, standing by his maintenance worker, who was painting over a Dragon Skull.

Shit, I thought as I climbed the stairs to speak with my friend.

"Some punks did it during the night," he said after giving me a warm embrace.

My mind raced as I followed him to his office chamber. He clearly didn't make much of it, but the pit in my stomach would not be ignored.

"How can I help you, my friend?" he asked after pouring us some cold water.

"Well..." I did my best to restrain the mischievous smile as I told him about my plan and my need for his help.

He grinned and tapped his fingers on the desk as he considered my request. "Are you sure the Ramirez's wouldn't mind a Jewish Chaplin?" He knew Nico was a devoted Catholic.

"Nico always held you in high regard, Rabbi. Same is true for his parents." My smile got the best of me. "Besides, who else would agree to my insane plan?"

Shemtov looked at his Vietnam photo for a long moment.

"If his family approves, then I'd be honored. The old uniform might still fit me." He winked and pretended to measure his waist with his eyes.

"Then it's settled." I stood up quickly. "I'm sure they'll agree."

"Hold up a moment." His voice stopped me in my tracks, and I watched his brow furrow as his eyes scanned me. "You are different."

He, too, knows violence.

A nod was all I could give him.

Custer rang me on my walk back to the van.

"We can do it. I got the place booked, and we'll get him from the morgue ourselves. But, there is one challenge." Just under his concern was his confidence in me. "We don't have any say outside of the military cemetery. You'll have to figure out how to get all your people to the gate."

"Yes, I've been thinking about that..." When I told him about my solution, he whistled and remained speechless for a long minute.

"You just get them to the gate."

"Yes, Sir."

"Glad to see that you're still in top shape." I understood his reference to my encounter with Moss. "Alfa is already stationed around the area and available for support if needed."

I miss them.

"About what you sent…" he started. "We couldn't get their faces, but we did a good job isolating the voices. RCC will download it to your chip."

So that I can hear you again and again.

"Thank you," I replied, feeling the urge to touch my ear.

"Don't thank me so quickly, Son. These fuckers are probably American citizens. I'm reminding you that no Directive Two is authorized at this time."

I'll wait.

"Yes, Sir."

The group from the morgue waited for me on the grass between the two homes at the Ramirez compound. They all stopped talking when I opened the front gate.

Dmitri wasn't among them.

Good. He's mustering up.

"I found a solution to the Dragon measures. We can bury him in the Los Angeles Military Cemetery. Neither the state, county, nor city has jurisdiction there." The family held each other as they listened. "The trick is going to be getting there."

They, too, were stunned by my plan.

Roberto looked to Paulina and Celeste. When they both nodded in agreement, he turned to me. "We're in. And thank the rabbi. Nico always liked him."

"Very well. And keep radio silence on this. Nobody outside this gathering is to be informed unless authorized by me," I instructed, barely noticing how quickly my old self had taken command.

Cel's gaze was intense, yet it didn't seem angry anymore, as I bid them all farewell.

I motioned for Emmanuel to come with me.

"Can you do it?" I asked after explaining his role in the plan.

He nodded, wearing the same sly smile that Nico always gave me. "Yes, Ese. I got this one for you, but there better be reckoning for this one day."

One day, I thought to myself but only nodded to Emmanuel before walking away.

Custer's words sniped at my thoughts on the walk home.

"Mask up, Fucker!" yelled some guys across the street, but even that wasn't enough to stop my thought.

How do I tell her?

Your home is your castle, and it should be. But when I crossed the threshold with this plan already in motion, I felt like a stranger entering my own home. That is, until I saw Ari's face at the top of the stairs.

Dani was starting to make dinner, so my timing was perfect for bathing the kids.

I love this time of day.

I felt the tension dissolve in my body and mind as I took a few stairs at a time and picked Ari up for a squeeze.

Our tub wasn't the largest, but it must have felt like an Olympic pool to Lil whose favorite game appeared to be trying to drown her daddy. I was already drenched and doubled over in laughter by the time Ari marched in, demanding his turn in the water.

I can't lose them.

The dinner was plain, which spoke volumes about the chef's state of mind. Dani's number one love language was cooking, but tonight she was using all of her energy to smile and hold us together around the table. When it was over, I offered to put them to bed, so she could relax. She'd been doing everything on her own while I'd spent my long nights in the studio.

Leelee drifted quickly but Ari squirmed.

"Buddy, what's happening?" I asked.

"Daddy, why is Uncle Nico dead?"

The tension returned and seized my throat.

He's not even five. How do I answer?

"Bad people did it, My Love." Dani's voice came from behind me.

I breathed a sigh of relief as she bent down, kissed Ari's cheek, and continued to stroke his hair gently.

His innocent face contorted with the meaning of her words. "But why, Mamma? Why did it happen? Uncle Nico is so good."

Dani looked up at me, dumbfounded, as our son's confusion and pain broke both our hearts.

Yes. His daddy is to blame.

I averted my gaze and pushed the pain aside to be present for my son, but it seemed all he needed was to ask the question in order to surrender to sleep.

"I love you the most..." I whispered my part of our familiar exchange in his ear before leaving the room.

"I'll take care of getting someone to watch all the kids here in the complex," offered Dani after I told her about my plans.

"Are you okay with this?" I asked, wondering to myself if I should have just waited until morning. We were in our bedroom after showering until our hot water ran out, and I had clearly shifted the mood.

Her eyes were wide, but her jaw was clenched as she nodded. "I won't lie to you and say that I'm not afraid. But this is good. I'm with you." She sealed her promise with a long kiss.

This was a rare break in the ocean of madness called our lives, and we were going to make the most of it, like we always did. She massaged the remaining tension out of my back and relaxation replaced it as her hands moved across me.

"What do you know about Victoria and Nico, Baby?" I asked.

Her strong hands stopped, but she didn't remove them from my skin. "All Cel ever told me was that Nico and Victoria dated back in high school. That they broke off before Nico enlisted."

I remembered that time frame when he was restless and in pain.

Could Victoria have been the issue?

"Did Cel ever discover the reason for their break-up?" I wondered.

"Not that I know of." Her hands left me, probably to get one of her essential oils, and I kept my tired eyes closed.

"It used to be bulkier back in Israel." Her tone was distant and when I opened my eyes and turned to face her, I cringed at the sight of my Rogue phone in her hands.

"It fell out of your jeans." She placed it on the nightstand and sat back on the bed, without breaking eye contact or saying another word.

I was deployed to the US embassy in Tel Aviv in 2012 when we began to date. Even back then, she'd suspected my parallel work with the Alfa team but never pried.

She deserves to know.

I sat up and moved close, taking her hands in mine.

"I'm going back, Dani." Each word tore me apart.

"When?" she asked, pulling her hands back and twisting her wedding ring.

"Right after the funeral," I replied, feeling a fissure beginning in me and between us.

She took a deep breath and did her best to smile.

"Growing up in Israel, we all understood the price of a spouse who serves. I never knew what and where you did what you did. I'm just happy that you decided to help."

If only you knew.

I turned out the light and silently thanked her with a kiss.

The old and new phones sat next to each other on my desk as I waited. When the former chirped that it had finished its data migration, I erased it and dropped it into a drawer.

Holden texted me a few times, checking in.

I don't want to lie to him, but what choice do I have?

I opened the radar on the phone, noticing the design was more intuitive than the old versions.

I guess it's time.

All the team members were within a few miles of my location. Taking a deep breath for the imminent plunge, I pinged them all for a group chat.

Dex was the most direct, "Sir, are you taking command of Alfa?"

"Not yet, remain in control," I wrote back and disbanded the chat.

Alone in the darkness of my studio, I shuddered with pain as I recalled every awful detail of his death and was immediately transported.

"Madison 46," demanded Jack. I was hung from a rafter after being beaten up repeatedly. The black bag on my face prevented me from bracing my body before each piercing strike. Each Federalist Paper was distilled into a few important sentences, which the Rogues had to know, no matter their state.

"The Constitution preserves the advantage of being armed, which Americans possess over the citizens of almost every other nation where the governments are afraid to trust the people with arms," I roared in pain.

"Good. Focus on the pain. Embrace it and find the right moment to strike back," came my father's voice.

"Night night, Bitch," interrupted the Demon guy's voice.

My eyes popped opened, and I sat forward in my chair, heart racing and stomach clenched.

My hand found the phone on the desk, and I turned on his death video and sat back in my chair.

Closing my eyes again, the *Sense* turned on, and every note and sound was studied and ingrained into my memory.

I sank deeper into my chair, emptying my mind of the sounds of the sirens and choppers in the air.

Where are you? Why aren't you talking to me?

PRE-GAME

I sprawled flat on my back on the living room floor, so the fun could begin. At only nine months old, Leelee's emerging personality was clearly taking after my queen's. She was determined to jump on my belly, and Ari abandoned his video game to join the fight, hooting with glee. We rolled and rumbled and laughed, as if everything in the world was right.

But it wasn't.

"Food's ready." Dani motioned with her head for me to move the children to the table.

While the kids ate, she pulled the tablet off the countertop behind her. "You've got to see this," she said as she clicked a video.

On the screen, the chyron reported that the Los Angeles mayor and some police commanders had gathered before city hall to meet the protesters for a dialogue. I sucked in my breath when all the bureaucrats took a knee on the stage while the mayor conveyed his utmost sympathy for "their pain and suffering" and mentioned nothing of all the destruction and lives lost as a result of their rage. The demonstrators shouted, raising fists, supporting the Comrades movement with other social justice slogans.

They're different from Ryse. More in the open.

"Disgusting!" snarled Dani. "The whole country is going crazy. This is *not* America."

I let the breath out and caressed her face.

"This *is* bad. But not everyone is falling for it."

Her face turned hopeful as I shared another video I'd found. A Florida sheriff had come out swinging, openly warning anyone who'd think to come and riot in his county.

"And he's not alone. Their governor and others like them are standing up and protecting their states."

I watched her relax a little before her bitterness spilled out again, "Not much help for us here in California."

A knock on the door saved us from that spiral, and I knew it was our neighbor coming to ask what time to come to watch over the kids.

"I'll tell her to come back in thirty minutes. I'm going to get ready now," I said, kissing her forehead and moving toward the stairs.

The black plastic cover had a zipper in the middle that opened smoothly, even though it had been years since the last time I'd used it. It was a sight to behold, every time I beheld it, requiring a pause. All three US flag colors. The blue jacket. The red trim. The white peak cap hanging on top of the jacket.

As I removed the plastic cover and touched the fabric, memories and mixed feelings flooded my mind and body. My decision to enlist after my conversation with Ulysses. Grueling bootcamp, special forces courses, and eventually officer school.

My eyes stopped on the Colonel's silver eagle insignia on the collar.

And the last summer, before it all began.

The studio door opened, and Dani and the kids walked in. She was in a black dress, her hair neatly pulled into a long braid.

So beautiful it hurts, I thought as she whispered to Ari and Lil, directing them to sit together on the sofa with her.

When I began to change, Ari bolted from the sofa and ran to my side.

"Can I help, Dad?" he beamed.

I can't let my guilt ruin this moment.

"Of course..." I directed him to get my dress shoes and other items from the closet.

As he handed me the last item, he asked, "Can I come today? I promise I'll be good."

But you're so young... I searched for the right words.

Jack used to joke that my training began earlier than the infamous Spartan Agoge. Back then, Spartan kids began their harsh education at seven. "You're not that lucky," he used to say when I tried pushing back.

I forced my bitterness aside.

"I know you're brave and good, Son. Your time will come, but it's not today."

Ari lowered his head, dismayed, until Dani picked up Lil and came over to pat his head.

"Look how handsome your father is." My queen's naughty smile was back, even if just for these few moments. She was right behind me and gently kissed my cheek as I stood in front of the mirror to check every detail.

"I'm here," called our neighbor from outside the studio, and Dani and the kids hurried out to meet her, leaving me frozen in front of the mirror.

A call came in from Jack. "You got the Eye for today. Let's get it done."

"We're with you, Honey," added Ali.

"Thank you. We're almost ready," I said, eyes still glued to the mirror, feet unwilling to move.

I never thought I'd see you again.

"Are you ready?" asked Dani.

"Yes, My Queen," I replied, trying to crack a smile while bracing myself for the unraveling.

We walked into the courtyard holding hands and were immediately noticed. Though my eyes were set straight ahead, I watched as the neighbors' eyes grew wide and heard the neighbors' whispers and Chelsea's sneer.

We acknowledged them with our eyes only before walking out of the complex.

"So bizarre," she grumbled as we crossed the street. "How your uniform affects them. What? They never saw a soldier?" A splash of anger dripped between her words.

It wasn't the time and place to explain or to join her in the upset about America's current relationship with those who volunteer to protect it and die if necessary.

"It's fine, Baby. I don't mind it." I opened my phone and scanned for any reported police activity on our predetermined route. Alfa's six red dots encircled us at various distances, creating a protective shield.

"They're pointing at you," whispered Dani as some guys heckled us from a parked car across the street.

"Don't worry about it." I squeezed her hand and suppressed a smirk when I saw Moss disguised as a bum chilling on the pavement as we passed him.

The jeers and sneers continued, even from some residents who hurried on Dragon-permitted errands.

"Is this how people treat soldiers in America?" she asked after some guy shouted that he'd like to see me die with my "cunt."

"This is the first time I've experienced this," I admitted, still harboring a murderous thought toward the last heckler. "My dad used to talk about how they were treated, returning from Vietnam. He couldn't believe the names he was called."

A text arrived from Custer.

"They got the body," I told her.

She bit her lip and nodded as we kept walking.

Holden's call came in right as we entered Nico's side street.

"Are you going to answer?" she asked.

"No," and I pocketed the phone and shook off the tension accruing in my shoulders.

"Is it smart to blindside him like that? He deserves to know."

"He serves those who enabled this to happen," I snapped.

But she wasn't an easy target. She stopped in the middle of the street and faced me, "Tanner Washington, you better take that back. You know better."

She's the only one.

"Fine, fine," I sighed. "But trust me, I'm doing him a favor."

"How so?" Her eyes narrowed, and I couldn't tell if it was suspicion or the way the sunlight strained her baby blues.

"Because he's about to be placed between a rock and a hard place."

It took her a moment, but her face softened as awareness dawned.

There was quite a bit of activity outside the Ramirez compound. The Taco Libertad van was decorated with Nico's US and USMC flags, and large vinyl posters showing him dressed in uniform were attached to both sides of it. About two dozen other men in the Marine's white cap and dress blues were talking and moving around.

Dmitri was the first to spot our arrival. His eyes grew wider when he saw me.

"Attention on deck," he roared and surprised everyone.

As they fell into attention, I released Dani's hand and walked to stand in front of them. I knew none of them, but it didn't matter. We were all brothers.

Dmitri advanced and saluted.

"At ease, Sergeant," I returned his salute and released everyone to return to their preparations.

"A Colonel, huh?" he asked quietly.

I grunted and shook my head.

"Tanner, my boy," said Shemtov, emerging from the crowd in his old Army uniform.

He gave a fine salute, which I returned with a smile.

"Thank you, Rabbi."

Roberto and Paulina were next to greet us. Celeste held back for a split second before hugging me tightly.

"Thank you," she whispered as we held each other for another moment before the final voyage began.

Dmitri began to organize the convoy according to my instructions as I walked to Emmanuel, who waited for me on his black cruiser bicycle.

"They'll be watching and looking to paint us as provocateurs," I told him after we rehashed his task.

He scoffed, "We'll see about that." Emmanuel turned and whistled at some other guys on bikes like his, and they all rode out to the street.

The convoy was finally arranged in silent attention. The decorated van was in the middle, with one car behind and one in front. The soldiers were organized in two neat columns on the left and right of the vehicles.

So many eyes were trained on me, including my beloved wife's. This was my plan and the "burden of command" sat like the world on Atlas's shoulders.

"Soldiers," I called to those who wore the uniform. "You represent the United States of America and its military as we honor Corporal Nicolas Ramirez on his last march. Our Rules of Engagement is only self-defense."

I felt my old life returning to me with every word uttered and honored by the men who stood before me.

"They will try to get us to react. But we will not fall. We will stand tall and do what is asked of us. Am I clear?"

"Yes, Sir!" the soldiers chanted in unison.

Some stunned neighbors came out with phones trained on us.

"Permission to speak, Sir," said Dmitri with a tight-lipped smile.

I nodded in return.

"Do we need to mask?" he wondered, allowing the sarcasm to slide through.

"You do as you choose. After all, this is a *peaceful* protest," I answered, my mockery eliciting laughs in return.

Dani got into the van with Shemtov and nodded at me.

I wish I could tell you it's all going to be okay, Baby.

"Mount up," I commanded and walked to take my place at the front of the convoy.

THE CONVOY

– Venice Beach, CA –
Wednesday, June 3, 2020

The march of a dozen soldiers echoed through the streets of my home town—the only place among so many others where my roots had been allowed to grow into the ground. Venice was where both our children were born and raised, and where Dani and I had built our loving nest.

And now...

I walked the dotted white line in the middle of the street. Behind me, the convoy rumbled forward with our sad display. The first onlookers gawked as we turned out of Nico's street. Residents who'd probably seen us from their windows. They trained their phones on us, some even walking with us, but the *Sense* didn't categorize them as a threat.

...I'm behind enemy lines.

Emmanuel's bikers fanned out around us, cruising forward protectively.

"This is a good distance, Emmanuel. Keep me posted if you need backup," I told him via recorded voice memo.

My earbud voice-activated my phone to stay connected with a few key people in the convoy.

As we approached the Circle, my heart rate increased.

"The convoy is going viral on social media with live feeds," said a younger female voice in my ear. "Alfa follows you."

The RCC sent me recorded updates via voice memos, which I cycled through when possible. The police were alerted to our position and both the media and LAPD sent choppers.

Let them come.

We entered the Circle and when we reached Taco Libertad, I held up my fist. Dmitri, who trailed me, stopped the procession and arranged them in front of the restaurant while ordering some of the soldiers to remain in position, facing outward.

The family emerged from the caravan and walked to the entrance. As Paulina placed flowers at the door under the police yellow line, she heaved in anguish and Roberto and Cel picked her up from both sides. Shemtov stood close, ready to help.

The Dragon Skull on the wall beckoned me. Roberto decided not to erase it or any of the other graffiti. "So they remember," was his only response when I inquired why he didn't clean up the place after the attack.

Noting the few dozen masked spectators gathering, *his* voice returned to me, "Kneel on your sacred flags."

Is he here, watching?

Out of the corner of my eye, I saw Emmanuel and his people handling two guys in Comrade printed shirts. I didn't see what happened, but they didn't get to us.

It was time to go and Dmitri followed my command to mount up. We were just about to move again when I spotted Todd walking toward us. Draped in the US flag, his face was somber.

"Let him in," I broadcasted to both Emmanuel and Dmitri.

My friend walked directly toward me and stopped a few feet away to appraise the uniform.

"They fit you well. I should have known." He sighed. "Can I join you?"

"Do you understand that you could be targeted for it?" I asked.

He smiled and extended his hands to the sky.

"What else is there in life but to follow what you know to be right?"

If only I'd known it in time.

I nodded.

"Only soldiers are allowed outside. Mount up in the back car."

As soon as he was in, the engines turned on and we began the march north.

Where are you, Holden?

The media coverage was slanted, of course, and the RCC gave me snippets of the vitriol—how we weren't masked and following the Dragon measures, and worst of all, shaming the military. Apparently, we were on par with the "fascistic police" who were obsessed with uniforms. Brett's live broadcast was among the few outlets praising our march.

"Police at nine o'clock." Dmitri's update cut through those coming from RCC.

We were on Main Street, just short of the Santa Monica boundary, when two LAPD cars showed up but didn't get in our way.

"Roger. Santa Monica PD will be next to show up," I replied, hoping that Dani and the rest were staying calm in the cars.

We entered Santa Monica with about a hundred spectators following on both sides of the street. Emmanuel broadcasted about "handling incidents," and the RCC and Dex reported drones a few moments before their arrival above our heads. It was no surprise, and it didn't matter who controlled them. The march continued.

LAPD squad cars waited along Wilshire Blvd, where the Santa Monica municipal area ended. Looking back, I marveled at our convoy and its tail, where the flags waved proudly in the breeze and the soldiers stayed at equal distances, keeping the three-car procession tight and neat. Many of our "camp followers" were antagonistic, offering a constant stream of heckles and curses, but no physical interactions took place.

Thank you, Emmanuel. I thought of Dani, as some woman with purple hair called me a Nazi. *Is this really America?*

"The police are set to block you before the 405," said Jack. "Are you ready for this, Son?"

When the freeway overpass came into view, I noticed the police barricade. Squad cars blocked both sides of Wilshire Boulevard, preventing us from reaching the cemetery's entrance, which was located just past the 405 Freeway overpass.

Here comes the rock.

"Hold," I broadcasted when we were a hundred feet from the police. Dmitri handled the convoy as Holden moved between the police cars.

Feeling her eyes on me, I turned to see my wife stepping out of the van, hand shielding her face against the sunlight. When our eyes locked, her subtle nod sent a wave of peace through me.

"I'm advancing. Nobody moves," I instructed.

The closer I got to Holden, the angrier he looked, even behind a mask. Eyes narrowed, his head tilted downward like a bull ready to charge. We met in the middle, a few feet apart, without a handshake or smile.

"What the fuck, Tanner? He's my brother too. How could you all do this behind my back? How could you steal my chance to grieve?"

His words were solid and trustworthy. He'd been my friend for many years, and we'd never crossed each other.

Today is different, Brother.

Holden fidgeted with his mask while he berated me for the illegal convoy. Eventually, he yanked it below his chin, nearly tearing it from his face.

"They're here, Cap." A voice came across his radio and stopped his angry torrent.

We both looked toward the police, where Victoria and a few city officials stood behind them. She was animated as she spoke on the phone.

Holden swiveled back to me.

"Break this down and send everyone home before I act. Think about all those you have led here and what happens next." His tone was caught somewhere between pleading and anger.

I looked at the convoy and all the civvies gathered among the soldiers. Holden was on his radio, but whatever was said didn't penetrate my inner turmoil.

Where am I leading them?

"Now is the time, Tanner. The mayor is pissed," ordered Holden.

I glanced at Dani again. Seeing her chin up and proud as she held Celeste's shoulders, I made the decision and turned back to Holden. "Yes. Now is the time."

I pulled the paper from my pocket and handed it to him.

"What the hell?" he asked after a quick review and one look back at Victoria.

"This is a military funeral we are heading to," I replied, a little too flatly.

He squinted his eyes. "Maybe so, but you're not on federal land right now. Are you? Stop the crap."

"What about the First Amendment, Holden? This is what a *peaceful* assembly looks like." I tempered the snark as I reminded him of his own words.

He bowed his head and shook it slowly.

"What do you propose then?"

When he raised his eyes to look at me, I saw the anger had been replaced with pain.

"The civvies go home, and the soldiers, the family, and the van are allowed to proceed to the cemetery."

It was the best available offer, and I hoped he'd take it and not force my hand.

Holden looked back for a moment.

"What happens if I refuse?"

> *Alone in the darkness, I rose to stand,*
> *no longer trying to touch the cave walls.*

"Try and find out," I answered without hesitation.

"*Yes,*" echoed the hungry voice.

He was struggling and fidgeting in place when Victoria crossed the police line and rushed forward. Dee and another cop ran after her, but when she yelled something at them, the two cops followed at a distance.

"What's going on, Holden? Why aren't they on their way home?" growled Victoria when she got to us.

"It's a military—"

He didn't get to say much before she cut him off with a loud bark, "They're not masked! This is a health crisis, and they're just trying to cause provocation. This is not the way to honor Nicolas!"

Holden pulled his mask back to its proper position as she tore into him.

I watched as Holden held his palms up to calm Victoria, his inner conflict written all over his face. When she kept at him, he glanced at Dee, who stood a few feet back.

"Listen, Vic, there is a way out of this..." He told her about our agreement.

"You better stop them right now, Captain. This is coming straight from the mayor!" she shot back.

Holden's chocolate skin turned a dark maroon as he struggled to contain his anger and pointed at the spectators who tailed us on the street.

"Look around us! We even have drones watching. Do you want to have LAPD on national news beating down folks on their way to a funeral? Do you want *your* picture and name associated with that?" He took a deep breath. "This is a good solution. Let them have the ceremony and defuse the situation."

Curses reached our ears, and I turned to see a raging Celeste being restrained by Dani and Roberto. She obviously wanted a piece of Victoria. Dani managed to wrangle her, but not before giving Victoria a death stare that would frighten even a man in uniform.

Oh, man.

"This is going to be bad, Vic. Let's end this before it happens," pleaded Holden.

The councilwoman turned her focus on me, her finger inches from my face.

"Is this your idea? To provoke and antagonize those who are hurt? Is this how you honor Nico? Getting his family and friends to march without masks or any regard for the pandemic?"

It took me a moment to fully register her words yet remain unclear about one thing.

"Who did you mean—who is *hurt*?"

Holden's head moved with the verbal volley, his eyes betraying his surprise at the turn of events.

Victoria stretched her arms out wide and swiveled around, gesturing toward the hundred or so followers on both sides of the street.

"Them, of course, and all those who were deeply hurt by what took place in Chicago." Her tone bled condescension, "Do you care about anything besides yourself?"

I shook my head empathetically.

"Chicago was horrendous. The cops are detained, and justice may be served upon those found guilty."

She stood more erect as though my words gave her strength.

"But protesting for justice has turned into riots, looting, raping, and killing. You say that you care for those who *are hurt*." It was my turn to point and draw attention to my loved ones in the convoy. "Well, take a close look behind me and do your best to remember who is hurt by *your* kind of justice."

Victoria seemed ready to speak, but I cut her off.

"And as for the masking, do you really dare come against fifty unmasked people, marching peacefully, while *covering* for hundreds of thousands of unmasked rioters? Do we terrify you because we don't obey?" I paused, refusing to divert my attention from her seething brown eyes. "So, Madam Councilwoman, I ask you: Do *you* care for anything but yourself?"

She bristled and was opening her mouth to respond when Holden intervened, "Vic, people are watching and filming. This won't be good for anyone. Let's finish it."

Sighing, she nodded with bitter resentment in her eyes, and I was certain I heard a snarl from behind the mask as she huffed away.

"Let me handle my end," I told Holden and turned back to the cavalcade.

"You should be proud of yourselves. Now is the time to go," I said at the end of my brief speech, announcing the plan.

Todd, Emmanuel, and the rest didn't like the news, but they all complied.

The police allowed the bikers and cars to depart down a side street, leaving the soldiers, family, and van alone in the middle of the road. Dmitri took a minute to rearrange us, and then we continued toward the barricade with Shemtov driving the van.

I nodded to Holden and Dee when we passed through, ignoring Victoria completely. My eyes stayed on Dee for a moment as she dropped her mask and nodded at me.

Brave girl.

Dmitri quickened to my side and whispered, "I'm glad you didn't release everyone to go home."

I followed his eyes to a lone masked man on the overpass above us.

He will always remain a Spetsnaz. Remember that.

"Let's get it done," I replied, neither confirming or denying his earlier statement.

SEMPER FIDELIS

– Los Angeles, CA –
Wednesday, June 3, 2020

"**H**ostiles on our six, over," broadcasted Dmitri.

I wasn't surprised when I looked back and saw our followers were gaining on us again. Holden was probably forced to let them pass the blockade.

"Roger that," I replied, looking ahead at the left turn into the military cemetery where police cars with flashing lights waited.

Our hecklers had caught up by the time we reached the intersection, phones capturing the play by play. Yelling curses. Wishing us to die. Desecrating Nico's name. And those were just the ones I heard.

Pussies.

The cops emerged from their vehicles and ensured we could make the turn without interference. Dee was among them, and she raced on one agitator and took him to the ground when he tried to rush in front of me. Our eyes locked, and I nodded my appreciation.

"Sorry for your loss, Alfa-leader. We'll remain outside." Dex's voice came over the team channel.

The cemetery was just a hundred feet ahead when the gate opened and an armed Marine platoon marched out and arranged itself on both sides of the road, facing outward in battle formation. Their lieutenant, a young Asian male, saluted and remained frozen until I released him.

When a siren beeped once behind me, I turned to see a sole police SUV driving toward us.

"Sergeant, take them inside." Dmitri nodded and left to confer with the lieutenant.

The SUV stopped about twenty feet from me, and Holden got out by himself. As he marched toward me, I noticed Dani's faint smile through the van's passenger window.

Looking at the Marines and the procession that had just entered the cemetery, Holden sighed and visibly struggled for words.

"You forced this moment, and now I'm asking your permission to attend his funeral."

It wasn't the place or time for our disagreements, hard as they may be.

"Permission granted," I replied and started toward the cemetery with him walking by my side.

Like Arlington and other final fields of the fallen, the Los Angeles Military Cemetery's expansive green lawns were dotted with endless rows of white rectangular tombstones. All the noise disappeared as we followed the US Marines' Honor Guard, holding the casket, toward Nico's final resting place.

The General and Dad came through. Emotion caught in my throat for a moment.

The closed casket was placed in the grave and draped with our nation's flag.

"Where is your Christian God now?" The Demon guy's voice broke through as Shemtov moved to the Chaplin position in front.

The family and Holden stood together while I remained with Dmitri and the soldiers. The Honor Guard took their position on both sides of the casket.

The guards shot three times, a tradition that originated in a bygone world where it was used to stop the fighting so that the dead could be removed. Though my face remained frozen, committed to my other family and life, I noticed Dani's frame shaking on the first shot and her eyes pleading with mine.

I'm sorry, Baby.

"Drones inbound," reported a masculine RCC voice in my ear.

My eyes caught them coming from the west and hovering above us, filming and recording the event. Media choppers joined them but stayed much higher.

Vultures.

Shemtov sighed and then smiled at the family before sharing what he had prepared for this sad and pivotal day.

"Genesis 22. And it came to pass after these things, that God tested Abraham, and He said to him, 'Abraham,' and he said, 'Here I am...'"

Time stopped and my body disappeared, leaving only my senses and mind.

Here I am.

The rabbi looked directly at me and continued, "And He said, 'Please take your son, your only one, whom you love, yea, Isaac, and go away to the land of Moriah and bring him up there for a burnt offering on one of the mountains, of which I will tell you.'"

Are you talking to me, Shemtov?

"And Abraham arose early in the morning, and he saddled his donkey, and he took his two young men with him and Isaac his son, and he split wood for a burnt offering, and he arose and went to the place of which God had told him."

Back in the tunnel,
the cold rock bed under my bare feet.
I felt the urge to lie down,
to cower from the moment.

"*No. You stand and face this,*" growled the voice.

"And Isaac spoke to Abraham his father, and he said, 'My father!' And he said, 'Here I am, my son.' And he said, 'Here are the fire and the wood, but where is the lamb for the burnt offering?'"

I'm here.

"And they came to the place of which God had spoken to him, and Abraham built the altar there and arranged the wood, and he bound Isaac his son and placed him on the altar upon the wood."

"And you think that this proves your commitment?" taunted the voice.

"And Abraham stretched forth his hand and took the knife, to slaughter his son."

My knees threatened to buckle,
eyes drowned in eternal darkness.

"And an angel of God called to him from heaven and said, 'Abraham! Abraham!' And he said, 'Here I am.'"

Here I am.

"And he said, 'Do not stretch forth your hand to the lad, nor do the slightest thing to him, for now I know that you are a God-fearing man, and you did not withhold your son, your only one, from Me.'"

"We shall see about that..." the voice whispered.

I felt my body again when Shemtov stopped and looked at the family.

"We don't know why the Lord decided to take Nicolas from us. But we'll take refuge because Nicolas died doing what he believed was right."

Cel wailed and would have fallen to the ground if Dani and Paulina didn't hold her between them. I ached to run to them—to help them, to comfort them—but that wasn't my role.

Shemtov turned his gaze back to me.

"So, ask yourselves, what will you do when God calls you to the altar, commanding you to give that which is the most precious of all?"

I can do this without losing them. I can!

The rabbi stopped and nodded at Roberto.

Nico's father drew a folded note from his jacket and read to us, voice firm but always on the verge of breaking as he told of his son's rough road into the Marines and the man he had become.

"He loved his neighborhood and his country," he continued, noting Nico's decision to enter politics. "And now, his campaign is over." Roberto shook and Paulina held him tightly. "He was our only child, and now he is gone." He barely got the last words out.

"Tanner, would you say some words?" Shemtov blindsided me.

"You could have stopped this, Hermano." Nico's words and sad expression echoed in my head, and I sighed and nodded.

"Nico was my best friend, and he remained with his eyes open while I shut mine," I started, feeling Dani's eyes and love holding me up. "He stood tall, never spoke a word he didn't mean to uphold." I looked at the family. "He loved like he fought—with all his heart and soul." My eyes rested on Cel's.

The drones buzzed closer, and the chopper's thump thump augmented the divide between the sacred and the profane. I looked up at them, wishing to drop them down with my pain.

"Kneel," the Demon's taunt brought me back from the sky.

They all waited as Nico's final moments assaulted my mind with vivid colors and sounds, finishing with the Dragon Skull, painted red on the restaurant.

"He showed me the way when I fell into the abyss all those years back," I continued, looking at the family, and then focused my attention on Dani.

Baby, I'm so sorry about what comes next.

She nodded with a faint smile.

"I failed you, Brother. I failed all those who love you too. I am truly sorry. No words would bring you back..." A surge of rage displacing my sadness, I echoed my brother's final words, "But hear this! This is my promise... Semper Fidelis!"

I saluted as the Honor Guard bugler advanced and played "Taps" on his trumpet. With each note, my current life crumbled to make room for what would come next.

The Honor Guard removed the flag, folded it, and presented it to Celeste, who held it close to her chest while she sobbed.

With the ceremony over, I walked toward the family and met Dmitri and Holden there. We hugged, allowing our separate pains to intertwine as one.

"Thank you, Rabbi."

Shemtov smiled sadly at me.

"It's been quite a day, Son."

"The mayor and the other cowards bent their knees to these assholes while trying to stop our funeral," I vented.

Shemtov stayed quiet as I turned to look at the casket.

"He died refusing to kneel."

"And how do you know that, Tanner?" I looked back to see Shemtov's eyes narrowed in suspicion.

Damn. I can't lie to him.

I stayed quiet, and he nodded after our moment of stalemate.

"What else is bugging you?"

"I hoped not to raise my hand on another, ever again, Rabbi."

"Are you going back?"

"Yes, Rabbi." I nearly choked on the words.

Laying a hand on my shoulder, Shemtov whispered, "You're answering *his* call, my boy."

"Was that why you shared the story of The Sacrifice today?"

He smiled sadly again but said nothing else.

"Since he died, I've wanted to ask you something." Roberto spoke slowly as we walked together, behind the family, toward the cemetery's gate. "It's hard for me even to say the words. I feel the old ugliness returning to me." Again, I recalled Nico's hints about his father's violent days in Mexico just before he stopped us and turned to face me, eyes searching mine. "But after hearing you at the grave...." Roberto paused. "Do I need to ask you at all?"

He deserves it.

"I could have stopped it, or at least tried. Now, all that is left is my promise. I will make sure of that," I replied flatly, sentencing others to death in my head.

"Will you? Or will you disappoint the old man as you failed his son?"

Here I am!

The voice laughed and dissipated.

After scrutinizing my soul, Roberto nodded and offered his hand, which I shook for a long moment.

"Then it's settled." He let out a long sigh.

And we began to walk again.

The gate was just ahead of us when I took advantage of the moment alone with him.

"What is it about Victoria and Nico?"

He stopped and turned to me, face fallen.

"Before, you blamed yourself for no reason. But I, his father, have failed him the most. When he needed my compassion, all I had was anger. Those kids..." Roberto gathered himself. "Leave her be. She suffered enough..."

Then he left, giving me zero chance to ask more questions.

Dani was at my side, slipping her hand into mine as soon as Roberto was gone. Celeste was close behind.

When we reached the gate, I was surprised to see two buses flanked by police. Holden marched toward me, Dee close on his heels. Over their shoulders in the distance, protesters were already on the road, their heckles and curses filling the streets.

"There are quite a few at the intersection as well. But we'll get you back safely," he promised.

I thanked the soldiers as they filed onto the buses and then turned to Dani.

"I'll see you at home."

I kissed her forehead to soothe the worry that spread when she realized we weren't going together.

Nothing but grace, this woman. In high heels and under duress, I thought as she ascended the stairs.

"Did the police find anything about the killers?" Dmitri's tone was menacing.

"No."

His face contorted as he slowly rotated his bull-sized neck to crack it.

"I guess we are doomed to become what we were, da?"

I guess so, I admitted, feeling the ravenous desire for revenge stir in my belly.

We embraced, offering nothing more before he saluted and joined his brothers.

When she was close enough, Celeste whispered, "Tanner, I'm afraid of what my words may have caused. Danielle and the kids need you..." She took a deep breath. "We all need you here..."

"No. You were right, and now I'm awake." I hugged her, wishing I could take away her pain. "Go now."

A TAIL

– Los Angeles, CA –
Wednesday, June 3, 2020

The buses were already moving when Holden looked back and realized I hadn't joined. Looking torn between his assignment and his suspicion, he shook his head as he jumped in his SUV with Dee.

The van sat alone in the empty parking lot and Nico's proud face stared at me from the large poster on its side.

I'm out in the open now. Just like you wanted me to be.

I rushed to remove the flags and posters and carefully placed them in the van where I removed my dress blues, folded them properly, and changed into the jeans and t-shirt I'd brought along for the next task.

★   ★   ★

The buses advanced to the intersection at a snail's pace, cops pushing on the protesters who tried to block them from leaving. I managed to catch up quickly and got behind the second bus.

Here goes, I thought as I watched the police in action ahead. Alfa and the RCC had been keeping an eye on the intersection, so I knew we were about to face some drama.

With at least three drones circling above us, the protest transformed into a mini-riot as frozen bottles were thrown at the buses. Cops did their best to push the rioters away from the intersection, but it was only a matter of time.

When one of the frozen bottles hit my driver-side glass without breaking it, I realized he'd not just tinted the windows, he'd reinforced them.

Thank you, Brother!

Holden's troops routed us to Wilshire Blvd, heading west toward the 405 Freeway.

Time to check on their abilities.

I surprised the police escort when I didn't join the buses that went up the freeway.

"UAV is still with you," the RCC operator updated me.

I looked around, wondering whether the drone pilot was in one of the cars nearby or behind me.

"Roger that."

The unmanned aerial vehicle didn't have a chance when I broke into a side street and backtracked, gaining distance from Wilshire Blvd.

"Possible hostile following you. Blue sedan," the RCC operator said.

"Permission to pursue and engage," requested Dex.

The sedan came into view on my left-side mirror. Fast ripples moved through my hands, making my fingertips shake slightly.

I'm ready to fuck someone up.

"Negative, Alfa-one," I answered Dex, recalling Jack's strict rules of engagement warning.

I made a surprise left turn into an alley, the sedan still behind me.

"Alfa-leader, proceed to the following coordinates," said the RCC operator.

My phone chirped, and a live satellite feed came up with my path ahead painted in blue. The van bounced over potholes and shook as I followed the zigzag path forward. Turning into a multi-level office parking structure, I took a ticket from the machine and entered.

It worked. The RCC and Dex reported that the sedan had missed my last move and sped past me.

"Proceed to the second level. Alfa-four is waiting on you," said the operator.

An Asian woman in her mid-thirties dressed in blue jeans and a black leather jacket leaned against the ebony motorcycle parked in the middle of three adjacent empty spaces. Her straight raven hair was down, but it did little to hide her gorgeous face. Two helmets waited on the motorcycle seat.

I parked the van next to her and opened my door, smiling at Jenny—our fastest operative, both behind the wheel and in hand-to-hand combat.

Beaming, she rushed to give me a firm hug.

"Good to see you, Alfa-four."

"Back at you." She winked and laughed, and my heart warmed at the expression of how far we'd come.

She used to hate me, especially during Hell Year, I mused, recalling the death stares she gave me during her Rogue course.

Jenny showed me around the bike and made sure the helmet fit me well before the bike's operating system authenticated me as a rider and we loaded the motorcycle into the van.

"I'll see you soon," she said and then melted among the cars.

"The media found your civilian number, and your inbox is full of their messages. If anyone manages to speak with you, send them to Camp Pendleton," instructed Jack.

He'd called as soon as the van left the parking structure.

"Yes, Sir," I replied, directing the van toward home.

"It was Ryse LA was behind today's events around the convoy. They have independent chapters in various locations around the country," he told me.

"Nico?" I asked.

"Probably," he replied.

The drones came to mind.

They got abilities.

"I need protection for my family," I said.

Jack was already steps ahead, as usual. He said Eli had insisted on providing a shadow, an undercover agent, to watch Dani and the kids.

"It would be better if they handle it. It's in their DNA," said Jack, referring to the Israelis' unfortunate history with terrorism.

"Sounds good," I agreed. "Thank you."

"Before we end, Son, how are you? Your readings have been all over the chart."

Damn chip. They always know.

"I buried my best friend today, Dad." I did my best to hold back my mounting anger.

He didn't respond immediately, maybe recalculating how much leeway was warranted on such a day.

"You've been listening to the voices samples quite a bit. Is that necessary?" he inquired.

"Waterboarding time, soldier boy," the Demon's voice interjected in my mind.

Always training me.

"What's my ETA, Sir?" I asked.

His loud grunt said it all, but he allowed me to deflect.

"Forty-eight hours to your flight out of Santa Monica Airport."

"Roger that."

My father had barely gotten off the line when Eli's call came in. He confirmed Jack's earlier comment about the shadow.

"I gave Dani the agent's number. She knows that we're protecting her."

"Thank you, Eli," I replied, some tension releasing.

"Don't thank me. Go hunt instead."

I couldn't help but smile at the savage tone that Eli measured so carefully in so many other arenas.

Brett Cohen's podcast helped me get my mind off the ticking clock inside me. He shared the sad story of a retired old cop murdered while trying to protect someone from rioters, and then praised Senator Garcia from Texas who made waves by calling for strict enforcement against the mayhem. Just before wrapping up, he talked about how former Defense Secretary Grayson rebuked President Stone who, according to him, was pressuring the governors to restore order in their states.

Ignoring my guilt and desire to turn off the podcast, I used the *Sense* to keep listening, analyzing, and looking to find patterns within the tidal wave of events.

THE CHAT

– Venice Beach, CA –
Wednesday, June 3, 2020

I left the van in front of the Ramirez home and rode home on the motorcycle, its modified design so quiet that it had taken me a moment to realize the engine was even on. The quick trip down the street didn't quite give me enough time to test its speed and suspension, but it felt good to be back on a bike.

Ari was waiting on the main balcony and ran inside as soon as he saw me rolling into the complex.

Like a damn scout.

I was barely off my new ride when our front door swung open, and he raced to check it out.

"Oh, Dad. It's so cool. Can I go on it?"

He bounced in a big circle around me, and his enthusiasm made me laugh for the first time in days.

Dani held Lil in the carrier, face smiling straight at me. But Dani's smirk had faded to tight-lipped concern by the time I looked up from my little man.

The phone, and now the bike. I know, Baby. I'm so sorry, I thought as I picked Ari up and put him on the motorcycle. As we made a small loop in the courtyard, my heart began to ache. I wanted this moment to last forever, but it couldn't.

Dani had made her famous lamb roast and before we all sat together to eat, she asked me to tell the kids about my departure during dinner.

"Your boy needs to hear it straight from you."

Lil was too young to understand, but Ari compensated for it with his keen sense of what was happening around him. He listened for a few minutes, eyes wide with shock and something else I couldn't make out.

"When are you going?" Ari asked to confirm a second time.

"The day after tomorrow, Baby," I replied, seeing Dani's slight nod.

"I'm not a baby," Ari said with a pout and crossed his arms for emphasis.

I reached out to tousle his long hair.

"I know. I know. But for Daddy, you will always be my baby."

"You're going back to the Army?" he pressed.

Gah, no. But I'll correct him another day... before he meets up with another Marine and finds out how we all feel about being called Army.

"Yes, and I'll be here in California. Very close to you." The lies kept rolling out of my mouth as I avoided Dani's eyes.

He kept quiet long enough that I thought there was a chance the matter was over, at least for now.

"Are you going back because of all the bad people?" His green-gray eyes looked too mature for his age.

Glancing in her direction, I realized Dani would be no help. Her face remained unreadable, almost as if she was waiting for the answer herself.

"Yes, Son," I answered honestly.

"Then why didn't you go to help Nico?"

I caught the gasp in time, but I couldn't avoid the total impact. It was as if the world had put on a boxing glove made of steel and hit me straight in the face. I used the *Sense,* unwilling to be lost in the moment. Dani reached out to grab my hand and squeezed it to steady me, but she didn't give me a rope out.

"I was afraid." The truth was all I had to offer.

Ari's jaw dropped in surprise. "Daddy? Afraid? Of what?"

Of what I used to be before you were born.

I gathered myself.

"I was afraid, and because of that, I didn't do the right thing. It was a mistake, and Daddy's so sorry. You should always do the right thing, even if you're scared. It's what being a man is all about."

Feeling my pain, my sweet boy slid out of his chair and hugged me.

"It's okay, Daddy. Don't be sad. I still love you."

"I love you the most," I whispered, gulping back the waves of regret, and tightened my arms around my most precious treasure.

"Just don't turn on the TV for a few days," said Dani. She was lying next to me on our bed, her head on my chest, and I was soaking in every detail before I had to leave her. Her gentle touch on my chest, her firm body pressed against mine, her silky black hair between my fingers. I enjoyed the scent of her favorite lavender essential oil on her skin and rosemary in her hair as she filled me in on the legacy media's frenzy regarding the funeral. In less than a day, the portrayals ranged from "careless mourners" to "fascist collaborators with the systems of oppression."

It was easy for them to build on the first false narrative of the "Taco Libertad incident." Nico had been made culpable in his death when "reliable sources" told pseudo-journalists about how vicious my dead best friend was toward the "peaceful protesters."

"Fuck them, Baby," she sneered as she propped herself up on her elbow and looked at me. "They call you 'The Soldier from the Funeral,' and they are right. You are him, and you honored Nico."

"Is that it?" I asked, breathing slowly to release the increasing pressure in my chest.

"No." She lowered her head back to my chest and told me about the many friends who'd decided to shun us, using social media to attack us openly.

"I can't believe they did it."

I smiled and playfully dug my fingertips into her ribs, "Like you said—Fuck 'em."

She wriggled and laughed lightly and, with the tension defused, we forgot about everything else for a moment and kissed.

It wasn't long before reality interrupted us again.

"I saw that you spoke with Roberto."

"I did." My tone was flat, signaling that it wasn't a conversation I wished to open with her.

Her brow still furrowed, she let the matter go and told me Celeste and the kids would move in while I was away.

"It's safer here," I agreed. "The agent will be here the morning I leave, and you've got the SOS number in case something happens. And..."

"Tanner, I got it," she interrupted. "My father has already made me repeat all of the security protocols back to him... twice!"

I smiled at her half-assed attempt to assuage her frustration and knew she would change the conversation quickly.

"Cel told me what she said to you before we left with the buses." When I didn't respond, she asked, "Was it me that caused you to go back?"

Finally, the real subject.

I wrapped both arms tightly around her as she began to cry into my chest.

"Even our son knows his dad was wrong. You all saw what I refused to confront, and now I'm doing it."

I held her quietly until the tears subsided and she released herself from my grasp. Tilting her head back a bit.

"The other thing you told Ari about California and the Marines..." She stopped mid-sentence.

It was a forbidden question with an answer she'd suspected since she'd first met me.

"If anyone asks, tell them to call the base," I grumbled, feeling the weight of the entire day in every bone in my body.

"My Love," she touched my cheek and pulled my gaze back to her. "I know you blame yourself. Only you can know how to find the way out of that guilt. I'll always be here for you."

ONE MORE DAY

– Venice Beach, CA –
Thursday, June 4, 2020

In the studio finalizing all of my preparations, I half-listened to the exposé on TV about the mayor's new commitment to cut the police budget, effectively giving in to the mob's demand to "defund the police."

Disassembled in front of me was my 9mm Wraith handgun, a weapon every Rogue carried. With a proprietary design, its sleek black polymer frame was light and virtually undetectable, augmented by a biometric lock, which only allowed one user per gun.

"In other news, Governor Knight now faces some criticism for not using the National Guard to protect the cities better..."

After finishing my kit, I moved on to the silver metal container in the closet by the safe—Dani's emergency box. She knew its code and had her fingerprint lock for a faster opening but had never had to use it. Inside, there was a 0.38 six-shooter revolver, extra ammo, and a satellite phone, fully charged by an external lithium battery. The longest I'd ever left my family was maybe a week to go surfing or snowboarding with friends, so this "toy box," as Dani referred to it, was there more as a protocol than anything else.

I smiled, remembering the last time we were at the range together.

She's become a very good shot, but I hope she never has to...

Anxiety replaced the warmth of the memory.

Uncertain and irritated, I switched to Brett's podcast. He was talking about new vandalism cases involving monuments and other symbols of our culture—all lumped together with what happened in Chicago. When he discussed the nightly riots in Seattle, I was too distracted to give it my full attention.

I need to tell her.

It wasn't easy or even allowed, but the pages filled up with what I could share about my culpability in destroying our world, my love for her, and my hope to redeem myself again. I sealed the letter in a double envelope, writing her name on the exterior and "only open if I'm gone" on the inner cover.

Feeling a bit of relief, I put her "toy box" back and grabbed my surfboard.

I need to clear it all out.

Todd was on his hill, US flags adorning its top on all sides.

"Tanner, my friend!" his voice boomed as he saw me walking toward him with my surfboard.

I thanked him for his support at the funeral, and he insisted that the honor was all his.

"It's a shame how they speak about him now."

Todd's frustrated expression and unusually combative posture intensified as he vented about all the media bias surrounding Nico's death.

"You be careful," I motioned to the flags around us.

His head bowed, he shook it a few times.

"No," he said, his black eyes blazing. "This is my stand, reminding people that our nation is good, even with all its imperfections."

I nodded and was ready to turn and head to the water when he surprised me.

"You're leaving, aren't you?"

"How...?"

"Drifters can smell it."

He smiled and patted my back, gently releasing me toward the ocean where the sets were glassy and powerful enough to send my shortboard up and down the lip repeatedly.

For those precious moments, there was no Tanner, virus, or guilt. There was no haunt of Operation Market. There was just the wave and the union of my body and soul.

Dani and the kids went to the Ramirez home to help Celeste pack for the move into our place, but I stayed back to call my brother after hearing fresh updates on Seattle and the growing unrest there.

Our conversation didn't start well, as Chad was both happy about my call and anxious to make me understand what he believed was good about the situation.

"I know they're rioting, but this is a natural social evolution toward something better."

"What the hell are you talking about?" I nearly forgot the original reason for my call.

"There is only one way in which the murderous death agonies of the old society and the bloody birth throes of the new society can be shortened, simplified, and concentrated, and that way is revolutionary terror." His dramatic radio voice didn't improve the sentiment.

Fuck, I thought as I realized its source. *What an idiot!*

"Listen, Man. Mob justice is no justice. Just don't ever quote Marx to Dad," I warned him before ending the call. "Talk soon."

I gotta talk to a sane human, I thought as I dialed Shemtov's number.

He sounded distracted when he picked up and admitted to being engrossed in a book, the subject of which fit the world's state of affairs.

"How does that book help you these days?" I asked.

"It provides me with both hope and trepidation," he started. "The chance for a hero to rise at the worst of times..."

And—

I bristled with unease and impatience and rolled the sudden tension out of my neck.

"...and the price and unknown consequences of victory."

My mind was too busy to deal with more riddles. In fact, it was still stuck on his Genesis 22 sermon. Fortunately, I heard the familiar voice in the courtyard and then a knock at the door.

"Rabbi, thanks for who you are, and please be careful," I said before hanging up and opening my front door.

"Hey..." I greeted Holden and immediately directed him upstairs and away from my studio below to no avail. His cop mind checked anyway.

"Are you going somewhere?"

I nodded.

"I'm reenlisting and heading out tomorrow."

His eyes widened, but only for a moment.

"Maybe it's for the best."

"Why would you say that?" I asked, sincerely surprised.

As he followed me up the stairs, Holden rehashed his great disappointment about the funeral and the deception. He didn't seem amenable to any explanations, even about my attempt to save him from problems with his employers.

"Your little altercation with Victoria hasn't helped either. So yes, maybe it will be good for you to get out of here for a bit before you get into more trouble," he grumbled as he sat down on the stool at the counter.

There was no point fighting, so I asked him about the drones. His face flushed red as he explained that the drones had been patrolling around his Pacific Division headquarters since the day after Chicago happened.

"We're not allowed to do anything about it!"

"Any news about Nico's case?" I asked as I poured him a glass of water.

He shook his head, admitting that he'd reached a dead end and the DA's lackluster attitude about the case wasn't helping.

"I wish his secret tape weren't missing," he added, eyes narrowing and scanning my face intently. "Will you stay out of this?" he wondered when I offered no response.

Roberto and Dmitri came to my mind, and I shrugged.

"As you said, maybe it is for the best that I go."

Holden didn't like my answer but nodded in resignation, took a sip of water, and shifted roles with me.

"How are the cravings... with everything going on?"

His question brought back Nico and his final dance with alcohol.

"I get urges here and there, but I'm fine," I answered honestly.

It was my turn to get some details, and I asked him about Victoria and Nico.

"Do you know why they broke up before he enlisted?"

Confusion crossed his face momentarily.

"All I know is that he still loved her after the breakup." He paused and raised an eyebrow at me. "Don't do anything more to get on her radar. It isn't what you need, Tanner. She has the mayor's ear, who has the governor's. She *alone* managed to stop LAPD that day. With Nico gone, she'll run unopposed and win next year and be on track to become the next mayor and who knows what after that. She's hungry for power—has been since we were young. She was always different from the rest of us."

His shoulders slumped and his eyes darkened with sadness.

"At least consider that she's also mourning. It can't be easy on her. She oversaw the negotiations." A big sigh escaped him. "I need to go." Looking at his watch, he started moving toward the staircase and turned back and leveled his gaze at me. "At the funeral, when you said Semper Fidelis... Was this just about echoing the Marines' motto?"

I knew I had to tread carefully.

"I don't envy your position, Holden. Your leaders have bent their knees and chosen their lot. Your time is coming too. I guess time will tell."

I regretted my colder tone of deflection, but it was all I could offer my friend.

BACK AGAIN

– Venice Beach, CA –
Friday, June 5, 2020

The faint vibration behind my ear informed me that my 0300 silent alarm had activated, but it wasn't necessary. I was already awake in bed, dreading the moment of my departure.

Dani stirred when I left the bed but remained asleep. My heart ached as I stood over her and our children who had found their way into our bed during the night. Lil was snuggled in close to her momma and looked so peaceful. Ari was also curled on his side, purring like a little lion, strands of his long blond hair covering half his face.

God, this is gonna hurt.

The studio door opened just as I finished putting on my street BDU. The RCC had modified the special forces "battle dress uniform" into a civilian-like dark khaki, which could be mistaken for cargo pants and a long sleeve shirt.

Quickly, I slid my Wraith handgun into my holster, but it wasn't fast enough. Her eyes squinted suspiciously for a moment, but Dani didn't break stride as she reached for me, her mischievous smile in full display on her beautiful face.

"I'm glad the kids allowed us enough time to play last night," she whispered as we kissed.

My phone chirped, and I glanced down to see the message from Eli.

"The agent is outside and ready," I told her as we allowed the sweetness of our night to dissipate. "One last check." I released her and walked to the closet.

Dani didn't try to hide her annoyance when I insisted she show me how she opened her secure box, handled the revolver, and activated the satellite phone one last time.

"All the numbers are already programmed here. Use it if I tell you or if the network fails for some reason."

"Yeah, yeah," she sighed. "What's that?" she asked, pointing to the sealed envelope.

Losing myself for a moment in her big blue eyes, my heart shuddered.

"Open this if something happens to me, and only if. Do you understand?"

She nodded, lips pursed and chin raised, and then did her best to smile as she followed me upstairs to kiss our sleeping children one last time.

The motorcycle purred quietly as I looked up to our balcony, where the love of my life stood alone against the dark sky.

I can do this and keep everything together.

I mounted the bike, put the helmet on, and waved to her one last time.

As I approached the keypad to punch in the code for the gate, the Israeli agent was pinged on my phone. Eli had synced their data with ours, and I looked up to see a black woman in a nearby car. She gave me a slight nod, which I returned.

Thank you for protecting them while I can't.

The ride to Santa Monica Airport was uneventful and the guard at the airport gate was sleepy when I arrived.

"Who are you flying with?"

"I'm flying out with Old Glory. It's a chopper flight on helipad four," I replied as I pulled out my printed confirmation. He read through and let me in.

Sarah Mitchell was doing the final preparations around the helicopter, a modified version of the Blackhawk. Faster and capable of longer distances, it also had a side mount for the motorcycle.

The young woman, in her early thirties, turned toward me when she heard the bike approaching. She was dressed in her black Old Glory flight suit with the company's logo of a Betsy Ross thirteen-star US flag in light gray colors on the back. Her brown hair was pulled back in a bun, revealing her signature smile.

"Hamilton 79," she called out as I pulled up.

"In the general course of human nature, a power over a man's subsistence amounts to a power over his will."

She jumped and hugged me as soon as I got off the bike.

"It's good to have you back, Alfa-leader."

For one bittersweet moment, I was back in Big Bear, hearing Ari's "Alfa under fire" with Nico laughing at my side.

"Are you okay?" Sarah's smile had disappeared.

I nodded.

"All is good, Alfa-five. Thanks for coming for me."

We mounted the bike on the chopper and took off.

Sarah was, among other things, our team's pilot. Between the military and Alfa, she had thousands of hours under her belt. As we lifted off, she set the coordinates for Cape Perpetua, Oregon.

"Are you ready for this?" she asked when she noticed my eyes on the flight plan.

It had been five years since my last time in Alfa's home base along the Oregon central coast—a brutal moment after Market.

"Only one way to find out, Sarah. Land me outside the Cape." I grimaced in her direction, hoping she would hear between the lines.

"Should have known," she replied, understanding my motive to land a good distance from the base.

As the world began to wake up underneath us, Sarah began to vent.

"When the lockdown started, it looked like the zombie apocalypse from up here. No one in the streets. Then Chicago happened, and suddenly the streets were on fire, clogged with hundreds of thousands. I just don't get it. How is this even happening?"

Clearing Los Angeles, she flew us over the Pacific Ocean, along the coast heading north. There were surfers in the water, but nobody else on the wide sandy beaches. Even with my eyes on the ocean, I fumed quietly about the millions stuck in their homes, getting infected instead of being in the open spaces where the virus couldn't thrive.

"I don't know the answer, Sarah. It's infuriating."

"How bad was it?" she asked, her tone softer.

Thinking about the Dragon measures, the closed-down shops, the shuttered schools, and the masking paranoia, I bristled and sighed my answer, "Let's just say that I feel free again, but my family is still down there." I didn't try to mask the conflict as I pulled out my smartphone to start my first task.

It was time to catch up. The RCC had sent me various reports, some at my request and many on order to study. We were just over the Oregon border when I discovered a trending social media post—an open letter written by Diego Columbo to President Stone.

Alarmed by the content, I researched the author, only to find Columbo's identity shrouded in mystery. My mind remained fixated and searching until Sarah cut through to let me know we were getting close.

Below us, there was just one big endless forest along Highway 101 as the ocean broke against the cliffs with infinite rage.

"Alfa-one, this is Alfa-leader. Come in," I called into my earbud.

"Alfa-leader, this is Alfa-one. Go ahead," came Dex's voice.

"Black Hills. Do you copy?"

It took him a moment before he responded, "Roger that, Black Hills forever."

"I can't believe I'm missing this." Sarah offered a fake pout as she began descending into the woods below.

When she had set us down in a small clearing in the forest, I adjusted my kit to make sure I was ready, knowing Sarah would take care of the rest of my things.

"Good hunting, Alfa-leader."

I stepped into the dense Siuslaw National Forest, leaving the midday sun behind me. The scent of red cedar and tall hemlock trees mixed with the salty ocean breeze, gently moving the sprawling ferns growing between the trunks. The sounds of small animals scurrying and birds taking flight stopped when I did.

"Close your eyes, Tanner, and listen." It was my father's voice from one of my early woodsman training courses. He taught me how to take a moment to sync with every geography and especially the ecosystems teeming with life, like forests.

I allowed the *Sense* to expand as my eyes shut to the world around me. Clouds must have obscured the sun beyond the canopy as the chill rose on my skin. The calming nothingness felt like home as a hunger for violence spread through my body.

Where are you, Beast? I can feel you!

Knowing that I was being hunted by the best, the old ripples in my hands traveled to other areas of my body, sending adrenaline to every limb.

"Did you just name me? I like it," the Beast growled in satisfaction.

My eyes opened.

Hux found me when I was forced into the open as I climbed the rocky mountain terrain. With only a moment to consider my options, the best choice was to hurry up until the thick foliage started again.

I'm g—...

He jumped at me from behind a tree and Jenny surprised me by materializing out of the bushes.

I lunged forward and managed to trip Hux, swerve, and kick Jenny straight in the gut. They were both down for a moment, which was all I needed to bolt away from them.

Shit. Shit. Faster.

Speed was now my best friend as I rushed between the trees, forsaking stealth for velocity. Every Rogue was trained in the martial arts to exhaustion and then reforged with specialized combat techniques. Panting, I stopped to rest next to a small cave opening in the mountain's face until the *Sense* warned me of someone's presence.

"Fight them inside," urged the Beast.

No. I'm so close. I'm beating them.

I gave one last look at the cave and continued my run.

A dark form launched from the side and knocked me hard to the rock floor. As I flipped back to my feet, I saw Moss in battle stance. My mind had barely processed it when someone else hit me from the side.

Both Dex and Moss waited for me. And as I rose to my feet, I heard a whistle from above.

Liam. Shit!

Dressed and face camouflaged in black, the young Rogue dropped on me from the tree above.

Pinned down, I struggled to get out from under him. But when Hux and Jenny arrived, I surrendered to their combined laughter.

"Exercise is over, fuckers," I called. "Well done, Alfa."

They all came at me for a group hug and I could no longer ignore the truth.

I'm home.

★ ★ ★

Liam Morales was our youngest operator at thirty years old. He was a small, lean, Hispanic man with black hair and eyes. Beyond his work as our team's cyber warrior, he was one hell of a scout that we all happily followed quietly along the cliffs of Cape Perpetua.

During World War II, the government feared the Japanese would invade the West Coast and built many military installations from California to Washington state. All these sites were eventually abandoned and overtaken by nature, except for the bunker right on the cliffs of Cape Perpetua, overlooking the ocean from its 800 foot elevation.

What would the original architects say if they knew how we have repurposed their design?

Liam led us into the concealed entrance, down a natural shaft, under a hemlock tree. Once inside, we were immersed in pitch darkness yet nobody turned on a light. Rogues were trained to walk and operate using all of their senses.

"Would you like to lead, Sir?" Liam stopped.

They're testing me.

"Yes, Liam," I answered and moved to the front of the small column.

There was no need to use my physical eyes. My memory alone told my feet and hands where to place themselves along the treacherous path into the earth as my lungs breathed in the familiar cold and salty air.

Extending forward, I was rewarded with the hard surface of the rock and searched the top right of the stone until I found the button. When the crackling sound of the rock sliding aside ended, I walked into the blackness beyond it.

Deep within the upper level of the old army bunker, we turned on our night vision goggles. It had been left in shambles.

Our padded combat boots barely made a sound as we moved deeper into the old maze-like structure and found the old elevator door with a "1776*" symbol imprinted into the metal. Each Rogue team had this symbol, with a corresponding star count.

I wonder how many teams there are.

The symbol always helped me refocus my thoughts.

I wonder what the early American revolutionaries would think about us and our mission.

When I stepped forward, the elevator sensor lit with green light as it scanned me and communicated with my chip. The old door hissed open, revealing a big enough space for us all.

"Welcome back," said Dex as he commanded the elevator to drop us even deeper into the ground.

Sarah was there when the door opened and bemoaned being left out of the exercise as Dex led us down a tunnel dotted with soft white lights. When we arrived in the mess hall, our food was ready.

I missed this.

Mealtime was an excellent opportunity to catch up with the team and thank Dex for leading them in my absence, as well as hear what they'd been doing. I quickly discovered they had all been on duty since the pandemic started and were curious about life under the Dragon measures. Liam used the big screen on the wall to project some of the current stats and give context to my story. It wasn't pretty, with almost one thousand deaths per day, but the fundamentals remained the same: age and comorbidity were the chief causes of fatalities while most other cases had recovered.

"This is insane!" blurted Moss after hearing the details of the lockdown in Los Angeles.

"Don't get me started about the damage to the children..." I told them about the preschool and Ari. They all shook their heads in disbelief when I told them about the parent meeting.

An hour in, I wondered when they would broach the topic that hung heavy in the air.

Will I be able to regain their full trust? What will it cost? I can't lose my family.

Soon, the discussion turned to Chicago and the riots popping up around the country. When the enthusiastic conversation dropped off suddenly, I looked up to see them all intently focused on me.

Nico.

"Then it's settled," I heard Roberto's words.

I need to be clear with them.

"Listen. I appreciate all you did during Nico's funeral. Continue with your questions. My reckoning will wait." I smiled at Liam when the look of relief crossed his youthful face.

Dex nodded at Liam, who elaborated on the growing destabilization in the country due to the Dragon, the measures, and now the social unrest and riots.

"Is there a question there, Liam?" I wondered.

Hux smacked Liam's neck, inciting quick laughter from us all.

The young cyber operator took a deep breath.

"Will there be DIR2 ops soon?"

All bantering ceased as the gravity of the question played out in all of our souls. The Rogue Doctrine, also known as "The Doctrine," had two primary Directives with their respective rules of engagement. "Directive One" handled all foreign adversaries, while "Directive Two" dealt with American citizens. In all the years of my service, there was only one time when I acted under the latter, and it was well-deserved.

"We'll see," I answered, recalling Custer's recent warning regarding Nico's killers.

"Here it is, Sir," said Dex as he opened the door to the commander's room.

The open rectangular space was about 800 square feet. It had an office set up on one end, and the other was dedicated to sleeping arrangements and the bathroom.

"You kept it the same."

He passed his hand through his thick dark hair.

"Well, I figured you'd return to us one day."

I circled the desk and dropped into my old leather chair for the full debrief that only Dex could give me.

"How about you, Dex? How are you holding up?"

I was the only married-with-children member of the team, but my second-in-command had family on the East Coast.

When he looked down and to the side, I knew something had happened.

"I lost my father in April. He was old and sick, and the Dragon just got him."

Oh fuck.

"I'm so sorry, Brother. I know you two were tight." I paused. "I didn't…"

"Yeah. I asked the RCC not to speak of it. You had enough on your plate already." His eyes darkened as his fist clenched on the desk. "New York state didn't allow me to visit him in the hospital or attend his funeral. He died alone, surrounded by strangers. And I wasn't there…"

Fucking tyrants! One day!

Unhinged by the sound of my friend's voice cracking with grief, I tightened my grip on the armchair.

"How are you, Sir? You had your share of grief," he asked after a long pause.

"Not so tough after all, soldier boy," the Demon guy's taunt reverberated in my mind.

"Sir, are you okay?" asked Dex, bringing me back to the present.

Although I had yet to meet any other Rogue teams, I was certain they followed the same rules. Every team leader had to be checked by their Executive Officer to ensure they remained operational and acted accordingly.

"Is this about that thing with Liam?" I asked, and my XO nodded. "As I said, that 'other' thing is my war and mine only. Let's focus on our assignments."

"Yes, Sir. I'll let you get settled." He forced a smile as he stood up.

When he had closed the door behind him, I pressed a button and a large screen rose vertically from the middle of the desk, which lit up as a touchscreen. It was time to call the Rogue Command Center, so I pressed the button to connect.

"RCC," came the female voice in my ear.

"Please tell the Commanders I'm ready when they are."

"Stand by, Alfa-leader."

TIME TO GET TO WORK

Custer and Jack's faces filled the large screen in front of me and our pleasantries only took a moment, as it was the acceptable language of our hard world.

"Thank you for all you've done for Nico and the family."

They both nodded.

"He's a Marine. He deserved nothing less than that." A smirk appeared on his face. "But while we're on the subject, it's important to note the 'fame' that you've attracted because of the funeral."

"The Soldier from the funeral?" I asked, missing the sound of Dani's voice already.

Jack nodded and told me about all the reporters who'd been snooping around Camp Pendleton.

"This is a distraction, but it may be turned into an opportunity one day. We'll see."

Custer coughed with a wink before he started with the real debrief.

"Various foreign players are currently destabilizing our nation. This is always true but augmented now with the pandemic, social issues, the election, and the animosity toward President Stone. Jack, please start with China."

Jack scratched his wrinkled, clean-shaven face.

"Well, Lee was right, and now he's working himself to death about this damn virus."

Old irritation rose up.

"It's called guilt, Sir. We should all know it."

Neither of them liked my comment but let it slide without rebuttal as Jack brought up the current database, which reconfirmed the Dragon originated in China and nowhere else.

"We don't know whether they did it intentionally or not."

"Well, they locked Wuhan from the rest of China while letting international travel continue out of the province. Intentional or not, they used it quite well." I didn't try to cloak my gut instinct on the matter.

"Thanks to the US legacy media, China seems immune with the focus on Stone's response to the virus instead of the virus's origins. This is only the tip of the iceberg..." He continued on about China's recent enaction of the "national security" law, purposely designed to deal with Hong Kong. Under its pretense, the country could place the island under martial law, but that wasn't the worst. "The way they wrote it would apply to any adversary worldwide."

There was a moment of silence as we each contemplated what it would mean for our divided nation.

"Did you get more on General Zhang?" I probed.

Jack shook his head.

"We know that he's involved, but nothing else at this moment."

"How about Baker?" I pressed.

Custer shook his head this time.

"No data on Baker. He's been hard to pin since the Charlton administration ended."

"Is there any other foreign power that might be involved in our mess at home?" I asked, leaning forward on the desk.

"Iran is possibly connected, but we're not sure yet." Jack's brow furrowed.

"Now, let's speak about domestic issues..." Custer began by identifying all the civil rights abuses across the country, which fell under the harsh Dragon measures, bringing up cases I didn't even know about. From priests being arrested for outdoor ceremonies to funerals without guests, it all disgusted me. "The First Amendment is under direct assault," finished Custer as my anger rekindled on Dex's sad story. "We're concerned that powers taken from the people will not be returned."

"And this is before we even consider the financial ramifications for the destruction of the middle class," chimed Jack before moving the conversation to the current social strife.

"We all saw the tape from Chicago, and anger is warranted. But there are various anomalies around the protests, which made us consider that there is more in play here." He clicked something on his screen. "Let's watch this short segment."

On the screen, I watched footage of the worst riots, looting, violence, and the legacy media explaining it all away as "peaceful protests." My blood heated to a soft boil as rioters forced people to salute with fists up after surrounding their cars or even hassling them in restaurants, monuments were vandalized, and the "defund the police" demands were shouted from street corners and media outlets.

Even with all my *lived experience*—a loathsome term that the Left loved to use—I didn't realize how sophisticated the domestic assault on our way of life had been and continued to be.

"And there are two entities we need to keep watching..." Jack turned our attention to the ones financing this mess. The first was a company named Pax Eden—a multi-billion-dollar corporation out of DC, which coordinated donations for left-leaning causes and politicians. The second was the Open Borders Initiative, also known as OBI, an international company with European roots supporting worldwide civil society groups. "They bail out rioters everywhere, finance the Democrats against Stone, and seek to change the justice system in America through district attorney races."

"Why DA races?" I asked.

"Why do you think Nico's investigation was squashed?" Jack's question blindsided me. "The Los Angeles DA is some prick named Neville Bernard. OBI financed him a few years back, and he's basically been preventing cases from reaching prosecution since."

Ah yes, that's why Holden was pissed about Nico's case.

"Now, we spoke a bit about Comrades and Ryse right after Chicago happened. But, here are some more details," Jack continued. "Comrades was first spotted around 2012. It began as a campaign against police brutality, which gained momentum due to some iconic incidents around the country. Shortly after its first spotlight moment, it evolved into a Marxist social change movement espousing everything from the 'erasure of debt' to 'equity-based education and hiring.'"

"Equity?" I was puzzled about the use of the word in this context. "Do you mean equal opportunity?"

Jack scowled.

"No, Son. This perversion means exactly the opposite—equal outcome. Let that sink in."

"From each according to his ability, to each according to his needs," I said quietly, referencing Karl Marx's famous words.

They both nodded sadly.

"As for Ryse, the original movement was allegedly started by the old Soviets in Eastern Germany to create shock troops against any fascists who might have still lived there after the war. But soon after, the group opened chapters throughout Western Europe, appearing in anarchist protests and bringing violence with them." Jack's voice was somber.

The white lightning on black background.

"The American chapters only started around the '80s, mostly around the American Northwest and some in New York. They solely operated around minor incidents, mostly surrounding 'anti-capitalist' cases," explained Jack. "It's an anomaly how they got from there to what we are seeing with these riots."

I immediately thought of the attack on Taco Libertad and the efficiency of those who sacked it.

Somebody trained them. But who? And why now?

"I'm sure you've noticed that both of these groups use communist-like symbolism in their verbal and printed messaging."

"And the Dragon Skull," I added.

"Yes, that too."

Custer interjected, "As for the upcoming elections, while The Doctrine is prohibited from taking any sides, we do want to point out a few things."

I leaned forward, surprised to hear them addressing this at all. During Hell Year, every Rogue learns that our mission requires complete impartiality toward political parties and their aims.

"First, there is this whole Western States Coalition, which we're keeping an eye on in case they toy with the idea of secession should Stone win again," said

Custer. "Then, there is the recent revelation about the 'Transparent Election Review.'"

"Who?" I asked, amazed at how much had transpired since my retirement.

Custer explained that TER was a short-term project involving current and former government officials, academics, journalists, and retired military leaders.

"Their exercise aimed to model various responses to disruptions in the 2020 Election."

"Disruptions? By whom? The Chinese?" I was lost.

Custer's response was grave, "No. The adversary in their wargame is President Stone and what he might do if he loses the elections."

"Who's behind this? Financing it?"

"It could be Deep State actors, but we're not sure. Regardless, we are only monitoring, not getting involved." Custer's tone was somber.

So many thoughts raced, my mind stretching to make all of the connections.

Speaking of Stone...

"Have you read that online post by Diego Columbo?" I asked. "He called it an 'open letter for the president.'"

Neither said anything, but I had their full attention.

"He claimed the Dragon measures were designed to establish a new world order called The Great Reset and that the riots are being used as a smoke screen for the Deep State to get Stone out of office while weakening state powers. All toward a regime change."

I thought they would laugh or at least shake their heads, but they did neither of those.

Did I hit a nerve?

"We know about the letter but nothing about its author. Why did you bring this up?" asked Custer.

Seriously?

"It's a rare opportunity. Scared masses would sacrifice the few for their safety. Even if this letter is fake, its content is troubling. What if this is all coordinated? A plan of sorts…" My voice trailed off.

"Listen, Son," said Jack. "This whole Great Reset is on our radar, but so far, it is just socialist talking points, masquerading as a wonderous answer for the damages done by the pandemic."

An odd sensation spread through me.

How did he know to focus on Chicago back then? Why is he stonewalling me now on Columbo?

Jack moved us to the next subject, effectively ending the discussion and its open questions.

"A confidential informant reached out to us— from Mexico…" He explained the CI was embedded in a Mexican Cartel and had some troubling news. The Cartel was working with some foreigners on smuggling into the US. "We don't know who is working with them from the US or what they are smuggling. But something is going on." Jack laid out the plan for a recon only mission, which centered around meeting the CI to understand the situation better.

"Yes, Sir. We'll act accordingly." I tapped my fingers on the desk.

"What is it, Tanner?" asked Jack, voice stern as a command. "Spill it."

Thinking about Liam's question over dinner, I told them we should seriously consider using Directive Two to engage domestic threats quickly.

"I know other Rogue teams are out there, and why you're keeping us apart. But, maybe it's time to get together and figure out what's really happening here."

Custer frowned.

"We need to stay focused on our foreign adversaries for now. Our facade is thin at best, and we cannot risk it for a preemptive conflict with American antagonists. Understand, Alfa-leader?"

Old Glory was our cover—a military contracting company that Ulysses had started three decades earlier. It allowed us to operate while disguising ourselves within the company's legal operations, so Custer was justifiably concerned.

But to what end?

"I understand. But with all due respect, Sir, what happened in LA and elsewhere is a new factor to consider."

"Maybe so, but for now, we'll remain in assessment mode." Jack closed the subject.

"We all need to get used to working with each other again," said Jack after Custer left our conversation. "There is much you don't know about the dangers we face and their roots. Be patient with us, and you'll have your chance to effectuate a change."

I leaned back in my chair, realizing he wasn't done with me.

"Your newfound fame might help us..." Jack focused on an online reporter named Ken Lim. "He was among the dozens of reporters who reached Pendleton, but he's not like the rest of the vultures. Not only did he provide some excellent coverage of the rioters' true face, but he also highlighted Nico and the funeral in an honest way."

"Any new information on that front?"

Jack confirmed that he also concluded that Nico had seen at least one of his killers before the attack.

"It's just hard to know beyond that, as there's no earlier footage. However, that Ryse LA chapter keeps on causing trouble. We've been monitoring them, and they are connected to so many incidents without any repercussion." He paused. "Will you be able to focus on your tasks?"

"I'll do my job. But I also gave a promise, which I intend to keep."

Jack sighed.

"And then there's Seattle..." When he brought up the rising tension with the nightly riots, we both concluded

Chad was probably safe as long as he was identified as an ally by the far-left forces there.

Ally! Another word losing its meaning to a fucked-up ideology.

"We play the long game, Son. Everything is on the table, including us being the last resort."

"Maybe you'll tell me where the RCC is located then...." I responded, jabbing at him for holding back the secret location of our entire command center.

"Maybe," he replied with a smirk before saying his goodbye.

The black screen retracted quietly into my desk, and I left my room. Once inside the elevator, I glanced at the ten buttons that led to other levels of our base. The last one was black and absent of markings. As soon as I pressed it, the elevator shot down into the earth.

When the doors opened with a silent crackle, the cold salty air struck me with full force. I made my way to the metal path leading to an opening in the rock.

"The Pit," as we called it, was a massive cavern at the bottom of the Cape's cliff. The ocean water filled half the cavern through an underground waterway, and the rest was a stony shore when the tide was low. As the footpath ended up on a natural rock ledge, about six feet over it all, I used an affixed metal ladder to descend and stood by the water's edge.

Reaching into the freezing dark liquid, old fears immediately assaulted my mind.

I broke to pieces here. Death is here.

It took all my mental force not to retract my hand in fear.

Where are you, Beast? Why did you want to fight in the cave?

DAMN HOT

– Mexicali, Mexico –
Sunday, June 7, 2020

The smell of gun oil mixed with cheap coffee hung heavy in our "safe house" while the team deep-cleaned weapons and checked gear.

I missed this so much, I mused as I paused to watch my warriors work in silence while the sweltering heat beaded on their brows.

We'd driven for forty-eight hours, from the cold northwest of Oregon to the boiling hot barrios of Mexicali, Mexico, just south of the California border.

When Dex nodded at me, I took a seat next to him at the makeshift desk so he could give me the mission parameters. An hour in, he pointed to the highlighted screen on his laptop, "This is the alley where you're going to meet the CI."

"Roger that," I responded and then turned back to the team. "Liam, we're leaving in ten."

Dex would stay behind to run the operation from the safe house.

It was time to change my appearance.

★　★　★

A few hours later, I was walking the streets, dressed in old jeans, a dirty brown long-sleeved shirt, and a mask that half-covered my two-week beard, darkened with makeup Jenny had applied. It never ceased to amaze me, the freedom that came with obscuring your authentic self within the shadow of another.

The sun dropped behind the horizon, its last rays painting the taller buildings bright red. Although Mexico had implemented its own version of the Dragon lockdown, it didn't seem to be as well-enforced as it was in California. Many people were in the streets, mostly unmasked, especially the children.

A sharp ache passed through me as I thought of my own kids.

Liam was my designated "wingman" and walked behind me to watch my back while the rest of the team was set as a "quick response force."

The target was ahead, just beyond a shuttered hardware shop. When I reached it, I leaned on the wall where the alley started. It was long, dark, and narrow, with debris and graffiti covering the buildings.

Darkness, I'm in the tunnel.
My bare feet feel some liquid on the rocky surface.
What is this?
I touch it and bring my hand to my nose.
Blood!

"Alley rhymes with Ali... Alley..."

"Alfa-leader, Alfa-one. Over."

Dex's voice broke through my mumbling and brought me back from the bottom of my memories.

"Go ahead, Alfa-one. Over."

Did he notice my delay?

"Alfa-leader, friendly on target, five mikes, over."

"Wilco, over and out," I replied and started to drift into the alley, dragging my feet as a drunken day laborer would. Liam clicked twice on the radio to tell me he was in position.

The CI was dubbed "Mr. Jones." He was a short, chubby man and had the face of a tired accountant, not a daring Cartel double agent. He spooked when I appeared quietly and immediately asked for his code in Spanish.

After authentication, he smirked, "Where did you get your Spanish, Gringo? You sound like a Colombian."

My blood pressure rose quickly, and I used the *Sense* to calm myself.

"I came to hear *you* speak."

His eyes remained narrow as he told me the story of how foreigners had been working with his Cartel lately. He didn't know anything about them or their ethnicity, but he fidgeted and looked around anxiously the whole time he spoke.

Jack had already briefed me that Mr. Jones had been a reliable confidential informant for many years, so I didn't suspect a betrayal. But something was off.

Whoever they are, he's scared of them.

The CI didn't know what the foreigners wanted to smuggle into the US, but he had the time and target location for the first shipment—right across the border in Calexico, California.

"The Cartel is doing the 'middleman' work."

"Do you know who is meeting the shipment on the US side?" I pressed.

He shook his head.

"All I know is that they are some revolucionarios."

Revolutionaries. Could it be?

We finished the meeting and went our separate ways.

"Something's wrong here. I request permission to have Alfa intercept the shipment."

I was back in the safe house with Custer and my dad on the line. They'd instructed us to return to base, but my gut feeling had me pushing against their order.

"Negative, Tanner. Return to base as scheduled," ordered Jack.

My frustration must have reached my face, as Custer released a grunt and smiled.

"Your request has merit, but it doesn't outweigh the risks. We can achieve the same goal by tipping the US authorities. And if this is Comrades or Ryse on the other end, they'll be targeted by the entire federal apparatus. It's a win-win for us."

He was always kinder. Memories of my training emerged and then receded. *But they're both wrong about this.*

"Yes, Sirs," I responded, unconvinced, and ordered Alfa to prepare for departure.

Sarah had the chopper waiting in an empty field across the border. We boarded and began our flight back to Oregon. It was an hour before dawn when we flew over Los Angeles and my heart constricted as I looked at the sea of tiny lights.

So close, but so far.

OUT FOR A RUN

The sand was cold and dense and my muscles screamed in agony as I pushed my body in a barefoot run along the beach, trying to outrun the haunts.

"Listen, Hermano. I gotta go. If something happens…"

Faster…

"This United States Marine Corporal Nicolas Ramirez did what he believed was right."

Faster!

"You should try it again," Nico's laughter faded with his last words.

"Arghhh!" I ran into the freezing ocean, losing no speed. When I was finally encased under the icy waves, a great roar escaped my lungs.

★   ★   ★

With only swim trunks on, my body shivered uncontrollably as I got out of the water and caught sight of the town beginning to glow in the morning light.

The picturesque town of Yachats boasted barely a thousand homes. It was nestled along Highway 101, the ocean on one side and the Siuslaw National Forest on the other. Cape Perpetua was less than three miles south of it, which made it Alfa's go-to place for a dose of civilization.

I hate the fucking cold, I thought as I jogged to my motorcycle, which was parked in a small inlet parking lot. I pressed my thumb against the saddle secure box and it clicked open after reading my fingerprint, giving me access to the much-needed towel, clothes, and phone.

I need to talk to her.

"Good morning, Babe...." I was walking to a local coffee shop where I suspected at least a few Alfa would be dining.

"Hi, Husband. Cel, it's him. I need a few minutes..." I could hear the voices of our children fade as Dani moved to a quieter part of our home.

"How are you, My Love?"

"I miss you." She paused. "I'm hanging in there, but so tired. Every day, we have new restrictions, but do they care about all the crime? No! And I don't know where that agent is, but at least Holden keeps checking on us. Even sent that young officer one time. She seems nice."

"You're not supposed to notice your father's people, Sweetie," I teased. "I'm glad Holden is keeping an eye out for you. And I agree, there's something special about his partner. She seems to care more than most."

When I entered the town and approached the main thoroughfare, I froze. About fifty or so older people demonstrated along the highway, carrying "Remember Chicago" signs.

"Your mom has been calling daily, which is nice because our friends have cut us off..."

I was only half-listening as I watched the useful idiots marching.

"Are you okay, Baby?" she asked. "You sound distant."

She senses everything, even if she doesn't know what I am.

"It's everywhere, My Love. This fucking mess has changed everyone."

Suddenly losing my appetite, I turned back toward the motorcycle.

"Maybe so. But some things never change. Your family is always here for you," she whispered as the children's voices reappeared in her background.

"Hey, Baby, I gotta save Cel. Call me again soon, okay?"

"As soon as I can. Love you."

She ended the call and I sat for a moment on my bike, staring at the waves, savoring the warmth my queen's voice always brought to my chest.

Jack's call came right before I turned on the engine.

"Something's happening in Seattle. Rioters there have declared some "autonomous zone." They're barricading it right now. Chad lives there!" His fatherly stress was palpable, despite his best efforts to speak as a commander.

"Is the city allowing it?" I asked, turning my bike toward the highway.

"Yes. The mayor ordered the police to vacate the precinct that handles that area."

Fucking crazy. How's this even possible?

I shook my head at the thought of it happening in my own hometown.

"Where's Chad? Is he getting out?" I pushed down on my own worries.

"No, he decided to stay and report from inside the zone. Your younger brother is finally waking up. He read me the draft of his article for this morning. He's finally questioning his ideologies."

"Really?" I pulled down on the gas handle to increase my speed, wondering why it was so difficult for me to believe that my brother could turn away from his beliefs.

"It's never too late to see the light," responded Jack, relief in his voice.

That was about me too, wasn't it?

"I'm minutes from base. Send it to me. Any news on the 'shipment'?"

"It's going down tomorrow night. We tipped some good people at the Border Patrol. Whatever's coming, those guys will stop it," he responded.

"Okay. Talk soon," I confirmed, making the right onto the dirt road that led to the top of the Cape.

★   ★   ★

The Capitol Hill Autonomous Zone was all over the news. It had all rolled out within a few hours as coordinated rioters blocked the roads to the Capitol Hill neighborhood in Seattle, effectively creating an area under their control. Just as Jack had reported, the mayor had ordered the police to leave their East Precinct station to "avoid needless conflict." One after the other, all the news anchors hailed the "historic peaceful protest against the system of oppression." They even called it CHAZ, following the rioters' lead again.

Seated at my desk, my blood boiled as news anchors related the "Comrades' demands" of the city. A video clip of a masked Comrade leader yelling about defunding the police and granting immunity to all who took over the zone played on repeat.

I can't believe this shit.

The RCC pinged me when Chad's article was released. My dad was right about the apparent shift. He pointed out his own liberal views and history while questioning the escalating violence and now the CHAZ phenomenon. I actually read it twice, not believing that my younger brother had taken such a bold stand.

To dispel my unbelief, I called him.

"You know me, Tanner. I do think that people have had enough of this police brutality. But this… this… whatever it is… has gone too far. The movement will only suffer with more violence," Chad confirmed. He was happy to receive my call and my words of support for his article but unwilling to consider leaving the city. "It's my moment, Tanner. I'm right here in the middle, reporting from the ground."

"Listen, both Dad and I support you. Just be careful. Okay?"

"Isn't that something…" he responded in a subdued tone before we said goodbye.

I felt for my little brother, whose worldview seemed to be collapsing underneath him.

My mom called while I was still digesting my chat with Chad, and we spoke briefly about him before her own maternal instincts took over.

"How are you, Honey?" asked Ali.

"It's hard, Mom. I miss them," I replied, deflated. "Thanks for checking on them."

"It's supposed to be hard, Tanner." Her voice carried both pride and sadness. "Are you okay? What is it?"

Just like Dani. They sense.

The nightmarish relapse from the alley in Mexicali returned, and I wanted so badly to tell her about it and get some answers.

What happened to me in Bogotá? Why am I rhyming these words?

"It's fine, Mom. I love you. Let me talk with Tami." I'd heard my sister's voice in the background, requesting to talk with me.

Ali didn't push and called for Tami, who asked her to watch Adam while she spoke with me.

True to form, Tami was anxious and driven. She voiced her concerns about the lockdowns and the successful approaches they were trying out in South Dakota.

"Oh, and Lynn asked me to send you her warmest condolences and tell you that she'd love to hear from you."

"Thank her for me," I replied, resisting another endless repeat of his death in my memories.

I congratulated her, pivoting away from Lynn and my pain, "I'm so happy about your work, Tami. We need litigators like you, who still care about the law."

She laughed.

"Who knows, Brother, maybe you'll need me one day. I'd be there, no matter what. You know that."

"I do, Sis. Love you."

I returned to my desk after eating dinner with Alfa. They asked me to stay for Poker, but Seattle was on my mind.

CHAZ had the attention of every news channel, and I noticed that several referenced Ken Lim, one of the reporters embedded within the zone.

The guy Dad mentioned.

Ken was undercover somewhere in CHAZ and had shared some scary footage. According to him, Comrades had already placed armed guards around the zone, checking the IDs of those who tried to enter.

In one day!

I smiled when Senator Garcia from Texas was shown petitioning the president to get involved in Seattle.

Texans know what this means!

But it was Brett Cohen's podcast that sparked some hope that people might wake up. He went hard against the mayor and the Washington governor, who surrendered the citizens of CHAZ to Comrades.

"We're going to have a problem here. We are placing the villain as the hero. You'd leave the hero no choice but to act like a villain."

"Well said," I mumbled as I turned off the podcast and the lights in my room to enter the pitch darkness.

Where are you, Beast?

FUBAR

– Cape Perpetua, OR –
Tuesday, June 9, 2020

It was early evening, and all of Alfa sat at attention in the control room at our base. Liam and Dex managed the technology while the rest of us just watched the operation on one of the giant screens on the wall. The Eye was tasked with this operation, and the live satellite feed was eerily precise as the three black trucks made their way from Mexicali to the border.

"Why can't we see into the trucks, Liam?" I asked, sensing tension creeping its way up my spine.

He nodded as he spoke with someone at the RCC in his headset and then turned to me, eyes wide.

"The trucks are coated with something that blocks our thermal imaging scan."

Damn it!

"Romulus, where does US Customs and Border Protection plan on stopping the trucks?" I called my dad by his official callsign through my headset.

"They're going to let them deeper into Calexico," replied Jack matter-of-factly.

Customer Border Protection had some tough agents working for them, but the use of the anti-satellite coating worried me. We all held our breath as the large vehicles inched their way toward the border.

Liam received an update from the RCC and relayed it, "Alfa-leader, we're getting reports on increased encrypted chatter across Ryse chapters in the Southwest. We broke through some of their messages, but they also use codes."

We're missing something.

My anxiety doubled.

"Romulus, can you get the CBP to stop the trucks right after the border?" I asked.

"Negative, Alfa-leader. We tipped them, and we cannot intervene and expose ourselves." Jack's tone was strained but firm.

Fuck.

I paced around the control room.

The trucks were at the border when the first report came in that protesters had begun to converge on the CBP headquarters. The RCC had the Eye refocused on the large CBP complex as hundreds of protesters began to block their main gate.

How the hell? Damn it. They're efficient.

"Romulus, isn't the timing of this surprise protest suspicious?"

"What do you suggest, Alfa-leader? We're unable to intervene even if we wanted to," insisted Jack, his tone still guarded.

I stopped pacing and gripped the back of an empty chair as we watched the trucks crawl past the border into Calexico.

"Romulus, can you scan the sides of the trucks for any invisible paints?" I asked.

"Standby, Alfa-leader." The line went silent for a long minute. "We got something. Sending your way."

As the grainy image came up on one of the other screens, I sucked in my breath. It was the Dragon Skull.

Fuck. Fuck.

I hit the control desk with my fist as I growled, "Romulus, they know about the ambush."

"CBP is about to roll on them in the next intersection," said Jack. "We tried to tip them to send more forces, but the protest blocks their base."

The trucks were just about fifty yards from the intersection when hundreds of people appeared from side streets.

I can't fucking believe this.

Chatter between Liam and the RCC increased as the trucks accelerated and the people opened to let them into the intersection and then closed on them as the trucks stopped.

"CBP is moving in, and the protesters have created a human shield around the trucks!" blurted Jack, suddenly realizing what was unfolding before our eyes.

A few dozen Border Patrol agents tried to get into the intersection but were held back by the protesters.

"More agents are coming from headquarters. They managed to clear their gate," said Jack. "ETA 10 mikes."

We don't have that kind of time.

The thought had barely crossed my mind when the trucks' back doors opened.

Every Alfa member in the room gasped as a couple hundred masked armed men emerged from the trucks and laid precise assault rifle fire on the CBP agents while using the protesters as shields. A pin drop could be heard in the dead silence of our control room as we watched the attackers kill or wound every CBP agent in less than two minutes.

Professionals!

After the rioters and attackers escaped in all directions, all that remained in the intersection were the downed CBP agents and some rioters who had probably been caught in the agents' return fire.

Looking at my team's stunned faces, I removed my headset and dropped it on the chair in front of me.

"Show's over, Alfa. I'll be in my room."

Alone in my room, I watched the news, marveling at how the media was reporting events within minutes of the massacre.

They were tipped. We got conned.

The bile in the back of my throat burned as all the chyrons and anchors spoke emotionally of the travesty of the "police brutality" toward the migrants and the peaceful protesters who tried to protect them. Nobody even mentioned the wounded and dead CBP agents.

My chip vibrated, and I could sense the tiredness growing in Jack as he admitted the operation's grand failure. "Good call, Son. On the Dragon Skull. Never crossed my mind. The operation details must have leaked somehow."

"It's California, Dad. They hate the federal agencies unless they hold the White House."

I shuddered at the mere thought of the coming election.

"Maybe so. Ryse is now openly congratulating the fight against the oppressors, protecting poor migrants," he murmured. "We're going to work hard to find out more. They worked like soldiers," he added, leaving the hanging concern in the air.

Who are they?

"What about your CI, dad? He might be in great danger now."

"I know. We have a plan in place to evacuate his family if necessary, but we need him in there more than ever. Pray that he finds something."

"We should have done it ourselves," I grumbled.

Jack was silent for a moment before responding, "I know it's personal for you. Heck, it's bloody personal for me too. But we still have operational boundaries. You need to get right with this fact, Alfa-leader."

I'm always in training.

"Yes, Sir."

A LEAD

– *San Francisco, CA* –
Saturday, June 13, 2020

"Almost ready," called Jenny from the bathroom.

We'd spent the previous few days on edge as the "Calexico carnage" coverage played nonstop on all major channels, faulting the police and law enforcement, and the stakes had gotten higher when our informant Mr. Jones reached out with another worrisome lead. He'd mentioned the "Chinese People Collective" as a possible connection with the Cartel smuggling, so the RCC had immediately dispatched us to San Francisco, where the CPC's national headquarter was located.

The bathroom door opened and Jenny walked out, dressed in a short skirt and a fashionable business jacket.

Liam whistled from the kitchen. "Damn, Jenny. I'd hire you myself."

"Douche bag," she grumbled with a smile as the rest of the team bantered away.

"You're a stunner, Jenny," I agreed, smiling even though my stomach turned the way it always did before sending a team member into undercover work.

After complimenting me on my homeless disguise, Jenny teased, "Just keep some distance from me, or I'll call the police."

"Poor cops wouldn't be able to do anything anyway."

My dark sense of humor made her shake her head as we both masked up.

At least there's one good thing about this pandemic—it's easier to hide.

I hung back about fifty feet as Jenny and I walked the neglected commercial street. We'd learned early in training the importance of connecting with the environment and the mission before fully executing it.

San Francisco, just like Los Angeles, had stringent Dragon measures and their impact could be seen on every corner. Homeless encampments, shuttered businesses, and dystopian signs about "doing your part for the community." If that wasn't jarring enough, the abundant display of Comrade symbols was enough to make us even more vigilant as we made our way from the safe house to the CPC headquarters.

"Alfa-four, repeat mission," I spoke into my earbud.

Jenny stopped ahead to adjust her high heels and started detailing her general knowledge, "The CPC is an American non-governmental organization. It was founded right here in San Francisco around the late '70s..." She continued to explain how the CPC was allegedly helping Chinese migrants assimilate into the states but quickly becoming influential in politics and matters advancing educational goals in universities across the nation.

"They have chapters across the country but are mainly located in Democratic-held states. They donate heavily to political races, California being the prime example of their success," she continued. "Right here in San Francisco, the CPC has the mayor and DA in their pocket." She pulled out a cigarette, dropped her mask to her chin, and lit it while walking around discarded trash on the pavement. "As for the colleges, the CPC has been donating to various social justice causes for decades. They have even opened a few educational centers around prestigious schools."

I shook my head as I recalled the warning, often attributed to Vladimir Lenin, that had clearly not been heeded by the institutions of America: "Give me four years to teach the children, and the seed I have sown will never be uprooted."

In between puffs, Jenny detailed how the CPC had become active in shifting the "Dragon origin blame" away from China and promoting the strict lockdown measures China had enforced while stoking the fires of social unrest right here in America.

"They've openly supported the Comrades movement since its inception, yet they've made it clear they don't condone violence to achieve social justice goals. There is no evidence of any crimes by them."

I removed the whiskey bottle from the brown bag and drank from it while dragging my feet behind her.

Still too easy to re-enact.

"How's the chocolate milk?" she teased as she dropped her cigarette and put it out before finishing the mission review. "The CPC CEO is a guy named Paul Shi who was born in 1977 to a successful migrant family from China. They escaped with nothing and made themselves from scratch right here in town."

My age.

She continued to recount how Paul had gone back to study in China after doing his undergraduate in Berkeley. "He got a graduate degree in international relationships from Peking University in Beijing and then returned to California straight into the CPC. No criminal background."

While stopped at the intersection, waiting for the light to change, she spoke to her role. "My mission is to answer a job posting, get hired, and see what I can learn."

She crossed the street toward the CPC's massive three-story, industrial-style building. It was surrounded by a six-foot stone wall that enabled controlled access for cars with a guard posted. The blood-red Chinese flag flew over one side of the gate, and its American counterpart was on the other. Jenny stopped and, leaning against a tall office building on the other side of the street, she lit another cigarette.

"I will never get used to seeing this flag on American soil, waved by Americans... of all people," she whispered in disgust tinged with pain.

Noting the octave change in her voice, I quickly recalled her harrowing tale of losing her mother during their escape.

Tying my shoelaces like an intoxicated bum, I responded, "Alfa-two will provide overwatch, night and day," thinking of Huxley in the office building with his favorite sniper rifle. "Get the job done and come back home."

"Wilco, out." She smashed her cigarette under her heel, pulled up her mask, and then crossed the street toward the imposing building.

"Don't worry, Son. We'll get her back safely."

I was back in the safe house, talking to Jack on my laptop. "Every Rogue is a trojan horse" was what we were all taught and trained to be, but it didn't make it any easier.

Tired of the elephant in the room, I addressed it head on.

"Do you think that it was the Chinese in Calexico?"

His face looked strained as he replied, "There's no evidence, but since Mr. Jones reached out, I'm a bit concerned." He sighed. "Speaking of concerns..."

He shifted the attention to the "Transparent Election Review" project, which had been disclosed to me during my first briefing. "We found out Baker was involved in that TER wargame. He's currently employed in the Department of Defense."

My body froze.

"He wasn't hiding his participation…" Jack was still trying to put the puzzle pieces together in front of me.

"Why would he do that?" I asked.

"Maybe because his old boss Grayson is running for president. I'm not sure."

Raging resentments crackled in my belly.

"We should have taken care of him back then. Why aren't we going after him?"

Jack shook his head slowly as he answered, "It's not so simple, Tanner. He's Deep State with quite a bit of power. You remember when I met General Tall? Well, Baker's the one who got the witch hunt started on him once our meeting was revealed."

"Is that the mistake you referred to during our Big Bear conversation?" I wondered.

Jack's countenance fell.

"It was my first time considering a move against their systemic power, but poor Tall was eviscerated before he could do anything to help." He grunted at the memory. "We never found who leaked the meeting."

So much going on. We're like rats in a maze.

"Dad, we've got to stop this. Let's do what we need to do," I pleaded, forsaking all official decorum. "Lee warned us back then, and look what happened. What if this is all connected, and we're missing the whole picture?"

Jack's expression had shifted from sad to annoyed.

"For the millionth time, Tanner. Directive Two is limited to near collapse. We won't be vigilantes in our country. Go to Pendleton and talk to Custer about it." His tone was final.

Reminding myself of my position and rank, I pushed down the fury collecting in my core.

"Any news on Ryse Los Angeles?" There was no need to explain to him my reasoning.

His expression softened as he shook his head. "No, Son. I'm sorry. We're always searching for clues about Nico, but nothing's turned up yet."

"Thank you for keeping up the search. Anything else?"

"The only other update of any consequence is personal." A small smile crept across his face as he told me about Chad's second article questioning the liberal argument for what had been happening since Chicago. "We've been talking daily. Can you imagine?"

It was apparent how happy it made him to be closer to Chad, so I forced a smile.

Look at you trying to be a dad. How nice.

OLD DOG

– Camp Pendleton, CA –
Friday, June 19, 2020

My motorcycle was parked a few hundred feet back from the entrance of Marine Corps Base Pendleton, on a side street just off the Interstate 5 Freeway. The saddle box was open, my official BDU uniform carefully folded inside.

Even after the long drive, I'm still not sure I'm ready.

The General had been in my life since before my birth. He was present during my childhood training and throughout the various stages in the Marine corps. He was hard like a diamond, but warmer than my father. He had never married or had children, and the matter had always remained somewhere in my mind.

Checking the time, I thought about my family, less than a hundred miles away, getting ready for breakfast and homeschooling.

God, I miss them.

I sighed and buttoned my shirt, stitched with my rank and name. When my phone chirped with a message from Holden, I slid it into my pocket and got back on the bike.

It can wait.

The motorcycle coasted slowly in the line of cars entering the base. As the guards checked each vehicle carefully, I thought about the conversation that likely awaited me.

The last few years had been hard on our relationship, as the General wasn't pleased with how things had turned out after Market and my retirement.

How long has it been since I've seen him?

The female guard snapped to a crisp salute as soon as I stopped the bike.

"At ease, Marine." I smiled and returned her salute as my mind drifted back to my days of being a guard here.

The long ride across the base called up dozens of memories and the unsettling contradictions between life in here and the one outside the gates. Within the base, the flag waved with dignity, the young men and women in uniform honoring it while working to protect their country. As my thoughts began to wander into a dark comparison with those who killed and looted on the outside, I tightened my grip on the handles. I used the *Sense* to steady myself against the rising swell of anger and parked the motorcycle in a lot by one of the live-fire exercise fields. Custer had instructed me to meet him at the usual spot, an unused bunker away from the main base.

The General waited on the first level of the dugout, looking out to the ocean in the distance. I approached the fit black man in his mid-sixties, whose presence was much bigger than our shared height and stature and whose bald head reflected the light coming through the wall's opening.

I snapped to salute, and he returned it with a smirk, making his hard face soft for only a moment. Swiftly, we descended into the deeper levels of the bunker, silent as ghosts.

He led us to the small room with an old desk and two chairs that we had used many times and lit the same ol' small lantern that cast weird shadows on the cold concrete walls. As soon as we sat across from each other, Custer turned on a noise scrambler and placed it on the desk.

"You've become quite famous on base," Custer mused after asking a few questions about Jenny and San Francisco.

"Yeah. I heard about the reporters. I even checked on that Ken Lim guy. As Jack said, he's been fair so far."

The General laughed heartily, and I enjoyed the rare and cherished event.

"My Boy, I don't speak about that. I'm talking about all the Marines who saw you on TV, honoring their fallen brother." He shook his head. "I even had to discipline a MARSOC team."

The Marine Special Operations Command were notorious badasses in the small special forces community.

"What did they do?"

"Protesters arrived at the front gate, carrying signs disrespecting Nicolas and the Marines, and the operators saw it on their way back from a run…"

"Oh." He almost didn't have to finish the story.

Custer cracked a savage smile.

"Yeah, 'Oh.' They beat the shit out of them."

"Spiritus Invictus," I repeated MARSOC's "Unconquerable Spirit" motto.

He nodded, and we savored a moment of ease before attending to business that brought us here.

"Are you staying sober?" His tone was flat and firm.

As my commanding officer in my official role in the Marines and the shadow one in The Doctrine, he had the right to ask.

"Yes," I replied, pushing down the memory of emptying the whiskey bottle with Nico back in Big Bear.

"Good." He smiled genuinely. "I was a bit concerned after he died."

Custer knew Nico was instrumental in my sobriety after my first marriage ended in a disastrous substance binge.

"Did he ever suspect your other life?"

The words from my last call with my brother haunted me. "Back there when you guys saved us. Your team, you, and what you all did... that wasn't any military? Right?"

"He did." I shoved my sadness out. "He saw what he saw when we rescued them, and it nearly broke his mind. It's why he fell back into drinking when returning stateside."

"Do you think he ever talked to anyone about it?" asked Custer, his words conveying the seriousness of the matter.

I shook my head as I answered, "Not a chance. Nico was also suspicious when I returned to serve after my recovery. He knew I was in the Middle East but never asked anything beyond razzing me on the subject of 'buying a bride' while I was there." I smiled sadly, remembering how he loved to roast me.

Looking satisfied, Custer switched our attention to the new difficulties related to the Dragon and the recent upheaval since Chicago. According to him, some Marines had been accosted in San Diego while on leave.

"We could have acted sooner," I grumbled, unable to hold back my old resentment.

He rolled his eyes, lips pressed.

"One of these days, you'll stop and seriously look at how you behaved after Market was over. Nobody forced you to leave the fight. It was you!"

We stared each other down for a long minute, but neither of us wanted to fight. So I nodded for him to continue.

"Jack told me about you wanting to go after Baker."

"Yes, and as fast as we can. If Grayson wins, he'll be much tougher to handle," I replied matter-of-factly.

Custer shook his head slowly, the same way my dad had just a few days earlier.

"You have no idea how vast the bureaucratic power is behind that son of a bitch. It doesn't matter whether it is Grayson, Stone, or even Washington himself. Your dad and I have both experienced that in the flesh."

What? Vietnam?

I thought about asking, but the General didn't seem in the mood to divulge any more details.

"What will happen with Old Glory if Grayson wins?" I wondered.

OG had been in business for decades, doing great work under Democratic and Republic administrations alike. It was an excellent smokescreen, which Jack and Custer had used to achieve The Doctrine's true mission since 1984.

Custer admitted he didn't know before he brought up the true issue at hand, "Jack also told me about your insistence on Directive Two."

I tried again, explaining all my reasonings, but the General remained unmoved, just like my father.

His final words were firm but kind, "You're emotionally invested, Tanner. But it doesn't mean that you're wrong. For now, we remain focused on *foreign* adversaries."

He must have sensed my dampening spirit as his voice turned warmer.

"It was never easy for you, Son. Unlike your grandfather and Jack, you had no choice in this matter. Regardless, your dad and I have waited, and now you're back. Just be patient."

I nodded, holding back the rest of the concerns eating me from the inside.

But what if you're wrong and we're wasting time?

PIT STOP

– Los Angeles, CA –
Friday, June 19, 2020

The sun made its slow descent on my left as the relatively empty road stretched ahead of me. There were a few "advantages" of the Dragon pandemic and easier traffic was one of them.

The ride from Pendleton was uneventful, except for the "new scenery." The speed with which the ad agencies had adapted to the new world was dystopian. Across countless giant billboards, models were all masked.

Nightmerica. Gagged and obedient.

My phone was fastened in the secure stand, just above the motorcycle's dashboard. The map showed one ping at the synagogue and another outside on the street. Dani was worshipping and the Israeli agent was watching. My wife was used to our devices being synced on the map app, but the Rogue smartphone made it only one way. I could always see her, but she'd never know where I was unless I or someone at the RCC decided it was necessary.

I'll see you soon, My Queen.

With a quick twist of the throttle, the bike shot forward.

Five minutes later, I parked in front of the synagogue, dismayed by all the trash and visible neglect on this once vibrant street. This evening's Israeli agent was a young male in a black sedan down the block who pinged me to acknowledge my arrival. The RCC had notified him about my appearance in advance.

Find any synagogue worldwide and they will all look the same on Friday before the sun goes down—festive and welcoming those who come to bask in the Shabbat's light. I had never cared for these things, even after the Jewish conversion, but I missed it greatly now as I took in the shuttered front doors and the few guys hammered and sprawled on the street.

The Dragon measures had explicitly forbidden religious gatherings inside and outside. Most temples complied, but some didn't. I crossed the street and walked around the synagogue to a locked side door in the fence. Shemtov knew about my surprise arrival and had sent me the code in advance.

Stealthily, I crept into the synagogue toward the back room where the Friday Kiddush blessing took place. I paused when a young child's voice prayed in Hebrew, "Sh'ma Yis-ra-eil, A-do-nai E-lo-hei-nu, A-do-nai E-chad.

Hear, O Israel; the Lord is our God; the Lord is one." It was Ari's voice.

The sweetest sound, I thought as I watched him from afar.

"Daddy!" he yelled as soon as he noticed me.

The dozen or so in attendance turned and smiled, Shemtov's being the grandest.

I didn't have a moment to acknowledge anyone else before Ari flung himself at me. Pulling him up to my chest, I held him close and kissed his wild blond hair.

Dani raced over with a giggling Leelee in her arms, and I was crushed under weight of their love.

"I missed you so much," I whispered to my queen as she allowed her tears to fall and kissed me.

"An outlaw, eh Rabbi?" I teased Shemtov with a wink.

We were both seated in his office while the rest devoured the potluck in the hall. Luckily, some chocolate chip cookies were distracting enough for the kids that we found a few moments alone.

Shemtov's eyes flashed behind his glasses, his face reddening behind the thick white beard as he slammed his fist on his desk.

"How dare they? I was ready to play along, to be a responsible citizen. We even closed the preschool, sending those precious children into lockdown in their homes." He took a breath, and his voice deepened to a near growl. "Then, they allowed all this madness in our streets, unrestricted by the virus and their measures. Outlaw, you say? Yes. I will not comply. The word of God will be available for those who seek it. Lockdown be damned!"

His outburst surprised me, as I'd never seen the rabbi mad. I nodded in appreciation, but he wasn't done.

"And of course, they 'canceled' me after Nico's funeral!"

I had to fix my face when his enthusiastic air quotes gave expression to my own feelings about the emerging abysmal term. It had become too easy to boycott and erase anyone the herd decided was straying from whatever orthodoxy controlled the narrative at that time.

Old-fashioned liberalism has twisted into authoritarianism.

"Dani's been telling me that I made us all pariahs. Sorry," I replied, failing to suppress a smirk, and we both had a short laugh. "You let me know if you ever need help, though."

"Fine, fine. Now, how are you doing?"

The rabbi held a very special place in my heart, augmented by the confidentiality of our conversations.

"I haven't hurt anyone yet, Rabbi. But this will eventually change. I'm afraid of what comes next." I turned my head back to the door, thinking of my family eating happily behind it.

"Have you given more thought to Isaacs's sacrifice?"

All I had for him was a shrug and a slight shake of my head.

Why am I avoiding this?

Suddenly, his hand reached for the worn Vietnam picture on his desk and he started to tell me about that time in his life. His voice sounded far away, almost disappearing into his past, as he talked about serving as a young chaplain and visiting a platoon positioned in an isolated, fortified camp upon a nameless hill.

"There was this Jewish kid from Brooklyn who asked for a rabbi, so it was my luck to go there to provide help."

His voice was full of sadness as he recounted how the Vietcong started a night assault shortly after he had arrived.

"That kid and I had barely sat down to chat when the mortars began falling on us."

Shemtov's eyes joined his voice in the distant past. He stared at the image as he continued, "I ran out with the rest of them to the foxholes but didn't know what to do. Soon, I ran back and forth, bringing them ammo as they did their best to hold back the attackers."

My breathing stopped at Rabbi's admission.

"I found the kid dead on one of my runs. Bullet hole in his head. I held him in my arms as more and more mortars fell around us. Then there was the silence, except for a few wounded crying out for their moms. Our position was overrun." A sad smile crossed his face as he touched the faces in the picture and pointed at a grinning boyish man with cropped hair. "This is the kid. That picture was taken right before the attack."

His face reddened again.

"I saw them coming up the hill with their bayonets, intending to finish us off." He paused and took a deep inhale. "I never hurt another man before that battle. Yet, that night, I heard God's command for sacrifice, and all I had in my chest was 'HERE I AM.'" A deep sigh escaped his lips. "All I was before that moment died as I waited for the Vietcong to enter the base and then jumped them from the back with a small entrenching shovel." He extended his hands toward me. "My hands killed three men, and, for some reason, the rest escaped."

He looked at me intently.

"This is what I had to do, and I would do it again if needed."

His story shocked me. Not only had I never seen this brutal side of him, I could hardly imagine it. But he wasn't done.

"Tanner, Elohim, our God, has chosen *you*, Son—commanding *you* to the mountain. You need to be ready..."

Anger pumped violently through my heart as I sensed an alien presence hovering in my mind.

Is that you, Beast? Say something.

Shemtov observed me silently until the door opened and Ari confirmed it was dark outside and time to go home.

The Ramirez clan was already at our home when we arrived. Dani had texted them about my surprise arrival, and they all showered me with love as soon as I reached the top of the stairs. Hugs and conversations made it easier for me to set aside the angst that had been growing since my conversation with Shemtov. Using the *Sense* to set aside the concerns and questions for another time, I lost myself in this life as deeply as I could.

"I've been helping Mom and Cel," said Ari when dinner was finished.

"He sure has been," agreed Danielle, winking as she dropped cooing Lil on my lap.

"Thank you, Ari, for taking care of the ladies when I'm not here." I reached over and held my hand up for a high-five until he slapped it with all of his strength and beamed a proud smile.

I played with the kids until Dani and Cel wrangled them toward the shower.

"I'll be right back," I said to Dani as she shuffled the kids into the bathroom and I headed toward the courtyard.

The agent knew to expect me by a tree in the shadow cast by a tall building, but he clearly didn't expect me to greet him and thank him for his service in Hebrew. I listened carefully as he confirmed my suspicions that there were no threats to the complex but there was more lawlessness happening around it.

"My dad is *always* on the phone with me. Even Ella is driving me nuts. I'm not used to this," murmured Dani, stretching out on our bed.

Dani's older sister, Ella, was a hard woman who lived with her family just outside the Gaza strip, which was run by the Hamas terror organization.

The kids were asleep and the house was quiet.

"It's kind of nice." A smirk sneaked across her beautiful face.

This is hard on her, I thought as I noticed a lone white strand in her otherwise jet-black hair.

I stretched out beside her and pulled her close, feeling grateful for the good father who watched over my queen.

Like Jack, Eli Peled was a rough and tough man to the outside world. But unlike Jack, he was a tender and loving father in his home. Dani had told me so many tender stories of growing up with him after her mom died from cancer. A grieving widower, he continued to be an amazing father to three young kids.

"It's getting even more ridiculous, Tanner..." She vented about the measures, the masks, the lockdown, and the general distrust in the streets since Chicago.

I listened and pulled her closer, hoping she wouldn't sense my growing anxiety.

I can figure this out. I don't have to lose them.

Words were nowhere to be found, so I pulled her onto me and showed her how much I'd missed her.

Holden arrived shortly after I texted him.

"They're sleeping," I whispered as I let him into the studio.

Sweat beaded on his dark skin, more indicative of stress than heat at this early hour. He looked tired and frustrated and didn't spend much time on pleasantries.

"My officers are under a whole lot of pressure. I have psyche evaluation requests stacked to the roof..." He shared how his command was fragmented and demoralized. "First the ridiculous measures, and now the 'Chicago Effect.'"

It's everywhere, I thought, recalling the demonstrators in Yachats.

"And it's almost impossible to get answers or support..." Holden admitted that nothing had advanced regarding the Taco Libertad investigation.

I wasn't surprised, but my blood boiled nonetheless.

"I wish I knew what happened there. It's eating me alive," he confessed, his eyes searching mine for hints.

No, Brother. I'm sorry.

"What's going on with you, Tanner? Are you back with the Marines or what?"

The question might have been innocent, but his pressed lips and narrowed eyes told another story that irritated me.

"You want to tell me that with all you're facing, you have the time to wonder about me? About the damn camera from Libertad? I suggest you get more concerned about appeasing the rioters and those who have enabled their lawlessness."

He sighed as he pushed himself up and out of the chair.

"What happened, Tanner? When did we stop being on the same side?"

It was a fair question, and he had earned the right to an answer.

"The day he died, Brother. The day he died."

Holden scratched his head sadly and turned to leave without another word.

NOT A MOMENT

The vibration at the base of my ear felt like a jarring fall from grace, and my eyes opened to the silent darkness of my home. Turning to the clock on the nightstand, I let out a quiet growl.

I just got here.

I rushed downstairs to the studio after a quick shower, knowing every middle-of-the-night call usually meant a quick departure. The gal from the RCC knew to connect me with Jack as soon as she heard my voice.

"It's Chad. Tanner, he's in danger," blurted my father, his tone unusually tenuous.

I listened as he explained that Chad had released an article—a scathing rebuke of the city and mayor for their "anti-police" stand and allowing Comrades and others to take over the Capitol Hill neighborhood, de facto creating an autonomous zone. It had trended on social media instantly, and he was in trouble.

"He's terrified. Said that he's been receiving death threats everywhere he has a footprint." Jack was beginning to sound distraught. "We immediately dug into it and he's targeted, Tanner. My *boy* is targeted by so many people who want him to die."

I'd never heard such concern in my father's voice, and it took a moment to register this side of him. He gathered himself during my speechless pause.

"'Comrades Seattle' is seeking his address openly. It's only a matter of time before they find him."

I gulped back the lump of anxiety forming in the back of my throat.

"Orders?" Knowing that an official request would center him further, I hoped it would do the same for me.

"Alfa is authorized to extract him under the 'Family Protection' clause in The Doctrine."

"Does this fall under Directive Two?"

It was my first time working under this clause.

"Scantly," replied Jack, irritation replacing his fear for a moment. "Your ROE is limited to self-defense."

It's something. I can work with it.

"Did Comrades note anything besides the articles? Anything from Ryse?"

"No, on both. Why?"

I spoke my concerns about Chad being connected to me as the "Soldier from the Funeral"—that it could mean more than just attacking my brother and my family.

"I'll talk to Eli about tightening the ring around them," he replied. "Chopper is already en route to pick you up. Get moving, Alfa-leader."

The line went dead, as did my hopes of spending the day with my family.

How can I even wake Dani for this?

Eli's words rang back with the answer: "Don't shelter her. She'll back you up."

The clock read 1:25 a.m. and the phone showed me Sarah's ETA at Santa Monica Airport.

She must have felt my absence already, as she was awake when I entered the bedroom and sat beside her.

"You're leaving, aren't you?"

The pain almost choked the words back, "Yes, Sweetie. I have to."

Dani sat up and kissed me gently.

"Just go. Don't wake the kids. It'll be hard enough."

She touched my face and then laid back on her pillow.

"I'll call you soon, My Love," I promised as I reached the doorway.

I softened my steps as I moved to take one last look at the two sleeping angels, made from the best of us, without the worst of me.

I hope.

Chad answered on the first ring, his anxious voice coming through clearly over my helmet audio. Hearing the fear in his voice, I twisted the throttle, making the motorcycle release its own growl as it sped toward the airport.

"I'm on my way, Chad. Can you relocate to another place until I arrive?"

"It's scary, Tanner. I'm an outcast. Friends refuse to answer my calls, and the rest want to kill me."

It took some time to shift him from fearful babble to a short-term solution.

"One of my neighbors agreed to let me stay there until you arrive. I can go there."

"Good. Go. Don't answer the door, and call us if anything happens."

Sounding more settled, he took a moment to tell me about Jack's repeated calls, "I've never heard dad so upset."

"He's proud of you and loves you, you fool. He's concerned for your safety, like every father should be."

It was the truth, and I pushed away the resentments that always surfaced when I thought about how different our childhoods were.

"We both are. I'll see you soon," I added before ending our call to focus on the airport gate ahead of me.

The chopper was fueled and ready when I parked by its hull. Liam and Moss jumped out to mount the bike to the side rack, and everyone worked at deadly silent speed. Sarah had us up into the air in less than five minutes.

"This is an evolving battlefield. Here's what we know," I started.

I just called it a battlefield.

I pushed the thought away, and we rehearsed the operation for the next twenty minutes while Sarah navigated us toward Seattle.

"We'll get him, Brother," assured Moss when the briefing was over.

I smiled, realizing that my agitation and concerns had probably perverted my briefing. Liam chuckled, his jovial self lightening the mood the way it always did.

Dex chose right.

I reflected on my XO's decisions on who to choose for the mission, grateful he was backing us up from the Cape's command and control.

"Rest up, boys," I instructed.

The chopper burned speed along the coast as it headed north. When I sat next to Sarah, she nodded, "As fast as I can, Sir."

Custer called to confirm they were checking on any connections between Chad and me.

"Don't expect any help from the locals. They're either hand-tied by the mayor or cooperating with the rioters."

Behind enemy lines. Just like the funeral convoy.

"Anything else, Sir?"

Custer sighed, his voice strained with concern as he ordered, "You just keep your head in the game and remember that you're on US soil. These are Americans." He ended our call, leaving me twice-warned about the consequences of playing outside my rules of engagement.

AIN'T YOUR WORLD

– Seattle, WA –
Saturday, June 20, 2020

It was still morning when the chopper landed at a small airport just outside of Seattle to start the rescue mission. The one-runway airfield was one of Old Glory's numerous facilities, and the guards knew better than to approach the masked guests who had just landed at their base and moved quickly into action.

Liam pulled my motorcycle off the side rack, Moss retrieved two more bikes from the nearby hangar, and Sarah refueled the bird.

"Does he know he's chipped?" asked Liam, seeing Chad's ping on my phone's map display.

"No. Neither does my sister," I replied. "Theirs are only for tracking location."

He grunted and rushed to help Moss with his tasks while I called Chad to let him know we were outside the city.

"People tried to get into the building," he blurted. "I'm safe at my neighbor's apartment, but she's afraid."

I slipped my shades on as the morning sun rose above the trees and blinded me.

"Stay quiet. Do not communicate or do anything online. We'll be there after the sun goes down."

The guys and I rode out a few minutes later, leaving Sarah and the chopper at the base.

Seattle looked just like Los Angeles and San Francisco— locked down, neglected, and accessible only to those that had no use for the law.

When are people going to wake up?

Thinking about the local politicians, my grip on the motorcycle handle tightened until my hand cramped.

The RCC got us a room at a rundown, fenced, one-story motel complex just two blocks from the Capitol Hill neighborhood. There were only three cars in the parking lot when we arrived, and the double-masked, white-haired older gal at the reception commented about how happy she was to see my face diaper securely in place.

"Some folks think they can disobey the measures. So disrespectful. We should all work together."

"Of course," I mumbled, careful to keep my back to the lobby camera.

Once inside our room, Liam opened his laptop and began connecting to the RCC network. He would work with Dex and provide us with reinforcement if needed, and Moss would be my wingman.

"I just don't get it. I wish I could ship all the snotty, masked brats to the Balkans or Somalia. Maybe then they'd appreciate what we have here," Moss grumbled while we set up.

Like all Rogues, he'd spent most of his childhood abroad while his father served as an Army attaché in various hotbeds across the world. His dark, boyish face was contorted, and his white teeth bared.

"They call themselves social justice warriors but they are a bunch of cowards. No different from all those gangs in Mogadishu," he said while strapping his concealed combat knife.

The team had been venting regularly to me, their minds struggling to comprehend what was happening to our beloved country.

Or maybe they're trying to get me to speak.

My ear vibrated, and I froze when the older male voice reported that Jenny had to bail out of the CPC complex after being exposed. According to the update, the Calexico incident, the CPC, and CHAZ were all connected.

"...one or more of those operators could be in CHAZ. Advance with caution. More details will be available after the op is over."

Relieved Jenny was safe, my mind raced with the implications of having those professionals from the Calexico firefight right here in town.

"...no connection was made between you and your brother as of this moment." The briefing ended with one bit of good news, "The Eye is tasked to help you with this operation. Oh, and check with your IT for enhanced capabilities. Godspeed, Alfa-leader."

The guys heard the same report in their earbuds, and Liam smiled widely as he combed his hand through his short black hair, stopping right behind his ear.

"Up 'til now, vibrations only signaled calls coming in. Now, the chip will vibrate in different rhythms and sequences to alert us to threats or other important things."

After he asked the RCC to send us a few sample vibrations for each different situation, I nodded in appreciation, "This is good."

"Wait up, there's more." Liam's smile got more mysterious as he reached into to his satchel and pulled out two black, folded contraptions about the size of a large phone and laid them on the dingy bed. "This is hot off the press."

He nearly giggled as he opened the first collapsible device to reveal a skull-like helmet. With thin black rods, a built-in mouthguard, and an eye cover, it looked like a hybrid of a Halloween mask and robot skeleton.

"Put it on, Sir," he implored. "It's made of titanium."

When I picked it up, I immediately noticed its light weight. "What's it called?"

"Flex cover, for now. It's a prototype," he added as he turned off the light in the hotel room.

It stirred as soon as I put it on—a hungry presence, satisfied with the device and the darkness we were in.

Beast?

When Liam pressed a small button under my mouth-guard, a light green Head-Up Display lit up on the hard eye covers. The word "SYNCING" flashed on the right edge.

"Give it a moment to connect with your chip, Sir. Once it does, the Flex will have the same capabilities as your smartphone and all of the new features. It will even sync with your Wraith for assisted aiming at multiple targets moving quickly." The young techie was talking fast, like a small child excited about a new toy.

Moss whistled as he pulled his Flex on.

"There is a built-in air filter, various spectrums for night vision, and a voice scrambler. Plus, its skeletal build protects the head against blunt trauma."

"How do I operate it?" I asked.

"Just speak to it. Like the civilian voice command on phones, but much better."

He showed me the list of commands.

"Night vision," I commanded. Immediately, the room lit through my HUD. "Nice."

"Yeah, each Flex recognizes and obeys only its user's voice." Liam turned on the light and showed us how to fold the Flex back into a small unit that fit into our cargo pants' side pocket in seconds. "Expect more from the eggheads. This is just the start, but it already works really well with the Eye. You'll see during the op."

"It reminds me of a skull," I mused, sensing the Beast's presence receding back to its lair as I removed the Flex from my head.

"It sure does." He grinned. "You can voice command it to collapse the eye covers and mouthguard to the back. If you were already wearing a hoodie and scarf, you'd look like one of them in a second."

Opening another duffel bag, he began pulling the rest of our allowed arsenal for the mission—smoke and flash grenades to add to the Wraith handgun and combat blade I already had on me. Anything else would have made us too noticeable.

As the sun reached the horizon, we turned our attention to disguising ourselves and making final preparations for the insertion.

Liam was right. Moss and I looked no different from all the masked assholes on TV. As soon as it was dark outside, my wingman slipped out ahead of me. His role was to provide me with a tight security envelope, augmented by Liam from the room, Dex in the Cape, and the RCC with the Eye.

I wore the Flex under my hoodie and knew it was worth gold as soon as my feet hit the empty street. Through the map display, I could see Moss's location and all other assets in color, coded to their threat level.

The noise from CHAZ was unmistakable, like a music festival gone wrong, even two blocks from the border of their "zone." Following the RCC's map, I scaled a fence between two empty apartment buildings, bypassing the barricade manned by a bunch of fucks with guns.

Where the hell are the police? These shitheads have a fucking checkpoint!

Inside CHAZ, from behind an overflowing dumpster, I looked into the main street bustling with people. It was just after sundown, and the party was hopping. Hundreds roamed, dressed for a festival, carrying signs, hooting, and hollering with joy.

While the streetlights prevented infrared imaging, the Eye displayed "red pings" on my HUD for those with weapons.

"Alfa-one, Alfa-leader, over," I called.

"Go ahead, Alfa-leader, over," responded Dex in my Flex's earbuds.

"Going in, Alfa-leader. Out."

I ordered the Flex to withdraw the eye covers and mouth guard, "Retract."

As I crossed the thirty feet to enter the street, I used the *Sense* to drift and join the stream of partygoers. Scanning the area, I could hardly believe my eyes—how a boulevard in a major US city had managed to secede from the Union without a shot fired. The businesses were looted, boarded or not. Comrade flags hung everywhere, and the only American flags around were desecrated, torn, or burned. My heart rate increased as I recalled the last time I'd seen a flag defiled and lying on top of my fallen friend.

Guards with red armbands traveled around us in pairs, masked and carrying shotguns and semi-automatic assault rifles. Thanks to the vibrations in my ear, I was always one or two steps ahead of them, pivoting between the various groups of dancing assholes.

Hearing the screams from some of the upper floors of the buildings around me, I shook my head at how the mayor had abandoned thousands of residents for the rule of the zone.

Could this happen back home?

Feeling my pulse race at the mere thought, I pushed it down.

It took me about thirty minutes to arrive outside Chad's brown four-level apartment building. Quite a few people were loitering around, and some were definitely armed. Moss alerted me that he was able to cover my entry and exit.

"Building layout," I whispered to my Flex after ordering it to protract the cover and mouth guard. The HUD quickly populated the structure's satellite view alongside the architectural plan.

Nice!

There was a back entrance through the laundry room, which was perfect, and I was about to move when some minor graffiti just outside the front door caught my attention.

"Zoom in," I whispered and then shuddered as the Flex's view made the symbol clear. The Dragon Skull stopped me in my tracks again.

Fuck.

Alerting Dex about the Dragon Skull, I hustled to the back of the building. It took me a quick minute to break in and then race up the stairs two floors to where Chad waited for me. My heart pumped hard.

Baby Brother, I'm almost there.

"Retract," I commanded the Flex, hiding my face under my hoodie and scarf as I approached the door.

Chad knew to expect my knock and opened the door on the first one. What I saw provoked a quick inhale, stopping just short of a gasp. My brother, known to be a fashionable hipster, was almost unrecognizable. His black hair was disheveled, his shirt was misbuttoned, and his blue eyes were wide with fear.

"Tanner! Thank God," he uttered. I hurried into the apartment and closed the door behind me.

As he hugged me, I wondered, *Did this atheist just say God?* The thought dissipated as I relaxed, relieved I'd gotten to him in time. *Damn it. I love this asshole.*

A short young woman with brown hair pulled back in a messy bun stood behind him. She fidgeted as Chad introduced us and then left us alone in the living room.

"Are you ready to go?" I asked.

He scanned me from top to bottom.

"Are you back working with him?"

"I'm back in the Corps, but this is family business. So, yes. He sent me over."

It was a deflection, and his eyes narrowed, showing me he understood it as such.

"You've never been honest with me about what you do for him," he grumbled.

Is he serious?

"Where is this coming from, Man? I'm here to get you out, and you wanna talk about this now?"

"I hoped you'd never go back to work for him, whatever you're doing." He sighed. "Even if it means saving me."

Dipshit. You don't even know what you're talking about!

I took a breath, pushing down my aggravation.

"We don't have the time for this shit. You ready to bounce? Is she coming?" I nodded toward the kitchen.

"No, she's not."

"Mask up," I instructed as I pulled my scarf up and covered my mouth. I felt naked without the Flex's abilities, but at least I had the chip vibrations to give me the heads-up on threats around us.

As I led the way to the back entrance, my mind gravitated to the Dragon Skull but was interrupted when the RCC updated me that there was increased chatter about Chad's location online.

"Some guys are gathering outside the front door," warned Liam.

"Stay here," I told Chad before walking to the back door where I whispered my instructions to Moss, Dex, and Liam.

"Who were you talking to?" asked Chad when I motioned for him to join me by the door.

"I've got some guys with me," I explained, looking outside the small window in the door.

When we heard screams and yells from the front of the building, I pulled him into the backyard.

"Go, go!"

Liam gave me verbal instructions as we sneaked from one structure to the next, and the vibrations did their part to alert me of roaming guards.

Every time Chad tried to speak, I silenced him. Somehow, we were being tracked by a few groups of armed hostiles, which blocked us from my original pathway out of CHAZ.

"Damn it," I cursed quietly when Moss reported that we had hostiles just a block behind us and another group coming on our twelve o'clock.

"What?" Chad was catching his breath while we hid behind a car with slashed tires.

Are you really breathing hard? Keyboard warriors!

Pushing my amusement aside, I admitted to him that we were being chased and needed a new path to get out of CHAZ. He surprised me when he pulled his phone out, popped his map app, and showed me a side alley in a small park right on the boundary of this nightmare.

"This should work. Residents have been using it to escape the zone," said Chad.

The voices of our pursuers grew behind us, giving me a split moment to decide.

"Lead us."

Chad ran forward, and I stayed on his heels as we crossed through a street party and approached the alley. A shudder coursed through me as he approached, and my hand shot up to grab his shoulder and stop him.

Alone in the tunnel. Unclear echoes in Spanish, bouncing, reverberating on the rocky walls.

"*Bogotá...*" muttered the Beast.

Shemtov's eulogy forced its way into my mind, "Genesis 22, And it came to pass after these things, that God tested Abraham, and He said to him, 'Abraham,' and he said, 'Here I am...'"

"*Yes...*" whispered the Beast with satisfaction.

"Alley rhymes with Ali... Alley..." I murmured, trying to stay present.

"What are you saying?" Chad waved his hand across my face. "Tanner! Wake up! Let's go!"

His words pulled me back.

"Stay behind me," I ordered Chad, pushing past him, still rattled by the shaking of my inner world. We entered the long dark alley, leaving the street party behind us.

★ ★ ★

We had about three hundred feet before the park at the end of the alley, and now Chad was on my heels.

"Alfa-leader, a dozen hostiles on your six o'clock about to enter the alley," warned Liam. "Alfa-three is parallel to your position, half a block away." His reference to Moss made me breathe a little easier.

I used the *Sense* to clear my mind completely as we entered the alley. It was about twenty feet wide and full of debris from a large open dumpster just ahead of us.

We're halfway through!

The "oncoming threat" vibration came in when Liam alerted me of a new group that had materialized at twelve o'clock.

"...they came from the building, so the Eye didn't catch it."

It's a fucking ambush.

My body coiled for action.

"You're boxed in, Alfa-leader," Liam confirmed.

I stopped our advance by the dumpster. Positioning Chad by the wall next to the dumpster, I stepped into the middle of the alley.

"Why are we stopping?" Chad's voice cracked with fear.

Is he ready for this?

"We're stuck, Chad. We have people coming on our front and back."

His eyes grew wide and his body began to fidget.

"How... how do you know?"

Luckily, there was no time for explanation. The yells and curses and the dark figures they originated from showed up on both sides of the alley.

I was about to tell Chad to get into the dumpster when a voice rose from the group behind us, "Yo, Chad Washington. Is that you there?"

"I know that voice," whispered Chad, his eyes squinting to see in the dimly-lit alley.

The ear vibrations told me there were plenty of armed men around us, and Dex had activated Liam to meet us.

One group stopped just about thirty feet from us. According to Dex, about ten of them, with three firearms. The other one consisted of a dozen men, also with a few guns. They all crept closer.

"Daj Morris? Is that you?" yelled Chad, surprising me when he left his hideout to face the group behind us.

"How did ya know?" called the guy in the middle of the group, masked and wearing all black.

"He's like a warlord here or something. I ran into him in heated city council meetings. I tried to interview him a few times," explained Chad. "Let me try to talk with him."

Nothing to lose.

"Fine," I said, opening my side cargo pocket with my right hand.

The guy named Daj took a few steps forward and told Chad they wanted to chat about his articles. When my brother lowered his mask, so did Daj, revealing a clean-shaven handsome black face.

"Alfa-leader, Ryse just made the connection about you and Chad. They're notifying Comrades in Seattle," said a male RCC voice in my earbud.

My body tensed, and the *Sense* lost its grasp on my mind for a moment.

I'm in the tunnel,
searching for something I cannot recall.
There is a growing growl coming from everywhere.

"...so now you're running like a rabbit, Chad boy, ain't ya?" Daj's taunt refocused me.

Chad's hands flew around as he responded, "This... this is crazy, Daj! I'm all for social justice, but not like this."

"Alfa-leader, a hostile shadow got into one of the buildings next to you," reported Moss, using the term reserved for operators who exemplified stealth tactics.

An image of the professionals shooting the Border Patrol agents flashed, causing my chest to constrict as it did when seeing the massacre on a live feed.

Is he from the smuggling?

Dex ordered Moss to pursue the shadow.

"You used to be an *ally*, Chad. Look at ya now..." sneered Daj.

One of the guys behind the young black man reached out to hand him a phone.

Fuck!

Daj listened for a long moment and then returned the phone to his guy, motioning toward me.

"Who that masked bitch, Chad?"

Chad looked at me, confused, and then turned back to Daj and stuttered that he didn't understand.

"Back," I commanded Chad and pulled him behind me.

Daj took one more step forward, stopping just ten feet from me.

"Yo! Yes. You. The quiet bitch! Drop your mask! Are you Chad's older brother? The soldier from that funeral? That you?"

A Rogue is trained to allow the other side to reveal while analyzing, but my focus didn't stop the slight tremble beginning in my hands.

"This ain't your world," he roared, and his minions around him and behind us hooted and laughed. "This is CHAZ, Motherfucker!"

I called on the *Sense* holding me together and within my rules of engagement while Daj gathered himself.

"I think you are that funeral soldier. Wanna go home? Save little Chad? Tell ya what. Your friend in LA choked on piss because he refused to respect. How about you kneel now, and we'll be even?" He laughed maniacally. "Then we'll let you go home."

What? Nobody saw the tape besides us!

"*Get him, no matter what,*" the Beast growled in command, shattering my *Sense*.

I twisted, grabbing Chad by his shirt and hurling him into the open dumpster as he screamed. As soon as my hands let go of him, they reached for two Rogue smoke grenades, shaped like a six-inch oval. Dropping one to my feet, I slung the other toward Daj.

"Protract." My command activated the Flex, and the eye covers and mouth guard clicked on my face.

Screams abounded at the sight of my helmeted face. *I know you all have seen a skull before!*

Rogue Dance is an advanced maneuver that allows the Rogue to hit multiple targets within a smoke and loud noise envelope. Trained to do it with our eyes closed, it was even easier with the Flex HUD, which painted all the hostiles in the darkness.

Daj tried to escape into his group, which raced forward to protect him. But I sped forward, combat knife primed in my right hand.

"*KILL!*" roared the Beast.

As I moved toward him, the *Sense* returned, reminding me of my limitations.

I expected to hear gunshots, but they didn't come as I plunged myself into the group. My knife slashed back and forth, scoring multiple wounds without killing.

"Help!" screamed Daj as my left hand reached him. I kicked one of the guys who tried to save their leader from me, cutting the arm of another.

"Tanner!" Chad's scream broke my trance and Daj managed to release himself from my grip and ran away with his retreating tribe.

When I turned back, I found Chad outside of the dumpster, blind and coughing in the smoke I'd left to protect him. Completely exposed.

Damn it!

One last look at Daj and the backsides of his men, and I raced back to Chad, dropping a third smoke grenade. He screamed as I pushed him onto the ground and put my knee on his back, pulling my Wraith while looking for targets.

The ear vibration started as silenced shots hit the pavement by us, and I dropped myself onto Chad, protecting him with my body.

"Shadow's opening fire. Looking for him," called Moss.

He can't see me like this!

I retracted the eye cover and mouthguard, closing my eyes and mouth against the smoke.

When the shots stopped, Liam came on the line. He said he was just a hundred feet ahead in the park and had chased away the few goons who waited there.

"Alfa-leader, a new hostile group is getting ready to enter the alley at six o'clock. Get out to the park now. Alfa-six is there! He cleared your path." Dex's voice was strained.

I pulled Chad to his feet. "We're running. Now!" I commanded over his incoherent babble.

We raced the remainder of the way.

"It's my guy," I told Chad when he cried out at the sight of Liam materializing in front of us.

Quickly, all three of us broke into the park, among the trees and away from the nightmare called CHAZ.

GUT PUNCH

– Seattle, WA –
Sunday, June 21, 2020

The sun began to ascend in the east, but dark clouds clawed against another day's rise. With Chad behind me, Liam and I rode to our forward operating base while images of Nico's dead face and the laughter of those who killed him haunted me.

I fucking had him!

The Beast growled but said nothing.

Chad's body fidgeted as we approached the Forward Base's guard post with the black and white Old Glory's Betsy Ross flag waving above it.

"I never knew that he had a base so close to town," he grumbled when we slowed down for inspection.

There's a lot you don't know, Baby Brother.

The two male guards who carried sub-machine guns nodded as they opened the gate for us after checking something on a hand tablet.

"Are you okay?" I asked Chad once we dismounted in front of the chopper.

Liam returned his bike while Sarah mounted my motorcycle to the side rack.

He looked all around and then back at me.

"My life in Seattle is ruined. How can I ever go back?"

"Are you talking about the paper?" I kept my other question to myself—the one about why in the world he would want to go back to a legacy media institution.

Chad wiped his forehead.

"Not just that. I know that I'm *canceled*, but I'm afraid for my life. They'll now connect me with you and the..." His words stopped.

"The funeral?" I offered, feeling the exhaustion of the adrenaline drop.

He nodded in silence, head and shoulders drooped. *Oh man.*

"You did something brave, and now you're paying. I can't say anything to change that, but things will get better." I placed a hand on his shoulder. "All that matters right now is that you're safe."

Chad smiled and, for one moment, he looked like that innocent boy I used to see during my visits home.

When Liam returned and began talking with Sarah, Chad's eyes tracked him.

"Why did you jump from the dumpster?" I wondered.

"Why did you jump on me?" he responded with a question.

"To protect you." I was confused.

"That's why I jumped out of the dumpster. I didn't know what was going on with you. All the smoke and screams... I was worried about you."

His words surprised me.

You thought about someone else. That's a good start, Little Brother.

"Why did you charge them?" Chad interrupted my internal debate. "I heard Daj talking about someone who died. Was that about Nico?"

"It doesn't matter, Chad. He'll get what he deserves for what he did to you and others."

His eyes narrowed and he leaned his head back.

"Is this what you're doing for Dad? These kinds of things?"

Fucking journalist to the end.

"Chad, this isn't an article that you'll write. Let's cut on this now." It was time to shift gears. "Listen, I'm proud of you and your position, and we'll make sure that you remain safe. Now, I need a moment."

I walked toward Moss who'd entered and stopped about thirty feet from us.

"Sarah, please call my parents and let them speak with Chad," I instructed before reaching my wingman for the intel.

"He was quick. I found him in an empty apartment. He had a concealed position overlooking the alley." Moss knew I needed to know what took place with the hostile shadow.

They knew.

"Turned on me when I entered and managed to spray me a bit. Escaped through the window onto another balcony or something," he continued. "Not sure what happened there, Boss. He was highly trained to evade. It feels like..."

"...a planned ambush?" I finished his sentence, and he nodded.

What should I do?

Resolved, I instructed Moss to head back to Seattle, infiltrate Comrades, and find Daj and the shadow.

"If I'm right, you'll find that shadow right by that punk-ass warlord."

Moss threw his head back in delight, revealing perfect white teeth at the name that suited Daj so well. Then he waited, holding me hostage to the moment.

Fucker.

"By my Independent Authority, Moss. There, you heard it!" I grumbled, holding back my amusement.

"Yes, Sir," he replied before he turned to say his goodbyes to Liam and Sarah.

I looked back to find Chad staring at me. He had Sarah's smartphone to his ear and motioned with his head for me to come.

"It's Dad. He wants to speak with you."

"You did good, Son." Jack's gratitude was quickly replaced with agitation. "We'll do the mission debriefing back at the Ranch." It was the first I'd heard we were heading there.

Makes sense. It's a good place to protect Chad.

"What is it, Dad?" I probed, feeling him holding back. He cleared his throat.

"It's about Danielle and the kids...." He must have felt my world begin to shake around me. "Relax, Son. They're fine and back home."

When my breathing resumed, I whispered, "Tell me..."

"There was an incident in Venice. You couldn't be distracted during the op..."

I used the *Sense* to steady my heart rate and not interrupt. The team must have felt it, as all of them stopped and stared as soon as I engaged it.

"Ken Lim, that online journalist. He's the hero of the day..." He explained that Ken had managed to catch up on the live online discussion between Ryse and Comrades about the connection between Chad and me. "There was something mentioned about the 'wife in Venice and harassing her.'"

A ball of fury exploded in my belly as Jack shared how Ken had reached out to LAPD's Pacific Division with an anonymous tip about Danielle. "The call was rerouted to Holden."

Sorry, Bud. It's not going to be easy.

I sighed and kept listening.

"Ken even tried to reach out to Seattle PD about Chad but was stonewalled due to the sensitivity around getting into CHAZ," continued Jack. "It took a bit of work, but we managed to pass Ken's encryption and authenticate his identity. He saved many lives, as we were able to act both in Venice and alert you in Seattle."

Thank God.

I felt gratitude for the man I'd never met.

"Anyway, Holden raced to Venice while trying your cell, which we answered. He gave the details as he'd heard them."

Hurry the fuck up, Dad.

I was tense and doing my best to keep myself together.

"We reached out to Danielle as soon as we got the call from Holden. She was on her way home from the beach with the kids. She'd already seen the two guys who trailed and began to hassle her and speed-dialed the SOS number right before I reached her."

Oh my God!

The pressure in my chest overwhelmed me.

"She dropped the phone, pulled out her pepper spray, and hit both assailants as soon as they approached. Good move having it in the stroller."

Thank God!

I let out a huge sigh of relief, thinking it was over.

"Your son apparently jumped out of the stroller and kicked one of them, screaming at them to leave his mommy and sister alone."

"Oh my God..."

This time, the words left my speechless mind.

"Yeah. They did great. The Israeli agent arrived a few seconds later and whooped those assholes before escorting Dani and the kids back to the complex."

"What did they haggle her about?"

The anxiety was taking over.

I did this. I did this.

"It doesn't matter, Son."

"Dad, what did they *say*?" My tone held the same finality that my father used.

"Something about a Nazi cop-lover husband and shit about Nico. They also threatened her sexually..." Jack's voice trailed off as my vitals spiked off the charts.

"And you let them go..." growled the Beast.

I relied on the *Sense* to keep myself quiet while Jack reported that Holden had arrived moments after Danielle returned to the complex, and she had told him how she scared them away with zero mention of the agent.

"I also told her you're 'engaged' and will call as soon as possible." He paused. "We also had a candid conversation about the agent and the joint-father operation to keep her and the kids safe." He paused again, this time longer. "Will Holden be a problem?"

It was a good question.

"I'm not happy with him, and he suspects me. But he's not a problem. At least not one that I can't handle."

He remained quiet, and I quietly hoped his next words wouldn't place me on a collision course with my friend.

"Fair enough. Now, let Chad speak with his worried mom. And you, call your wife."

Dani answered on the first ring, her voice hushed, which told me that the kids were still asleep.

"Baby, just wait a sec. Going down to the studio."

When she began to sob, I allowed the *Sense* to dissipate, and anger swiftly replaced the calm.

"You had him..." taunted the Beast.

"You should have seen Ari. He's so brave. Jumped into action. We need to remember that." Her voice steadied a bit as her momma pride took over. "Did your dad tell you everything?"

"He did. I know they attacked you because of me. I'm so sorry, Love. So sorry." It was almost impossible to keep my own voice from cracking.

It's my fault. All my fault.

"It is. But not in the way you're ready to accept," corrected the Beast.

"Don't you dare, Tanner Washington! Whatever you do out there, you do for us *all*. I know that in my heart. Come back to us when you can, Baby. We're safe, and my dad told the agent to stay with us."

"I'll be home as soon as I can. I love you." I winced as my voice broke.

We hung up after I thanked the agent, who confirmed the mission had evolved into a tighter ring around my family.

"A few more calls," I said to Sarah when I saw her look my way.

They were all by the chopper waiting and it was evening in Israel, but I knew my father-in-law would have answered from the bowels of hell.

Anxious and ashamed that I'd failed to protect his daughter, I still had to ask him.

"I know what happened and that you're 'back at work.' We got this. Don't worry," insisted Eli before I could say anything.

Here goes nothing.

"Eli, what if I send Danielle and the kids back to Israel? At least until things are calmer here?"

He laughed for a moment and then wondered out loud if I'd had the balls to run it by Dani.

When I admitted I hadn't, he calmed down and spoke seriously, "I already tried it. I was about to order my agents to bring them all home when she made it very clear what would happen if I tried." His tone was that of a proud but subdued father. "She's a feisty one. You know neither of us will be able to move her on this. Focus on your tasks. And let me and Jack help with securing the family. We've got them."

"Thank you, Eli." A moment of relief released my shoulders, allowing for a deeper inhale than I'd been able to take since Jack's call.

My next call was to Holden.

"Thank you, Man..." I expressed my gratitude for everything he had done and tried to end the chat quickly but failed.

"Do you know who called the station about it?" he wondered.

You don't stop.

"No clue," I responded.

"And then this person answered when I called your cell. I didn't know you have assistants, Tanner."

He was fishing, so I put the ball back in his court.

"Will this attempt on Dani give you the power to start moving the investigation forward? They obviously attacked her because of the funeral. We've been targeted."

"Right now, Tanner," Holden sighed. "Unless those assholes actually kill, there isn't much I'll be able to do. The DA won't allow any such actions."

I recalled hearing about the DA, Neville Bernard, during my first briefing and my anger got the best of me.

"Well, they fucking killed our brother, Holden! Something has to be done!"

"What aren't you telling me, huh? You suddenly want to talk straight and all?" Holden's heat rose to match mine.

I allowed the *Sense* to rein it in and thanked him again, but he wasn't buying my deflection.

"This isn't over, Tanner."

"At least we agree on one thing, Brother."

"Five minutes," I called to Sarah, and she started getting them all prepped for the flight.

"How are you, Sir?" asked Dex when he answered.

"Tough. How's Jenny?" I deflected further investigation.

He confirmed she was safe and back at base and then updated me that Moss was already working on his "new assignment." It was apparent that he had more to say.

"Independent Authority, Sir?" he asked at last.

"Yeah."

"Here we go again," he replied with a gruff sigh, obviously recalling the last time I'd used that maneuver. "Can I update the RCC on that?"

He waited. So loyal.

"Yes, let them know. Please update me live when you hear from Moss. I need to take Chad back to the Ranch."

"Yes, Sir. Anything else?"

An image of the small flask he always had on him flashed quickly through my mind.

I could use some of that right about now.

"All good. Talk soon," I answered, squashing both the urge and call.

MIDAIR TALES

– Eastern Washington State, WA –
Sunday, June 21, 2020

The weather didn't improve as we made our way east. Dark clouds loomed, and I watched Sarah do her best to avoid turbulence from the co-pilot seat.

Chad was back with the team. When I looked back and made a phone sign with my fingers, he nodded in response and Liam placed headphones on his head.

"Sarah, I need a private channel."

She executed my request promptly.

"How are you?" I used the helmet microphone, observing him for another moment before facing forward.

It took him a moment to figure out how to use the headphone.

"I'm anxious, Tanner. Look at what I've done, what you all had to do for me…"

The thought of stopping his guilt trip crossed my mind.

But maybe this is his wake-up moment.

I looked straight ahead into the gloomy morning as I waited for him to continue.

"It's hard. I believed in so many things... CHAZ was the final straw..." He gulped. "Don't get me wrong. I still hold many of my old convictions. I'm just not willing to give my hand to the violence, which my side now provokes."

Are you waking up?

"I really want to thank you, Big Brother," whispered Chad after a long pause. I looked back and our eyes locked. Noticing the emotion filling his eyes, I smiled and faced forward. "You made me feel safe back there in the..." His words trailed off.

"It's okay, Man. First time is the hardest," I started, realizing that he had never been in combat. "Besides, it's Dad you should credit. He was on the lookout and got us all moving in time."

He kept quiet for a while, and I didn't push.

"I guess I'm also anxious about going back *home...*"

It sounded like that last word made him as uncomfortable as it made me.

"It was different for you," he continued. "You were just there for a few months, and then you enlisted. I was barely nine years old when Dad moved us there." His pain distracted me from any self-reflection. "I waited, counted the days, until I could get out of there! I never wanted to be a farmer or live in the middle of nowhere." His voice was heavy and filled with confusion.

It had been years since Chad had entrusted me with one of his "monologues"—those precious moments when he self-analyzed his inner world and his place in the one outside of him. It took creativity and a sharp mind, which I admired.

"It's Dad. It's always been. I never got over his disappointment in me. Do you think that he actually sees me as a man? A real grown man?"

"Tell me a bit about your growing up there. We have time to burn," I probed, stepping around the mental trap he'd laid out for me.

"Fair enough," he answered with a chuckle.

I watched the horizon and listened carefully as Chad described the first days of "taking over the Ranch from Grandpa" as a culture shock for him and Tami. He continued for an hour, and I enjoyed imagining all these family moments, almost touching them through Chad's well-honed storytelling skills. If I couldn't have the childhood full of normal everyday events, at least I could imagine it as if I'd been there for it.

His tale seemed to be wrapping up when he went off to college.

"Thanks for sharing, Chad. It meant a lot."

When he laughed coldly, I turned back to look him in the eyes.

What was that?

"You're just like him—hidden in plain sight." Chad smirked. "You fool most people, but not me."

"Why would you say that?" I turned and sat back in my seat, eyes on the endless land ahead and body tensing up again.

"Because you always deflect away from your life," he replied evenly.

"How about you take a damn moment to appreciate all you have? Fuck. You had a childhood, Man!"

It's not his fault. Don't blame him for all your shit! I chastised myself, fully aware this minor example of his eternally resentful questions and comments was hitting up against my growing angst about my own family and the impact of my double-life on them.

I used the *Sense* to shift my mind away from misusing my pain.

"Listen. I'm sorry. It's been a lot."

I looked back, and he nodded at me.

"You okay, Tanner? What's going on?" he pressed after a moment.

This is real.

In broad strokes, I told him about the attack on Dani, leaving out all the sensitive details.

"I'm... I'm so so sorry. And so happy that nothing awful happened..."

His sincerity touched my heart, and I silently savored the rare moment of brotherly love.

We must have both decided to stop the conversation there. Neither of us broke the silence on our private channel while the chopper kept cutting eastward, carrying us and our demons toward a place neither one of us recognized as home.

THE RANCH

"**B**lack Hills, coming up," reported Sarah on the open comms.

It was late evening, and the world was black with the vast emptiness that doesn't exist in California.

When I looked back, I saw Liam's eyes closed and Chad looking out his window. He must have sensed me as he glanced my way in the cabin's dim red interior light.

He knows we're close.

I nodded and turned back to look out my side window. Our conversation weighed heavily on me. It was difficult to compare his mindset to mine. He grew up there and yet resented everything, while the Ranch was hallowed grounds for me. It was more than my birthplace, even though I'd never lived there. It was where all Rogues had to go through one last test—the Black Hills Final War week.

Thinking about the vast forested hills, memories of Grandpa and how that iron-made man had started it all with Grandma consumed me.

He and Chad never got along.

My brother, like others, had seen Grandpa as a grumpy, scowling, old man. But I was lucky to have known Ulysses—to appreciate and even love him. As for his sadness...

Grandma.

I recalled being nine years old when my parents sent me from Bogotá to be with my grandparents. My recollection of my grandmother, Debra Washington, was dim. A tall, white-haired woman who always smiled and sadly died in a car accident mere days before the rest of my family returned from Colombia. We'd had a few days alone, just him and me. Seeing him—the respected patriarch of our family and a man I didn't know well—going through hell and back left its mark.

It was tough to watch him carry and deal with that amount of pain.

"Over the Ranch," called Sarah, exchanging a quick glance with me.

"If not you, then who, Tanner?" My grandfather's immortal words echoed as I stared into the dense black forest beneath me. It was how he used to end our many conversations about the Nazi death camps, communism, and the choice to fight for freedom. He never tried to convince me to do anything, but those words were enough. I remembered sitting across from him at eighteen years old, having just returned from my dad's nine-year post in Israel and feeling the full weight of these words as I considered the possibility of continuing the family legacy of service to the country.

Ulysses knew about "my training," and I'd always wondered why he seemed so unsettled about it. It obviously wasn't his idea.

"Your father is preparing you for what your country might call upon you to do." His words were the final straw. The following day, I told them all about my decision to enlist.

I was just a kid.

Jack accelerated my training in the few months leading up to my recruitment date. There were many days I didn't even enjoy the main home or a tent, for that matter.

Did they know I caught them checking on me? Did I know they prepared me for the course?

"Five mikes," called Sarah.

I gave Chad one last nod and smile and braced myself for *home.*

Sarah set us down on the landing pad in the empty pasture. It was brightly lit against the pitch dark of the night. There were a few parked cars on the road nearby, and their doors opened to us as soon as Sarah killed the engine.

Mom, Dad, and Tami waited, dressed in thick coats. When Chad stepped out of the chopper, the ladies converged on him quickly.

Giving them a moment, I looked at my team and noticed that Sarah and Liam stood erect and in disguised attention. My eyes moved from them to the object of their focus.

Of course.

They knew my dad as "Romulus." Like the rest of the team, they'd met him once before, when they successfully finished Hell Year here in the Ranch's unforgiving terrain.

Jack grunted with a smile, motioning with his head for me to handle them, before turning to join the family hug.

"There's a cottage before the main house. Take a break there once you're done," I instructed Liam and Sarah. They nodded and returned to finishing with the chopper.

As I grabbed my things, I took a few extra moments to collect my thoughts and address the subtle anxiety I always felt on this land. Once I was calm enough, I walked to the small clan that waited for me.

They look so happy, even Dad.

Almost as soon as we'd all piled into the car, my mom blurted, "Lynn and Jerome are joining us for a late dinner..."

A familiar wave of warmth passed through me.

As soon as we entered the two-story ranch house, I dismissed myself to the guest bedroom my mother had prepped for me. I wanted to call Dani, but I decided to wash the day off first.

I knew she'd probably be putting the kids to sleep and I wouldn't have much time, but I needed to hear her voice.

"Hello, My Love..."

While she updated me, I observed my body in the mirror. Red from the scalding shower with fresh black bruises on my upper arms and right leg, I pushed away thoughts of the alley and Chad's screams.

"You sound good, Baby. I'll be home soon..."

As soon as we said our goodbyes, I grabbed the jeans and red flannel button up.

Time to be a cowboy.

The sounds of glee and wine reached me as soon as I left my room.

"Tanner. Finally, Son!" Jerome was the first to spot me as I reached the bottom of the stairs and entered the dining room located at the heart of the home.

Shoulders back, I walked toward the man who had been grafted into our family long before I was born, noticing he hadn't changed much. In his mid-sixties, he was still fit with the same dark eyes that had always been hard and true. The only difference was the white beard and hair.

"Where's Clara?" I asked.

Jerome and his wife were my parents' best friends from high school.

"She had to help with the grandkids," he motioned to Lynn behind him, "so this one could come."

When he stepped out from between us, that familiar warmth returned.

Lynn was beautiful. Tall and slender with long blond hair and piercing blue eyes, her assertive presence commanded attention in every room, even when she was simply dressed in jeans and long sleeve shirt.

She's barely changed since high school, I mused.

Nodding at Jerome, I walked past him to hug my summer love of decades past.

"It's so good to see you," she whispered in my ear.

"You too," I responded before letting her go. "You ready for this?" I rolled my eyes toward the table full of family.

"Do we really have a choice? Always at the ready." She smirked as she half-saluted.

The table was full of freshly baked bread, cured sizzling red meat, and salads. I suppressed a chuckle, wishing I was there to see Liam and Sarah's surprised faces in the cottage when the kitchen staff took the same meal to them, together with our best wine.

They deserve the break.

Mom directed the conversation, as always, but everyone fell into it easily like two families that had known each other for generations.

"We were happy that you all came back finally..." Jerome recalled our return to South Dakota after my dad had retired, and they all laughed when Ali reminisced about our time abroad.

"Bogotá..." whispered the Beast when she mentioned Colombia.

I can't remember anything! I internally screamed as the empty space of the lost memory tried to swallow me at the table.

The Beast laughed. *"Finally. Was that hard?"*

"Alley rhymes with Ali. Alley..."

Ali's eyes sought mine from across the table. My silent prayer stopped when she smiled sadly at me.

She knows. Why isn't she saying anything?

"Fine. I'm ready to learn, okay?" Chad responded in jest to Jerome's jabs about his lefty values and CHAZ.

"Well, I cannot tell you how grateful I am to have Tami working with me..." Lynn used her natural political prowess to redirect the conversation and winked in my direction to invite me to join our decades-long quest to keep the peace while fighting for freedom.

★ ★ ★

"Care for company?" called Lynn from behind me.

I'd left them all once they'd gotten to the desserts. There was too much wine on the table for me to hang around, so I'd found myself a perfect spot on the outside covered deck.

She stood next to me, her shoulder almost touching mine.

"Do you sometimes wonder what would have happened if you hadn't enlisted?"

I had to go. I never forgot about you.

I searched for words but none came.

Graceful as always, she changed the topic, "I'm sorry about your friend, Nicolas. What really happened?"

I told her what everyone knew, hoping my darker emotions remained hidden.

"It's not over, is it?" she probed, scrutinizing my face.

She was dear to me, enough to warrant a truthful answer.

"No," I replied without offering anything else.

"There's a lot that isn't over." Lynn smiled sadly. "It seems to be just beginning, in fact. I'm just glad we both have good and kind people around us..." She spoke about her husband, Rick, and their three kids and the challenges of being the "governor family."

"You also have a beautiful family. That viral clip of Danielle giving that death stare to the councilwoman. Oh my God! I'd love to meet her one day!"

"You two would love each other, for sure. You've got the same fire that burns for all the right things..." I glanced up at her, grateful for the moment of reconnection, and noticed her nose wrinkle the way it always did when she was upset.

"What is it?" I asked, refusing to let her smile the moment away.

"It's a lot, Tanner..." Lynn admitted, in a hushed tone, how challenged she felt by all of her tribulations since the pandemic had started.

"You know, that friend of mine—he admired you. He even showed me your video clip when you said the state wouldn't infringe on the Constitution."

Lynn took a deep breath, her eyes wide as she processed the compliment Nico had sent her from beyond his grave. Suddenly, the distraught individual was transformed back into the powerful governor who spoke freely about all the pressures to close down South Dakota and her absolute refusal to do so.

"I don't believe the Constitution has given me the power to lock people in their homes, take away their livelihoods, and shutter their children's schools. So we're protecting vulnerable cases and the elders while doing our best to live an everyday life through this nightmare."

"What about the riots?" I wondered.

"We had none. The First Amendment allows folks to protest peacefully, so we made sure that can take place." She paused. "But I've been thinking... It's funny how the world's most successful military contract company, run by our parents, is right here in South Dakota. Did you ever work with them?"

"It's cold. I'm going to grab us blankets," I replied with a tight smile, trying to deflect as I realized how little she actually knew about Old Glory.

"You know what we're planning for July Fourth?" she asked when I returned with the blankets.

She forgot about Old Glory.

When I shook my head, she told me they were planning a massive ceremony at Mount Rushmore. "We need to send a clear message that our history—our very past—will not be toppled. It's worth preserving. We can learn from our past mistakes, take pride in our accomplishments, and forge a better way forward united as Americans..." She was covered with a thick brown blanket, hair dampened by the fog that rolled around us, but her voice rang clear like a true leader's.

A president's, even.

"It's a good place we got here, Boy. It's worth fighting for." Grandfather Ulysses's words during my very first visit to the mountain with four presidents' faces carved in it resounded in the dark night. I remembered him sharing how he and David Norton, Lynn's grandpa, had worked for a time on the carving of Rushmore before Pearl Harbor sparked their enlistment.

And now, his granddaughter is an emerging leader for the country they loved so much.

"Your mountain address could very well end up being a rallying call. It's the place to do it." The inherent symbolism would add to the profound words I knew she would say. "It could very well be the last American bastion..."

My words, unguarded in the easy connection between us, exposed my deepest worries, and Lynn's brow was furrowed when I looked up.

I said too much!

"Would you stand with us if such a grave day would be forced upon us?"

Too overwhelmed to answer, I studied her face, which became both serene and resolved.

She's like Nico. Free.

"There you are!" Jerome's voice boomed behind us as he opened the patio door. "Time to go, Sweetie."

Whew.

I wished them both goodnight as Lynn smiled and hugged me one last time before they entered the house to say their goodbyes.

When I stepped in behind them a moment later, Ali and my siblings were tired and ready to go to bed. But my dad was wearing his boots, a smirk, and deep resolution in his blue-gray eyes.

We're so the same. Fine. Now it is.

The Ranch lights glowed like fireflies in the distance when I looked back before following my father into the rocky ravine.

Our night vision sets enabled us to quickly find the cave mouth concealed along one of the stone walls, and we stepped inside.

I had heard rumors that hundreds of tunnels, if not more, lay beneath the great expanses of the Ranch. Only a few had been revealed to me, but this one I knew very well.

"You can take it off," said Jack a moment before turning on the light.

We were at the end of a tunnel, which opened into a larger space where a dim red light hung from the ceiling above a few stone seats. He motioned for me to take one and started right in with his debrief.

"There were no arrests made after the attack on Dani, but we'll watch more and keep the agent with them."

I nodded calmly, but my stomach turned on itself.

I can't lose them!

"What is it, Son?"

"Shackles, Dad. It's like shackles. This worrying about them and their safety is driving me insane." My father didn't say anything, but there was no hiding his thoughts. "I know. I know. You warned me about this."

"Our families are the source of great strength and dangerous weakness. You call it 'shackles,' fine." Jack took a deep breath. "I did the same as you, and so did your grandpa before me. Having a family is everything."

"But not Custer," I commented, positioning my remark as a question.

"He chose differently," was all my father was willing to offer before turning the conversation to Ken Lim, the journalist. "This promising young man has done dangerous undercover journalism work in some of the nastiest far-left organizations..." He highlighted Ken's recent reports and support. "They call you vigilantes now." A touch of amusement played in his voice.

"What?"

"The whole thing in the alley created quite a mess. There were no videos, but there were enough who came forward with scary stories. They've dubbed you vigilantes, taking matters into their own hands against the rioters." Obviously annoyed, he went back to Ken. "He played a pivotal role in providing another narrative for the emergence of such a phenomenon."

"Really?"

"He quoted someone saying, 'We're going to have a problem here. We are placing the villain as the hero. You'd leave the hero no choice but to act like a villain.'"

"Yeah. Brett Cohen's words. He and Ken work together sometimes." I recalled hearing it while on leave in Yachats.

"Anyway, we'll keep a good eye on that Ken fella."

He ended the subject, and gave me enough time to pick the next.

"How is it to have him back in the house?"

"I hope your brother is finally ready to help out..." He revealed to me his intention to find a position for Chad in Old Glory. "He seems ready after what he saw back there. I want to take a chance on him."

I opened my mouth to wonder out loud if that was such a good idea.

I shouldn't let my jealousy ruin this. Maybe this scared him enough to really change.

"You got my support, Dad. What's next?" My body screamed at me to go to sleep.

Jack switched to Jenny and the CPC.

"She got the secretary job on the spot, but I didn't have time to spend on this. I authorized a data grab op."

Rogues could use their chips to access any online or Bluetooth systems, provided the chip had enough time to break through encryptions. Once the connection was established, the chip could siphon data and broadcast it, pending local abilities.

"With Seattle heating up, I ordered the escalation," explained Jack. "She stayed late one night and grabbed the data..."

The story got stickier. Alarms and sirens went off, trapping Jenny on the upper floor.

"She thought she saw that CEO, Paul Shi, directing armed guards around the facility."

He smirked as he explained how Jenny managed to evade her pursuers and escape the compound without a single punch.

She's so fast.

"What did we get?" I asked.

"Well, those operators from the shipment did go through the CPC compound," confirmed Jack.

"Through?" I wondered, still not admitting my concerns about the invaders' identities.

"Yes. They were sent out everywhere. But most importantly, we found that the Seattle Comrades chapter requested help. The CPC then committed to sending one 'adviser.'"

The implication hung in the air, my mind recalling the silent shots hitting the pavement around us in the alley.

"It seems the CPC is working with China..." He fidgeted a bit as he admitted that the operators could be Chinese, government or private.

You could have let me stop them. We had the chance! I fumed in the dimly-lit space, glad he wasn't watching my heart rate on a screen.

"How hard are we going against the CPC?" I pressed.

"Tanner, this is an American company employing Americans. Furthermore, they have everyone owned and compromised, from the governor down to the city council folks. They are *off-limits* for now."

I wouldn't say I liked the verdict, but my father moved the conversation back to Seattle. This time, he wanted my analysis.

"Dad! It's almost three in the morning," I grumbled.

"That's a 'you' problem. Let's hear it. Did you like the new toy?"

Man...

"That skull design scared the bejesus out of those dipshits. That on purpose?" I smirked at the memory of their faces. "Jokes aside, the system has great potential."

"Did they see your face?" he asked.

"No. I was masked and then used the Flex."

"Good. Good," he nodded, avoiding my question about the design choice. "Now, tell me what wasn't in the official report."

"This is an operation, Dad. It might look like a party gone wrong, and those on the streets are pretty much that stock. But there is careful planning for these moves."

Like a test run or something.

"From the Dragon Skull on his apartment building to the alley, it felt like a perpetual trap."

"That operator they sent from San Francisco could have been involved in all of this," conceded Jack.

And they're now spread across the country.

"Why did you go after their leader, Daj?" he finally asked.

"He knows about how Nico died, Dad. I don't know how, but he knows something!" I rose from my chair and paced. "If it weren't for Chad, I would have gotten him, Dad."

Jack watched me quietly for a few minutes before motioning me to retake my seat. He seemed to be vetting his words, but he took too long.

"Will you tell him how much you crave killing again?" wondered the Beast.

"Is that why you decided to give Moss his new assignment?" Jack finally spoke.

"Only as a secondary goal. My main one was to find that shadow operator. I figured he'd probably be closer to the plate and the two missions could be handled at the same time."

"Fair enough, but only scouting. Maybe Chad can help. He knows all those players." Jack's voice was full of hope as he spoke of his youngest son.

Maybe.

"It didn't take you very long, Son." Jack's statement reminded me of Dex's and Moss's before him, and their same resigned reaction to my issuance of the Independent Authority order.

"I did what I deemed necessary... in both cases," I replied flatly.

He chuckled with the superior air of a commander.

"Just that we're clear that you're confined to DIR1. Watch out for making this a habit. Understood?"

"Yes. Sir."

His tone and brow softened as he promised, "We'll help you get them all, Son."

I nodded, relaxing back against the hard stone wall.

What else, Dad? I closed my eyes, longing for sleep, while I waited for him.

"She still looks like that tall, beautiful youngster who sneaked out of the house at dawn. Did she ever tell you I caught her once?"

"We were kids, Dad. Just kids in another world." I grinned at the thought of what that exchange went like until the amusement turned to something else.

Did I hurt her?

"Our relationship is three generations old, Son. Grandpa had David. I have Jerome. Always remember that the Washington and Norton families are one," he directed without tying the third circle openly.

When his phone chirped, he murmured. "Just in time."

The light footsteps drew my gaze to the doorway as a shorter man entered the room. When he took off his NVG, I recognized Lee Wu's smiley face.

"It's good to see you," I stood to hug the Chinese scientist renegade.

"You too, Tanner," he replied and nodded at Jack, who motioned for us to sit.

Lee was in his mid-thirties, small but strong in mind, with short black hair and eyes dark with secrets. I knew he was somewhere around the Ranch since we'd brought him here after Market, but we hadn't seen each other since.

"You made the right call, Tanner. Without Lee, we would have been groping in the dark."

Ah yes, the "tip."

"Tell him, Lee," Jack prompted the scientist.

Lee's eyes and tone shifted with distress as he explained, both in English and Chinese, the actual utility of the outbreak.

"It's a Bio-emp. They used their people to create a mega-spreader event and then unleashed it on the world." His eyes fell one last time as he finished, "I have great shame. I created evil."

"What about all of the Dragon measures across countries? What's your take?" I asked, my own guilt and humiliation warring for my attention.

Lee sneered and cursed in a dialect of Chinese I couldn't understand. Switching to English, he referenced the lockdown, the forced masking, and the school shutdowns.

"It's about power. Obedience. Not science..." He insisted that protecting vulnerable populations while allowing the rest to get herd immunity was the best approach. "The lockdowns are only prolonging the virus and making it adapt."

"They did all this without a shot fired," I grumbled. *Diabolically genius.*

"Are there vaccines being developed?" I asked.

"Several," replied Lee, detailing the top player as some multi-national big pharma called Zenergia. "But it won't help. A vaccine will lower the mortality but not stop the spread. The virus will mutate even faster."

"Giving governments an eternal reason to hold emergency powers," affirmed Jack.

"I was a fool. I believed him when he recruited me to the Peking University of Science..." Lee shook his head in despair as he explained how, after Market, General Jun Zhang had recruited him for the Dragon project. His emotional pain was palpable.

It's bad enough that I didn't stop it. How would I feel if my creation had ruined the world?

"Tell me more about him. It's been a while," I probed, hoping to ease some of his discomfort.

According to Lee, General Zhang was a ruthless yet charismatic leader educated in the West.

"He spoke extensively about the 'unpaid debt' that Western countries owed China for the colonization..." Lee's voice began to tremble when he detailed the human trials. "I didn't know, or maybe it was easy not to think about it. But when I saw them, hungry and demoralized..." His voice trailed off.

Jack and I gave him a moment.

"My second mistake was to believe Americans wouldn't do such a thing," bemoaned Lee. He had taken a significant risk reaching out to the US embassy, which had ended with him being interrogated by Baker during Operation Market.

He hoped for something else.

"'Work with me, Doc. I'm one of the good guys,' he said." Lee quoted Baker from their session together. "It was like talking with a spider when I'm already stuck in its web."

Jack stayed quiet, as if he were waiting for something specific to be said.

"Why did you save me, Tanner?" asked Lee.

Painful memories rushed forward—what happened there, after, and the "now."

"You didn't bargain for your life. You just asked me to kill you, so you wouldn't be used for further evil. I reckoned you were owed a chance at redemption."

"Thank you, Tanner. Not much has changed. I'm still a liability if they ever catch me," Lee replied somberly. He stood to say goodbye and then paused. "Sometimes, I wake in the middle of the night. I'm scared and can barely breathe. All that I can think of is that they are here—their flag, their vile philosophies, their tyranny. And that this great nation has fallen and the rest of the world with it. We must fight back, Tanner."

His words sent shivers down my spine. All I could do was nod in agreement before he bid us goodnight and left.

"We built a nice cover story for him, for at least living on the Ranch freely." Dad's tone was warm, and I could tell he was fond of the young scientist.

"Custer told me that other Rogues died because of my decision to take him with us," I admitted with a heavy tone.

"It's true," he confirmed but added nothing more.

Lee's words had replaced my fatigue with resolve.

"They're waging a shadow war against us, Dad, and weakening us from within."

"We're working on it," he nodded.

But this was my opportunity to push more.

"Time is running out. There's a plan in motion. The Dragon is the method, the riots the fuel. But there's more to it."

"Explain," insisted Jack.

"There's a playbook, Dad. This is well-organized, financed, led, designed in advance. Regardless of how and who released the virus, the play was ready."

"Go on." He shifted uncomfortably in his chair.

"I don't know the final goal—the agenda—but I know this. We must go after our citizens. Our side is involved beyond China. I fear these are all flare-ups, a warm-up for a grander destabilization."

CHAZ...

"Your Grandpa came back different from the war," said Jack. "He got it into his head that we must prepare to save the country." He sighed, affording a small smile. "It took me being called 'baby killer' during and after Vietnam to understand."

I leaned forward.

He rarely speaks about these things.

"We were used up and cheated by both our superiors and the public," grumbled Jack. "Then radical socialist forces began their long march through the institutions, effectively transforming this country from within, using the universities and colleges as the breeding ground." Still visibly upset, he finished, "Much of your gut intuition is spot-on, Son. But it is far more complicated than you imagine. You'll have to be patient until we find the solution."

My head nodded, but my mind remained perturbed by the thought that had haunted me since he'd called me about Chicago.

What are you not telling me?

WHAT MATTERS MOST

"**A**ll history has been a history of class struggles, of struggles between exploited and exploiting, between dominated and dominating classes at various stages of social development..." The voice quoting the fathers of communism belonged to a smooth-talking black woman in her late twenties. She was introduced as a Comrade spokeswoman and interviewed on one of the leading morning shows. The male anchor nearly drooled as the woman lectured him about the need "to change the system." They spoke specifically about CHAZ, and both agreed that the experiment was "mostly peaceful" and even a possible model to learn from.

Little fucks. I should've slept.

The kitchen was the place to be if you wanted to be loud early. It had its own wing of the great house with a small table and chairs and a large wall-mounted TV. I'd been sitting there since the chat with my dad, drinking one cup of coffee after another.

At least I showered.

"Good morning, Baby," said Ali as she walked toward me, dressed in jeans and a heavy coat. "I'm ready for some coffee and a walk... Shall we?"

I nodded as she poured a hot cup and took her first sip. Then she grabbed my arm, and we both walked out onto the gravel path.

The Ranch home was built at the top of a gradual hill, and the double front doors opened directly to the east where the first rays of red light painted the tall cliffs in the distance.

"He didn't leave you time to sleep, did he?" she asked a few seconds into our walk.

Ali never opted for the underground locations that offered secured spots for conversations. Instead, she was always outside carrying an activated noise scrambler. I'd spotted it in her thick coat pocket when she had put her arm in mine.

"No. He didn't," I admitted with a chuckle, noticing again how my body and mind were always more at ease when I was with her.

We spoke of the dinner, seeing Lynn, and the incredible bond between our families for several minutes before she paused. We walked another long stretch in silence until Ali brought up her growing relationship with Danielle.

"I love her tough-cookie side. God Bless her for that." She squeezed my arm and looked up at my face as she reflected on how they handled themselves during the attack. "And your blood runs in Ari, Tanner. Keep an eye on that."

My heart dropped at her words, but I nodded reluctantly in agreement.

As always, she had led my thoughts into pastures of her design and waited for my response.

"I'm going through something. I told Dad about it last night. I'm not coping well with not being with them. When I'm not working, and sometimes even when I am, I can't stop worrying about them." I tried to pull the fresh morning air deeply into my lungs. "It's like shackles, Mom. And I'm worried it's going to..." I couldn't finish.

Why do they terrify me?

Her arm tightened on mine again as we took the path leading to a nearby hill.

"He told me about it, but not his response."

"Dad recognized the fear and said only that having a family both helps and weakens. But he never brought up the option of breaking the shackles..."

"Is that a valid option to consider?" she wondered, eyes betraying her surprise.

"No. No," I quickly retorted. "I feel bad about how I left them. Besieged, vulnerable, abandoned by friends."

The red glimmer in the east grew higher on the rocky plateaus as we neared the top of the grassy hill. The sky was without a single cloud—a rarity.

"Your father's right. Your family is everything, whatever the cost," she started. "But this goes *both* ways. We're proud of your decision to serve again, but it doesn't help when you're living in fear of hearing the phone ring about a loved one."

We arrived at the top and sat on the small wooden bench bolted into the rock and I glanced at the helipad in the distance, noticing the chopper had some lights on and a small fuel truck was driving toward it. Liam and Sarah were working on prepping for our upcoming takeoff.

Good kids.

Her eyes tracked mine.

"They missed you."

I nodded, silently reflecting on how she always knew more than she ever admitted. "I missed them too."

Farm animals began to move through the fields in the distance, but my mind continued searching the contents of my chat with Jack.

"Mom, did something happen to Dad and Custer in Vietnam?"

She turned to look at me, eyes slightly narrowed above her faint smile, and asked, "Why would you ask that, Tanner?"

"We were used up and cheated by both our superiors and the public," Jack's words echoed, and Custer's remarks about the power structure behind Baker played alongside them, "Your dad and I have both experienced that in the flesh..."

"A hunch," I offered.

She looked up to the sky, shielding her blue eyes for a moment. I thought about the satellites and how once I realized I was being watched, it was hard to resist gazing up. It was an involuntary movement, akin to the urge to touch my ear when I realized I'd been chipped.

"It was a cruel war, like them all. Nobody returned the same." Ali's voice was distant in events long past. "You ask if something happened? Yes, and it placed your father on the path he's on. Same goes for William," she added, referring to the General by his first name.

Shemtov's words joined the inner choir, "All I was before that moment died as I waited for the Vietcong to enter the base…"

"I remember meeting Ulysses for the first time and praying your father would never have that haunted look, and then Vietnam happened. Now, my son looks at me with the same eyes."

Three generations already. The thought was too painful, so it was pushed down, almost without any effort applied.

"Dad seems happy to have Chad back," I changed the subject.

"I was troubled about their relationship for years. Chad never understood why your father has been gentler with him. He was jealous through his teens, envious of the… special time you got with Jack. He took it the wrong way."

Unlike my father, who openly discussed my childhood training with me, Mom usually sidestepped the issue unless I pressed it.

"Chad didn't know I forced your father to stop it after you," she admitted with a long sigh.

My heart quickened when her face suddenly looked many years older.

"When was it, Mom?" I asked, hoping her moment of reflection would grant me more details.

"Right after we finished in Bogotá."

Her eyes now locked on mine, I could tell she was holding a puzzle piece I needed and wondered if this was a subtle hint.

What happened that you finally stopped him?

"At least he didn't get the eyes. Right, Mom?"

I knew it was a cheap blow before it left my vocal cords, and it was confirmed when she flinched, as if I'd smack her across the face. Quickly, she stood and looked at her smartphone.

"Too far to the nearest location," she grumbled to herself.

Does she want more privacy? What's going on?

When I got to my feet, she faced me and grabbed my shoulders.

"Tanner, I'm sorry for everything we've done to you," she whispered, her eyes wet. "I haven't given up... I'm working on it."

Maybe she'll tell me. I momentarily considered using her apparent guilt about me to learn more. *I could ask about Bogotá.*

The words were just forming in my mouth when Tami's hoot ended our conversation.

We turned to see my sister making her way up to us, carrying a small picnic bag.

"Outdoor breakfast," she called with a broad smile.

I was in my room getting ready to leave when the call arrived.

"She died," said Moss. "Right after the evac. Brutal."

Chad's female friend, who'd sheltered him, was murdered for her good deed. And nobody was taken into custody because the murder had happened within CHAZ. The police barely cordoned off the apartment before being chased out by community leaders.

Oh no, what's this going to do to Chad?

"What about the targets?"

Moss confirmed he'd already managed to infiltrate the Comrades, but he hadn't seen Daj or the possible operator sent from the CPC.

I told him to stay on course and then went searching for my father.

Damn it. Where is he? We gotta go.

Jack was in the barn, working on an old green tractor while talking on the phone. He ended it quickly and spoke before I could, "I know. I'll get him, and we'll talk to him together."

It took minutes to locate my brother but only a moment for him to collapse into the hay-covered earth when he learned the fate of his friend.

Jack instantly bent his knee and stroked Chad's black hair as he spoke, "It's okay. It's not your fault. Go and wash your face." His tone was warmer and softer than most had ever heard from this man. "Go on now, Boy."

I took a deep breath as we watched Chad amble out of the barn, shoulders slumped and head down.

"It might help with his transformation," Jack whispered soberly.

Ever the architect.

He turned to face me, all warmth and softness gone from his face and voice when he asked, "Did you follow my instruction?"

Moss. Recon only. I know.

I nodded, resigned.

"It's time for me to go, Dad. Are we good?"

His face was furrowed with worry, but he offered a crooked smile.

"Go home, Son."

The sun was up as the chopper charged west. Liam dozed in the back while Sarah focused on the flight, leaving me free to answer Dex's call. After we arranged to meet at the base in a few days, he shifted gears.

"How was it for you to be back?"

My second-in-command was more than a friend. He was a Rogue brother.

"A wild ride," I answered. "Family is intense."

My heart stuttered as I recalled the details of his father's death.

"I'm sorry, Man..." I started, but he interrupted me.

"All is good. Thank you. I'll see you in a few days. Enjoy the rest, Man."

Dex's question remained with me after the line went dead, and I sought answers in the endless forests and hills below us—answers to questions that had plagued me for a long time.

What do I really know about The Doctrine and this crazy family of mine that created it?

It was evening when Sarah dropped me and the bike at Santa Monica Airport and I rode out to see my family.

Not much had changed. Vacant, dirty streets filled only with the feeling of lawlessness, and the few cars on Lincoln Boulevard driven by masked individuals.

Back in crazyland.

The female Israeli agent, a young redhead, nodded from the shadow of a tree when I arrived at the gate. I lifted my fingers from the throttle to signal back to her before turning toward home.

Dani was waiting for me in the courtyard, and my heart raced at the mere sight of her in her favorite red shorts and white tee.

Somebody ratted me.

"Care to take a ride with me, Fair Lady?" I asked as I stopped the bike by her bare feet and marveled at her natural beauty.

Zero makeup and a messy bun. And I'm sunk.

"Stupid husband," she blurted with that smile as I removed my helmet. "I can only wait a little bit to have you," she whispered after a passionate kiss.

"Me too," I panted back before sliding off the bike and following her inside.

"It's a BBQ for you, Daddy!" called Ari with glee when he saw us coming up the stairs.

After all the kids had greeted me with enthusiastic hugs and high-fives, I said hello to Roberto and Paulina who were taking care of the food and hugged Celeste before she left to help Dani with something. Nodding at Dmitri and Emmanuel, I figured they'd been drafted to entertain the kids.

An hour later, full of homemade Mexican food, all the men were seated in my studio.

"She okay?" Dmitri asked about Danielle and the attack and casually mentioned seeing a "female guard" outside.

There was no point in holding back on it, so I told them we all have security and none of them pressed further.

"I'm glad Cel is with Danielle." Roberto's eyes had dimmed since I'd last seen him, and I noticed the muscles tightening in his jaw as he spoke. "There's not much to report here. Same bullshit. No news about Nico's investigation."

Emmanuel added a colorful curse in Spanish and shook his head.

As the venting continued, the grieving father's eyes remained on me, silently asking me if I remembered my promise. I nodded at him, and he relaxed back in his chair.

Before I could say anything more, Dani yelled down the stairs, "Mister! If you're home, then you help. Yalla…"

Oh boy.

I bathed the kids, marveling at how much older they seemed.

I'm already missing too much!

"Put us to sleep, Daddy. It's your turn. Your turn!" cheered Ari as I pulled his pajamas over his head. Lil just clapped her pudgy hands, understanding her big brother's request.

Dani laughed and walked out, leaving me helplessly roped into a multiple books session, which put Lil to sleep. When I closed the third book, my son's eyes were still open and focused intently on me.

He's a little man.

I stroked his long hair strands away from his face as he bit his lip.

"Do you want to tell me about what happened?" I asked.

In a flash, he sat up and faced me.

"I wasn't afraid, Dad," he started, reminding me of my own admission during our chat before I left. I listened as he told the story from his almost five-year-old's mind.

Damn it, Boy. You were so careless. I could've lost you!

"I'm proud of you, Son. You did something… even if it was *not* allowed." I ground my teeth to emphasize my subtle warning.

He nodded with some relief, but his brow remained furrowed.

"What is it? You can tell me."

I patted the bed, and stretched out to face him as he laid down.

"They said bad things, Daddy. *Really* bad words."

His eyes shifted slightly, indicating embarrassment at the simple recollection, and my blood boiled as I witnessed my child's pure response to evil.

"They said things about Uncle Nico." He shook his head. "I'm not allowed to say those words, Daddy…."

Oh my God.

"Ari. I'm so sorry. Someone will stay with the family from now on when I'm gone," I assured him, pulling him into a hug.

"Grandpa Eli's friends. Mommy told me already," he responded, sleepiness finally beginning to take hold.

"Did you catch the bad people?" he asked.

"Why would you ask me that?" I pushed down the gushing pain and guilt.

I made a promise.

"So you'd be back with us. I love you, Daddy..." His final words slurred as he closed his eyes.

Closing my eyes, I pulled him closer and whispered, "I love you most," wishing I could infuse his little body and giant soul with an impenetrable sense of safety.

"Your son senses what you refuse to consider. All roads lead back to the same place..." whispered the Beast.

What do you mean?

My eyes popped open in frustration, and I wiggled myself out of my son's embrace, put a blanket over Lil in the crib, and left to find my wife.

Danielle sat on the edge of the bed, a strained smile stretched across her stunning face. I kneeled in front of her and wrapped my arms tight around her waist before planting a soft kiss on her lips.

"Tell me," I invited, bracing myself for what was to come.

She spoke a little about the physical attack, but admitted it was the words had been haunting her sleep.

"Put your mask on, Bitch! Where is your soldier boy now, Cunt? We can bury another Marine!" Dani finished quoting her assailants and her body shuddered. "What happened to us? What happened to this place?"

I tightened my embrace, using the *Sense* to sequester the rage for another time.

"It's the lockdown!" she answered her question. "The Dragon measures divided us. This virus is scaring people to do bad things!" The words left her lips in a growl.

No, Baby. It's the people, not the virus, that caused this.

"And...?" I prompted, feeling there was more to the storm needing to be voiced.

"I feel alone sometimes, but I'm fine... How about you?" She pulled back and lifted her hands to hold my face.

I let out a big sigh as I sorted out how much I would share about Chad and CHAZ before giving her the redacted version of the evac operation.

"Oh, that thing on the news..." she started.

Busted...

"...something about vigilantes fighting with rioters in an alley." Her eyes narrowed and her bottom lip quivered.

We held each other's gaze for a long moment until she released the tension with mocked exasperation and laughter.

"How was it to be back in South Dakota?"

She moved to the other side of the bed and pulled me up with her. As she nestled herself into my side, I began to tell her all about seeing the family and some about Chad's journey ahead and my dad's architect-like plan for my brother's future.

"Why are you always doing this?" She didn't try to hide her frustration.

"What?" I tried not to give away how defensive I was feeling before I even knew the accusation.

"You speak of your home as a foreign place, even when we went to visit. No connection. I just don't understand... It's amazing there. Why don't you...?" When she turned her head and saw the look on my face, she stopped.

"Not my favorite topic, Babe..." I responded. "But while we're on it, is there any possible way I might be able to convince you to relocate to the Ranch..." I paused and braced myself again. "...or Israel?"

"No way, Tanner. Israel's measures are just as bad and I'm not leaving Cel behind, not after she lost Nico that way. They all need us here. We'll go if you go, or we'll stay. This is our home."

All the Israeli fire that had drawn me to this woman had established its hard boundary, and I knew any further attempt to convince her would be met with its shadow.

Should have listened to Eli.

I nodded and kissed her gently.

"Holden's around a lot. Still fishing for info, but we love him." She shifted the topic again.

As I listened, I noticed the numbness in my chest at the mention of my friend.

Better this way.

"Tanner Washington." The fire chastised me after a long pause. "This is your friend, your very good friend." I sighed but she continued, turning my face to hers. "I'm proud of you, Honey. But it took *you* time, right? Be patient with him."

Exasperated, I decided I couldn't take any more.

"I thought you could only wait a little to have me?"

In two quick moves, I had her on my lap and utterly distracted from all of our worldly cares.

JUST LIKE BEFORE

– Venice Beach, CA –
Tuesday, June 23, 2020

"**G**et a bird for tomorrow at 0800," I spoke into my earbuds in a hushed tone.

"Roger that. Enjoy your moment with them," Dex replied warmly.

On cue, little footsteps pounded across my studio's ceiling.

"I'll catch you later."

When I opened the door, Ari launched himself at me from the fifth stair.

"Good morning, My Little Warrior." I wrapped my arms around his little body as he reached up to kiss my cheek. "Don't try that with anyone else but me, okay?"

"Okay, Daddy. I know you're the only one strong enough to catch me."

I don't know if it was his words or the neck squeeze that melted me to my core.

"There are lots of people strong enough, Son, but you can trust *me* to always be there."

"I know, Daddy," he said as I carried him upstairs.

I didn't want to be late for breakfast or the waves.

"Some masked guys, all in black, came by. They tried to give me some trouble," Todd grumbled as he squinted his eyes away from me and in the direction of his newest display. We stood on his hill surrounded by American flags of all sizes, from a small lawn-size to full three-by-five foot heavy canvases.

"What kind of trouble?" I pressed, noticing Holden's police SUV rolling slowly up to the beach station.

"The funeral. Many consider me a traitor," sneered Todd. "But have they cared to listen to my words? I was always on the side of the brave, the faithful, and the men and women of God. No... I think I will stay right here, on this very hill."

His tall dark silhouette stood a bit taller against the rising sun behind him as he made his decision.

"Be safe and don't mess with those black-clothed goons, especially if you see a white lighting symbol."

I squeezed his shoulder and headed toward Holden, shortboard in hand.

His eyes were tired and sunken just above the black LAPD mask. When he didn't offer his hand, I nodded toward the short concrete wall overlooking the break-water surf spot.

"I really appreciate how you helped with Dani," I offered sincerely.

He only nodded before mumbling, "Interesting move on the personal security."

"Do you blame me? We're left to fend for ourselves."

Holden looked sideways at me for a moment and then exhaled loudly, inflating his mask.

"Do you know who called the station with the tip?"

You couldn't resist.

I shrugged and shook my head slowly, keeping my eyes on the ocean where a nice set was coming.

"What's going on with your brother in Seattle? He still making waves?" he asked, sending my mental defenses up.

Just check somewhere else. Nice.

"He ditched town and headed to our family ranch in South Dakota," I answered flatly.

Holden scratched his head the way he always did when he was uncomfortable.

"Did he tell you anything about those vigilantes?"

"What again?"

His eyes remained narrow as he told me about the news from Seattle.

"Oddly enough, shortly after we got the tip, I heard about this reported gunfight in an alley in that autonomous zone. I figured your brother would know."

Fuck.

"I'll ask him next time we speak," I answered, barely holding back the sneer.

"Cap!" Holden and I turned to see another large black male officer. "Should we wait for you?"

"Nah. I'll be on the radio." Holden's voice was as exhausted as his countenance.

The officer nodded, turned, and entered a squad car with his female partner. As I watched them drive away, Dani's words haunted me, "I'm proud of you, Honey. But it took you time… Be patient with him."

"How's the morale in your station?" I warmed my tone.

Holden groused about it being low due to the "defund the police" movement and its effects.

"There are some businesses these days that refuse to serve us! Can you imagine?"

Hope rose in my chest for a moment, and I decided to go for it.

"Have you stopped to consider who's enabling this madness?"

"It's the president! He's stoking the fire… inflaming the protests!"

Holy shit.

I tilted my head back in disbelief and tried to keep my cool.

"Stone? Really? Not all the corrupt politicians from this neighborhood up to the state capitol?"

"They did their best with the riots." Holden's tirade about the difficulties of local rule since the pandemic broke out stunned me. "We didn't want another Chicago on our hands."

"Really, Holden? Is that what happened? It seems that enough of your leadership decided to take a knee in front of the same assholes who attacked your officers and killed law-abiding citizens."

The implication hung like a thick fog between us.

"Any progress?" I asked at last.

He shook his head.

"Fucking Chicago ruined everything." Turning to make eye contact, he continued, "Would have been good to at least see what happened in the restaurant."

A wave of irritation passed through me.

"Yeah? What would you have done if you had it? Not admissible, right?"

He pulled down his mask to reveal his dark skin flushed a reddish purple.

"You better be careful, Tanner. You sound more and more like him."

You motherfucker.

"Well, he was right, and I didn't listen."

Holden raised his mask and stood as he ended the conversation, "Whatever, Man. Go have fun." Done, he walked back toward the station.

My blood boiled as I entered the tumultuous waves. The sets were three-to-four feet, breaking fast and strong, yet my focus wasn't there.

A wave rose and crashed on me while paddling out, ripping my board from underneath me. It was during those two or three seconds under the dark water, when every surfer knows to curl in, elbows protecting the head, and let it pass, that the Beast decided to speak.

"You want to scream? Then scream!"

No! I'm not ready!

An hour later, I was on my way to the synagogue.

Dani had taken one look at my face when I returned from the beach and insisted I go check on Shemtov.

She always knows, and it's cute how she made it about me checking on the rabbi.

The bicycle ride was nothing short of disheartening, especially after returning from the open wilderness of the Ranch. The businesses were mainly shuttered, with food establishments doing their best to shift their operations to pickup and delivery.

Riding without a cloth of obedience elicited the usual number of heckles. The worst was the man in a business suit, screaming at me through his mask while his two children, not older than five, stood next to him gagged and droopy-eyed.

Lee warned us. Fucking China and anyone else who had a part in it!

Noticing a few tents on the pavement in front of the synagogue, I continued to the side gate, punched the code, and got my bike inside the fenced courtyard.

Shemtov, dressed in an oversized black buttoned shirt over long pants, sat in one of two chairs amid the discarded wooden toys and structures.

"Come, my friend. Let's enjoy the afternoon sun. At least they can't take *that* from us," he boomed, a wry smile on his face.

"Have you seen any more Dragon Skull graffiti?" I asked after a few pleasantries.

He shook his head.

"How are you?"

Shemtov's voice always relaxed me into a spiritual embrace.

"I recently had a moment thinking about Genesis. Your eulogy."

He steadied his glasses.

"What was the trigger?"

My mind conjured the memory of stopping Chad from stepping into the alley in Seattle.

"Violence and fear."

Shemtov nodded, and his face softened.

He's not going to push on this.

"There has been no progress in Nico's case," I said after a moment.

"How does it make you feel?"

The rabbi's genuine care melted my defenses.

> *Alone in the darkness, the weight of my*
> *failures makes my feet so heavy.*

"Guilty. I could have done so many other things. I could have run to join him inside," I admonished myself, clenching my fists as the pain reached them.

"Is this your only source of misery?" he asked, shielding his eyes from the sun so he could search mine.

My mental defense was about to rise when a great resignation held it back.

"Say it, Rabbi. You've earned the right."

"I think that the virus haunts you. That you know it, somehow," he offered gently.

"I'll tell you something, and you will hold it inside as the token of my trust. Yes, I know the virus. I even had the opportunity to do something about it, but I left the fight." The sudden surge of emotions forced me to take a breath. "At the time, I was angry. And maybe I just wanted out, and that was my reasoning. Whatever it was, I left when others remained on the battlefield."

"What else, Tanner?" he asked, earning my respect for not probing beyond my admission.

Beast, are you there?

I gripped the chair tightly and refused to allow the *Sense* to calm me down.

"Every day, I feel closer to the edge. It's an abyss of violence, separating my life into two. It is a ticking clock that I'm doing nothing to stop—only delaying."

His hand reached my shoulder and squeezed it.

"Why are you delaying it?"

Don't you see? Really?

"I'm afraid, Rabbi. My family is the most important thing in the world. I cannot... I *will* not turn my back on them."

Shemtov paused, but only for a moment, while I stared at the ground.

"Isn't doing whatever you do... done *to* protect them?"

How can I explain this to you?

His hearty laugh broke the tension briefly, and I looked up into his amused face.

"You are more Jewish than you can even imagine, Tanner. Our people's story is like a tapestry of mistakes, sadness, and a few triumphs. Remember Tikkun Olam."

His eyes remained kind as he referred once again to the Jewish concept of "repairing the world" with actions that can improve ourselves and those around us, but there was something else as he held my gaze.

"Why do you bring it up again?" I challenged him.

Through the confusion and swirling words that haunted me, "You could have stopped it, Hermano," I couldn't do anything else.

"Because you'll eventually have to forgive your past mistakes and then focus solely on the repair."

"You sound like my wife," I protested.

Shemtov laughed, but then his face turned serious again.

"Give more thought to The Sacrifice. Elohim gave us the freedom to choose. That is true for both the easy and the hard times. It's what makes life so grand and so painful. As long as you draw breath, it's not too late."

DEBRIEF

– Cape Perpetua, OR –
Wednesday, June 24, 2020

It was late afternoon when Sarah dropped me off at the farm.

The official way to base was through a two-hundred-acre chicken farm up the Yachats river, just a few miles northeast of the Cape. That's where the chopper landed and motorcycles always waited in the nearby hangar. It was a fenced area at the back of the property, so we never encountered the farm hands.

I thanked Sarah and sped away from the property and into the Siuslaw National Forest, heading south-west. The thick woods calmed my tired mind until the salt in the air and the large metal gate with the "Private Property—No Trespassing" sign made their appearance.

When I looked in the direction of the concealed mounted camera on a tree ahead of me, the gate slid open, barely making a sound. Slowly, I drove into the forest until an oversized, old-looking shed appeared. The double barn doors hissed and opened upon my arrival, and I rolled into the space with reflective silver concrete walls and other bikes lined up. I parked and made my way to the stairway, concealed doors, and tunnels that would take me to the base.

I'm back in the L...

"Say it. Don't stop," insisted the Beast.

My body froze in the darkness of one of the natural tunnels that led to the upper level of the old bunker—the upper level that Alfa had named.

"The Lair," I whispered into the empty air.

"Who am I?" the Beast whispered back.

The *Sense* rushed in on my command, emptying my mind and raising my defenses as I kept walking.

I hadn't even set my backpack on the bed when I heard the knock.

"Come in," I called and turned to see Dex and Jenny at the door.

I hugged Jenny and smiled at Dex before offering them seats and circling the desk to take mine.

"They're mostly American Chinese, but there are others as well..." Jenny briefed us on her mission. She only had a few days on the payroll, but her impressions were extensive. "There is a very strong social justice atmosphere, but the upcoming election is hovering above all matters."

It was no surprise to us that Stone was hated while Grayson was hailed as the new hope for the country. As for the Dragon, the CPC's general attitude was fighting to clear China from any wrongdoing while supporting the communist country's strict pandemic mitigation measures.

"You can get into serious trouble if found unmasked, even in the restroom," grumbled Jenny. "They are heavily pro-lockdowns."

No surprise there either.

"The big news is that I met Paul Shi, the CEO. He interviewed me personally, which was a surprise opportunity..." Jenny let the sly smile cross her pretty face.

"Did you get anything?" I asked, sensing she was holding onto something.

"Not at first. Our first interview was professional and almost ridiculously catered to make sure that I felt safe and welcome at their facility. Paul was pleasant and warm."

I knew something was up when Jenny sighed, pinched her small nose, and looked at Dex, whose bushy eyebrows raised once back at her.

"You can say it. He just told you so with his damn eyebrows," I jested lightly.

Turning back to me, she let out a big sigh of relief.

"I did see Paul again before my evac. It was just a short interaction in the cafeteria where he was commenting to many staffers about the protests and the need to help them reach their goals. He was eloquent and smart. But I sensed it..." She paused, still uncertain about her words or maybe whether she should say them. "There's something about him that is just like you, Sir." Fixing her eyes on mine, she let the words come. "You're both natural-born killers." Her tone was dead serious, absent of malice or intention to offend.

"And yet, you are blind..." whispered the Beast.

My stomach clenched against the implications of their words.

"He's very charismatic and quite admired in his company. They treat him like the leader of a movement. Politicians, media, and even big businesses line up to talk with the 'progressive CEO.' I was so surprised by the mission acceleration, I did something to trip a wire," said Jenny, referring to the "data grab" operation and getting noticed by the CPC security.

"Any other thoughts, Jenny?" I probed, sensing more unease.

"There's something so unreal and twisted there. It's like a miniature parallel universe. One that America did not win..."

Dex and I exchanged a knowing look, agreeing to let her speak.

She took a deep breath and placed both her hands on the table, her black eyes flashing with flames.

"I now understand why you are asking for DIR2. I wouldn't say I like it. Not a bit. But I know now, and I... support you."

"Thank you, Jenny. I'm grateful for your work and so glad you're safe. We have quite a mission ahead of us."

"Yes, Sir," Jenny smiled and took her leave.

Dex waited for her to leave before he made his suggestion, "The team is due for a chat as well."

"Yeah. Get them assembled in twenty," I responded, my mind still troubled by Jenny's remarks.

Where am I leading them?

We sat in the conference room, Moss synced up with us from the "field."

"We've been running for days now. Now that Jenny is safe among us, let's take a moment to dial out and look at the big picture," I started.

The first item was a reminder of our mission and the apolitical stance it required.

"To protect the Constitution, we must stomach all those who gain power according to it and as long as they adhere to its sacred terms and conditions."

But for how long?

I pushed down the nagging thought and updated them on the meeting with Lee.

"He's eaten with shame over it."

And so am I.

The team grumbled about the insanity our country's citizens had been enduring since the onset of the pandemic with the Dragon measures, Chicago, and the riots erupting.

"It's a regime change." Huxley's deep voice boomed, and his words elicited an even deeper silence. The big guy wasn't keen on these types of chats. He preferred the exhilarating freedom granted by combat, so he'd caught us all off-guard.

"Explain, Hux. Do you mean the Dems?"

It was a fair question, considering the Democrats threw their weight and massive resources behind the Dragon measures and support for the protesters. The cost didn't matter as long as it was against Stone and the Republicans.

He scratched his head and gave Liam, who made faces at him, a mocking growl before he answered, "On the surface... yes. But deeper than that. Maybe bigger than parties. Maybe."

They all looked at each other while I remained focused on Huxley, something about his insinuation prickling me.

Moss chimed in after a long pause, wondering if his mission scope might expand. There was no doubt about the implications of his request.

Directive Two.

"We need more actionable data to get more... rope." I treaded carefully, fully aware of the implications.

Moss's whistle was reciprocated with chuckles.

Just planting the seeds.

"Will we finally work with other Rogue teams?" Dex wondered.

Our mission required complete decentralization, which was the reason we had never operated with others like us.

Even when they were right behind us, cleaning up my mess and sacrificing their lives to get us out of China, I thought to myself somberly.

"Wouldn't that be something," I replied, smiling as they all nodded in hopeful agreement.

Dex consulted his smartphone while everyone left the room.

"The CI in Mexico made contact. We're on mission lockdown until further orders," he reported.

"Very well. I'll see you at breakfast tomorrow."

Once in my room, I took off my sticky clothes and showered. When I heard the chirp of my phone, I turned off the scalding hot water and dried myself off.

Tami had texted that Lynn would be on the news soon, so I dressed quickly and clicked on the TV.

The governor was flanked by police and National Guard as she addressed the state about recent calls to attack Mount Rushmore as "just another monument to topple."

"I have news for anyone considering coming here to hurt our heritage. It's a one-way ticket!"

Presidential, for sure. My heart swelled with pride and affection as she walked away from the podium.

"Well done, Governor," I texted her as another news story took over the screen.

Out in Seattle, CHAZ's leaders agreed to break down the zone as "the mission was accomplished." Their *mission* wasn't hard to figure, as the Comrade female spokeswoman was out there again, wearing a shirt with VOTE GRAYSON on the front.

The definition of insanity. I clicked off the TV and picked up my phone. *I need to hear her voice.*

"Baby?"

"Yes, My Love. How are you?" I asked and allowed her voice and passionate update to settle me like nothing else could.

BEHIND THE LINES

We'd sailed into Ensenada's small port just three days earlier, carrying large duffel bags. The Baja Mexican surf town was eighty miles shy of the San Diego US border and full of American college students on summer break.

The Pacific Ocean roared up the rocky brown cliff in front of our beach house while the team prepared, checking their gear and catching some sleep when possible.

Our target was a large compound just a few miles into the desert. A known Cartel headquarter, left alone by corrupt local police. The Eye was tasked to help us, so we had the luxury of ascertaining our informant's location before beginning the mission.

Mr. Jones had managed to get one SOS out before his phone went dead. He was still alive, as the Eye had picked him up a few times, in various locations across the expansive hacienda. My dad suspected it was related to Jenny's operation in the CPC—that they must have traced his footprints in something.

Unbelievable. I was still stunned by the news that Mr. Jones had been chipped with a GPS tracker, even though my dad had assured me informants were grateful to know we could find and rescue them. *Gotta have your eyes on everyone, right, Dad?*

Alfa did a good job reconning the area, but there was no easy way to get close to the compound without being noticed and potentially losing Mr. Jones for good.

Fortunately, luck was on our side. Big parties were scheduled for the next evening, so there was a good chance that many of the Cartel goons would be in town partying.

Barely enough, I thought, looking at the live feed from the compound. About a dozen operators stuck together and stayed away from the Cartel guys. They were always masked and carrying assault weapons, and they moved like soldiers.

Fucking China. If this is real... then...

My chip vibrated at the same time I heard Dex call, "Sir, incoming."

"They're tightening their grip on Hong Kong. A windfall of the 'Great Pandemic...'" Jack started our call with some recent updates about China, which only increased my agitation.

"Are you ready?" he asked. "This is a tough one, Son. But we owe the man a chance at freedom, and we desperately need to know if there's more news."

I looked back at the living room where the rest of Alfa sat looking at me.

"You're more than likely sending us against China…"

"Good chance," he replied, failing to cloak his concern.

I know you, Dad. At least some…

Seeing Alfa all nodding silently, predatory smiles crossed all of our faces in unison.

"Yeah. We're ready."

Jack was satisfied as he switched the subject to a recent situation in the States.

"A couple with young children had rioters entering their private yards. The father walked out, waved his shotgun around, and told them to leave. They left him alone, but the district attorney ordered the police to arrest the father on multiple charges."

What the…?

I didn't have enough time to properly digest the story before he sent me a quick video clip for the next update.

It was from Portland. Comrades and Ryse foot soldiers were assaulting the police after being accosted for painting "kill all police" graffiti on government buildings.

"Insane…" I could barely hold back my anger.

Switching the topic one final time, Jack mentioned July Fourth and how Lynn had been preparing for her Mount Rushmore address.

"She's getting a lot of media heat for that. Definitely Jerome's daughter!"

"I heard a part of that speech when I was at the Ranch. She's..." I paused, wondering if I should speak the words out loud to my dad. "...presidential."

"Yes, she is," he agreed before ending the call.

BLOODY RIDDLES

– Ensenada, Mexico –
Friday, July 3, 2020

The Cartel Compound, sitting alone in the desert, was visible from our vantage point on the rocky hill. A few tiny houses and the main villa were surrounded by an eight-foot white wall. We'd taken the dirt bikes, leaving Sarah back with the chopper, and had set up on top of the hill once the sun went down. We dug into the hard earth, anti-satellite camouflage nets strewn above us and the bikes.

As our intel suggested, we watched as a whole Cartel convoy full of well-dressed men headed to Ensenada.

"RCC confirms operators remain in the target, in one of the smaller homes. Five more Cartel guards roam as well," reported Dex. He had his tablet open while he managed communication with the RCC.

"Roger that," I replied.

"So, who do we think *they* are?" asked Liam, getting only silence from the rest of us. We all knew our cyber warrior wasn't asking about the identity of those who guarded Mr. Jones.

"I don't know if those are Rogues," I replied. "I already told you that a few times." My grumble only elicited more chuckles, Liam's mimicking an old scary TV show trailer's music.

When Jack gave me the mission parameters, it was clear that our job was to insert, retrieve Mr. Jones, and retreat. But he remained mum on a few key questions: Who exactly would provide the distraction and smoke, "opening the door," and defend us from being attacked in the back by outside forces?

His response had been full of amusement, "They won't fail. I'll tell you that."

The team continued their banter while I remained fixed on the growing knot in my stomach.

I'm about to do it again tonight.

"Like she said," whispered the Beast, reminding me of Jenny's words, *"Natural-born killer."*

The implications reverberated through my mind and body.

Just in time, the RCC signal ripped me out of my endless riddles and forced the team to wind down their banter and prepare to insert.

"Protract," I commanded, and Alfa echoed the order. Our Flex helmets closed down over our faces, with their HUD covers and mouth guards.

"Zoom in x2," I instructed, and the compound grew on my display. We were all mounted on our bikes, waiting for our cue.

The Hacienda was the only place with lights on in the otherwise black nightscape, Ensenada's bright lights further in the distance in the other direction.

"10, 9, 8..." the ticker began on my HUD.

"They won't fail. I'll tell you that," Jack's words resounded in the empty waiting.

Nameless and loyal.

"...2, 1."

I saw a flash of red light a mile from the target.

Ground missile!

A colossal explosion erupted in the compound.

"Go, go, go," I commanded Alfa while zooming out my HUD to accurate distance and augmented vision.

We rode down the hill like fiends, our paths marked on the Flex display for us to follow. Whatever hit the complex had a kick. From a distance, we could see the entire side of the wall and attached building were both destroyed and torched as our coordinates took us around to the other side.

"Incoming smoke," flashed the RCC alert on my HUD with a chime.

I love this system.

Just as we stopped our bikes about twenty feet from the white wall, smoke mortar bombs plastered the compound.

With the Eye tracking the moving personnel in the compound, we were given an insertion spot free of guards. I was the first to reach the wall, extracting two small climbing blades from my utility belt.

No going back.

I growled and climbed up, feeling the adrenaline push harder through my veins with every reach.

A thick blanket of smoke covered the place, but our HUD provided us with the mission checkpoints as we advanced toward the structure with Mr. Jones.

Hux searched for an overwatch position while Liam, Dex, Jenny, and I fanned out in teams of two with blades and silenced Wraith guns ready to eliminate any combatants quietly. Jenny was with me.

"Hostile down."

Calls started on the comms while my wing woman surprised a Cartel guard with two bullets. We advanced through the smoky courtyard, closing in on the one-story Spanish-looking home.

Using the Flex display, the Wraith locked on a Cartel member running across the yard. Only took one shot to drop him. It was satisfying to see him fall, yet the hunger for more consumed my core.

Other operators stood their ground, covering the windows and looking to the courtyard. They weren't ready for Huxley's 0.50 Cal sniper rifle, synced with the Flex capabilities and the Eye above us. The big man managed to take a few of them, even through the walls they used for hiding. We had no time to waste.

"Dance," I called for the execution of the Rogue's bloodiest hand-to-hand tactic.

Leaving Hux outside to keep covering us, the four of us ran from opposite directions, jumping into the target through different windows.

Launching myself through the broken glass, I tucked into a roll. The masked operator turned in my direction. He most likely couldn't see me, but I saw he was holding an automatic weapon.

My combat knife was faster and my throw was accurate—into the base of his neck. When he dropped, I rushed to pick up the blade.

"Yes," growled the Beast, sending more adrenaline through my veins and eliminating everything but the mission from my mind.

My HUD told me the insertion story as the blue dots removed the red ones across the home. The final operator died by my hand with one shot to the face.

"No KIA," called Dex, confirming the team's vitals on my display.

Thank God.

We found Mr. Jones battered and wounded, tied to a chair and gagged.

A three-minute countdown began ticking on our display, alerting us how long we had to get back to the bikes.

"Scan hostiles," I commanded.

"On it," responded Liam as he rushed out of the room.

"We can't take him on the bikes," grumbled Dex as he opened his med kit to work on Mr. Jones.

"On it," Jenny answered and disappeared out of the house.

While everyone worked, I headed to another room and found one of the dead operators Liam had just scanned while he worked fast to grab the faces and prints of each of the operators.

I wasn't surprised to see a mid-thirties Chinese male face.

Liam looked up at me and paused. Even though his face was covered by the Flex, I got the message.

Yes. China. Everything changes.

The smoke began to dissipate across the overrun compound, the only sounds remaining were those of the fires spreading into the structures.

Dex and Hux carried Mr. Jones out of the house while Liam covered their rear. I led us to the large black pickup truck that Jenny had appropriated from the Cartel. As the boys set Mr. Jones in the back seat, the rest of us mounted all but one of the bikes.

Ten seconds. Just enough.

Adrenaline peaked and blood pounding in my ears, a pyre rose inside my soul—the rush of killing fresh on my hands and mind—as Alfa waited on my command.

"Let me hear you," commanded the Beast.

Not knowing how the Flex would react, I roared anyway, and the voice scrambler turned my growl into the sound of rolling thunder. Alfa roared back.

★ ★ ★

The burning compound disappeared in the distance as we sped toward the evac point in a wide ravine where Sarah would meet us.

"He doesn't have much time," whispered Dex when I arrived at the truck.

I removed the Flex and opened the side door to see Mr. Jones laid across the back seat, bleeding steadily from his abdominal wounds. Jenny helped to prop him up as I pulled myself into the seat next to him, the remnants of the battle dispelled from my body and mind as soon as I saw his face contract in pain.

"You, again. Amigo..." he greeted me weakly with a cough.

Certain he was dying, he quickly updated me in Spanish. He'd discovered the Cartel worked with the Chinese sometime after our last meeting.

"I don't know how many of them we got into your country, but we also got whole groups of poor migrants across..." Mr. Jones revealed the other smuggling operation done on behalf of the Chinese.

"Do you know why those were selected?" I asked, puzzled.

He coughed and shook his head. "We just moved them across and gave them to the revolucionarios."

Like fucking insurgents!

"I don't know what happened. But suddenly, they began to suspect everyone. People getting tortured and killed..." Mr. Jones depicted the abrupt change in the relationship between the Chinese and the Cartel when a leak was suspected.

"Something happened in California right before it started," he added.

Damn it. Jenny's CPC op.

Mr. Jones's vitals faded and Dex's face confirmed it.

"Anything else?" I pushed, knowing in my gut that the mission comes first.

He nodded weakly and told me in a little more than a whisper that he managed to get one word related to the revolutionaries. Something about "fellow travelers."

"Will you honor your word about my family?" asked Mr. Jones through the death rattle taking over.

"Alfa-leader, Romulus. Put me on speaker." Jack's command came through my earbud.

My dad told Mr. Jones, in Spanish as well, that the deal was already honored. The family had been picked up and transported to a safe location in the States.

"They will know no financial difficulties," promised my father over the speaker. "For the rest, I'm sorry."

Mr. Jones thanked him and looked back at me.

"I was a bad man until my eldest was born. My son changed me. I wanted to make amends and protect my family. Your people found me shortly afterward. Maybe I was wrong to believe I could do both at the same time..."

Angst spread through my chest, but Mr. Jones took one last breath and passed before I could interact with it.

The air changed and dust rose as Sarah landed the chopper nearby.

I closed Mr. Jones's eyes.

"We're taking him with us. His family deserves a grave to visit," I called into the group channel.

"He stood by his word all through the years. We even offered several times to end the mission and move him over," said Jack through my flight helmet comms. It was clear that Mr. Jones's death pained him and Custer.

Sarah flew us as close to the water as she could as the sun began to rise on our right and the Pacific Ocean remained still in the darkness to our left.

"The night is your friend." The training mantra swam through my mind as I stared into the cold, dark water, searching for more than a proper reply to my father.

"Why didn't he?" I wondered about the stranger who'd died in my care, his blood still on my pants.

"He still wanted to make amends..." sighed Jack.

Yeah. That one.

"I assume you saw it all live." I sensed the tiredness spreading through my body.

"Yes," he answered. "You haven't lost your touch, Alfa-leader."

Some part of me enjoyed his praise but it was just specks of dust, blown out in the next moment.

Like you trained me to do.

"The Chinese actions are acts of war. This is not the issue," said Custer, taking over the debrief. "The key point is the lack of hard evidence and the ability to prosecute the case openly."

"What about the 'fellow traveler' code name?" I pressed, hoping to get something from them.

"Soviet roots. Later becoming an accusation of being a commie in the '50s. What else?" asked Jack.

"Organizers..." I mused.

"We'll keep an eye," assured Custer before shifting to the elephant in the room. "Whether those were private or Chinese government forces, they're already within our borders, and now they will be more careful."

Jack promised to get the data scan results as soon as possible.

Fists clenched, I let my agitation rise just enough before I spoke, "We have to act before it's too late. The Chinese couldn't have done all of this without help from our side."

They need to see this.

They were both silent for a long moment.

"Daj will remain the sole DIR2 case, under limited authority," offered Jack, changing the direction again.

With CHAZ winding down, it was becoming harder to track Daj, but at least we had a little rope from command.

"By the way, Chad's been sharing some insights to help us better understand the Left's more radical wings..." Jack admitted to considering offering Chad some work, at some capacity, in Old Glory. "Who knows, he might end up helping us nab Daj."

He's mine first.

The sun had finally reached us, dispelling the last of the darkness as Jack and Custer talked and my mind drifted to the words spoken in his final moments.

Fellow Traveler.

When the idea struck, I bolted upright in my seat and interrupted, "I've been studying the riots quite a bit, creating an indicators list of the signs leading up to them. I'll revise it to include the Chinese special operation operators. Can I share it with the RCC?"

"Of course," said the General. "All right, go have yourselves a happy Fourth of July. I gotta run."

"Are you heading home?" asked Jack when Custer had exited the call.

"I am."

I smiled at the thought of surprising the family.

"Good. Happy Independence Day. It's the perfect holiday to remember why and for whom we fight."

"Happy Fourth, Dad."

I glanced at Sarah, who was immersed in her low flight north, almost surfing on the waves, and then back at the rest of Alfa who were laid out and snoring.

Taking a long deep breath, I closed my eyes and laid my head back against the seat, thoughts of my family transporting me to the back seat of the Cartel truck.

"Maybe I was wrong to believe I could do both at the same time..." Mr. Jones's final words collided with the echo of Shemtov's voice, "Here I am," threatening to spiral me into the abyss.

JULY FOURTH

– Santa Monica, CA –
Saturday, July 4, 2020

The sun was midday bright and the air was salty and crisp. I changed into jeans and a black t-shirt while Sarah refueled the chopper and Liam retrieved my motorcycle from the secured garage Old Glory rented from Santa Monica Airport.

"Did you catch some rest?" Sarah looked concerned.

"Why would you ask that?" I wondered, securing the Wraith into my concealed holster.

"You thrashed in your sleep a bit," she replied.

I shrugged, unwilling to admit what had returned to haunt me.

She wished me a good time with the family, as did the rest of the team.

The ride home was depressing. It wasn't just the closed businesses and neglect. There were zero symbols of freedom. I was used to the small number of American flags in this area, as it had been the case for the two decades, but this was different.

People here are ashamed of their country.

The thought struck me like a slap in the face for all who'd ever fought and sacrificed for our blessed nation.

Nico died for this!

My blood boiled and the Beast growled as I recalled Sarah's question and the memories that were harder to keep out while sleeping.

No. I'm heading home.

I used the *Sense* to push away the anger and clear my mind.

The black female agent pinged my smartphone from her spot under the tree by our complex's gate, and I gave the signal without slowing down.

Thank you, Eli.

Once inside the courtyard, my sour mood lifted the moment I saw the US and the USMC flags hanging from our second-floor balcony's rail.

The bike was barely parked when the front door swung open and my family clamored toward me. I lifted Ari with my right arm before pulling Dani and our little one into a family hug. Lil was stuck between us giggling.

"Did you like the flags, Daddy?" asked Ari, pushing his long hair from his eyes.

"I sure did. Thank you all."

I smiled at Dani, who beamed back.

"Tell him," Dani nodded and whispered to Ari, who blushed momentarily.

Looking up to get a better view of the flags, Ari's words hit me at the same moment my stomach turned with recognition, "They belonged to Uncle Nico. Tia Cel agreed..." His voice turned a bit uncertain as he observed my face the way only one's child can.

"You're the best son in the world." I squeezed him tighter, determined to save him from knowing that just under the pride I felt for him, my guilt pummeled me. "Now, what are we going to do together to celebrate Independence Day?"

Summers in Venice were a time to behold with throngs of visitors, colors, lights, and vendors selling art and beach memorabilia. But that wasn't the case anymore.

I pushed the stroller with the kids in it and Dani at my side. Luckily, the kids were happily oblivious to the boarded-up shops and posters calling for everyone to adhere to the Dragon measures.

When we reached the ocean, we saw quite a few people spread out across the miles of sandy beach.

"The police aren't enforcing this crap," grumbled Dani.

I nodded, thinking about how delicate the sacred covenant is—in a free society—between civic leaders and those in uniform.

Defund the police, right?

We went to our favorite spot right by the towering structure of the lifeguard headquarters, just off the jetty surf spot.

"Sorry about your friend."

The lifeguard captain was a pretty woman in her early thirties, brown hair pulled back in a bun, who'd come to speak with me when she saw us setting up on the sand. Venice is a tight community, and she knew me from the neighborhood.

I kept my eyes on Dani and the kids playing closer to the water as I replied, "Thank you. How's it been to serve these days?"

The captain looked around before whispering, "It's been hard. My staff isn't willing to enforce most of the shit coming down from city hall. It's insane! They want us to scoop up a lone swimmer but do nothing when protesters surround our station."

"Really? You?" I was surprised.

She shook her head and sighed.

"We wear the uniform, even if those are red bathing suits and trunks. So, they've lumped us with the police and even vandalized the station."

"Insane is the right word. I'm sorry it's happening to you and your staff. For what it's worth, *we* appreciate your service."

"It's worth a lot." She smiled. "Thank you for *your* service. Hope you and your family have a happy Fourth, Sir."

It was a great day, sitting with Dani, watching our kids play in the sand.

Ari was digging a hole about ten feet away, when Dani nudged me and pointed with her head up the beach. My eyes followed hers to a group of adults and some kids carrying picnic stuff. They were all masked, including the little ones.

I nodded at Dani, dismayed that we had reached such a sad state—that our separation grew and became visible.

"Folks are scared," I offered, thinking of the recent death and infection stats, as I watched them set up their chairs close to where Ari played.

Dani pushed against me with her shoulder.

"Nah. They lost their damn minds. I understand masking if done properly in close quarters and around vulnerable people. But this?" Her hand rose to gesture, but she caught herself in time and retracted it.

One of the big guys approached Ari and said something to him. It was impossible to understand what they said through the mask, but easy to see Ari's body recoil in distress.

I was out of my chair and at his side in moments.

"You can't play here if you don't have a mask..." The man's words reached me as I arrived. Ari turned to me, his sweet face confused, slight redness creeping around his face.

He's trying not to cry. This motherfucker.

"Behind me," I instructed Ari, reaching with my right hand to help him out of his hole while keeping my eyes on the big guy. Luckily, Ari didn't stage a rebellion.

"We're all doing our part. You should, too." The big guy's tone was condescending and accusatory.

A strange cocktail of rage and exhaustion coursed through me. It wasn't a physical sensation but a mental and emotional one.

Fucking little tyrants everywhere.

"Next time, consider finding the parents instead of scaring the little kids," I responded evenly.

"I can't fucking believe it!" He raised his voice and shook his hands in the air.

Behind him, I saw two other men from his group pointing and starting to move toward us.

Use the Sense. It's a distraction.

"Aren't you tired of this shit?" provoked the Beast.

"We're both breaking the law right now on the sand of a closed beach during a lockdown, so let's not be righteous. You have miles of open beach. Put some distance between us."

It wasn't the nicest thing to say, but it wasn't an invitation for violence either.

The big guy stammered something in his growing anger, "...you fuck!"

As his face reddened and he took one step toward me, his friends quickened their pace to join him.

Time stopped, and I heard Sarah's words, "You thrashed in your sleep a bit."

"You can't escape what happened to you..." the Beast said.

My body stiffened and my fists were up when I turned back to find Ari a few feet behind me.

"Run to Mom!" I commanded and returned my focus to the idiots.

If they were smart, they would have circled me. Instead, they came as a pack, flexing and hooting.

I remained quiet, the *Sense* slowing the events to a crawl.

Come on, you fucks!

A smaller hand touched my shoulder, ripping me out of the time-stop.

Danielle!

My body knew before my mind could interpret the physical sensation.

"Alley rhymes with Ali... Alley rhymes with Ali..." she whispered into my ear.

I was shocked by how Dani had managed to get to me unnoticed but not by the impact of her words. Some of the tension in my body released while I kept my eyes on the three guys, who kept up their aggression but didn't move closer. Their wives were also calling them to relax.

Both her hands were now on my shoulders, her body touching mine, as she whispered into my right ear, "Please stop."

The Beast howled and receded.

I took a deep breath, watching the guys look at each other as my body relaxed into a natural posture, arms down at my sides.

Glancing down at the hole Ari had dug, I pointed at it while I kept my eyes on his.

"You cross this, and you become a threat to my family. There's no going back or need for that. Walk away, and we'll keep to ourselves."

The big guy took a breath and nodded to his friends in agreement, and we walked back to our families.

Dani smiled up at me as we walked, but her face was strained. She extended her hand to take mine, and we both smiled at the sight of Ari standing in a protective stance over his little sister.

Little Warrior.

Assaulted by Ari's endless questions before we even made it back, Dani caught him with one of her mommy looks and stopped the questions with three words: "We'll talk later." Then, she gave me the wife look, motioning for me to wrap up our little camp to head home.

And you, My Queen.

The Ramirez family knew how to throw July Fourth parties, but this one was a dark shadow of the past. I watched Roberto grilling for our two families, noting the rage and exhaustion that tensed and slumped his shoulders. Paulina, Celeste, and Dani took care of everything else, absent of the playful banter and laughter that usually filled their collaborations. The kids appeared less affected as they played before dinner, and I'd zoned out at the table after finishing my meal.

We miss you, Brother.

"Nico used to love this governor from South Dakota who never locked down her people." Celeste's voice pulled my focus back to the conversation, as she shared Lynn's divergent approach to the pandemic and the recent wave of riots. "She's giving an address on TV from somewhere important. Want to see it?"

Paulina stayed in the yard with the kids while the rest of us followed Roberto into their home just in time for the event.

I smiled as the projectors illuminated the four presidents carved into the mountain's side and the stage that had countless US flags waving behind it. As Lynn approached the stage, I suppressed my laugh when I saw she'd opted for rancher jeans, a white blouse, and flowing hair under her favorite cowboy hat.

She really knows how to relate to the people.

"My fellow Americans and South Dakotans, Happy Fourth of July..." She started her address speaking about the difficulties our forefathers endured in creating the country before summarizing our history. "We have made great mistakes and done marvelous things. We atone for our past and aspire to do better now and in the future. We are all Americans, even now, through our nation's great pains."

Lynn's words reverberated through the living room, promising that we'd prevail against it all. When it was over, I looked around and saw the price that we'd all have to pay reflected back at me as Cel succumbed to deep sobs, Roberto shook his head and sunk deeper into his chair, and Dani became the comforter in the room.

"She was amazing..." Dani raved about Lynn while I pushed the stroller beside her.

I might as well...

I stopped the stroller and looked down at Ari, hoping he was not about to see his mom whoop his father.

"What?" she asked, looking up at me, eyebrows narrowing.

"Well," I started with a chuckle and decided I would be safer if we kept walking and talking. "I met Lynn when I was eighteen, right after my dad got us back from Israel, and our families are really close." I glanced at her and was relieved to see her more curious than anything else. "The bond started with my grandfather and hers—Ulysses and David—and has been passed down with each generation. Jack and her dad, Jerome, were raised as friends, and Lynn and I..." I summarized our brief romance. "And now, we're both continuing the legacies of our families in our own way. I'm proud of her and glad to see she's surrounded by good people—her husband and now my sister is working for her."

Dani took a moment to digest everything and then responded, "I'd like to meet her one day."

You're amazing.

"She feels the same way. When I was at the Ranch, she said she'd seen footage of my badass wife and hoped to meet you soon."

I paused to tug her closer and kissed her.

"Badass..." she repeated with a sly smirk before changing the subject. "Did you call Holden?"

I shook my head.

"Any chance we can open that relocation conversation again?" I wondered out loud after another minute of walking in silence.

"We only leave with you."

Her tone told me she would not budge, but I had to try anyway.

"What happens if I'm away when you need me?" I grumbled.

The recent beach incident with the big guys was in her eyes when she looked at me and probably mine as well.

"We... I've never seen you like this..." said Dani quietly, turning to face me.

My stomach caught fire, and I wanted to lash out in frustration.

What the hell did you want me to do?

She must have read my face and said the exact words I needed to hear, as she always did,

"You did the right thing. You stood by your boy. But I have never seen you like that..." Dani repeated her words, but this time, they carried another meaning altogether.

I used the *Sense* to keep the indignation from taking control of my exhausted mind and started walking again.

"Where did you learn those words? About the alley..."

She sighed and looked aside for one moment as she stayed in step with me.

"From your nightmares, Baby."

Feeling exposed, I asked the question that needed not be asked, "When did it start?"

"When he died," she offered quietly.

We reached the stop sign just a few blocks from our gate.

"Every time, you eventually get to the part when you say those words. Repeating them again and again. Then relax back to deep sleep."

I pushed the stroller into the street, processing her admission.

"I never planned on saying anything. It just came out of me when I saw you like..."

We stopped again, eliciting grumbles from Ari about the constant stops. I turned her to face me again and held her face with both hands, so I could drown in her baby blues.

She's the only one...

"*Who could stop you...*" came the faint guttural voice.

"I never thought I'd go back to fighting..." I stopped, unable to finish my confession.

"Stupid Husband. Just kiss me," she commanded.

And I was saved again.

LIMITED APPROVAL

When we woke from a night full of fireworks, Dani and I saw maddening reports of destruction. The riots didn't care about Independence Day or the day after.

After breakfast, we played with the kids. She looked up each time I checked my phone, betraying her concern about how long they would have me around.

Am I really here?

The urge to return to the fight grew larger by the minute, and she knew it.

Eventually, Dani saw something on her social media and forwarded me the post. It was a "call to action" from Comrades in Portland, asking people to gather by a federal court.

Shit.

I shared it with the RCC and slid my phone into my pocket.

"Let's go to the park!" I cheered, scooping the kids into my arms.

We had fun, but I kept my eyes on the sun passing through the sky.

They come out at night.

We got home before dark, and I turned on the TV while Dani got Ari into the tub and Lil stayed on the floor next to me and played.

The Mark O. Hatfield United States Federal Courthouse in Downtown Portland was under siege. The majestic building, towering above most others with its sixteen stories and engraved with the words of liberty, was now surrounded by hundreds of rioters. Only a thin ring of federal police officers in riot gear separated them from the building itself.

Fast little tyrants!

Dani joined me and her jaw clenched, her eyes occasionally finding mine as the chyrons reported.

The news cut to an interview with a Customs and Border Protection commissioner-deputy—a tough-looking woman in her fifties.

"Where's the mayor? Where are the cops? Why is nobody coming to help?" she raged at the reporter about the total no-show of the local government, leaving the court to fend for itself.

"Is this happening?" asked Dani, pulling my right arm around her.

Before I could answer, the ear vibration began.

Of course.

Tension rose in my spine.

"I need to make a call, Baby."

She nodded without pushing for an answer to her question.

Because she just got it...

★　★　★

"Your indicators list was spot-on," said Jack, referring to the notes I'd sent the RCC after Mr. Jones died. "We don't know much, but enough to consider Portland a 'mega-event.' It could spill to other locations."

I was down in my studio, pacing.

"Do we know anything about the leadership?"

"Nothing on the Chinese front, but we did get a ping on the 'Traveler.'"

Hearing the usual sirens outside the complex, I used the *Sense* to dim out all distractions from Jack's voice when he mentioned the RCC had intercepted some comms suggesting a "Traveler" in Portland helping with the "court."

I froze.

"Is it Daj?"

"Possibly," answered my father after a quick pause. "Both Comrades and Ryse are heavily coordinated on this court action, and we know the mayor and governor both held off any locals from helping. And of course, they're supported by their city council and progressive DA."

Cowards!

"Any indications on time frames for this?" I asked.

"All data suggests that whoever is planning this is going for a long nightly siege on the feds. Looks like they want to make this place the next Chicago if they can," he sighed.

The hunger rushed from my belly into my chest but was controlled by the *Sense*. My commanders made decisions, and mine was to listen and execute.

"You leave at zero-five hundred," he started.

About time.

Jack ordered Alfa to Portland under the guise of Old Glory surveillance training with the Department of Homeland Security. It was easy to arrange, as they had been providing training to various law enforcement bodies for decades.

"Your DHS contact is Agent Shida Saam. She's the one who requested Old Glory to help with surveillance around the court. She's a good woman," he added and then stopped himself from saying more.

"Your ROE is strict 'self-defense,' The Traveler is your only DIR2 approval."

I took a breath to quiet my frustration.

"Chad will be ready to help ID Daj if you find him," he offered in a warmer tone before continuing.

We were tasked with insertion into the crowds to provide intel for Shida about dangerous threats for the court and its defenders. Tracking the "Traveler" was our parallel mission.

Turning on the TV, I muted it, seeing that fireworks had already been thrown at the court. There was so much smoke, it was hard to see what was going on.

Fuck.

"Ken's undercover there. He's been sending some damning footage. He was even attacked one time but managed to escape. Keep an eye out. You might cross paths with him."

I acknowledged it, somewhat distracted.

"You should start preparing your family for longer deployments," he said toward the end of our chat.

My heart ached as his words reached my ears, but he was right. And I knew it.

"Will do," I replied, feeling wholly torn between my two lives.

DOWNTOWN SIGHTS

The blazing afternoon sun greeted us as Jenny drove the black van through Downtown Portland. We all looked somberly out our tinted windows at the city self-destructing before our eyes. Streets filled with homelessness and neglect. Boarded-up businesses, many with those cowardly signs, showing support to those who loot at night.

White flag.

I shook my head from the front passenger seat.

The last few days had been filled with prepping for undercover deployment, and it was time to execute our mission. The dashboard screen led us into an alley just behind a motorcycle repair shop with a high chain-link fence. When the gate slid opened, Jenny slowly rolled us into the lot where two Old Glory guards dressed as mechanics acknowledged us on comms but kept their distance.

The repair shop was a two-story concrete building with giant garage doors. Jenny navigated to the leftmost door that immediately rolled up, revealing bikes of all kinds and in all conditions. We retrieved our duffel bags quietly and followed Dex, who led us to a concealed entrance and staircase that took us into a basement level.

The door hissed, and the neon lights flickered on across the high ceiling. I'd never been to this forward base, but it was just like the other installations. Metal frame bunk beds on one side and arsenal and shelves of accessories on the other. A command room at the back, by the restroom and showers.

The team spread out, bantering on about who got to take a dump first, while my mind churned on the masterminds behind all this.

Romulus and Remus.

I thought about my father and Custer's choices of callsigns.

"How fitting," I muttered quietly.

The outside camera confirmed the sun had set. I looked at my team, all but Dex hooded, masked, and dressed in black.

"Hux, Jenny, you're team one. Sarah and Liam, you're team two. Dex remains in command and backup."

They remained quiet, but we all saw the elephant in the room.

"We're on US soil, and the danger in Mission Creep is valid. So, stick to the objectives, and Dex will handle any data transfers to DHS. That's it."

They nodded, but nobody moved.

What now?

"No backup, Alfa-leader?" wondered Hux in his deep rumbling voice.

Dipshit, who was your demon during Hell Year?

It was hard to keep the smile from rising as I shook my head.

"You start the fun without me. I'll go and see about that DHS agent contact."

Our safe house was about a ten-minute walk from the courthouse. Like the rest of the team, I had the light-deployment setup: Wraith, combat blade, and an assortment of non-lethal accessories. We had been authorized to have the Flex folded and ready, but it was only to be used if conditions required.

The street was dark, dirty pavement and tall apartment buildings towering on both sides, and the traffic was moving toward the court.

Where are your parents? I wondered at the groups of hollering younger crowds.

A shuttered corner grill restaurant came to view, and I saw someone standing by the overflowing dumpsters behind it. When I got close enough, I saw the tall, slender woman wore dark pants, a jacket, and a dark Muslim hijab head cover, extended across her face. Only her eyes were showing.

When I pinged the DHS agent on my device, she reached for her phone and then looked up at me. Giving a slight nod, she walked behind the dumpsters.

According to the file I'd been sent, the DHS agent was in her forties, but the olive-skinned woman that stood before me seemed far younger, her striking brown eyes and hair shining brightly in the night. As she removed the face cover, there was instant familiarity and warmth in my heart. She reminded me of Dani in her beauty and grounded presence.

I dropped my mask and pulled down my hood.

Jack had surprised me before the mission when he'd instructed, "Show her your face. We can trust her."

"Tanner Washington." I extended my hand to shake hers.

She smiled and shook my hand firmly as she reciprocated, "Shida Saam, DHS."

The agent didn't waste a moment in voicing her needs.

"We're experiencing more and more cases of sophisticated attacks on our officers…" She described the fireworks mortars, high laser beams, smoke, and even Molotov bottles that we'd only briefly seen on the news. "Whatever footage you can get would help us understand what's happening around us, so we can better protect the courthouse." Her brow was furrowed in anger. "It's maddening that it's happening, but this is the mission."

"What the hell is going on?" I asked as an eerie déjà vu sensation spun down my spine.

"Let's go fuck 'em up! Remember Chicago!" a male screamed, eliciting cheers from across the intersection.

"The election..." Shida sighed. "It makes no sense, and *I'm* a Democrat. Tanner, nobody is coming. We were even advised to abandon the courthouse so the streets would inflame further."

My blood boiled at this blatant betrayal by the local government.

The fucking election. Cowards!

"Have you heard about OBI—the Open Borders Initiative?" she probed.

I kept quiet so no lie would be needed. She smirked in return and confirmed the same data that Jack and Custer had relayed.

"They funded the DA, and she refuses to enforce the law. It doesn't matter how the evidence is presented. It's happening in any city with these district attorneys that OBI has financed."

Yeah. Like that motherfucker DA in LA.

We heard more and more people passing through, hooting and hollering about their destination—the courthouse.

She wrinkled her nose in visible disdain.

"The media is covering all of this. We're presented as the 'stormtroopers' while rioters who blind cops with lasers are not even charged if caught."

"Who leads it on the ground?"

"All of them," Shida grunted. "Portland has a long history of Ryse activity. Comrades also joined, and now I'm hearing about this other group, 'Western Jihad.' This is before you factor in all the criminals and gangs taking advantage of the lawlessness."

Unfucking believable.

I shook my head in disgust before I responded, "The team is already embedded as of tonight. We'll provide the goods, and you keep me updated on anything new."

I pulled my hood up, thinking our conversation was over.

"I've worked with Old Glory many times and have much respect for your father."

"When did you meet him?" I wondered, holding off on the mask.

She smiled warmly.

"It's been over a decade." Shida took a deep breath and adjusted the hijab on her face. "Be safe out there."

"Inshallah," I replied with the Arabic "God willing" prayer.

"Inshallah," Shida whispered back and left with me behind her.

LONG MAY SHE WAVE

Morning maintenance crews worked hard to clean the grounds surrounding the Mark O. Hatfield United States Courthouse. Discarded signs, broken bottles, and fresh graffiti were just the tip of the iceberg.

I sat on the sidewalk, watching this morning ritual, disguised as a drifter. It was my favorite go-to, allowing me to sit idly, close to the target, without being approached.

It had been almost two weeks since we'd started this deployment, going out nightly, melding into the shouting crowds, providing DHS with a better picture of their nightly siege. Our work helped the feds thwart some dangerous attacks, but we had found no trace of the "Traveler."

Alfa was already back at the base in their bunkbeds, snoring, but I hung back to see it all in daylight.

Some lady dressed in a business suit passed by me, smiled, and dropped a $5 bill by my feet before continuing into the court-barricaded entrance. The powers that be had decided to move the regular security checkpoints outside the building, complete with a federal police officer.

Standing up, I stared at the massive structure a few more moments, warmth filling my chest in the cool morning air. It gave me hope that this symbol of our national resolve remained open, even though it was attacked every evening.

"How's working with Shida?" asked Jack.

The small desk's digital clock told me it was almost 5 p.m. We'd all gotten some good rest and were getting ready to go back out when he called.

"She's effective and clear." I stretched my neck, moving the stiffness out of my body. "How do you know her anyway?"

Despite a short chuckle, his voice remained severe.

"That's a tale for another time. What I can tell you now is that her family escaped Persia as the ayatollahs took over in the revolution and turned it into Iran, and she chose the hard route of joining DHS shortly after 9/11. Not an easy decision back then or now." Jack paused. "She is a good, freedom-loving, strong woman..." His tone revealed his affinity for her and what she brought to missions. "Like that one you have at home."

"Yeah, I thought the same thing when I met her." I was smiling, even though talking about her only magnified the ache.

"What's your analysis thus far?" Jack brought us back to a more serious note.

I pointed out the similarities I had seen between Los Angeles to Seattle and Portland.

"They effectively create an AZ around the court every night!" The "autonomous zone" acronym had become a general slang term among the rioters and those who countered them. "Every night, their tactics become better, more organized, and bolstered while no local government comes to help the court and feds."

"What else?" he asked as I watched Liam trying to punk Hux and getting slammed on the floor in response.

They gotta get some action once in a while, right?

"The Dragon Skulls seem to be painted for multiple purposes. Sometimes as stage areas and other times for swarming a target. They do it during the daytime before the mobs converge." I put my Wraith on the desk for cleanup and oiling.

"What else?" he probed.

My irritation grew, and I stopped breaking down the Wraith.

"The media drives me nuts. We're there every night and see what they're doing—the fireworks bombs, frozen bottle projectiles, mortars, and lasers. Those poor cops are being assaulted, abused, and even blinded! And the media cover for it, with Democrats egging them on!" I raged against the rioters' impunity in harassing ordinary people on the streets, in the restaurants, surrounding their cars. "They're making people raise their fists and photograph it for social media. It's insane!"

"It has been..." Jack sighed, "challenging for the feds to work without state support. Same situation wherever the Dems control the levers of power, even at the highest levels of government unfortunately."

Deep State...

"Any word on Baker?" I asked, noticing the increasing agitation in my body.

"Nothing about the riots. He's probably heavily invested in the Grayson campaign."

His words hung until I broke the silence. "Stone is pretty much boxed in on both the pandemic and the protests."

"Maybe so," he replied. "But... he's not the first president to face world-changing adversity funneled into a political attack by the opposition at home."

His explanation was reasonable, even logical, but his immediate dismissal of the subject irked me.

Really? Just normal opposition... Sure, Dad.

He switched the subject.

"The scans came back. MSS."

Damn.

Stiffness and agitation were immediately replaced with a chilling sensation in my spine. The infamous Chinese Ministry of State Security had many branches dedicated to preserving the Communist Party and its hold on the country. But for us, it was also personal.

"Same fuckers as Market?" I asked.

"Yes," replied Jack.

"Still commanded by Zhang?"

"Still," he responded. "It has been hard to get intel on him."

The sensation erupted into rage at the insanity of the moment.

"They're waging a destabilization operation. We must do something."

"We need something strong, Tanner." He was frustrated. "It has to be hard proof that, if exposed, would survive the Deep State and their efforts to squash it."

The only ray of light was that the Chinese involvement had forced Romulus and Remus to shift their attention to US soil, which I supported.

"Your Portland operation is proving valuable. Maybe Alfa-three will find that Traveler after all," said Jack.

Moss had come into town just a few days ago with his Comrade buddies. It was good to know he was close, even if we hadn't seen him. But my dad was really only reminding me that the mission comes first.

"Maybe."

"Fucking MSS," grumbled Hux.

"Market," Dex sighed.

The rest looked around each other, digesting the news.

Yes. MSS in our own fucking home.

We were seated around the kitchen for briefing before heading back to the courthouse.

I scrutinized them all, internalizing the implications of our haunted past as it crossed each of their faces, until I got to Jenny.

The team knew that Jenny had lost her mom while escaping China, but I was the only one who knew it was the MSS who'd tortured her to death. When I saw it in her personal files, it was one of the reasons I picked her for the Rogue course.

They did your mom really bad, Jen. We both have accounts to settle.

She looked up at me, and I gave her a slight nod.

"Listen up," I clapped and got their attention. "Our mission remains the same. We go out, looking for DHS targets, and keep our eyes out for the Traveler."

"So that cute DHS agent gives us brownies," quipped Liam, looking insulted. But nobody laughed.

"Focus up! It's all up to us, Alfa. We need to find more and fast. We need to get that Traveler. It's the only way to get some… free rein."

This implication brightened all their faces, except for Dex's.

I can't fool you. Yes. I want that fucker to myself too.

"Fuck the police!" screamed the masked, blue-haired woman beside me who couldn't have been more than twenty years old. Hundreds more joined the chorus. Once again, I thanked the virus for creating such a convenient environment for blending.

The team was spread around the courthouse, forced to do nothing about 99 percent of the attacks against the officers. Feds sealed within the property occasionally sent officers in riot gear to squash a fire or to prevent the rioters from breaking the fence.

Thousands upon thousands of people squeezed together, some masked and others not. They used a ring of "human shields," usually women carrying peaceful signs and wearing bright shirts. Behind them, the real assholes kept lobbing rocks, fireworks, and the occasional Molotov bottles.

Where are all of the Dragon measures now? Social distancing? Lockdown? Hypocrites! I used the *Sense* to manage my never-ending visceral reactions to the constant rush of insanity.

We kept informing DHS about attacks, but there were too many of them. Some Alfa members grumbled on the private channel about being "chained," wishing they could do more. I allowed the banter, as it was valid, and it helped them release some steam. Besides, Dex, who stayed back, kept everyone in order.

"Alfa-leader, RCC, over," came a female voice in my earbud.

I pinged them back twice, tapping my earbud as I took a few steps back from the front rows of rioters.

The RCC woman reported a black male carrying a US flag and being surrounded. "Be advised. The live-stream is coming from Ken Lim's personal social media account. It could be him filming it." She pinged the man with the flag on my map app.

No orders?

I waited a moment.

He's testing me!

The Beast lurked, but no words were offered.

Fuck that!

I whispered my order to Dex to prevent further debate.

I passed through the yelling crowds like a blurred wisp. It wasn't hard to find the man surrounded by screaming baby tyrants.

The medium-size black man was probably in his thirties, wide-shouldered, and bearded. Holding a wooden pole with the US flag on it, he stood tall and said nothing as the rioters yelled at him to "remove the fascist piece of shit flag" and "mask up!"

Scanning the circle, I realized the screamers were normal rioters, except for the one black-clad goon with the Ryse white lightning on his mask. He was agitating the crowd to push on the black man with the flag and was visibly frustrated that no one did more than yell.

I started moving when I saw him pull out a blade and hold it close to his pants and out of sight.

I see you, Motherfucker.

"Then do something," rumbled the Beast.

When he stepped into the ring and then toward the man with the flag, I rushed forward, knocking two screamers into the empty circle. Rioters yelled, and the Ryse goon turned in time to see me enter. He lifted his blade to strike, but I ran and sent the knife clattering on the concrete.

He didn't have a chance to regroup before I kicked him, breaking his right kneecap. Collapsing to the cement, he howled in pain. One more kick crushed his right hand.

The prickling sensation on the back of my neck alerted me to a threat. I turned to see another Ryse fighter tackled and kicked in the face by Liam. The small Alfa fighter quickly melded back among the screaming crowd and disappeared.

The whole takedown took less than ten seconds, and everyone watching was shocked. The man with the flag nodded at me before he departed. Turning back to the courthouse, I saw another small guy masked, his Asian eyes fixed on me. He nodded and quickly vanished into the crowds.

Ken?

I rushed out of the space and back among the throngs of rioters, who kept advancing.

Only when I was back in the crowd did I realize that Alfa had been around me the whole time. I pushed down the nagging thought as I moved back into the fray, *Where am I leading them?*

It was close to 1 a.m. when Shida called for help about the advanced high-grade lasers being used to blind the federal officers protecting the court. I looked up at the nearby building and saw the green beams targeting them.

"What are you asking me to do, Shida?" I whispered.

"Whatever Jack allows you…" she responded and then had to hurriedly end our call, as she was among the defenders herself.

Romulus surprised me and gave us a limited DIR2 authorization to catch whoever was doing it.

"And then?" I asked him, blood boiling and body aching to act.

"We'll see when you get there," he responded flatly.

Dex plotted our path to the tall office building right across the street from the courthouse. When Alfa converged on the building, we were separated but aware of each other's hidden location.

The rioters must have broken the plywood that held the doors shut, as they had black-clothed masked guards roaming near the opening.

Glancing up, I saw the lasers taking down the feds from the third or fourth level of the building more clearly. Adrenaline spiked and my right hand instinctively moved to the Wraith concealed on my side.

Damn it! I retracted my hand back, sensing the Beast's desire for mayhem.

Using the *Sense* to focus, I gave Alfa my orders and they pinged back as I pulled down my hood and removed the Flex from my cargo pants pocket.

"Protract." My face was immediately encased within the Flex.

"Alfa-four, now!"

A second later, a smoke grenade exploded among the guards.

Thanks, Jenny.

We rushed into the smoke, using the Flex to find the coughing guards and knock them senseless with a few punches and kicks.

"Go... go... go!" I roared, leading the rush into the dark building.

Without the Eye tasked to help us, we had to check both the third and fourth levels. Hux was the first to find the laser overwatch nest, but whoever operated it had long been gone.

Shida called to thank me while Hux and Liam stomped the lasers to pieces.

"You bet," I replied, noticing my frustration peaking.

They were here!

We arrived at our safe house as the first rays of light began to push on the darkness. Once inside the machine shop, I hung back.

"You guys go ahead," I told them.

As my tired team ambled into the underground FOB, I stayed topside and pulled out my phone.

"Are you okay, Baby?" asked Dani.

Last night's sights haunted my memory, fueling my fear for my family, but I did my best to deflect her worries and promised to call again soon.

I've got to sleep.

Jack reached out once I was downstairs by my desk and most of Alfa was dead asleep in their beds. He sent me a link to Ken's social media feed with the video clip of the incident.

"I'm starting to like this kid."

The man with the flag was a Marine named Ishmael Harris. He'd done two tours in Afghanistan before returning to live in his hometown Portland. Ken had covered Ishmael's lone flag protest, but he didn't mention anything about our "intervention."

My dad was justifiably impressed with Ken, but my mind was still on Ishmael and his bravery.

Another free man. Like Todd and...

It was time to sleep when the RCC forwarded me an update on my "points of interest" list.

The article was about the World Forum on the "Great Reset," which Pax Eden hosted. I recalled Jack's briefing on this multi-billion entity that financed left causes and politicians nationwide.

Pax Eden's CEO was a woman named Claudia Kruger. She was quoted extensively when it came to re-imagining the world economy because of the Dragon and the lockdowns.

"We need to take advantage of this point in history..."

My blood raged in response.

First, destroy the world. Second, take advantage of the situation, in the name of socialist utopia. Fuck that!

As I closed my eyes and used the *Sense* to calm my system enough to rest, my mind's racing slowed. In the silence, just before drifting into sleep, I recalled another detail from Columbo's open letter. That anonymous post had warned of this exact thing—a new world order labeled as "The Great Reset"—and Jack's odd response when I'd brought it up still unsettled me.

You acted the same way about the Chicago incident. What are you not telling me?

GRINDING PAIN

The sun was setting behind the buildings, its last rays making it challenging to see the Hatfield Courthouse in Downtown's landscape. Huxley and I were lying on the carpet, looking out the window of the three-story office building. His advanced thermal binoculars were positioned on a tripod in front of him.

"Weird not having my gun," he grumbled, eyes scanning from our high perch.

After the high-grade laser fiasco a few nights earlier, RCC had approved an overwatch nest minus the sniper rifle. It wasn't hard to find an abandoned office, as most employees operated from home during the lockdown.

For their safety, of course.

"I know," I commiserated, silently reflecting on my impulse to use the Wraith when we stormed the building.

Hux turned his face toward me, eyes wide and red.

"I'm watching them every single night—destroying, attacking, and burning. They say it's their right, but I don't recall any of that being in the Constitution." He shook his head and returned to the binoculars as he murmured, "I just don't get this hate for your own country."

His bewilderment saddened me. Like all of my Rogues, Huxley didn't grow up in the States. He hailed from Norway, where his father, a US Army Colonel, was deployed for almost twenty years. I had never understood why Jack and Custer recruited Americans raised abroad, but I was beginning to see their wisdom.

Kids raised here don't know how good this country is.

"How's your sister doing?" I asked, hoping to switch the subject.

Huxley's twin sister had been diagnosed with the Dragon earlier that week, and the big guy had a rough day until he was certain she was handling it well.

He lowered his face from the binoculars to say a quick prayer in Norwegian, and I smiled even though the only word I understood was "Jesus." When he was finished, he turned to me with a tight smile.

"She's okay. Luckily, they live in the Tennessee countryside, and folks there aren't afraid if you got the Dragon. Just keep your distance until you heal." His handsome face contorted. "It didn't get my sister, but it got many others. Dex's father. We owe them a payback for that, for anyone who had a hand in this!"

Yes, we do. I nodded.

Hux returned to watching the courthouse and pointed to the "human shield" assembling. Through my small, folded binoculars, I saw the women dressed in bright-colored shirts beginning to form a ring with signs in front of the court.

The show begins...

Seeing the naive women willingly setting themselves up to provide cover for the upcoming nightly violence sparked the anger lying dormant in my chest. I couldn't understand this tactic that had originated in the Middle East, and the atrocities I'd witnessed when we lived there and later during my deployments with the Marines.

"Have you seen any symbols or flags of that Islamic group, Western Jihad?" I asked.

I'd requested data from the RCC after Shida had mentioned them, and we'd found their insignia of a crescent moon pierced by a curved scimitar sword on a green backdrop. The RCC had confirmed that Shida was correct that the Islamic group was somehow involved in the events here.

It may be the land of tyrants and endless wars, but it's also the birthplace of civilization and two of the strongest women I know.

Hux shook his head and promised to keep an eye out for it.

We watched as darkness enfolded from above and the riots erupted below. Removed from the screaming and violence, it was even more obvious that the whole thing was coordinated and organized. Hux pointed out a few times when it was clear that orders were given to the human shield that moved in unison to protect a bunch of rioters who advanced to throw fireworks at the feds.

"Their leaders are probably in a building nearby watching from above," he murmured.

Knowing Hux was right, the tension in my spine began to build as I scanned the other tall buildings around us.

"Look. Right there by the fence. The vet with the flag again," he called out.

I zoomed in and saw the black vet standing tall and quiet. Ishmael Harris hadn't shown up again since the night we had intervened to protect him. This time, he was smarter, placing his back against the fence the feds had erected around the court.

"Do we know *why* he's doing this?" Hux was dumbfounded.

"No. He has no political affiliation, either. He's fed up with the riots and decided to do more than just post about it." My words dragged pain into my body.

"Why are we fixated on him, Sir?"

It was a valid question. I'd instructed Alfa to keep an eye on the Marine vet and protect him if needed, and Jack had approved my "mission creep" with a warning, "You won't be able to save them all, Son."

"Oh shit... I'm sorry," apologized Hux as the answer struck him in my silence. "I wasn't thinking."

When my fist hit his shoulder, he stared at me.

"Stop it, Hux. You did nothing wrong. Ishmael does remind me of Nico and others who stand up for the right thing—for this country."

He smiled, and we both looked down again in time to see some protesters beginning to hassle Ishmael. With the federal officers close to him, on the other side of the fence, he was safe for the moment.

"You're envious of him, aren't you? His freedom to act," mused the Beast.

The guilt in my chest seemed to increase in weight with the accusation.

I fucked up everything. Market 'til now.

"And yet, you remain afraid and shackled," challenged the Beast.

I can't lose them!

"How come we got approval to protect him?" wondered Hux.

Fortunately, his question quieted the intense internal whipping.

"Romulus thinks Ken Lim will be nearby."

We'd received Ken's photo, so we would be able to identify him.

I wonder if that was him, I thought as I recalled the small masked Asian man who nodded at me when I first protected Ishmael.

"Where to?" he asked when I rose to stand.

"Got a date," I responded, proving that Liam's jokes about Shida had stuck.

Hux's laugh sounded like thunder breaking against a mountain as I walked to the door.

We walked along the boardwalk park, the darkened Willamette River reflecting the city's regular evening light display. Shida's face was covered with her hijab, and I was hooded and masked.

"The 'human shield' tactic they're using. It's familiar to me." I paused. "You told me Western Jihad might be involved here in town. What do you know about them?"

"Ah yes. A US-based group that sprung first from some radical left chapter at Berkeley and then other universities. They're known to support the Hamas and Hezbollah terror groups, but we've never caught them doing actual violence," explained Shida. "If your insinuation is right..." She left the words hanging between us.

"Did you see the mayor and the police chief bending their knee in front of city hall?"

"They're a disgrace. They do that while our officers are under attack, just a few blocks away." Her tone resonated with the disgust rumbling in my belly. "And don't start me on the brainwashed kids attacking the court. I still remember my parent's stories of how the mullahs fooled the students into thinking that bringing down the Shah would usher in a new age for Persia. Same bullshit." Those last words were shoved through gritted teeth.

I like her.

"How're the other agencies?" I kept the question vague, uncertain about how knowledgeable she was.

She laughed lightly through her hijab.

"I used to think that Deep State was something mentioned in movies to make us believe in conspiracies. And of course, when I trained to become an agent, we were told that disgruntled conservatives conceived the term, especially during the Charlton administration. It was easy to believe it for a very long time."

"And now?"

Shida stopped and turned to the rail, staring at the broad river that cut Portland in two.

"I can't escape the feeling that there's a coordinated effort to remove the president," she whispered. "And I say that as someone who also voted against him and has disliked him. I cannot believe this would be enough reason to allow this madness to happen."

The fucking election again.

Some joggers dressed in fashionable gear ran by us, huffing and puffing in masks.

We've lost our minds.

I swear she rolled her eyes at the joggers before continuing, "I've spoken with a lot of cops here in town. They're furious they're not allowed to help us. Truly forsaken. Morale is gone, and many are filing for early retirement or quitting." Her grip on the rail tightened. "Some cops are even doxed with those scumbags coming to their homes and their kids' schools."

I grimaced at the new cowardly "doxing" tactic. Posting people's private addresses and other personal information, leading assholes to harass their targets in places they should feel safe.

"If this," Shida pointed toward where the riots blazed just a few blocks away, "catches nationwide, we're screwed. And I'm not just talking about the riots. I'm talking about the Dragon measures and everything else being shoved down our throats in its name."

We were quiet for a long moment, individually digesting the sad state of our nation.

"We need more Ishmael's..." I told her about the Marine and his brave stand in an effort to bring some light into the darkness.

"Are you protecting him?" she asked, hand raised to remove her hijab but retracting back.

I nodded but offered nothing else, noticing the tension returning to my body.

"Because of your friend, Nicolas?" Her soft voice tread carefully. "I remember you from the funeral. It was everywhere on the news."

I dropped my head and closed my eyes against the horrors I'd seen a thousand times already.

"I know that you're not supposed to be here. You're an active Marine Colonel, not an Old Glory employee," she added quietly.

Her words reminded me of some of the questions that lingered unanswered: Why did Ken place himself by the vet? Did he make the connection about me like Shida had? Was he stalking me?

I turned to look at her, recalling how Holden had suspected me since Nico died.

There's something different about her, but can I trust it?

Maybe she understood my silence, or maybe it was something else. Regardless, her words conveyed her position, even if through a riddle.

"You took care of those lasers and have saved our asses many times over the last few weeks. I'm not talking to you now as a cop, but a friend." She smirked. "Your father taught me the need for acting in the shadow."

I'm going to take my chances.

"It is about Nico," I responded, leaving no room for further questions.

She quieted down, looking at me for a moment.

"How did you meet my father?" I asked, recalling Jack's deflection on the matter.

Shida removed the hijab enough to reveal a mischievous smile.

"Let's do that when we both have the time for confessions."

Moss was seated in the kitchen, surrounded by Alfa, bantering away when I arrived. But they all quieted down when they noticed me in the doorway. Dressed like a Comrade dickwad, with the red soviet symbol on his black shirt, Moss stood up with a full white grin plastered across his boyish black face.

"I don't know whether to hit you or hug you." I mocked a grumble and returned his embrace. "It's good to see you, Brother."

We all sat so Moss could detail his undercover work inside Comrades.

"They *believe* their shit. We're talking about pure Marxist philosophies, adjusted to our times..." He told us Comrades had a concealed headquarters near the court in some closed and boarded retail shop. "They just broke in and took over. No fear of the police."

"Were you able to locate him?" I asked, fully aware of how my question brought everyone to standstill attention.

"I think so." Moss nodded. "He's always masked, and I'm not close enough to the plate to speak with him. But I think he's in town."

My heart rate sped up.

"How about the MSS operators?"

He shook his head as he explained, "Everyone is masked and disguised. No way to know. But there are Ryse fighters from Los Angeles."

I had to use the *Sense* to calm my vitals as Moss described the joint coordination to attack the court on July 29th.

Six days! Will the Demon be among them?

After glancing at his watch, Moss told us he had to go. The team took turns embracing him, and Dex took an extra moment to hold his face like a father would and warn him not to do anything stupid.

He's a good leader, I thought, seeing how naturally Dex cared for everyone. *Me included.*

"I'll be in command," I said as soon as Moss left. "You go to the court, and I'll join once I'm done."

They all looked back at me, anxious to know their next order.

"I'm requesting to let Alfa handle the raid." My tone was firm as I addressed Romulus and Remus.

"Absolutely not," answered Jack, explaining that beyond the DIR2 limitations, there were too many other risks. "This is US soil we're talking about. What would you do if cops surrounded you? This is right by the court!"

Custer interjected, "Give the details to Shida and get the feds to raid the place."

"What about the MSS? If they're there, it could be a bloodbath like Calexico," I responded. "What if it gets leaked out? What if they catch Daj but can't get anything out of him?" Pissed, I pushed harder. "Ryse came all the way from LA. They have a greater plan. We need to know what's going on."

"Valid points, Alfa-leader," agreed Custer.
But??

"You're getting personally involved. Maybe it's because of that Marine with the flag. Maybe something else. But you need to cool down and think straight. We're not about to sanction an all-out war against American citizens. They deserve court of law and whatever punishment it determines if they are found guilty."

I took a deep breath.

"Yes, Sir. I'll pass the details to Shida."

"Very well. We'll talk soon," replied Custer before he left the line.

"You're right about this being an organized effort. Chad is definitely giving us good insight into it..." Jack explained that my brother, now officially hired into Old Glory, had been helpful in analyzing various cases and providing valuable input for how the Left thinks and organizes. "He's driven to help, but he's still haunted," he added, noting how his friend's murder in Seattle had torn him up and his fears of returning to his old place to pick up his stuff.

Little brother waking up to reality. It sucks to wake up, and he really has no idea just how awful reality is.

"Okay..." agreed Shida on the secured line when I'd finished briefing her on the upcoming attack, the Comrade headquarters location, and my interest in Daj Morris.

"If you come across the Ryse fighters from LA, I'd like to know," I added without clarification.

"Anything else?" she asked.

Images from Calexico returned to my mind.

"Shida, there could be trained foreign military operators involved."

"Are you serious?" She sounded stunned. It took her a moment, but she regrouped and said she'd do her best to arrange the raid. "I'll make sure you can see what's going on, so you can tell me if those people you're looking for are there."

"Thank you, Shida. Inshallah."

"Inshallah," she returned, her voice somber.

I'm going to find you, Motherfuckers, if it's the last thing I do. Mission first, and you next.

MULTIPLE TARGETS

– Portland, OR –
Tuesday, July 28, 2020

The team was snoring after a long night at the courthouse, but I was still awake with Dex in the command room. The Eye gave us a direct live feed of the Comrade headquarters in Portland. We couldn't see into the building's first-floor hideout, but we had a good view of the grounds around it.

"Having the Eye for this op frees Liam to use his drone to get us sound," said Dex, eyes glued to one of the screens.

Alfa-one was right, but there was also the other side.

"Romulus doesn't want to use the Eye too often. The Chinese could end up detecting our satellite if they triangulate its path with events they suspect us being involved in," I reiterated my father's warning and the part he'd left out.

Our "side" could track it too.

"Thank God Moss IDed the bastard in time," Dex's voice was as tired as his medium frame looked bent over the desk after hours of hypervigilance.

It had been five days since Moss brought us the news of the alleged attack, which meant we only had one day left. Shida had delayed the raid until now to give us time to ascertain if Daj was there. Luckily, Moss had confirmed the night before.

"It hasn't been easy for her to hide the op, but who knows if she's succeeded," I responded, my frustration with the corrupt local government bubbling in my chest.

Dex cursed the Portland district attorney and I didn't correct him.

Yawning, I pushed myself up off the comfortable chair and turned toward the door.

"Keep me posted if anything changes. I'm going to catch some sleep."

He turned to face me, bushy black eyebrows raised in concern.

"Yeah. You'll need it for tonight."

Lost in the tunnels,
echoes in Spanish reverberate and haunt me.

A hand touched my arm and yanked me back from the tunnels I'd been traveling in my mind since Nico's death. My eyes opened to Dex standing over me, eyes searching mine for answers to whatever questions had been inspired before waking me up.

"Moss's been in touch. See you in command," he said and walked away.

Did I do it again? I recalled Sarah's comment about thrashing in my sleep on the chopper. *Was it Bogotá?*

The Beast slinked around my thoughts, lurking and watching.

Glancing at my watch, I saw it was almost five o'clock and raised my head to find Alfa working on their gear around the armory and kitchen areas.

"Hi, Sunshine," called Liam, using his sweetest tone. The rest of them laughed as I sat up slowly and made my way to my room.

After the cold shower finished waking me up, I joined Dex in command.

"Daj is inside the target. Moss managed to confirm it. We have a photo," said Dex when I reached the door, his voice taut with concern.

Yeah. He's a good leader.

I grabbed my chair and pulled it closer to him, squeezing his shoulder as I sat down.

"Moss is the best at this shit. He's got this. Now, show me the photo."

He took a breath and managed a smirk before turning back to the screens and bringing up a photo of Daj Morris. The same handsome black face I recalled from the alley. He was smoking a cigarette alone.

"Romulus got your brother to double-confirm the image."

I knew Jack felt Chad deserved to know that DHS was about to go after Daj after what had happened to his friend who'd sheltered him.

"Send me his photo. I'll share it with Shida when we meet."

Dex turned to face me.

"What's the plan?"

I wanted to get everyone ready around the Comrade headquarters, but that would have meant forsaking the courthouse and Ishmael.

Of course, it's only a few blocks away.

"Keep Hux at the courthouse. The rest come with me to the target," I responded and rose to leave the room.

Shida had asked to meet in an unmarked van parked on a side street. A male agent stood outside with black aviator shades and opened the back doors to let me in.

The van's interior had been converted into an advanced command post complete with gadgets and screens. Shida sat at its center without the hijab, her straight brown hair falling to her shoulders.

She laughed at my reaction.

"Did you think I wear it all the time? I love my religion but don't cover unless I need to."

I smiled and took the seat next to her.

"All right. How are we looking?"

Her smile vanished and her pretty face hardened.

"Locals somehow learned about our op, and now the mayor's office is trying to stop us with all the regular social justice bullshit."

A flame ignited in my belly, but I resisted reacting.

She must have noticed something.

"Don't be a cowboy. We're still on. I never told them the date and time."

I relaxed, but only a bit.

"How do you know you don't have a leak? If you do, they'll know."

"It's the best we have, and we're only a few hours out." Shida shrugged. "I'll look for your... targets."

"That reminds me. Pull out your phone." I pulled Daj's photo up on my phone and then initiated a locally secured transfer to hers.

"This is Daj Morris—the man we're both after."

Her eyes narrowed as she inspected every detail.

"We'll find him," she said with a determined smile.

Sarah was a backup sniper when she wasn't piloting, and she deftly set up her gear as soon as we arrived in the second overwatch position across the street from the Comrades' target building. She had the same binoculars tripod that Hux used.

We'd commandeered another empty office on the fourth and highest story of the shuttered building for a second overwatch location. Liam was on the roof, preparing his drone. Jenny roamed between our positions, providing security.

Dropping to the floor to take her position for the operation, Sarah peered through the binoculars.

"Did you know I saw Ryse back in Germany?"

"When?" I knew Sarah had been born in West Berlin while her mom, a long-serving US diplomat, was stationed there with her husband and their kids.

"I was six when the wall fell. I don't recall much about that, but I do remember seeing some goons with that lightning symbol of theirs," she said, eyes focused on the target below.

I recalled Jack's briefing about the group's soviet roots and how they spread into the west.

"Did you see much of them afterward?" I asked, knowing she'd been raised in Germany until her late teens when her family returned to the States.

She turned to face me, her usually bright blue eyes darkened and narrowed.

"Unfortunately, yes, I did. Those assholes used the German reunification to spread across the rest of the country. Some of my friends were beaten up by them when we all went to see some free speech speaker from England."

My fist clenched and a sneer sneaked out.

"Possible hostile drones," called Dex on our comms. The Eye IDed them, and Sarah pointed out where they were flying around the target.

Clever.

I confirmed back to Dex and then alerted Shida, who was less than an hour from launching the raid.

We were quietly watching the action around the target, waiting for the DHS operation to begin, when the ear vibration caught me off-guard.

Why not regular comms?

"Tanner, Ishmael might be in trouble," said Jack into my earbud.

Sarah turned to look at me, realizing I was receiving information on a private line.

I rose and walked back a few steps.

"Tell me."

"Got the lead from Ken. Ryse is about to do something to Ishmael. It's your call, Son," he said and got off the line.

Damn. Damn. Damn. Another fucking test!

I held my hand up to Sarah and reached out to Hux in the first overwatch location. "What's happening with Ishmael?"

It took him a second to reply, "Some guys in black are yelling at him. He's turning away to leave. Wait…" I felt my guts twisting. "They're following him."

"I'm seeing more protesters around the target," said Sarah, but I barely registered it as I paced around the room.

"Are you going to let another Marine down?" The Beast snarled its uncontested question.

Fuck. Fuck. Fuck.

A decision formed in my ocean of pain.

"Stay here with Liam," I told Sarah. "Jenny, come with me."

"Remember Chicago!" Jenny and I ran down the stairs and into the street, passing hooting rioters who were too busy enjoying the mayhem to pay any attention to us.

All we knew was the general direction Ishmael walked, so I asked the Eye to help us. Luckily, they found what looked to be an altercation in a side street a block north of the courthouse.

"Get the soldier! Fuck him up!" A group of men dressed in black surrounded someone on the pavement next to a building.

"Flex," I whispered to Jenny as we stopped behind the melee. "No killing." I ordered my Flex to protract. "Go... go... go."

Racing forward, we barreled into the group from the back and broke through their ring to find Ishmael on the ground. His eyes were closed and his flagpole was broken in half beside him.

No. No. No.

"Protect him," I ordered, pushing down the anxiety exploding in my chest.

Jenny dragged Ishmael to the wall behind me and then joined me.

There were about twenty of them, and even though our Flex spooked them, they weren't afraid with the numbers on their side. Their leader, a fat fuck with a football helmet, roared for them to attack us.

Jenny and I dropped to battle stance with fists up.

"Get them!" yelled the leader, and the goons advanced, brandishing chains, blades, sticks, and clubs.

Ishmael grunted behind us, probably coming back to consciousness.

"No killing?" confirmed Jenny on our private comms, her tone tense.

"What's stopping you?" the Beast demanded.

The battle cry came from behind the Ryse fighters and they looked back just in time to see a giant man wielding a trash can like a battering ram. He looked like a mighty Thor!

HUXLEY!!!

"Charge!" I roared through the voice scrambler, and Jenny rushed forward with me.

The Flex HUD transformed the mayhem into a precise fight, painting Jenny and Hux in blue and the rest in red. Hux managed to drop three of them before my fist knocked out another. Jenny swiveled between the rioters like a vengeful goddess, breaking fingers and limbs as she moved at a ridiculous speed.

Those who could began to run away. The fat fuck was the slowest. I jumped and pinned him down to the cement, face up.

"Kill him… He will harm others…" the Beast insisted.

I yanked his football helmet off to reveal his acne-laden, sweating face. My hand lifted his helmet, ready to smash it straight into his face.

"Mommy..." he cried.

"Don't," a new voice interjected, breaking the spell.

Ishmael was on his feet again, supported by Jenny and Hux.

"I'm fine. Let him go," he said, his voice tight with pain.

The Beast howled as I took a deep breath and allowed the football helmet to fall from my hand and clank on the cement.

"Get the fuck out of here!" I said to the Ryse fighter. As soon I pulled myself off him, he didn't waste a moment.

Yeah, run to your mommy, Asshole.

As I watched him run, I noticed a small, masked figure watching from a distance.

Ken?

When I nodded back, the figure ran after the fat asshole.

Ishmael was battered, but not broken. He picked up the flag and pole and looked at the three of us in our Flex helmets. I wished I could open the helmet and see him with my eyes, but that wasn't an option.

"Who are you?" he wondered after thanking us for saving him.

Time stopped, and all I could hear was the sad tones of Taps. All I could see was the image of *his* casket.

We saved him.

I took a breath and activated the voice scrambler.

"Semper Fidelis, Brother. Go home now."

"Semper Fidelis." He saluted before turning to hobble away.

Why did I say that?

"Tanner, we're ready." Shida's voice came through my comms and stopped my reflection.

"More rioters are converging around the target building." Sarah's clipped tone came over the other comm.

Shit. Shit. Shit.

In sync, the three of us took off our Flex and began to run.

Sarah was right. Hundreds of rioters ran toward the Comrade headquarters. We blended among them until we got to our overwatch building and sneaked into it.

"It's starting," Sarah said the moment she heard us enter the room.

We rushed to the window in time to see the unmarked cars screeching to a halt outside the building and pushing on the rioters that blocked them from entering the headquarters.

I was about to order Alfa down to the street when Shida and her agents managed to break into the building and keep the rioters from following them inside.

Ten minutes felt like thirty while we waited for the call from her.

"Somebody ratted us out," she grumbled, admitting their operation leaked. DHS didn't find anyone inside, but they did find explosives and weapons. "I'm sorry, Tanner. I know you wanted them, but at least we foiled a big attack."

I hung up the call, feeling an emptiness hollowing out my body.

Liam ran into the room, his drone in hand, and blurted, "You gotta listen to what I got, Sir."

He connected his drone to the laptop and started the video, zooming in on a masked group at the back of the Comrade headquarters.

"This happened just moments before the raid started. I didn't focus on this group, but the drone recorded them anyway. Took me a moment to isolate their conversation from the rest of the noise, but listen to this."

One voice, in a familiar foreign accent, told the rest to move the operation to the other "targets."

I looked up at Alfa, and we shared the same thought. *Chinese?*

The second voice thanked the accented man and "allies" for their support.

Liam had already run the voice through the RCC and Jack.

"It's Daj Morris."

I had to use the *Sense* to calm down as the feeling of failure began to upend my mind, but it was the third voice that got through all my defenses.

"I'm going back to LA," said the last voice.

I didn't need the RCC to confirm it, as I'd heard this voice countless times. It was Nico's killer, the Demon.

My rage erupted like a geyser, making it impossible for me to hear Dex's update that Moss had retreated with Daj and his people.

I will end you.

"You have to," growled the Beast.

AVERTED NOT SOLVED

It was early morning outside our underground base, but we hadn't slept since returning from the streets. On the TV screen, the talking heads on the morning news spoke about the DHS raid and the munitions found inside the Comrade headquarters. It was a rare moment of honesty, as even the extremely liberal anchors were forced to admit it was too much. The next segment was about how the raid had forced the governor and mayor to send local troops to protect the courthouse so that the feds could stop fighting with the crowds every night.

"About time, Assholes," grumbled Jenny, and the rest of the team nodded in agreement.

I watched their tired faces and felt their frustration. We'd scored a victory last night, preventing the attack and protecting Ishmael, but got nowhere close to figuring out who was doing it. They all wanted to stay and make a difference, so we waited for Romulus and Remus to contact us about our next move.

On cue, the chip vibrated in my ear. As I rose to walk to the command room, I could feel all eyes on me.

"Are you good to talk now, or do you need rest?" asked Jack, in an almost-fatherly tone.

"I can speak," I replied, managing the agitation in my chest.

He congratulated our efforts on thwarting the attack and the excellent side effect of forcing the locals to address the courthouse's protection.

"This whole charade has been an effort to hurt Stone. It made him look terrible with all the nightly fights." He took a deep breath. "As for Ishmael, I'm glad you saved him, but who knows how long that victory will last. After all, he will continue going there, won't he?"

I had to agree with him and hoped the feds' departure would deescalate the situation enough to ensure Ishmael's safety.

"Who leaked the op?" I asked, allowing my impatience to get the best of me.

"We don't know for sure." Jack grunted. "Maybe the mayor's office, but it could be the DA or even Deep State actors within the DHS. Tough to know."

"Whoever did it instructed Comrades to use the rioters to mob up on the target and disrupt the op," I grumbled.

"Probably so. As for the drone recording, we did confirm the voice of Nico's killer as one of the three, but you already knew it was him." Jack's voice was as final as his conclusion.

Anger flaring, my fists clenched. I used the *Sense* to calm down, not wanting my father to see my vitals spike.

"I'm sorry, Son. We'll do our best to find anything we can about him."

Quickly, he switched to Chad and his concern about telling him that Daj managed to escape their grasp.

"At least he's at the Ranch," I replied.

He's a pain in my ass, but I'm glad he's safe.

"Yes. He's safe, and I'm grateful we have Ken on the ground and helping," said Jack. "His alert about Ishmael's imminent attack started with a cryptic post. He took a picture of Ishmael and wrote 'Semper Fidelis' underneath it. The RCC caught it."

Nice...

"We took a chance and used an anonymous profile to reach back to Ken about his post, and that's when he told me Ishmael was in danger." My father chuckled. "Any thoughts on why he'd hang around Ishmael?"

Recalling my recent observations of the online journalist and his work, a conclusion morphed in my mind.

"I believe Ken stayed by the vet to protect him and lure us out." I stopped, wondering how much further my father would go with his questions.

"Us?"

Damn.

A Rogue is trained to answer the whole truth, no matter the question. Trust is everything. But it didn't make it any easier.

"Me. He stayed there to find me," I said, letting my tired head drop and stretching my aching neck.

"Explain," he commanded.

"The use of Semper Fidelis. That message was meant for me," I admitted my conclusion. "He took it from the funeral video. Those drones must have recorded it."

"What does the message mean?" he pressed, unrelenting.

I lifted my head and relaxed back into my chair, allowing my tiredness some respite, before it would claim me into the nothingness of sleep.

"That he knows who I am. His digging in Pendleton. The tip on Dani and Seattle. The rumors of the fight in the alley. Everything since," I answered, my respect for Ken growing as I pieced it all together.

"All that is probably true. But you're not addressing what those words *actually* mean for you and why Ken would choose them."

"Kneel!" The Demon's voice boomed as my mind projected Nico charging his killer, yelling, "Semper Fidelis!"

What are these words for me?

"The promise you made to the old man..." whispered the Beast.

But it's changing... expanding. What is it then?

The Beast's laugh reverberated and dissipated into a distant echo. All that remained was my commander's silent presence.

"Well, he got his confirmation. Didn't he?" Jack mused as my silence lengthened.

"Yes. He must have seen the first fight to save Ishmael. The small guy who nodded at me," I said, awaiting my father's decision on my deflection.

"This brings us to the next topic, which Ken has some relation to as well," continued Jack. "The vigilantes are trending again."

I knew rumors began in Seattle after the alley fight with Daj, and the two scuffles around Ishmael had provided fresh material.

"Did anyone catch us on film?" I asked.

"Not that we know of, but those Flex have seriously spooked them. They call them 'Skulls,'" he added with a short laugh.

Skulls...

His gruff tone returned, cutting my thoughts off before their conclusion.

"We're not thrilled about this vigilante matter, but we're willing to let it play out for now."

"We'd like to stay in Portland. The courthouse party isn't over."

"Negative, Alfa-leader. You and your team are all heading for some R&R." He sighed. "We rang their bells, whomever we are fighting. It won't hurt to give this a break."

"It will be good to see them." My disappointment about the mission's end was replaced with warm anticipation in my chest.

"Family is everything," he agreed. "How are you doing with the urges?"

Are you my backup sponsor now?

He meant well, even if his question was laced with his needs as my commander.

"I feel it here and there. Rebirth is coming up—nine years since the last drink."

Images from Big Bear resurfaced—Nico and I pouring the full whiskey into the drain. When my father didn't push, I allowed the truth to come out.

"I miss him, Dad. I miss him so much."

"I know, Son. I know..."

The late afternoon sun painted the world red for us as we met on a five-story building's roof overlooking the Hatfield Courthouse from above. I nodded toward the empty streets.

"Will they riot tonight?"

Shida, covered with her hijab, shrugged as she answered, "Probably. But if I had to guess, we'll see the intensity reducing, both on the ground and in the media. Mission almost accomplished."

Her words hung between us, a testament to our shared feeling of incompletion.

Scanning the area, I saw Ishmael limping to the fence with his flag on a new pole. Shida noticed my attention had focused, and her eyes tracked mine.

"Your guy down there was interviewed by police today," she said.

I froze for a split-second.

"What for?"

Shida told me about a large brawl on some street close to the court and that Ishmael was the victim.

"He told the cops he was saved by a few masked people who beat up the rest." Her eyes searched mine as she spoke, her smile barely hidden.

"Can you ask the locals to keep an eye on him?" I asked, returning her smile.

She nodded.

"Thank you. We need to protect those who are truly free and find more of them."

"The country is changing." Her face turned serious. "I feel it in the air. With every passing day, our common values shrink away. Who would have imagined that from all places in the world, youth here, in the most blessed nation on earth, would chant 'Death to America'? My family risked everything to come here, believing that America was the safest place in the world. But now, I see a growing mob rule egged on by politicians, financed by shadow groups, and sanctioned by compromised law enforcement leaders. My parents watch this on TV at night, and they are scared. I can see it on their faces—the return of a nightmare."

"What will you do?" I asked, both inspired and afraid of the guilt.

"I'll fight it with all I have in me." Her face flushed red, voice determined, before she turned and smiled. "May we cross paths again, Tanner Washington."

A free woman...

We hugged, and she left me alone to witness the darkness fully envelop Portland. I looked at my watch, anxious to see my family—to hold my wife and kiss my babies.

But there's so much more now. I could feel it piling up in my chest. *The guilt...*

"How long will you keep up this charade?" wondered the Beast.

HOME ALONE

The bright morning sun burned the darkness away as I opened our airport storage garage and rolled out the black motorcycle.

"Enjoy your time with them." Sarah appeared at my side. "We're happy to have you back, but we feel for you as well." Our pilot sniper's tone was motherly and earnest, and my eyes dropped for a moment.

None of my Rogues had kids or were even married. It was the recommended price for this line of work, which I didn't pay.

"Oh, stop it," she said in mock exasperation. "Children are a blessing, and so is a good marriage. It means that much more that you chose to return and command our team."

"Thank you, Sarah. Godspeed," I responded, truly honored by her empathy.

Abandoned.

I shook my head at the still-empty streets, riding slowly toward home along Rose Ave.

California remained a hotbed for new Dragon infections and death cases. The local and national stats were showing that besides vulnerable people, the absolute majority of the cases ended with a recovery. But only the exceptions were newsworthy. The heavy boot of the state government was in full force.

I could identify the food joints that had shifted to pickup and take-out options. They were surrounded by masked people huddling and maintaining personal space.

Together but apart.

I grimaced at the marketing slogan that so many companies chose to use.

Just a few blocks away, my heart grew heavy, fingers letting go of the throttle as though this moment could be somehow avoided.

I entered the Venice Circle and stopped in front of Taco Libertad, opening my visor to take in the sad sight. Boarded up with a heavy new metal door.

My eyes shifted to the middle of the Circle, the island of art installations, the spot where Nico and I had stood three years after he'd returned from Afghanistan. He'd held odd jobs, battled alcoholism, and suffered every night. Then, a few days after he stopped drinking, he'd asked me to join him.

"My father built it from nothing. It's where he met my mom, and how he supported our family. I owe them for the last few years. I'm going to work here, just like in the old days," he'd said. It had felt like he needed that anchor, and he was right. His life kept turning around, getting better...

Until he fucking drowned.

My bitterness intensified as some other part of me wondered what the family would do with this place. When I saw a guy in white overalls holding paint and a large brush on a pole walk to the side of the building, I followed him. The painter opened a tarp on the pavement and arranged his tools in front of the empty side wall of the restaurant.

I recalled one of Dani's comments about a tribute mural planned. It should have been a positive thought, but emptiness was all I could feel.

The male Israeli agent gave me a slight nod when I rolled by our complex's gate. He was in the usual spot, under the tree in the shade between our complex and the next building. I raised my visor and nodded back.

A few masked neighbors were talking and waved as I rode slowly through the black asphalted courtyard. I raised my right hand in return.

Are we still good?

I parked the bike inside the garage and closed it, feeling a little sad that nobody screamed my name or ran downstairs. The app showed Dani and the kids were at the Ramirez's.

That's what happens when it's actually a surprise visit. I paused and gulped. *Visit.*

My eyes gravitated to my colorful surfboards, neatly stacked on the rack, as I removed my helmet with a sigh.

Being alone in our rowdy home felt like stealing a moment from life. I took a long hot shower, grabbed shorts and a tee, and headed to the kitchen for breakfast.

I stood clueless in front of the open refrigerator. Cooking had never been a strength. "Men…" I heard one of Dani's regular one-word jokes and smiled until sadness gripped me.

I can't be without them. I can't do this.

My chest felt like it might burst, and I allowed my head to drop, absently closing the fridge and retreating a step.

I was still frozen in my kitchen when the front door opened and I heard Lil cooing and Dani and Ari arguing.

Life energy returned to my body, and an involuntary smile rose as I turned and got down low to greet them. They all saw me when they reached the top of the stairs and, as usual, Ari was the first to reach me and shower me with hugs and kisses.

"Go to Daddy. Show him how you walk," Dani encouraged Leelee, who stood holding my wife's left hand. "Look, Honey."

Leelee smiled, her blue eyes fired up as she wobbled into my open left arm. I picked them both up, fatherly pride replacing the sadness in my chest as Dani closed the circle, her eyes misty.

"You can't speak about all your secrets. Fine! So fuck instead. But you need to bring it out!"

We'd just put our kids to sleep and retreated into our bedroom to get ready for bed when her words leveled me. I turned to face her and found her standing by the closed door, hands firmly on her hips.

"We just had a great dinner... what...?" I stumbled on my words.

She growled and rushed forward to slap me across the face.

"She sees what you hide..." taunted the Beast, causing my blood to pump harder through my entire body.

"Show me who you are. Let me help you carry it," she pleaded, her tone a mix of sensuality and rage.

"Let me in..." insisted the Beast, and I allowed it into the inner sanctum of my decision-making.

I grabbed her roughly and lifted her to our bed, tearing the clothes off her body so savagely, she yelped.

My body froze at the sound, and I pulled back, terrified of hurting her.

"Yes, that..." she hissed with a smile.

Gone was the guilt, the suffering, the endless weight. Raw power coursed through my hands as I ravaged my wife, buoyed upward by her desire.

★ ★ ★

We collapsed to the bed, my body spent. Her pure energy had pushed on my darkness, giving me a temporary respite behind a shield of unconditional love.

"I felt you, Baby. I got you," she whispered, placing a gentle kiss on my neck before getting up. She was close to the bathroom when she looked back over her shoulder with that sly smile, making sure my eyes remained on her naked body.

She's the only one...

The Beast's satisfied energy receded, leaving me happy, exhausted, and stunned.

"We should go camping," she called from the shower. "Fuck the lockdown."

"As you wish, My Queen," I whispered as I stepped under the hot water with her, a renewed hope filling me.

I can do this. I can hold onto this.

NORMALCY

– Venice Beach, CA –
Sunday, August 2, 2020

The family SUV's back door was open, various boxes and the tent arranged neatly, and the radio was on to keep me company. My body was relaxed and worn from the intense nights with my wife and the dawn patrols I'd been surfing since arriving home just a few days earlier.

When the radio host reported on some lockdown protests in Berlin, Germany, I turned up the volume in time to hear the anchor say, "Thousands of people demanding an end to the lockdown flooded central Berlin..."

Finally!

"Baby..." called Dani as she came out of the house, holding several Israeli passports on the other side of the car. "Why are we taking these with us again? It's domestic travel."

There was an answer to give her, but it would have only spooked her further.

"We just need to have them, Honey, wherever we are." I reached my hand through the cab for her to pass them to me.

Her eyes narrowed.

"Like the gun you carry all the time now and that earbud…"

My hand froze in the air, eyes locked on hers. I nodded without a word.

She sighed, managed a faint smile, and handed me the passports before returning to the house to finish getting the kids ready.

Thank you.

I'd just finished packing the SUV when the sound of the gate opening caught my attention. I turned to see Holden walking into the courtyard, dressed in his dark blues.

Man, he looks tired.

"What's up?" I met him at the end of my driveway.

"A neighbor got me in," said Holden. "My officers told me they saw you surfing this morning. I figured to check in, as we haven't spoken since June."

What a surprise.

I pushed down my resentment and smiled, hoping for a better chat than our last one.

It started okay, with him admitting all the new policing challenges that the lockdown and Dragon measures had created.

"But that's not the worst of it. Not even close," he grumbled in a pained tone. "It's how they view us since Chicago. Something is broken, and I don't know how to fix it..."

Seeing his frame hunched, voice defeated, and far from the truth, I used the *Sense* to manage my increasing inner conflict. When he caught on, anger hardened his face.

"What are you looking at me for?" he demanded.

Here we go... damn it.

It was a pointless question, as we both recalled how our last one had ended, embattled over Nicolas.

"You knew damn well he had to be stopped, but you stayed cautious and quiet. He should have never stood his ground with those assholes. For what? For a flag?" He raised his voice, face flushed a dark purple.

I sighed and took a moment to measure him. Sweat beaded on his forehead, unshaven stubble, dark circles under the eyes.

"I fucked up, Holden. Biggest mistake of my life..." He bristled and I shook my head. "But stopping him? We all failed him by not standing up *with* him! Damn it, Holden! You think that fighting for the flag wasn't worth it? You should rip that one off." I pointed at the small US flag patch on his uniform. "Maybe replace it with the California flag. It fits you better."

"What the fuck?" he reeled.

The *Sense* kept my anger focused as I spoke, "Your mayor bent his knee to them. He allowed it to happen!

Our dead brother saw it first… he knew it was wrong…" I stopped, unable to continue containing the raw pain that rose at the words "our dead brother."

His shoulders dropped, and he gave a slight nod. But his eyes still had some riddle in them.

"Have you been following those vigilante rumors? Seattle? Now Portland?" he asked.

My irritation grew a knot in my neck.

It was so much easier to talk to Shida.

I shook my head and grunted.

"Where have you been lately?" he pushed, his eyes searching mine.

"Where my country needs me. You?"

Holden's face flushed again but then calmed down instantly when he raised his eyes.

"Hi, Ari." He softened at the sight of my son, waving with a smile.

Shit.

My head turned to see my son's angelic, curious face observing us from the balcony.

"Happy birthday, Little Man. I hear you're gonna celebrate in the woods this year?" Holden rallied as much uncle energy as he could.

"Yeah, Mom and Dad said that I can't have a party this year."

His little pout broke my heart.

I'm sorry, Buddy. They wouldn't come, even if we invited them.

"Well, I'm sure you'll have a good time in the forest. All kinds of cool animals there. I want to hear all about them when you come back." Holden smiled weakly in my direction. "I gotta go."

My eyes stayed on my old friend as he walked away and my irritation was replaced with sadness.

At least you don't see this, Brother.

I looked up again, but Ari wasn't there anymore.

How much did he hear? I wondered, reflecting on how he'd looked at me after the July Fourth beach scuffle.

I took a deep breath and called into the house, "Let's go, family!"

We used Interstate 5 to head north toward the Redwoods. When the noon glare hit the driver's side, I looked back to see both kiddos napping soundly.

"They ate a lot of lunch."

Dani glanced at me through large round shades.

"Would you mind if I put a news podcast on?"

I knew what her response would be the minute the words were out of my mouth. She turned to look at me and raised her shades to show me her gorgeous blue eyes filled with defiance.

"Music, Tanner Washington. Music."

I smiled and complied. It wasn't just her who'd stopped me from "working." Dex had told me to stop checking in for updates earlier that morning too.

We laughed, talked, and enjoyed the songs until the kids woke up as we entered Arcata.

★ ★ ★

We drove north of the bustling college town and deep into the woods.

"Look how tall they are," Dani directed the kids' attention to the great trees as we slowly drove into the thick forest that cut off our access to the dying sun in the west.

When we arrived at the small campsite, Dani and Lil took a walk while Ari tagged along with me. We set up a large tripod with a light projector to increase visibility for setting up camp.

"Did you learn this in the Army?" asked Ari, perched on a container to watch me.

"Marines, Son. Marines," I responded with a mocked grumble. "But no. I learned it when I was about your age."

"Wow. So cool."

Shivers assaulted my spine, recalling how "uncool" it was.

No tent. Alleys, under bridges, shrubs... always so cold.

He continued with more and more questions about the service, especially what and where I was during it.

He heard something when Holden was there.

"Enough with the questions," I said gruffly. "I need to get this done quickly."

Ari rose from the container and walked sadly back to the car. My eyes followed him momentarily, as guilt over my impatience with him set in.

I wonder what he's carrying, and then I cut him off. Damn it, Tanner.

The tent zipper sounded so unnatural among the sounds of the forest. Reclined in a lawn chair, I turned only my head to see Dani emerge. Her long black hair was disheveled after the hard work of putting the kids to sleep and she was wrapped in a blanket. Even though it was August, it was chilly outside.

She plopped down into the empty lawn chair next to me and reached for a quick kiss before settling in. We stayed quiet for a minute.

"This feels like the old world. Sane again," she whispered as she leaned toward me.

Her head rested on my shoulder while my mind unpacked what she'd said.

They need some peace, and so do I.

"We can stay here for a few days. Don't need to drive anywhere."

I kissed the top of her head gently.

As we relaxed into the easy sounds of nature, Dani reminisced about our time in Israel before our move to America. "Before we had children..." We whispered sweet memories until Ari began talking in his sleep and Dani rose to take a quick look.

When she took her spot next to me again, she whispered, "I'll wake you if you have a nightmare, Baby. Don't want the kids to get scared."

I inhaled deeply at the reminder of my vulnerability while sleeping.

"Hey, don't go there." Her strong hand grabbed my arm. "I never pushed or asked."

I let out the breath and nodded. Dani hadn't pried since revealing her knowledge of my mom's "alley rhymes with Ali" mantra.

"I can sleep outside. No problem."

She snorted in laughter as she teased me, "So 'man' of you!" Sliding her hand down to mine, her tone became more serious. "I want you to know you can tell me. I'm here for you."

Images and sensations of our last few nights of passion warmed me.

You're my greatest strength and weakness, Baby. The only one... who can stop me.

"The nightmares are because of Bogotá," I replied, opening a small crack into my chamber of secrets.

"Colombia?" she wondered.

"Yes. When we lived there, before he moved us to Israel. I was nine..."

"How do you know the nightmare is about Bogotá?" she pressed.

"Because I feel like a kid, and it's all in Spanish," I answered. "I never remember it. All I get are fractions of images and sounds."

She said nothing, her other hand gently stroking my arm.

"There's an alley. It's dark. And there are screams of a young kid," I continued, trying, for the millionth time, to see if I could recall anything more. "Those words you used on me during that fight... my mom invented that mantra to calm me down when I'd have these nightmares. It worked. Eventually the nightmares just stopped, somewhere in my early teens."

Dani nodded, but her mind seemed to be focused on something specific.

"Who's screaming, Tanner?"

Her question rattled me like an earthquake from within a sealed tomb.

"*Now... we're getting somewhere...*" whispered the Beast, like one of the sounds of the forest around us.

Crawling in the nothingness of the tunnels.
Should I search for him?

I had to use my *Sense* to regain my composure. "I don't know. I don't know who it is."

"What *do* you know, Baby?" she pleaded lovingly.

"That I was attacked there one day after school. My parents found me in an alley unconscious. Didn't remember anything when I came to."

"Did you ever ask them for more details?"

"No," I admitted, feeling unexplained shame heating my skin.

"It started again after Nico died, decades since your last ones…" she started but held back, looking at me.

My mind returned to seeing Nico's death for the first time, hearing the Beast's words, *"This is the second time, Tanner. Find me. You know where."*

"There, it's the same look. What's the connection between Bogotá and Nico?" she pressed. "How do you feel right now?"

Guilty.

"Like changing the subject," I responded, and she nodded after a moment.

I closed my eyes, willing my body and mind to settle into the ease of nature.

"Did you know I had a crush on you when I was little?" she asked, blindsiding me.

"What, as a toddler?" I teased, unclear where she was going. She was barely two when we moved to Israel during my dad's deployment there and I was almost ten.

"Of course not! I'm talking about when you left. I was about eleven years old. Do you remember what I told you the morning you all left for the airport?"

I searched my memory of that day, so far in the past. There *was* something about the beautiful girl, with the long black hair and blue eyes, but it evaded my mind.

"I don't recall, My Queen. Can you tell me?"

She shook her head.

"I have a feeling it will come back to you."

Her riddle rattled in my brain, but at least the subject was closed now.

Of course, my relief was short-lived as her next topic was dropping everything and moving back to Israel together.

"We can start all over. Leave the pain behind. Let's do it, Baby."

"Let's see," I responded, troubled by my inability to shun her idea on the spot.

How committed am I? Can I leave this all behind?

CAREFREE

It was around midday when we returned from looking for creatures in the creek near our campsite.

I had Leelee tucked in my left arm while Ari and Dani walked on my right. My wife turned to me and beamed without losing track of our son's long monologue about why we should go to town to get ice cream, and my heart swelled with happiness. The moment filled every ounce of my being, leaving no room for all that haunted us outside the great woods.

This is everything.

We got the kids cleaned up and ready for the evening routine, and I prepared the cooktop and got out the dinner ingredients while Dani got the kids dressed in the tent.

As the last ray of sun retreated behind the thick foliage and darkness took over, a slight shiver ran down my spine.

It likes the darkness...

Ari's cry and Dani's angry voice stopped my train of thought, and I turned to see my son stomping toward me, with my wife's explicit instruction to "discipline him for not listening to his mom."

"Chair, now," I grumbled at the wild blond-haired hippie child.

His sweet face began to turn, but I shook my head, dissuading him from doing anything but what he was told to do. Ari mumbled something as he sat on one of the lawn chairs.

"Tell me what happened."

Ari grudgingly admitted that Dani forbade him from annoying his sister, and then he did.

"So you disobeyed your mom?"

He took a deep breath, a hallmark of the beginning of another monologue. I shook my head again, doing my best to keep a serious face. Then I raised my voice so Dani could hear I was doing my job.

"Yes or no, Ari."

"Yes," he grunted in frustration.

I stopped messing with the cooking stuff and brought one of the chairs to sit by him.

"The moment you disobey us, you break the rules —our constitution."

His eyes grew wide. "What is a consti..."

"Constitution," I completed his question while my mind regressed to my own childhood lectures of civic duties that Jack started doling out around Ari's age. It was drilled into me as my young body began the excruciating training program my father envisioned as my education.

"Dad…" said Ari, pulling me back into this fatherly moment.

Oh boy.

"A Constitution is an agreement. It has all kinds of rules that tell us how to deal with each other. Our country has one that tells people how they can treat each other, and we have one at home. For example, you must do as your parents tell you."

I suppressed my smile again when his brow furrowed.

"What happens when people don't listen to the… consti… tution?" he asked after a long minute.

His question puzzled me, as it seemed he was talking about more than his infraction with Dani.

"Why do you ask?"

Ari lowered his eyes and then looked to the side.

"What is it, Son?"

He looked back at me, trying to keep a brave face.

"All the bad things back home, Dad. Why nobody listens to the Constitution?"

My blood froze as my little warrior's brutal honesty left me speechless.

A Rogue is trained to cherish, serve, and protect the Founding Documents. Our nature and mission are mixed into one dangerous path. But when was the last time I thought about this?

An answer was needed from me, and his eyes told me there was no wiggling out of it. I looked back toward the tent, where Dani made funny sounds to Leelee's delight.

I guess I'm on my own for this one, but I just can't right now…

"Come and help me cook," I said with a cheerful voice, rising from my seat and extending my hand to him. "We'll even get you a marshmallow before Mom sees."

His eyes brightened at my bribery, unaware of the shame that tore through me like a storm.

★　★　★

Camping life tired my family early. Even Dani collapsed into a deep sleep while putting the kids to bed in the family tent.

I sat relaxed in the chair, checking my phone for news and updates until I saw it. A rare video from a detention center in China that held Uighurs, a small ethnic minority in the communist state. I leaned forward and caught my breath as I watched the short clip of a thin, beautiful young Asian-featured woman pleading for help. She claimed she was a model before she was thrown into the facility for speaking out against the government. She pleaded with the world to get involved in what the Chinese were doing to her people, especially now, during the world Dragon pandemic.

"They use the virus on us... please help us..." were her last words before the video ended.

I turned off the phone, reeling from the presumably dead woman's words. A sensation of evil danced in my mind, forcing me close to the memory of Nico's killers' voice. The *Sense* helped me to center my thoughts, but thinking about the Demon reminded me that Moss was undercover and in great danger.

The tent zipper opened slowly and Dani emerged, wrapped in her blanket. She kissed me before sitting down to enjoy the reality we'd created together momentarily in the forest over the last few days. If she felt my unrest, she didn't address it.

"We need to go to town for shopping," she muttered. "We'll get him the ice cream."

The sensation of the Beast returned for a moment.

I don't want to see other people.

"As you wish, My Love," I responded and kissed her.

STAY BACK

We got the kids into the SUV quickly with bribes of pancakes and hot cocoa in town. I was about to start the engine when a wave of fear stopped me. It had no images or words, just feelings of loss and grief ripping through its tide.

"I love you." Dani reached across the console and squeezed my thigh.

"Let's go... let's go..." pleaded Ari from the back seat.

The *Sense* cleared my mind, and I turned the key and pulled away from the campsite.

Civilization met us as soon as we exited the ancient forest and got on the road to Arcata. Nobody spoke—a rarity I wasn't about to squander.

"We must feed them before getting supplies, Baby," whispered Dani, her look daring me to mess up her plan for our day.

She found us a restaurant with a nice outdoor area. In the old world, that would've meant a fantastic patio to enjoy. But in the Dragon world, it was the difference between keeping your business alive or shuttered for good, especially in California.

The eatery was on a lovely street with several other restaurants and coffee shops, all of which were using the pavement and sections of the road in front of their establishment. These parklets had been used nationwide to boost the nearly dead restaurant industry.

Those who destroy and then offer help.

The bitter thought provoked a slight head shake from me as we stepped out of the car and onto the pavement.

"We're the only ones without masks," whispered Dani, shifting Lil between arms.

I was looking around, affirming her statement with a slight nod, when the ear vibration surprised me.

"I need to make a call."

I stopped us before we reached the boarded-up retail shops, and Dani nodded and kept the kids by the closed shop's front door.

I tapped on my ear bud to receive the call, my eyes scanning the street.

"We have a multi-casualties event in Chicago involving the police..." started the female RCC operator voice.

A knot formed in my stomach. I looked back at Dani with a forced smile and raised my finger for one more minute.

The operator continued, reporting that, according to current knowledge, a police car carrying two officers had been ambushed in the early hours of the morning. SWAT had been called in, and a young boy had died in the crossfire with the assailants.

I was limited in my ability to speak in broad daylight, but one question persisted.

"Besides the boy, did any of the police or attackers die?"

"Negative."

Something stinks.

The knot tightened as I turned back to see Dani with her phone out, eyes wide as her finger scrolled. The kids were getting restless, but she paid them no heed.

"Thanks. Out," I said into my earbud and killed the call.

She looked up at me, her brow furrowed. "Chicago?"

I nodded, and she turned the phone to show me a video of the riot. At a quick glance, I could see that social media was exploding with "killer cops" and other derogatory comments about the murderous police.

Fuck.

"Can we eat already?" grumbled Ari, and Lil joined in by clapping her hands.

It's a small town. We're far from there. We have time.

Resolved, I grabbed Ari's hand and walked until we reached the white picket fence surrounding the outdoor area of the place Dani had chosen. The building was boarded up, but a metal screen door was open, where the waiters were bringing food and attending to the twenty or so people on the patio.

"I need to ask you to put on your masks until you get to your table."

The young female hostess was barely understandable through her mask.

Grumbling, Dani reached into her bag to pull out two blue cloth masks and handed me one.

"What about the kids?" asked the hostess.

"Over my dead body," responded Dani firmly. "Where's the manager?"

Scanning the street, I was paying little attention to my wife's increasing ferocity with the young woman.

The hostess buckled and we wore our masks as she led us to one empty white table among half a dozen others. When she left to get a high chair for Leelee, the kids got closer to Dani to look at the menu.

I stared blankly at a menu while the RCC sent me a voice memo about the growing evidence that Ryse and Comrades had both mobilized their various chapters to respond to Chicago, propagating a lie about the police and the incident that cost the life of the young boy.

"Tanner!" Dani's voice broke into my thoughts. "What do you want to order?"

"Pancakes, of course," I replied as another young woman arrived to take our order.

We did our best to keep the peace between our two hungry, bickering monsters and were delighted that our food came out quickly.

We were only halfway into our meals when the RCC updated me about a growing protest in Arcata, one of the many springing up across the nation following the shootout in Chicago. Dani looked at me, eyes questioning.

We need to go.

"Kids, let's finish our breakfast and get on the road."

Dani's eyes widened at my suggestion and she turned her head around the street.

"Can we get the check?" I asked a male waiter when he passed by.

He nodded and disappeared into the restaurant.

The next ear vibration reached me as the kids finished their last bites, and I paid our bill. The male voice warned that the riot was getting into our area just as my ears picked up the first screams in the distance.

Following my lead, Dani jumped up from her seat and pulled Leelee onto one hip as I picked up Ari. She followed me to the parklet entrance, and we both looked left and right to the edges of the street. Both sides were full of protesters with signs yelling.

I glanced at my wife's strained face, realizing my impossible situation.

She can do this.

"Get everyone inside the place," I commanded as I pulled my mask up to cover my face. "And mask up. Ari, go with your mom and obey her *every* word. Remember the constitution."

I set him down and held his gaze long enough to see his fear transform into resolve.

Her jaw clenched under her mask, Dani took his hand and turned around to rush all the patrons into the restaurant.

"Everyone get inside. There's a riot starting out there!"

The stunned hostess was the first to move and help her clear the patio, leaving me alone outside.

"Yalla, Yalla, inside." Dani's herding skills elicited another, more amused, shake of my head before I turned my eyes back to the street.

Patrons across the street had been caught in the middle as one restaurant after the other was swarmed. Some ran into the buildings and closed the doors, while others remained seated and encircled by the rioters. It wasn't clear what had happened, but my eyes saw several of them being forced to raise their fists in the Comrade-style salute. One woman who refused was punched in the face and so was her husband who tried to help.

Bastards.

The knot turned into a nuclear fissure, exploding fury up my spine. My right hand was on its way to my concealed Wraith on the small of my back when I then heard the door behind me open and saw Dani marching out without the kids.

"Remember Chicago!" The familiar screams and howls resounded between the buildings.

She stopped, eyes blazing in my direction.

Damn.

I retreated twenty feet through the patio, keeping my eyes on the growing mayhem outside.

"Why are you outside?" she whispered. "I could use your help. The owner is a dick."

As memories of Taco Libertad besieged from outside resurfaced, righteous fury warred with fear.

Squeezing my shoulder, she used the same tone she'd employed with the hostess earlier, "Damn it, Tanner. You can better protect us inside, and you know it!"

Her words may as well have been a cold slap across the face.

I looked back, reassessing the situation with the plywood-covered windows and metal screen door, which had a deadbolt handle.

"She's right," suggested the Beast.

I nodded as I pulled my mask up, giving one last look at the encroaching riot and then followed her inside, closing and locking both the door and screen behind me.

The crowd inside huddled toward the back, one older couple watching over Ari and Leelee.

"What should we do?" Dani asked as soon as the deadbolt engaged. I looked through the doors to the street and then back at her.

"Lock the back door. Get one of the waiters to watch over it. Keep them quiet," I instructed quickly, focusing on the rioters who had reached our restaurant and begun trashing the patio.

Even with the noise of tables being turned over and chairs crashing against the ground, I could hear Dani arguing with someone with a high-pitched male voice in the back of the restaurant. My eyes remained on the door, a wave of anxiety infecting my body from its core.

The ear vibration refocused me, and I accepted the call.

"What's the status?" commanded Jack.

I looked back, seeing the couple with our children. Lil was okay, but Ari's face was anxious.

He's scared.

Just past where he stood, I could see Dani in the kitchen arguing with a medium-sized bearded masked man. I told Jack the situation, using the *Sense* to keep my vitals from exploding with the rush of anxiety.

"It's coordinated, a wave of secondary riots from coast to coast, tied into what's going in Chicago," confirmed Jack. "We're hoping to see Arcata police moving in soon. I had to order Alfa to stand down from intervening."

Dani pointed at me, and the man bristled but nodded with drooped shoulders. Then she disappeared into the back, with a male waiter following her.

"Yeah. They won't make it here in time," I responded, shifting my attention between the door and the back where everyone stood. "I need to go now."

A long moment passed before she returned to the main room, checked on the children, stared hard at the bearded man, and then joined me by the door.

The hooting and howling outside increased and some rioters occasionally banged on the plywood covers and metal screen door.

"The back is locked. It also has a heavy metal door. What's next?"

In another life, this woman could be a Rogue.

A big bang rattled the place, and the crowd yelped in fear.

"We hold and wait for the police," I answered. "Was that the manager?" I lowered my voice to a whisper.

Some of her tension evaporated with a slight smile and nod.

"He wanted to open the door, saying he's an 'ally.'" She did nothing to hide her disgusted mockery.

We both glanced at the kids and returned to face the door.

"Why did you point at me?" I asked as another intense bang came through the plywood.

"I told that coward that you were the man he had to go through if he wished to weasel out."

I suppressed a chuckle and shook my head.

"What happens if they get in?" she whispered, allowing her fear to lace the words, but take none of her strength.

Cold rage reverberated in me, recalling what Taco Libertad looked like after being ransacked.

"You can tell her," whispered the Beast.

"I'll stop them," I replied, feeling my mask drop for a moment.

"Stop? How?" she asked hesitantly, her eyes again betraying that she didn't recognize the man standing before her.

"How do you think?" I growled, surprised by the resentment fueling my words.

The bangs continued, but our eyes didn't waver as she crossed her arms defiantly and my irritation surged.

Yes. If they come, I'll kill. This is what I do! This is what YOU insisted I do!

Police sirens interrupted us and the banging outside, and the rioters began to retreat.

We rushed our shocked silent kids to the SUV, seeing the police dispersing with the last rioters. The ride back to the campsite was quiet, as everyone tried to digest the experience.

We'd barely gotten out of the car when Jack's call came in.

"We lost contact with Moss," he started, his voice tight.

I breathed against the invisible steel hand that squeezed my heart and kept it from pumping while Jack told me that we got his location and he was most likely being held against his will.

"Where?"

"Chicago. He got there earlier today and sent one SOS before we lost contact."

A tsunami of guilt hit me.

While I'm in the woods relaxing.

"Orders?" I asked, looking back to see Dani and the kids watching the squirrels that clamored about our site.

Jack detailed the rescue mission and coordinates for my pickup, and then I made some requests for my family before we got off the line.

This is impossible.

I hung back by the car and watched my queen play with our kids, doing her best to erase the events of the last hour from their mind.

"Stop being shackled. You have a brother to save," growled the Beast.

I sighed and walked over to my little family.

"It's time to go home. Let's pack it up."

Dani's eyes searched mine a few moments before she quietly nodded and stood up to help.

Impossible.

No one liked my news, but Ari took it the hardest and complained the most.

"We haven't talked about what happened," Dani spoke in a hushed voice between Ari's monologues.

Hearing Brett Cohen's voice, I turned up the volume to hear his live show, and gave her my "not now" look.

He reported on the growing riot in Chicago and the lie spread about the police ambush, painted as brutality instead.

Turning the volume down a bit, I glanced at her pretty face and reached for her hand. The map app beeped, and my eyes returned to look at it.

"You did good over there," I answered, offering an olive branch and a way out for me.

I slowed the car down to a stop on the side of the empty road.

"That's not what I'm talking about, and you know it," she replied, uninterested in my deflection.

"Come out with me."

I reached for my door handle, using the *Sense* to center my mind.

I have to get them to safety. Then I can focus on Moss.

Thick forest walls towered on both sides of the one-lane road.

Walking around the car, I pulled her close.

"I have a hotel booked for you in Mendocino. It's not even four hours from here on the coast. An Old Glory team will find you and drive behind you tomorrow morning. I want you to stay on Highway 1, avoiding big cities."

"Are you gonna say anything about the restaurant?" she asked, dropping her head onto my chest.

"No," I replied, frustrated with her insistence on digging into the incident.

Lifting her face, she looked left and right.

"Are you getting picked up here?"

"Sort of," I grumbled as I pulled my phone out to forward her the hotel reservation handled by the RCC.

"Is this about Chicago?"

Her question dug at my growing anxiety, and the Beast laughed at my discomfort.

"Yes, and enough with the questions," I replied.

She remained quiet, and I looked back to see her mouth agape.

The restaurant scuffle resentment resurfaced in my chest.

It was you who wanted me to act! Damn it!

"Help me tell them goodbye. Please," I whispered, using the *Sense* to hold my harder emotions at bay as I pulled her closer.

She nodded into my chest.

The kids cried as I hugged them goodbye and my agitation dimmed Dani's kiss.

Impossible, I thought as the car disappeared beyond the bend.

Taking one look at my map, I allowed the fury to explode in my chest and increase my speed as I ran into the woods.

FASTER

– Over Iowa, IA –
Friday, August 7, 2020

The small jet sped eastward into the growing darkness of the night. All of Alfa was dressed in black urban insertion BDU and silent for most of the trip.

Dex double- and triple-checked everyone, and I had to ask him to take it easy.

His worry about Moss is bleeding out to the team.

"He's strong..." I whispered to him, my hand squeezing his shoulder to transmit some calm from my nearly-tapped-out reserve.

I looked at my app, confirming Dani had entered the hotel, and sighed with relief as my eyes reviewed the Old Glory update that a team had met her there.

"Alfa-leader, incoming from RCC," Sarah's voice called from the cockpit.

I offered one last shoulder squeeze for my second-in-command as I stood up and walked past the neatly-stacked gliding parachute packs arranged along the side plane door to a small cubical office space.

Romulus and Remus were on the line and projected onto the small computer screen on the desk. Both of their faces looked more tense than usual.

They care about Moss too.

Custer began the briefing with details on Chicago. He knew it well, as he had grown up there in the tough South Side. He spoke of the gangs, the current corrupt mayor, and the district attorney, who, like the other OBI-financed prosecuting colleagues, refused to press charges against many criminal cases.

"No surprise that the police there are extremely frustrated," he added somberly before turning our attention to the mission. "We have one asset on the ground—my nephew, Nils Custer. He's a CPD sergeant deployed around the riots with his unit. Romulus will take it from here. Get our boy back, Tanner. I'll see you at Pendleton soon."

Custer left the line, and Jack began to detail the mission.

"Moss is your main target. Nothing else matters..." He said Alfa-three was in a large warehouse near the Magnificent Mile area. "His vitals are strong, but there's indication of injury."

"Do the police have any reach in that area?" I asked, looking at Eye's live feed of the streets full of people and mayhem.

"Negative. They retreated after the ambush ended, and the mayor prevented them from returning to the riot zone." He shared the scene with the now burned and tagged police car left in the middle of the road. "Remember your DIR2 is limited. Do whatever you need to get Moss, but avoid collateral damage."

"Do we know why he moved into Chicago?" I asked, knowing well that while undercover, a Rogue could go without a sign for a long time.

"Something about being on Daj's tracks," Jack started. "But he also suspected some operation was planned in Chicago."

My memory returned to the footage Liam's drone had caught outside the botched raid in Portland and the accented man who spoke about other "targets."

"Like an ambush with zero dead cops or attackers and a dead boy to inflame the streets?" I wondered.

Jack conceded, adding to the mystery that a high-powered sniper rifle was used to immobilize the cops around their car, forcing them to return fire into an apartment building.

"The MSS could be involved in this," I grumbled, and he nodded without adding more.

"Your insertion should put you on the ground by midnight. Once there, you'll be within their zone without outside support until you connect with Nils at his position outside the riot area."

"We'll get him back," I responded, and we ended the call.

Left alone in the small room, all the pieces locked into place.

"Moss was ratted out," growled the Beast.

I know.

A BRIDGE TOO FAR

– Chicago, IL –
Saturday, August 8, 2020

"**P**rotract swim," I commanded the Flex, and only the eye cover came out, creating sealed diving goggles as I approached the plane's open door. Chicago's lights twinkled far below.

Not even three months ago, I was at home with my wife watching the motorist die at the hands of cops, and now I'm here.

"Good luck," called Sarah over the comms.

"Go… go… go!" I shouted, rushing and jumping into the black.

I opened the gliding parachute and the Flex's HUD lit the path for me and the other four Rogues being dropped over the great lake, just east of Chicago.

We paraglided westward over the black water in radio silence. It was my first combat jump over US soil—a red line I had never imagined crossing.

No matter how much they drilled it into us during the Rogue course, nothing could have prepared me to see my own country as a battlefield, its people divided into friendlies and hostiles.

One mile to shore, I pinged the team to release the parachutes and drop into the water. Luckily, it was summertime, so the temperature didn't shock my body. We activated the mini-swimmers engines we'd strapped to our chests, dove deep, and swam to the small, empty beach.

Live feed from the Eye was displayed on our HUD, showing all the action just a few blocks west toward the Magnificent Mile corridor, now held hostage as a riot zone. In the time it had taken us to reach the shore, the mayor had ordered the bridges lifted, hoping to stem the growing riot which gripped Chicago's famous shopping street.

I contacted the RCC once we'd finished disguising ourselves for the insertion and was told Moss's signal remained in the same shuttered office building in the riot zone.

Alfa huddled around me in a protective circle, vigilant while getting their light arms concealed on their bodies. We were all hooded and masked, hiding the Flex underneath.

"Let's go," I called and ran toward the boardwalk.

"The four horsemen of the apocalypse," quipped Liam, inciting a kick in the butt from Hux.

Our path took us up toward the north edge of the Magnificent Mile corridor, but we eventually had to cross through the riot zone.

"Remember Chicago! Fuck the police!" Screams rose from the boulevard teemed with rioters as they looted and smashed up the shops. There were no police in sight as we melded among them, moving like a pack of sharks in the dark waters of mayhem. The only engagement from the crowd ended with Jenny knocking a man out cold when he aggressively placed a hand on her.

It took us some time, but we reached the six-story glass-windowed office building. At least a dozen masked guards roved around the entrance, dressed in black, their concealed weapons obvious to us with the help of the Eye.

Across the street, we kept to the shadows while Liam deployed his stealthy mini drone—an oval-shaped black military-grade model that made minimal sound as it shot out toward the building. He kept talking with the RCC until it was confirmed that Moss was underground, most likely within the parking structure underneath the office building.

The team had been on edge on the flight, but the tension had become palpable with every step closer to our brother. When Dex muttered a curse, my attention split between the rare display of emotions from my second and the mission.

"Fuck," grumbled Dex as my HUD flashed "incoming from Romulus."

I raised my clenched fist, signaling for Dex to keep his shit together.

My dad's voice broke into my Flex's comms as the RCC projected the building and parking lot layouts on the HUD.

"He's hurt. We don't know how bad. His vitals are steady but concerning." He paused. "Ryse and Comrades are radio silent on this."

"Because they're ordered to be," I answered, insinuating the worst case.

It's fucking China, Dad! Wake the fuck up!

"Probably," mumbled Jack. "But even worse, they know someone is after them…" He updated me on the convoy of vans spotted entering the underground parking only minutes before we'd arrived. "We don't have much time. He might bite the tooth if those vans are meant for his transfer."

It killed me inside to know my father was right—that my brother would soon have to make the decision to crunch the cyanide tooth every Rogue has to prevent being tortured and broken beyond the chance for immediate rescue.

Don't do it, Moss. We're here. Just a few more minutes, brother. We can protect the mission and save you.

"The guards don't look like MSS. It would help…" I offered, realizing what was about to take place.

"It's our analysis as well. I'd have been surprised to see them gathered in one place to guard Moss," he said, leaving us both with an uncomfortable conclusion.

They're gathered for what then?

Jack briefed me on the evac planned for Lincoln Park, less than two miles north of our position. Nils Custer would be holding the intersection through which we'd cross into the park.

"That's it, Son. Dead or alive, bring our boy home."

Using the *Sense* to manage the pressure that had quadrupled with his last words, I looked again at the layout, silently strategizing the breach plan.

"It won't be pretty. Front assault is what I have for them," I cautioned him.

He protested quietly, "You have DIR2 authority to get him out and evac the team. Is this clear enough?"

The Beast growled in satisfaction, primal freedom coursing through me. I didn't know how long of a rope I'd been given, but there was only one way to find out.

"Clear."

As soon as Jack was off the line, I called Alfa on our channel, "Listen up."

As I explained my plan, there was dead silence on the comms.

They're shocked, I thought as I observed Dex's expression. *They can't believe we're doing this either.*

"What's with the surprised faces? I'd burn the world to get to any of you," I muttered at him, knowing the rest heard it on comms.

He flinched as though I'd slapped him, but then nodded as a vicious smile replaced the shock. The rest of Alfa repeatedly pinged the comms to voice their silent support.

"Protract," I called, and the Flex closed over my face. "Spread out. Thirty seconds," I instructed, and the HUD began the countdown for us all.

"4... 3..."

Jenny and I sneaked across the street and hid near the target entrance. Pulling our Wraith guns, we locked them on the nearest guards, claiming it on the HUD for the other Rogues to see.

"*Finally,*" said the Beast.

"2... 1..."

I glanced at Jenny crouched beside me.

Two smoke grenades exploded by the building entrance, but the Eye kept our targets' lock active, unhindered by the smoke. We all opened fire, and the HUD showed a dozen red-painted hostiles drop in rapid succession to five.

Jenny and I holstered our guns and grabbed our blades in sync. With a quick nod, we raced alongside the side of the target while Liam, Hux, and Dex rained fire and dropped two more guards, leaving three to us. Alfa stopped firing as soon we reached the smoke.

I ran by the first choking guard and swiveled around him, slicing his throat open. Jenny took care of the other two before we pivoted and ran into the entrance. The next three guards had just entered the lobby from the door we were heading toward. I pulled my Wraith and doubled-tapped the first big guy while Jenny took the other two.

"You're upping me," I growled and heard her laugh.

Liam remained outside while Dex and Hux entered the parking lot through the car tunnel. Jenny stayed to monitor the lobby and elevator as I raced to the side door that lead to the stairs.

We knew Moss's signal came from the underground area but didn't have the actual location. My plan called to lock down all access points while we searched each level of the underground structure.

I slowed my descent down the stairs when the power was cut, thanks to Hux, who'd found the utility room.

"Found them. Last level..." whispered Dex into the channel. He reported vans with engines on and a few people milling around. His HUD showed Moss's signal very close.

I was at the bottom of the stairs when the door opened one level below me, casting white light into the darkness and squarely onto me. Whoever it was, he started to yell and used his flashlight to blind me. My HUD surprised me with the instant automatic darkening of the display, and the assisted aim lock enabled my Wraith to split the hostile's head with one suppressed shot.

Everything accelerated as Dex called out that he was engaging. I jumped over the dead man and pushed the door open a crack.

Sporadic emergency white lights blazed from the concrete walls as the vans tried to get out. The giant had reached the scene and joined Dex in pinning them down with his submachine-gunfire. There were at least ten enemy targets when I opened with direct fire, flanking the surprised hostiles from the side.

We decimated their ranks like a scythe in a wheat field. It took less than twenty seconds, and I called for a cease-fire before I rushed forward and began opening vans in search of our friend. We found him unconscious and bound in the trunk of one of the vans.

"Found one alive," murmured Hux on the comms.

"Leave him to me. Kill the rest," I said as Dex carefully pulled Moss out of the van. "Exfil in two mikes."

The young black male guard bled from multiple bullet wounds but wasn't in grave danger when I arrived. Hux towered over him where he leaned against one of the vans. As he walked away, some suppressed shots were heard as the rest of the still-live guards were executed.

The guard shrieked as I got closer to him and looked away.

Jack's words about the rumors of vigilantes wearing skulls elicited a sly smile as I pulled my knife out and bent down to eye level with him.

"Speak the truth, and I won't have to force your words out," I snarled through the voice scrambler, allowing the blade to rest on the guard's right thigh.

When he started with bravado and cursing, I plunged the serrated blade into his flesh and began to slice him slowly. His screams reverberated in the structure, and I gave him a moment, glancing back to see Dex getting Moss on his feet and listening to Liam and Jenny's updates on the incidents they'd taken care of above us.

The guard was ready to talk when I turned to face him. He admitted he belonged to Comrades and that his team was tasked with driving Moss to San Francisco. I pressed with my questions and some more twists of the blade, but he spilled nothing more than harrowing screams.

"We're good to go Sir," called Dex, holding Moss between himself and Hux.

Screams turned to laughter as the guard's chest heaved.

"The revolution is coming, Bitch!"

The taunt reminded me of my grandpa's haunted eyes as he cryptically prophesied, "It can happen here, Tanner. Right here. We have to be ready."

Raging fire ignited in my heart, and my left hand shot forward and grabbed his neck, choking the laughter out of him.

"Revolution?" I whispered, intrigued by the choice of words. The Beast lurked, waiting on my actions.

No time for this.

"My name is Tanner Washington, and I sentence you to death for treason," I said, shoving the blade into the guard's throat as his eyes widened and stilled.

Finished, I shook my head and stood up to inspect Moss. His face was badly bruised, only one eye open enough to look back.

"I'm good..." he managed in a cracked tone.

Relief washed Dex's face.

I smiled and patted his cheek.

"Let's go. I'll lead."

We reached the lobby to find Jenny with a few more recent bodies added to her count.

She definitely upped me. I suppressed a proud smile. *Wicked speed, that one.*

Together we broke out through a side entrance, Liam converging on us, covering the rear.

Shouts of alarm rose inside the building, and the RCC confirmed they saw armed hostiles converging back on the building from the riot zone.

"We gotta go fast," I instructed Jenny.

"Yes, Alfa-leader," she responded and took point as we filed behind her.

I texted Nils Custer, using the Flex voice command, as we scurried between buildings, avoiding the large groups that mostly moved toward the riot zone in the other direction. Custer's nephew texted back that all was good.

The park was just ahead and a Chicago PD car sat in the intersection, lights off. There was one cop outside of it, which the HUD confirmed as Nils.

We raced past the masked cop who nodded without saying a word. Once inside the park, I stopped us in the woods just outside the open baseball field.

With Alfa creating a protective envelope around us, I sat by Moss who Dex had propped against a tree trunk. My second was still by his side, ensuring his bandages held while we waited for Sarah.

"He had an accent. A pro..." Moss described the masked Asian man who'd tortured him for details. "He and Daj talked with me once I was caught..."

Moss didn't know what had happened with Daj afterward, but his best assumption was that he went to the streets to help with their operations.

"I have no idea how they got me..." As Moss told us about being discovered and surrounded, Dex and I exchanged a silent look.

"I think my chip got some data. I turned it loose when they arrived," he said, stopping the chuckle when he realized how it hurt.

Even without a connecting device, Rogue's chips could conduct Bluetooth hacks into nearby devices, siphon data, and store it locally on the chip until an upload is possible. If our enemies knew us, they would kill us on sight and melt our heads to ensure our chips were destroyed.

"You did well," I told him, squeezing his shoulder until he yelped. "Good. You're alive." I smirked and rose to take in what was happening around us.

The sounds of the riots didn't reach our position, but there was no peace as choppers of all sorts buzzed overhead and endless sirens left no room for silence. I was under a tree, needing a moment to sort out my thoughts.

"Somebody ratted us out," Shida's words haunted me.

Dex walked over to me.

"They hurt him bad, but they didn't hit any vitals. Smart. They needed him to survive the trip west."

"Yeah," I replied, distracted.

"We're compromised, Sir," he grumbled, not elaborating as he rarely did.

Unease ran down my spine. My XO was correct, just as Shida had been. But neither of us knew to what extent.

"Twenty mikes for the bird," called out Liam on the comms.

Sarah was coming in hot with the stealth chopper, which was ready for her once she'd landed the small jet on a nearby secured airstrip. Old Glory personnel had moved our gear and vehicles between secured locations.

I looked at Dex and nodded.

"Get ready for evac."

Inside, the Beast growled in satisfaction with my inner thoughts.

He cocked his head slightly and whispered, "We are *all* leaving? Right...?"

Damn. He's onto me.

"I need to call Romulus," was my only response.

He held my gaze for another moment before nodding and leaving to arrange the team for exfil.

"Absolutely not," rumbled Jack slowly. "We're lucky to get Moss alive, but we also left a pile of bodies." Jack shut down my plan to stay on the ground and hunt the Traveler. "How many more will die if you enter their zone and find Daj?" His tone carried a tinge of suspicion.

"Answer him..." whispered the Beast.

"As many as needed," I responded quietly, sensing my growing desire for vengeance and mayhem.

"Damn it, Tanner! This is not the moment for it unless you can somehow present operational logic!" he snapped.

Calm down. This is Romulus!

My body aching for violence, I allowed the *Sense* to hold back the Beast, even as it howled in dismay.

"We need to find out how Moss was captured. There's a leak, and you know it." I held my tone down.

"Go on," he relented.

I laid out the obvious questions: Why was Moss being transferred to San Francisco? Who was the "accented man"?

"Anything else?" he asked.

I heard the dead guard's last words, "The revolution is coming..." and my stomach lurched.

What do I need to include?

"Something is coming, and we don't know what it is. This is my final argument to stay."

Liam announced ten minutes for the chopper's arrival. Out in the park, Hux and Jenny ran patrols around us while Dex remained at Moss's side.

"The media has already reported rumors of 'scary vigilantes' attacking and killing peaceful protesters within the riot zone. It's a clusterfuck, as the police are still trying to get to the scene of your little battle," groused Jack.

Dad and Custer, belonging to another generation and its etiquette, rarely cursed. But when they did, they meant it with all their hearts.

"Did anyone post photos or videos?" I asked.

"Negative."

"At least we know these assholes are in control and cleaning the scene. Don't be surprised if this thing is silenced," I replied.

"We'll see," snipped Jack. "As for your points, most likely, we're dealing with China, which will explain the transfer to San Francisco. That 'accented man' could very well be MSS. We know that one has been working with Daj since Seattle."

The Beast pushed against my forced calm, but it didn't suggest interrupting Romulus.

"We have no idea where Daj is. He could be anywhere among tens of thousands of people in the street." He stopped and changed his tone. "Let's examine what we got from the data grab and see whether we are compromised as you have suggested."

The hint of predawn played in the dark skies above. I looked at the empty baseball field, recalling the strict Dragon measures employed in this city.

How long since kids have played here?

"Anything else?" asked Jack, his tone tight.

Dread replaced my sadness about the shuttered park.

"Could the Chinese connect Moss to Old Glory and Market?"

We knew that Moss was photographed, but his prints weren't taken. Regardless, everything would lead to his fake federal agent credentials, which would withstand most outside inquiries.

"Who knows? Zhang is no fool," admitted Jack quietly, and we both spent a silent moment reflecting on the murderous head of the Chinese Ministry of State. "But we don't have time for this now. "Get out of the Windy City, and we'll talk soon. And don't forget there's a reason for our rules."

Damn it. Was he listening to my chat with Ari?

"Bird incoming," announced Liam.

I walked toward Dex, who'd propped Moss between himself and Hux.

"We're heading to South Dakota to drop Moss at a medical facility," said my XO.

The chopper's rotors made a shallow, suppressed sound as Sarah landed the black helicopter in the middle of the field.

I stayed on the ground, twenty feet from the chopper, providing cover until the last of the team was secure onboard.

"Alfa-leader," Sarah called. "We're ready for you."

"If you stay, we can begin ending this," the Beast suggested.

My boots remained planted into the grassy field.

"Alfa-leader..." repeated Dex on the team channel.

I turned to see six sets of eyes staring at me from the chopper, and Liam already beginning to get out of his seat and grab his gear.

No, you don't. This shit is mine to bear and fix alone.

"Coming up," I called and ran to join them.

EVERY MOMENT COUNTS

The sun began its descent as the Old Glory medical facility, a double-story white rectangular building, appeared on the outskirts of Sioux Falls. Looking back, I saw the team still huddled around Moss lying unconscious on the chopper's floor. He'd begun having problems breathing thirty minutes before our scheduled arrival and now wore an oxygen mask and laid still as the team continued to check his vitals.

As I turned around to face the front, I observed Sarah's intensity increasing. Her eyes were focused on the lit helipad as she communicated with the ground staff about Moss's deteriorating situation. She landed us flawlessly, carefully bringing her wounded brother to the earth.

We're lucky to have you.

I patted her shoulder and turned to face my team.

"Mask up," I called on comms. All of Alfa hid their faces, as it was the standard procedure whenever working closely with Old Glory personnel.

The side door swung open as the medical team rushed over with a gurney. Alfa helped to carefully place Moss on it, and then they rolled him back quickly into the facility.

"I'll handle our accommodations," murmured Dex.

I nodded, knowing we were all staying until we learned Moss's fate.

"Ouch," yelped Liam when Hux smacked the back of his neck. "I didn't..." he complained.

"You thought about it," concluded Hux, with a growing smirk.

I sighed like an exhausted parent observing children who teased each other mercilessly, but it was a show. I was glad they managed to hold onto some levity, especially now.

It was a long night. Alfa waited outside the operating room, and Jack and Custer checked in periodically for updates. We'd been told Moss had several issues, but the internal bleeding had to be handled first.

I watched my Rogues pace, wring their hands, and tap impatiently, their dominant emotion suffering.

"It will change..." whispered the Beast, making my heart race with desire and concern.

When the door opened, a masked Asian woman dressed in dark gray scrubs emerged. She didn't flinch, even with six masked warriors converging on her.

Of course. She's worked with Rogues before.

"He's stable and going to make it." She paused. "He was obviously tortured, and the hard drugs they used could have ended him."

She'd barely finished talking when Alfa barreled past her to see their friend.

I shrugged at her and followed suit.

To see Moss laughing and bantering with Alfa made my heart swell. When Dex looked back at me, he knew it was time to shoo Alfa out and make ready for liftoff.

Moss watched them leave and turned to face me. I wasn't surprised to see his famous smile fade from his bruised face, even though he was bandaged and stuck with a few tubes.

I moved to the bed and gripped the rail.

"Let it out."

He looked down momentarily and then turned his eyes back to mine.

"I fucked up, Sir. I got caught and didn't complete the mission. But they didn't break me."

"They sure didn't." Relief filled the space between us. "Now, let's go over your last steps."

We rehashed his moves over the last few days and found nothing that could have revealed him.

There's a leak!

"Don't be hard on yourself, Man. I think we may be compromised," I whispered, and his one open eye widened. "Now. Focus on recovering. Nothing else."

He insisted on gripping his arm in mine, and I was happy to feel his iron strength, even when bedridden.

"I'm coming back, Alfa-leader," he growled, slowly lifting his body to sit up.

I bared my teeth in a vicious smile.

"I'm counting on it."

The early dawn light surprised me as I walked outside the glass doors to the helipad. Alfa was huddled near the chopper in hot debate with each other until they saw me walking toward them.

Something's going on.

I recalled the Beast foreshadowing my team's state of mind.

Dex gave the rest a stern look, which silenced them.

"We need to address this," he said, motioning me toward the facility.

My XO was reasonable and rational, and I could feel the raw anger smoldering in his statement.

I looked past him to the rest of the team.

"Anyone else? Don't be shy."

"Like you did with that guard," grumbled Hux, implying more than anyone could admit openly.

"Someone's been ahead of us since Seattle," said Dex, and the rest nodded at the dark reality of a mole within the ranks.

The memory of Nico putting his weight against Taco Libertad's door, holding it from buckling, resurfaced. All I could see was him smiling up at the camera.

"Tanner..." Sarah placed her hand on my shoulder.

I refocused, nodded at her, and scanned their faces. "Anything else?"

It was Jenny who pointed out the elephant in the room.

"We're fighting China, and the debt is growing."

Everyone looked at each other, knowing full well we were all feeling the impact of Market, the Dragon Virus, and everything that had happened since. As for me, the added guilt of my poor choices weighed like lead in my chest.

"Anything else?" I asked, carefully looking at Liam, who'd kept quiet.

He fidgeted uncomfortably, but eventually squared his shoulders and spoke, "We know your family is in danger while you're here with us."

Sarah nodded emphatically, a faint reassuring smile on her motherly face.

His words hung between us, connecting my past departure and the dreadful present.

"Can you promise them to fight 'til the end?" taunted the Beast.

I can't lose them.

My eyes dropped momentarily. I wished to reassure them all that nothing would come between us, but I decided against it.

"I heard you all and need time to think. I'll get a car and head to the Ranch. You fly out to the Cape for some R&R."

MOMENTARY DRIFT

Interstate 90 cut into the endless hilly landscape of the Badlands National Park. Driving a sedan from the medical facility, my mind nearly convulsing with unsolved riddles, I decided it was a perfect time to catch up on what had been happening in the world.

Brett Cohen ran a long piece that started with the riots in Chicago, which had begun to simmer down. He contrasted the actual violence with the wall-to-wall legacy media blackballing of it.

"Funny enough, the only thing they cared to report on, as the Magnificent Mile was looted and destroyed, was an undocumented rumor of vigilantes attacking peaceful protesters."

The conservative podcaster was correct. Even Jack had admitted as much in one of his periodic voice memo updates, "You were right, Son. Not a word on the battle or the bodies."

Brett highlighted Ken Lim for his bravery in his undercover reporting.

"Without him and others like him, the rest of us would be forced to believe the media and the lies about what's happening on the ground."

Brett also commented on Senator Garcia from Texas, one of the Republican senators China blamed for "daring" to ask questions about where the virus originated.

Who is this Garcia guy? This is the fifth time I've heard his name.

The early noon sun illuminated the rocky hills, reminding me of the hard navigation training I'd endured here once upon a training.

"As for China, they are using their new security law to clamp down on Hong Kong even harder," continued Brett.

Cringing through his update, I was relieved when he turned his attention to the Dragon pandemic back home.

"New infections are at record levels, but the deaths trending down from their winter peak…" He went on to lament about the strife around the restrictive Dragon measures and the contrarian approach of some Republican governors. "You cannot force 'safety' on people without forcing them to relinquish their freedoms."

Exactly! Thank God he's brave enough to say it.

Brett switched to the nationwide riots, reporting them currently on a low simmer, with the exception of nightly scuffles in Portland. The mayor there had to discover the hard way that even after the feds left, somehow, the violence didn't stop.

I recalled Jack's original briefing regarding Ryse's American roots in the Northwest and NYC.

"Portland could be where they train..." suggested the Beast.

Brett's voice and my surroundings faded to the background.

For what??

"You could have stayed in Chicago..." The creature's taunt faded to a whisper.

I growled into the empty air, my attention pulled back to the road as a family car passed on my left. A young boy about Ari's age looked at me through the window, and dark thoughts dissipated.

"Last news for today is that Senator Dwayne Jackson accepted Grayson's invitation to run with him as his Vice President..." Brett didn't try to hide his skepticism as he shared his thoughts on this surprising political move.

I grimaced, remembering Chelsea's admiration of the New York Senator.

She loved his support for the Dragon measures. Is this what bugs Brett?

The show ended, leaving me in the silence of the car, those dark thoughts waiting on the outskirts of my consciousness, trying to solve the riddles.

"We need to address this..." I could still feel the intensity of these words from my second.

It's becoming personal for them. Like...

"Like you did with that guard..." Hux didn't hesitate to point out my escalating violence, forcing me to face the creature behind it and the model it presented my Rogues.

Where am I leading them?

My heart rate increased, and I used the *Sense* to calm my vitals.

I need to talk with her.

I reached for my phone, keeping my eyes on the road.

No. I can't!

"Kneel on your sacred flags!" The Demon guy's voice echoed and rattled me further.

My mind then switched to Ishmael, standing tall with the flag. I relaxed a bit, grateful we'd managed to save him in time.

"Someone's been ahead of us since Seattle..." My blood boiled again as I recalled Dex's confirmation.

We almost lost Moss!

Gripping the wheel tighter as I took a turn, I thought about the attacks on Chad and Danielle.

I've been targeted since the funeral...

Endless questions wove like strings pulling on new strings without a destination.

Arrghh.

"*Stop your whining and face the chaos...*" the Beast sneered.

The trance broke, and I felt my hands spasming at the grip on the wheel. Releasing the tension from my hands and my shoulders, I focused on the crisp white clouds dotting the open blue skies and took a deep breath.

My reprieve didn't last long. Anxiety crept into the emptiness of my mind, filling it with random soundless images from Portland, Seattle, and now Chicago.

"The revolution is coming, Bitch!" The last words of the dying guard resurfaced and reminded me of the eight-hundred-pound gorilla in the room.

"We're fighting China, and the debt is growing." Jenny knew that gorilla well.

Yes. Lee warned us, and China fucked us and everyone else. Fucking Zhang should have died!

The thoughts scrambled again, as my mind searched for additional clues.

How deep is Baker in with Grayson? How involved is he?

I hit the wheel with frustration.

"What am I fucking missing?"

"The Great Reset," echoed the Beast before it receded beyond my reach.

"Fuck…" I muttered, my foot pressing for more speed, as if I could outrun the spiral.

"We know your family is in danger while you're here with us."

My heart rate was getting away from me when the phone rang. I answered it quickly, as though my life depended on it.

"Are you okay, Baby?" asked Dani as soon as the line was established.

It was the first time I'd heard her voice since my abrupt departure from that empty road in Northern California. If she was still affected by our last encounter, her caring tone didn't show it.

My eyes closed for one moment of pure darkness and then opened.

"Beating myself up, Dani. About many things."

"That's why I called. I felt you...."

I'm so lucky to have you.

The thought should have warmed me, but all I felt was the cold fear of loss.

"I was the one who wished her husband to step up and help." Her tone was soft. "It's been painful to realize the price for my wanting, but I don't regret it. I know you fight for us, the family, the country. I know it with all my heart..."

"You know things, eh?" I managed to find some space for playfulness.

Her laughter lightened my suffering, if only for the moment.

"Did you remember what I told you when you left?" she wondered.

"When I was eighteen and you were *ten*?"

She laughed again but didn't relent.

"Did you?"

My tired mind offered up a blurred memory.

"No, Baby. Got nothing..."

She chuckled and said, "You already had this hardness about you, but you also had a childish side."

"Those were good years," I replied, remembering how Jack had allowed me to have the life of a teenager if my training remained my top priority. At the memory of my dad's wrinkled face and gray-blue eyes, anger erupted in me.

I didn't choose this!

"And He said, 'Please take your son, your only one, whom you love, yea, Isaac, and go away to the land of Moriah and bring him up there for a burnt offering on one of the mountains, of which I will tell you...'"

Shemtov's words cut through the memories like a sharp blade tearing open the ground underneath me.

Alone in the darkness of the tunnel.
Eyes open, seeing nothing since I got here.
Fear that I will never see again grips me.

Beast?! Where are you?

"Tanner..." Dani's voice found its way into my mental spiral.

"You let your love weaken you...." the Beast admonished me, returning from its lair.

What does it mean? What do you want me to do?

"Baby?" she called, this time her tone tighter.

"I need to go, My Love. I promise to come home very soon."

TIMEOUT

– Black Hills, SD –
Saturday, August 8, 2020

It had been a while since I'd driven into the Ranch, and as I turned off the state road, something stirred inside.

The gravel road carved into the forested black hills made smooth, quiet driving impossible. It was meant to be this way, but it didn't affect my speed. I only slowed down when I saw the guard post—a camouflaged concrete oval-shaped structure, which was even harder to spot with the descending sun directly in front of me.

A bearded man wearing an Old Glory khaki uniform emerged, carrying an assault rifle fitted for night vision. He approached my lowered window to verify that the face matched the one my scanned chip had put on the small tablet connected to his left arm.

"Welcome home, Sir," he said, falling into attention.

"At ease," I replied before I stepped on the pedal.

This isn't my home.

There were two more checkpoints to cross in the Ranch's multilayer defense system. Jack had never revealed the full extent of the design, which he'd perfected after taking over the Ranch from Ulysses.

Because they grew up here. Unlike me.

The resentment dissipated after the last guard cleared me and my eyes caught the last rays of sun glaring over the proud waving flags.

"Feel it, Tanner. No words…" Ulysses's words echoed.

I was ten, just new to the Ranch, when he had taken me to see the "Flags Mount." Grandpa had used a small hill above the final bend before the main house and created a mound with three silver flag poles for the US, South Dakota, and Gadsden flags. The yellow field flag had the words "Don't Tread on Me" emblazoned under a coiled rattlesnake.

If only everyone lived by it. We wouldn't be in this mess.

Continuing over the low hill, something stirred again as the two-story Washington estate came into view, nestled at the flat top.

Enough with this.

I parked the car next to Tami's black family van but didn't reach for the door handle. My eyes fixed on the wide heavy wooden front door, all I could hear was Dani's voice: "You speak of your home as a foreign place, even when we went to visit. No connection. I just never understand…"

It's not home.

The door opened, and my mom stepped out. She wore jeans and a brown blouse, her soft auburn waves stopping at her shoulders. When she waved, my hand reached for the handle, reinforced by her presence.

She was at my door, arms outstretched, by the time I pulled myself out.

"It's good to have you home, My Son."

Ali led me to the dining room, her arm wrapped under mine, where Tami waited with cooing baby Adam in her arms.

"He insisted on staying up to see his uncle," she yawned, rolling her tired eyes at the tall, blue-eyed man behind her. He fumbled forward and extended his hand for a firm handshake, which I gladly accepted.

"Good to see you, Henry." I smiled at my sister's kind-natured, awkward husband.

Chad was next to join us.

"Look at you, Little Brother. You look like a rancher." I could hardly believe my eyes. Gone was the hipster Seattle clothing and style. Jeans, a simple tee, and work boots matched the hair now combed without any gel to keep it tight.

He smiled, arms outstretched for a hug.

"Thank you," Chad whispered. "But don't expect me to change so easily."

He means this.

I moved in and hugged him, hoping his honesty would lead him on the right path forward.

Noticing Lee standing behind Chad with a smile, I separated from Chad with a grin and moved to embrace the former Chinese scientist, my mind refocusing on the next riddle.

Dad exposed Lee to Chad?

My surprise grew when we reached the table, and those two sat beside each other, laughing like good friends.

My dad was last, as always. He stood tall as I walked over to him, holding his glacier-gray-eyed gaze. When his hand extended, I clasped it.

The man who taught me how to shake a hand.

"It's good to have you home, Son. Let's eat."

"Boys, come with me to the study." Jack put his napkin on the table as he rose from his seat. He kissed my mom, said goodbye to the rest, and walked out of the room.

I looked at the empty hall, where my father had disappeared, and back to my brother who looked back and shrugged.

Okay, so first time for lots of things.

"Go on, boys," said Ali.

We stood up and Chad gestured for me to lead.

Jack's office resided within the heart of the home, shuttered from the outside. The heavy metal door was propped open, and the yellow sunlight blazed into the dark hallway.

We found him in his chair behind his dark brown oak desk. When he motioned for us to take the two guest seats on the other side of it, Chad moved forward, but my eyes were still taking in the place, as I always do when visiting.

Three of the four walls were covered with pictures in both black-and-white and color. They carried my family's rich history, from Ulysses working at Mount Rushmore with David Norton to photos of my angelic towhead baby daughter that Ali must have printed and framed.

The last wall, behind my father, touted a huge oil painting of General Washington crossing the Delaware River on his way to the Battle of Trenton and Princeton. Memories of Ulysses and my father's discussions of that daring Revolutionary War move filled my mind. I remember feeling the reverence they had for the General who had defeated the Hessian auxiliaries the British garrisoned in Trenton and helped prop up the Continental Army's morale when it badly needed the boost. As a young man, I'd asked my father why he loved that picture so much, and he'd answered with an unsolved riddle: "So I remember that there is always a chance, always another way, to come back into the fight."

"Sit down, Tanner," commanded Jack with a smirk.

Chad and I exchanged one more uncomfortable, stunned look as I lowered my body into the chair beside him.

"You both look like rabbits in a headlight," he grumbled with a sly grin. Looking at Chad, he said, "You earned the right to sit here with us. What was before is no longer."

My brother smiled slightly as he replied, "Yeah, dad, you are the best teacher."

Wow. A lot has changed.

Jack shifted his gaze to me and raved about my brother and his help in Old Glory.

"We've placed him in our analysis division, emphasizing US events."

Even though Old Glory was completely segregated from The Rogue Doctrine, I was still surprised at how quickly Chad had been adopted into the "family business."

My thought evaporated as my father broke the surprise.

"Chad will now give you his first-ever analysis. He worked hard on this," said my father proudly.

Chad smiled and cleared his throat.

"Dad, can you turn on your office projector?"

Jack clicked on his small remote, and a wide black screen descended from the ceiling. My brother attached his phone to it and began his presentation.

His slides told the tale from the Dragon's beginning to this moment.

"The virus, the measures, and then Chicago worked like a tinder box and a match. This is before you even address the hatred toward President Stone."

He looked uncomfortable, rubbing his neck for a moment.

"Go on, Son. You're not there anymore. You're here, with us," assured Jack, understanding Chad's plight better than I did.

My brother nodded and continued, "Both sides view losing the election as an existential threat, and this feeds the loop of the protests and Dragon pandemic."

It was well into the night, and my body was tired, but Chad's lecture was fascinating as he managed to articulate the perfect storm, which blew up across the nation after the motorist died in Chicago back in late May.

"Like it or not, there is now a generation of young Americans who don't view their country like us in this room. For them, it is an exploitative nation, which uses a heavy boot on anyone who doesn't toe the line."

It was remarkable to experience my brother's transformation since his escape from Seattle—enough to forgo any remarks for his past opinions.

"One last thing before I wrap up. I want to bring up the issue of the vigilantes."

My body remained relaxed, but a silent alarm bell went off in my spine. Jack remained impassive, but that's just who he was.

"Go on," prompted my father.

Chad derided the phenomenon, openly suggesting that the effect of attracting right-wing violent copycats is severe, whether it is true or not.

"We have enough issues on the streets without people taking the law into their own hands. The best way to beat this is through civil discourse, not violence."

He's not wrong. The problem is that all his old buddies prefer burning to talking. They're making it almost impossible for us to save this country without violence.

The realization bugged me as my own doubts constantly crept up.

Where am I leading Alfa?

I looked at him, searching his eyes for more context between his words. He smiled.

"It doesn't mean I don't appreciate how you saved me in Seattle. Sometimes you must use violence..." He looked down at his own admission. "Thank you for believing in me."

Warmth spread through me, and I reached out to squeeze his shoulder as I responded, "Of course."

Jack thanked Chad, who understood it was time for him to leave.

When the door closed behind him, my father praised my brother and their growing relationship.

"I'm glad it's working," I replied sincerely.

He pressed a button, and the only door made a tightening sound and fresh air entered through the vent above.

"I saw that Lee and Chad are buddies. Is that safe?" I wondered out loud.

Jack waved his hand.

"Lee's cover story is excellent, so I allowed them to meet, and their relationship grew naturally." He took a deep breath. "Now, let's talk."

"No sleep again, eh?" I grumbled.

"That's a 'you' problem," he replied and started the briefing.

I pulled myself to attention and told my body to suck it up.

★　★　★

"I talked to Moss's doctor again. He's a strong young man, and he didn't crack. The rest will heal."

We both rejoiced at the outcome of the rescue, but it felt a little too much like moving from one fire to the next, praying not to be burned alive each time.

"Tell me about Chicago." His tone was measured.

My eyes shifted to Washington, proudly standing on the boat carrying him and the soldiers across the treacherous river crossing.

How low we fell...

I pushed all of my disgust aside to answer my commander, "Just like the other sites, they're getting better and better at creating these zones of control. Local governments are frozen..." My report continued, covering the "accented man" who tortured Moss and the leak that had probably revealed him. I highlighted that he was to be transferred to San Francisco, noting my concerns about Zhang's involvement and a possible connection to Market. I grumbled over the fact that Daj was nowhere to be found and the cryptic "revolution is coming" from the guard I executed last.

He thanked me for the report.

"His chip did manage to grab some interesting details about Ryse and Comrades and their work with other organizations across the land. We can't tell what they're doing, but there is a high level of coordination."

"No actionable data?"

My father rubbed his tired eyes.

"Well... we did get some references to 'migrant resettlements' aimed at big cities. The 'Travelers' are mentioned as the ground coordinators."

I remembered Mr. Jones's help exposing us to the Chinese dabbling with smuggling certain migrants into the states.

Were migrants directed to Chicago? If so, why?

Jack probably read my face.

"We did find some traces of encrypted communications. We suspect that Chinese technology is involved."

Just say China, Dad.

He shifted in his seat.

"As for the 'leak,' The RCC concluded that Moss was captured due to advance intel on him..." He started with the possibility that Old Glory was ratted out to the Chinese by Baker or other Deep State actors.

"Even so, how would they know about Moss specifically?" I rallied against the unlikely option.

Jack shrugged.

"You were all disguised and masked during Market, but maybe Baker managed to film some or all of you. We don't know for sure." It was a scary notion to entertain. "If this is true, then that asshole broke our agreement," he said, not offering details into whatever he and Baker had ironed out after Market.

"What's the other possibility?"

His eyes widened in concern.

"Moss has somehow tripped a defense system we cannot see."

No other options?

"What? Spill it, Son," he barked.

"I'm just worried that we're missing the picture, Dad. You heard my rumble already, but hear it again..." I laid out all that concerned me, trying to tie together a picture, many parts of which were hidden behind a veil. "My team and I are eager to get to the bottom of this. Just let us work," I uttered, knowing well that my real request was loud and clear.

Give us Directive Two!

"We're back to the vigilantes conversation, I see...."

My anger bubbled at his comparison, but the *Sense* held it back.

Jack's face suddenly softened.

"Listen, Son. I do understand your passion for it. Frankly, you're more correct than wrong. But you've got to exercise patience. We're dealing with many unknown factors, accelerated by old grievances *and* Marxist theories."

He pointed at an old color photo with an older Ulysses, tall as my father, his long white hair, a mustache, and burning gray-blue eyes conveying the intensity of his spirit. Grandpa stood next to a younger Lieutenant Jack in an aviator dress uniform.

"My mom took that photo. I'd just returned from Nam..." his voice went down an octave as his memories returned. "My dad slapped a protester moments before we took that picture."

"Why?" I was stunned but not truly surprised, recalling the crazy stories I'd heard about Grandpa over the years.

"That protester rushed me and started cursing the service and uniform I wore. He didn't know Grandpa was right behind him." My dad chuckled. "Grandpa told him, 'You got slapped because you don't deserve a punch.'"

We both laughed.

"Things looked bad back then as well. We must remember this and not jump too quickly to start a war we can't end."

It wasn't what I wanted to hear, but there was no room to advance.

"As for China, we still don't have any actionable proof that could be handed to the government to act upon. All we have are riddles, the latest being the effort to remove Moss to San Francisco and this migrants operation."

"What was the deal with Baker?" I pressed, determined to find the leak that led to Moss's capture.

"Market was a shitshow, but we both agreed that China was the bigger enemy." Jack sighed and shook his head. "He was to keep us out of the Chinese crosshairs while we remain quiet about the virus and Lee."

"If China knows about us…" I started.

"Yeah…" he replied.

"Would they connect us to the raid in Mexico? To Calexico's failed Border Patrol ambush?"

"We did some good work to place the blame on rival cartels."

"Then what?" I asked. "We can't be waiting here for them to discover more."

"Leave this to Custer and me." His sly smile returned. "We've been thinking about introducing you to other Rogues…" This admission got my full attention, but he added nothing more.

"What about the home front then?"

"I'm helping General Tall with the Deep State witch hunt against him. In return, he'll open some doors with the administration for when we're ready to expose whoever is going against the country domestically."

My irritation grew.

"But what happens if Stone loses? Would we go to Baker's benefactor with whatever we find? The Dems are practically handholding the rioters, egged on by the media, who whitewash everything."

His eyes narrowed, but he had no immediate reply to my question. When he finally spoke, his tone carried an edge.

"Even so, we'll buckle down, close the hatches, and not start an all-out war against our people." His eyes softened again as the commander was replaced by the father. "Those who killed your friend will not enjoy our mercy, however."

I grunted and recoiled back into my chair, recalling my mind-wrecking drive and all of those unstoppable thoughts.

"Anything new on 'The Great Reset'?" I asked, remembering the Beast's insinuation.

He frowned and shook his head.

Of course not...

"Anything else, or can I send you to sleep already?" asked Jack.

I'm so tired, but we have to address this shit.

I mentioned that Texan Senator Garcia could be a future ally, and Jack promised to look more into him before I moved back to the upcoming election, "And what are you making of Dwayne Jackson? He's going to run with Grayson...."

"It's not surprising that Jackson is well-received in Washington and got some fame due to his pro-Dragon measures position..." He offered more details about Jackson's recent ascent from working in the State Department during the Charlton administration to the prestigious US senator seat from New York.

"Did he work with Grayson back then?" I asked, recalling that the current Democratic presidential contender was our Defense Secretary.

"Not that we know of. They were from different departments after all," replied Jack. "Anyway, you go home and rest up. Custer wants you to visit him soon to keep up your 'active Marine Colonel' facade."

Just one of too many facades, I thought as I pulled myself out of the chair and said goodnight to my father.

RUNS DEEP

The alarm rang, and I squeezed my eyes tighter as I reached out to the bedside lamp for my phone.

Damn. Already...

The soft morning light pushed against the predawn darkness and my ever-growing tiredness. I slowly blinked my eyes into focus as I took in the room with the large wood frame bed, desk, and windows looking out at the Ranch from the breathtaking second-story view. Grandpa had given me this room when I was with him after Bogotá.

Feeling the tug of exhaustion pulling me back, I forced myself to the shower.

Revived, I opened the closet and found the few jeans and shirts I'd left there through the years. My mind was already spinning on the information my father had shared the night before as I dressed. Hurriedly grabbing my few items, I walked downstairs to the front door and found my parents outside on the deck, sitting beside each other.

It warmed my heart to see my parents keeping up this daily routine I remember witnessing since we'd moved here more than three decades earlier.

They noticed me and motioned for me to join them.

"Do you want coffee, Sweetie?" my mom asked as she rose from her chair to hug me.

Though her words were full of love, fear over my deteriorating state of mind was all I could feel.

If I sit and talk, I might break and say things…

"It's okay, Mom. I'd rather head out."

Ali's hands gestured toward the still-dark world outside and then looked to Jack for support. My father just shrugged with a smile and stood to give me a warm farewell hug. After kissing my mom's cheek, I set out.

I walked into the gray-black world for several minutes, willing my feet to keep moving. The truth was that I wanted to sit down with them, to confide in them about my growing storm, which had my family in its path. But the fear forced me onward.

I'm not going to lose them!

Sarah was coming to pick me up with the Old Glory jet. My favorite way to the airstrip was one I'd perfected through the years. Instead of taking the roundabout road, I crossed through the hilly forested area. The pine trees grew from the rich terrain and looked like majestic sentinels on city walls. I climbed and climbed, knowing it by heart, until the chill ran up my spine.

I'm being watched.

My body crouched and my right hand flew to pull out my Wraith.

"Don't shoot, Tanner. It would be a waste of good coffee..."

Jerome.

Happiness swelled in my heart as I holstered the gun and walked in the direction of the familiar voice.

Jerome rose from his perch to shake my hand and hug me.

"Sit," he gestured toward the two small lawn chairs and the boiling pot on a small cooker and the active noise scrambler on the ground.

"How...?" I asked as I lowered myself into the chair and accepted a small tin mug of black coffee.

Jerome laughed.

"Boy, we all know about this path of yours. Figured you'd leave as soon as you could..."

His white-bearded face was suspended in a smile, but his eyes conveyed much more.

He senses my itch to leave.

I sighed and took a sip, realizing there was no way to evade his ambush.

"I'm not from here. I'm not like you—like them. I don't belong..."

He threw his head back, snorting in a half-laugh and half-admonishment.

"Pile of shit, Son. You were born here, on this very land," he said, pressing his finger against the rock. "Your blood runs deep within these hills, whether you realize this or not."

Conflicting emotions collided within me, and I realized one of them was hope. I leaned forward, ready to listen to him and understand further all that was hidden from me.

The old man sighed and shook his head, his eyes suddenly sad and his tone low.

"I was here... for your ceremony..." His voice trailed off, as he appeared to be calculating whether to tell me more.

Ceremony?

After a few moments, he smiled.

"He waited for you to return. We all did."

Questions swirled in my head, but the old friend seemed to have an agenda.

"I want to talk with you a moment about my girl," he started, sitting forward to set his elbows on his knees.

Suddenly, I felt like a teenager getting caught by the girl's dad late at night and it must have shown on my face, as he laughed again.

"Oh, come on now. I'm not talking about your not-so-secret fling."

I laughed with him, feeling foolish but also relieved.

His face turned serious as he made eye contact again.

"I wanted to ask you for something for when my time comes and I'm not around."

My heart raced again at the thought of this man not being a presence in Lynn's life.

She may be a badass, but she's always been Daddy's girl.

"She's a fearless leader, Tanner, such that we don't even deserve. But her enemies... they will only keep growing, especially if she does what I think she'll do..."

"What is it, Sir?" I asked.

"Please watch over her once I'm gone."

My heart dropped.

I'm not whatever you think I am.

"Man up or lose the moment," growled the Beast.

"Of course I will, Sir," I said, shaking his hand.

"Thank you, Son." He smiled. "Now get on to your plane and back home to your family."

LIKE A STRANGER

– Santa Monica, CA –
Sunday, August 9, 2020

The time difference had worked in my favor as the morning sun blazed above. Seated on the motorcycle pulled out of our storage at the Santa Monica Airport, the engine purred quietly beneath me.

"Why are you still here?" wondered Sarah as she passed me on the way to the restroom.

Shrugging, I looked at the clock and realized I'd been on the ground for more than thirty minutes.

Why can't I go home?

My heart yearned to see my family, but my body remained frozen on the bike.

I placed the helmet on and voice commanded a call to Custer.

Sounds of heavy machinery and soldiers reached my ears before the General's deep tone did.

"Good morning, Colonel."

"Is it a good time to come by?" I asked, pained over my proximity to my family and my inability to drive toward them.

He paused and softened his tone, "Come on by, Colonel. I'm in the field. Just check with my office when you arrive."

Thank you.

Warmth displaced my anxiety as I got off the bike to retrieve a spare uniform from storage.

Custer's office contacted him when I arrived, and a young MP arrived with a Humvee to drive me over to where he commanded a live-fire training with infantry, aerial, and armor units.

The explosions increased in frequency and volume as the desert road took us closer to the rear of the exercise. Upon arrival, the major pointed to a lone hill, a bit away from the action.

"Colonel, the General is up there waiting for you," she said with a smile.

The BDU fit Custer's lean and erect older frame like a young man's. The crown of his bald black head glistened in the sunlight as he turned to face me coming up the hill and motioned for me to join him.

"You came in good time," he said, handing me a pair of powered binoculars. We watched in quiet admiration as the exercise ran its course in the distance. Tanks blasted their targets, assisted by Marines who worked among them. Combat choppers flew overhead, adding their missiles and short cannons to the symphony.

"Do you miss this?" asked Custer, eyes still on the drill.

Did he sense that?

We dropped the binoculars and turned to face each other.

"I do miss it. The world is simpler. You know who the enemy is, and you're allowed to kill it."

He chuckled as though my words had touched on something completely different, as he activated the noise scrambler in his BDU pants pocket.

"Well, it's good you show your face here, so people actually believe you're working for me," he said.

We quickly debriefed about Chicago, Moss, and his recovery. When I thanked him for the help with Nils, the General shook his head, face flushing momentarily.

"They suspended him indefinitely the next day. Said he voiced too much opposition to the mayor's handling of the riots."

My blood boiled thinking about the lone cop who stood by the car the night we got Moss out of Chicago.

"He definitely had the chance to apologize for what he grumbled in the station, but he didn't bow," Custer snorted.

"Of course he didn't." I smiled. "Same stubborn streak."

"Watch it, Colonel," he uttered, his eyes smiling. "So what brings you here?"

His question was expected, but a precise answer wasn't. Memories of Nico, Ishmael, and Todd surfaced, my guilt rumbling just beneath all of them.

"I want to do more, and it's eating me from inside. Why are you stopping us?"

"Is this why you're not home right now?" he sighed.

His question irritated me, even though there was no chance the General tried to provoke me.

"Why didn't you start a family?" I asked, surprised at my daring.

Custer cocked his head and nodded slowly.

"Fair enough."

He looked again through his binoculars and called his aide to inform him he was indisposed.

"What do you know about our time in Vietnam?" asked the General.

Ali's words echoed, "It was a cruel war, like them all. Nobody returned the same. You ask if something happened? Yes, and it placed your father on the path he's on. Same goes for William."

"That you two were there and changed afterward," I replied.

He laughed.

"Ali... those are her words." His face turned serious and sad. "But she's not wrong either."

Custer started his story with meeting my father in flight school and their instant chemistry.

"We grew up quite differently. Him on the Ranch, and me in Chicago's South Side. But we just knew...."

A few choppers flew above us, and the General continued, "It was the end of the war, and we were paired up and sent over as soon as we got our wings..." Custer described the humiliating condition of the long war, seeing all the blood and suffering for a collapsing mission. "The morning of the incident, Jack and I were on patrol when we were suddenly ambushed by a dozen or so Chinese warplanes."

Chinese? I never heard about them being involved in Vietnam besides the financial aid they gave to the north.

"We didn't have time to consider the implications as they rained fire on us..." The General detailed a harrowing dogfight that ended with ten Chinese planes down and two still flying. "It was a bloody miracle that us two rookie pilots stood their superior numbers. The last two bogies flew off, but our victory was short-lived. Your father's plane was too damaged, and it was clear he had to eject."

"What happened?"

Custer chuckled as he recalled those moments.

"Only Jack can calm you down while his plane is on fire. Anyway, he ejected and told me to return home."

"How did he calm you?"

"He said that he knew how to traverse hell and that I should go back and get support." The General shook his head. "This was the first clue about your father's dark side that I hadn't seen during flight school..."

Dad only hinted at how Grandpa had "trained" him to fight during his youth.

"I tried to radio back for support, and our carrier commanding officer, Admiral Benson, actually got on the line and ordered me to fly back immediately."

Why haven't I heard his name?

"Those were hard moments. You're ordered back to safety, and your body begs you to do as you're told. But I couldn't..." his words trailed with his memories. "Anyway, I faked a distress call that my plane was also damaged and ejected."

The General floored me with his admission of serious insubordination, and it didn't seem like the story had even started. The sounds of the live fire faded.

"Did they send the choppers for you?"

He shook his head, eyes dropping for a moment.

"Far from it. Although the Admiral wanted to mount up a rescue mission, he was ordered to stand down and not risk any further casualties."

"Casualties?" I was blown away. "Didn't they know that you managed to evac?"

He raised his hand, signaling for me to hold and listen.

"Luckily, we found each other in the jungle quickly, thanks to your father and his outdoor experience..." Custer detailed how the two pilots found themselves over a hundred miles from the collapsing border with South Vietnam. "We had our comms but were far from anyone who could hear us. Frankly, it was too dangerous, as the enemy could triangulate us at any moment. It wasn't clear whether the Chinese knew about our ejections, as they'd happened after they retreated, but it mattered little."

His face hardened as he recalled my father's synopsis of the situation.

"After calling me an idiot for joining him in 'hell,' he promised me that he'd get us home." Custer smirked. "I never truly understood how Ulysses molded your father. He looked like another roughneck rancher who maybe loved hunting too much. I just had no idea…"

Yeah… that's Grandpa, for sure. I miss the crusty old man.

"We managed to evade everyone for a while, but Jack insisted we poke around as we made our way to the border. It's how we discovered the Chinese working with the Vietcong at a large depot base…"

He detailed seeing the Chinese People's Liberation Army convoys dropping tons of weapons and supplies for the victory-driven North Vietnamese forces.

"It's also how we were discovered," grumbled Custer as he described a two-man Vietcong patrol that saw them spying on the convoys.

"They were just kids, barely in their teens," said Custer. "I was frozen, but your dad downed them both with headshots."

He blinked his eyes as if the images were fresh.

"I'd never seen a man die so close, even though my bombs and cannons had killed many already…" The General continued to explain how the two pilots fought their way down south, killing many more along the way. "And the grand finale still waited for us."

The radio crackled, and the aide called Custer to inform him the drill was over. The General responded to him and then got back to his story.

"We were about ten miles from the border when our luck ran out. The Vietcong had us surrounded on top of a heavily forested hill. We barely had any ammo left and were exhausted from a few days with very little sleep and food. Jack tasked me with the radio efforts, as we were close enough to be heard and on a high vantage point."

"What did he do?" I asked, wondering about the younger brutal version of my father.

Custer smiled viciously.

"He got our defenses ready for the night assault on our position."

The General said the only message he got was that they must reach the border on their own, as no rescue was possible due to their location.

"Was it true?" I was stunned by this abandonment of US troops behind the line.

The General nodded sadly.

"Does that ring a bell for you, Colonel?"

Market! Damn it! Anger spiked in me for a moment.

Custer continued, not allowing me a moment to dwell on the connection between the two events, "Just before nightfall, it was clear that we'd get no rescue.

I'll never forget what your dad told me before they arrived…"

My body tensed up, new and wild thoughts racing as I learned the origins of the two men who'd eventually started The Doctrine.

"Jack said, 'We're probably going to die here, but if we make it, then everything changes,'" recounted Custer with a long sigh. "In retrospect, that was the night your father laid the foundations for the 'Rogue Dance,' as he gave me the last of our ammo and only kept his blade while telling me that I'd have to bloody myself further."

Custer recounted the final battle, where the two fought a brutal melee on the hill.

"We killed and killed, but they kept on coming. Jack kept one grenade for us if all else failed."

Oh my God.

A shiver ran down my spine.

"But just as dawn broke, a new force joined the fight and eviscerated the Vietcong from the back. A Marine special force unit had reached us."

"I thought no rescue was possible…"

Custer snorted in disgust.

"It wasn't. The Marine commander brought us to the border and swore us to secrecy about the rescue, no matter who asked us. He sent us alone to finish the last trek ourselves."

What the hell?

"Who sent him? Who authorized it?" I was speechless and tried to tie the story to anything I knew.

"Admiral Benson risked being court-martialed, jailed, and probably worse," replied the General with reverence on his face. "Anyway, your dad said it was okay for me to tell you the story, but do us both a favor and don't bring it up with him unless absolutely necessary."

I nodded, more confused than anything else. There were so many questions swirling.

"Why did you tell me the story? Why now?"

He squinted his dark eyes and grunted.

"You asked tough questions. I'm offering some answers. It all started with Ulysses returning from the war, worried about where the country was heading..."

The death camps... the soviets...

"Your dad used to laugh at your grandpa's intense seriousness. He told me all about it during flight school. But after the incident, your dad changed. And so did I. We both understood your grandpa better."

More riddles.

Custer shook his head, and lowered his voice as he said his next words, "Now, it seems as if your turn has arrived..."

My mom's words reverberated in my head, "I remember meeting Ulysses for the first time and praying your father would never have that haunted look, and then Vietnam came about. Now, my son looks at me with the same eyes."

"Little did we know how we had been betrayed by the very people who sent us to fight an enemy, which they then refused to acknowledge as being present," continued the General. "Already, there was a well-entrenched Deep State that wanted to cozy up to the Chinese and 'work things out with them' instead of calling them out for being what they were and are."

"Who told you that?" I pressed.

"The Admiral. He warned us and pleaded with us to remain quiet, else great danger would come to our doors."

Wow.

"Do you see now? We've been in this struggle for decades, carefully working and preparing for a time when we'd be needed to step up and protect our American way of living."

Because we are betrayed by our own...

He reached out with his right hand to squeeze my shoulder, reminding me how strong he was, even in his late-sixties.

"Market was hard on you. I understand you more than you can imagine," he said softly. "He was just like you, consumed and driven to engage. The Doctrine was what kept him sane. That, your grandpa, and Ali," said the General with a chuckle. "None other could whoop your father to silence."

I was amused, thinking about Dani's power over my decisions.

Maybe that's why I can't go home.

"This has been a long-running battle, which we started and you'll hopefully lead to victory one day." He took a deep breath, and his tone firmed up. "You must be patient. They took their time plotting and getting ready. Not for nothing, they called it 'the long march through the institutions.'"

"But when do we act?"

My anxiety piqued.

"You'll know when the time's right. All your training, hard as it was, was meant for this moment in time. You must stay focused and work the way forward beyond the mayhem. It's how we've survived until now."

I blew my breath out in frustration but couldn't let this moment be wasted.

"Who is Benson? How come I've never heard about him?"

His eyes narrowed again, but the faint smile remained.

"The Admiral made The Doctrine possible," he replied without offering anything more.

I need more.

"How exactly did you convince an admiral to be involved?"

He tilted his head, and his smile disappeared.

"Why are you asking this?"

I might as well.

"Because I feel you're hiding more about what's going on now in the country," I replied.

The General crossed his arms, his face remaining stoic.

"Since when do you have this *feeling*?"

"Since he called me that day about what happened in Chicago," I answered.

His smile returned, and he seemed impressed.

"Some stuff will be just between you and your dad."

What does that mean?!

When Custer didn't offer more, I pressed elsewhere.

"Then why no family?"

His face grew sad and he looked at the hilly brown earth.

"Your father was already married during Nam. Everything changed, and we embarked on the road leading to this conversation. You ask why I didn't build a family. Well, I decided to adopt you all as mine. It was enough to keep me awake at night without adding more fear."

His words released the demonic fears in my mind until I heard the Beast laughing in the background.

"I can't lose them, Sir. It's not an option..."

"Today is not the day to face your decisions. Go home to your family."

What the hell does he mean?

Memories of Nico's funeral, the promise to his father, and all that had happened since haunted me all at once.

I fell into attention and saluted the man who commanded me in both worlds of my existence. He returned my salute and then dragged me into a hug.

"Go on now and leave this old man to reflect on life," he said.

I walked down the hill, glancing back one last time to see the General standing alone, looking into nothingness. A surprising wave of pain and affection hit me all at once, requiring me to use the *Sense* to force my legs to find my way home.

IT'S ME

The ride to Los Angeles from Camp Pendleton was silent, save for the racket in my mind. The General's words had left me confused and reflective about Romulus and Remus, their past, and their devotion to saving our country.

The Venice Boulevard exit loomed, and I gunned the throttle as I got off the freeway. The expansive three-lane road started around Downtown LA and ended at the boardwalk in the heart of Venice Beach. I entered the road as the sun glowed red, and for a few moments, I recalled my infatuation with this area in my early years.

I should drive by the restaurant, I thought but didn't turn my bike in the direction, sensing the thin fabric of my thoughts and the volcano bubbling underneath them. *Later.*

When the complex gate opened, the black Israeli female agent strolled by and nodded casually as I rolled in.

As I parked outside our townhome, I saw lights on the second floor and heard kids laughing and Dani and Celeste doing their best to rein them in. It should have made me smile, but all I felt was awkward and disconnected.

Get a grip!

I chastised myself for almost knocking, found my key, and unlocked the door.

"Daddy!!! Daddy!!!" Ari yelled when he heard the door open and ran to the top of the stairs. A wide grin spread across his face as he barreled downstairs and lunged at me.

I dropped my things in time to catch my little boy and pull him to my chest.

"I missed you so much," I told him as I tightened my grip and kissed his head, overcome by his pure love and innocence.

"Daddy... Daddy..."

This time, it was the sweet voice of my Leelee, who stood at the top of the stairs, held back from running down by my gorgeous wife.

"What a surprise," whispered Dani to my ear after I kissed my towhead princess and held her and my queen close.

Celeste and her kids, David and Odalys, welcomed me warmly. The children's faces didn't have the luster they once did, and it dawned on me with great pain that they just saw their friends calling "Daddy" and it hurt.

Fuck.

"Where are my hugs?" I asked Nico's kids, opening my arms, determined to channel their father's love into their small beings. I tightened my squeeze when I felt them linger and didn't let go until they made the first move.

Dani served me dinner and then wrangled the kids, giving Celeste and me a moment to catch up at the table.

"It's been very tough, Tanner. The homeschooling, the lockdown, and the constant heckles for not being masked. I can deal with all of those, but the empty bed every morning..." Her voice was sad and full of the same longing I'd felt in the arms of her children moments earlier. "Some days, the only thing that gets me out of bed is the knowledge that David and Odalys now only have me."

Her words pierced my thawing heart.

Brother. I failed you, but I will not fail your family.

I leaned forward and reached out to hold her hand.

"He's gone, but you will never be alone. I promise you that."

Her eyes teared, and she nodded slowly.

"You know, his mural is done, but it gets constant abuse and vandalism."

My blood boiled.

"What kind of vandalism?"

"The usual crap about cops, hate for the country, and symbols." She sighed. "Always symbols."

"What kind?" I pressed quietly.

Sensing how my hand had tightened on hers, I relaxed my grip and sat back in my chair again.

She described the Comrades and Ryse symbols, but there was something else she didn't say.

"What is it? Is there more?"

She looked to the side, ensuring the kids weren't hearing anything.

"That scary Dragon Skull occasionally. Just like when they killed him…"

Skull… They use it to scare people. Fucking bastards!

A memory of the dying guard in Chicago and his fear of the Flex returned.

Monsters frighten assholes as well…

"Tanner…" Celeste's voice brought me back from the dark abyss of unending riddles.

I used the *Sense* to calm down and asked her to be careful and only go there with an escort. She smiled and mentioned that Emmanuel always backs her up on those cleaning trips.

Glancing at the clock on the dining room wall, she sighed again.

"It's time for me to go. I'm sure you and Danielle have a lot to catch up on."

Celeste called Roberto, who came to pick them up.

"It's good to see you, Tanner," he said, his eyes dim and his age suddenly showing more as he hunched over to help the kids into the car.

I'll keep my promise, Roberto. I almost had him.

Dani and I put the kids to bed, but even the multiple stories and countless kisses didn't help clear the dark weight left in me after hearing Celeste's pain and fear.

"Are you okay?" Dani asked when we closed the kids' room door quietly.

The question was blameless and well-meant, but a spike of rage and resentment coursed through me.

Yeah, besides all those I killed since last seeing you and the hunger for more blood!

"I'm good, Honey," I gently kissed her. "I just need a moment. I'll go out for a run and come back."

She smiled and nodded, but her expression told me she'd heard everything I was afraid to say.

The Venice boardwalk hadn't been safe at night since my early years there, but the pandemic and the riots had quickly taken it from unsafe to hellish. My run started at the closed-up police beach station where I wanted to check on Todd, who wasn't on his hill.

Night time. I hope.

The sound of the waves breaking in the darkness reminded me that it had been a while since my last surf, and I sighed and began running north along the boardwalk.

The camps and tents dotted the sand and pavement, reminding me of some third-world places I'd had the "pleasure" of being deployed in. The drifters and homeless people owned the boardwalk, having a nightly party without any cop in sight. They allowed me to run through them with only a few heckles about not being masked.

Really?

As I ran past the retail stores, it saddened me to think about how all the hard work put into creating a business was now replaced with the feeding hand of the government that doled out stimulus checks, basically paying people to stay at home.

We're printing money, debasing our currency, and ruining people's spirits. Fucking politicians!

I stepped up the pace, fueled by the growing anger at everything happening to us, the country, and the world.

Fucking China and all that were involved in this!

"What about your part?" whispered the Beast, and shame reverberated through me with each word.

"Arrgh..." I growled and turned away from the boardwalk back to Main Street, which would take me back home.

My feet raced faster and faster as I tried to put a stop to the mental spiral with exhaustion. As I approached Venice Circle, my body froze, seeing Taco Libertad from across the roundabout.

I pulled up my neck gaiter, masking my face, and strolled toward the shuttered and sealed restaurant, each step feeling as if it were in thick wet cement.

I almost gasped when I saw *his* eyes. Nico's image covered the entire side wall, dressed in a Marine uniform, an American flag behind him. My heart pounded as my dead best friend looked at me.

Getting close enough to the wall, I saw all the recent vandalism marks that had been painted over. My hand reached forward, palm open, fingers stretched to feel the painted rough siding.

The bottle is still full, Brother. But it's not easy—not without you. I don't know how long…

The memory of pulling Dmitri and Nico out of the deep, dark well they hid in from the Taliban resurfaced, quickly replaced by the words he spoke to me in Big Bear.

"You could have stopped this, Hermano," echoed the daydream version of my slain friend.

My heart raced in my chest as the Beast prowled for more territory. This time, I didn't use the *Sense,* wondering what would happen if I didn't stop it from enlarging its presence in me.

"Yo, Dipshit!" The angry male voice broke my descent into chaos, and I swiveled to see two masked men in hoodies.

"Whatchya doing here?" growled the larger one.

My anger simmered as I glowered back, "Free country, Fucker."

He bristled, and his hand moved to just beneath his sweatshirt while the smaller man tilted his head in my direction. My right hand dropped down, ready to pull the combat knife strapped to the small of my back.

"Stop your hand, or die here and now," I commanded.

"Oh shit. Stop, stop!" the smaller guy told the larger one, hand moving quickly to keep him from advancing. He dropped his mask. "Tanner! It's me, Emmanuel. Fuck. Too close..."

The rage subsided, and I dropped my neck gaiter and advanced to hug Emmanuel and shake hands with the guy who'd almost placed himself in my crosshairs.

Emmanuel confirmed Celeste's story and said they had been watching the mural at night.

"It's so fucked up, Homie. I can't recognize this place anymore," he said.

We both looked at the mural, each full of torment.

"This isn't over—just delayed until those killers are found. Right?"

So many emotions clashed inside, but I was saved from answering them when a police car entered the circle. Emmanuel and his friend quickly melted into the alley behind the restaurant, but I remained standing.

When the police car stopped in front of me, I saw Officer Dee in the passenger seat and another male cop in the driver's seat.

"Good to see you, Tanner," she said, her pretty black face fully visible, with her long hair up in a bun. "Is everything okay?"

Warmth replaced my cold anger as I recalled how the young cop had shown bravery. She allowed a smile to rise, and it felt like she'd like to speak with me further.

"I'm okay, Officer. Just heading home after a run," I replied.

She nodded, and they drove off, leaving me with my feet planted where my old life had ended.

DISPLACED

– Venice Beach, CA –
Monday, August 10, 2020

It was just after midnight when I entered the home quietly and tiptoed up to our room. As the hot water hit my sweaty body, I deeply inhaled and resisted the impulse to cough.

Finally clean and ready for bed, I checked on the kids, who were sound asleep. Dani was still snoring softly when I crept gently into bed. Careful not to disturb my queen, I slowly moved my right leg close enough to feel her warmth before I dropped into what I hoped would be a deep sleep.

★ ★ ★

"Me alone," grumbled the Demon
as he advanced toward Nico, fists up.
In the dark alley that looks like a tunnel,
a young boy is screaming in pain.
My body frozen with fear.

I close my eyes, my neck throbbing and inflamed.
All of Alfa looks at me with sadness.
My eyes open again, and the alley is still there,
but now I see the Dragon Skull painted in
red blood on the road.
"Who am I?" the Beast growls.
"Alley rhymes with Ali... Alley rhymes with Ali..."

"Alley rhymes with Ali... Alley rhymes with Ali...." My angel was holding my head, caressing my face slowly, whispering the words that had brought me back before.

I opened my eyes and kissed her hand, and we both dropped back to sleep without another word.

The late morning sunlight warmed me until I woke up naturally to a quiet house.

When I reached the kitchen, I found Dani's note that she had taken the kids to the Ramirez hacienda.

I paused at the counter and took in my surroundings. Everything remained the same, but something was amiss.

I can't remember how it was before.

The search for my pre-pandemic world upset me enough that I spilled some of the boiling coffee on the floor.

"Damn it," I growled, noticing my needless anger.

My phone rang and I reached for it with one hand while grabbing paper towels with the other.

"Hey, Sleepyhead," she giggled until she realized my mood was slightly sour. "Go surfing, Baby."

Thank you for not mentioning last night.

"I will. Love you," I replied and was grateful when I heard the click.

Dressed in my spring suit and holding my shortboard, it almost felt like something I could recall.

The last week has been a lifetime.

My feet remembered their way to the beach police station, and my heart swelled seeing Todd on the hill with his flags. He was deep in a conversation with a few folks, so I just waved to him, and he returned it with a wide smile.

My next stop was the station, where I said hi to the cops and asked them to pass a message to Holden before turning to the big waves breaking in the distance.

The swell was strong, and many surfers were ignoring the stringent lockdown order about being at the beach. After saying hi to some who knew me and mentioned not seeing me for a while, I made haste for the water.

Wave after wave, my body united with the board, leaving nothing else. No past, no future... just the present.

Eventually, I looked back and saw the lone black cop waiting for me on the beach.

Time's up.

★ ★ ★

When Holden handed me one of the coffee cups he held, I accepted it with gratitude. He was masked, but after he looked around, he lowered it under his chin.

At least that.

"Heard from Dee. Said she saw you last night by the restaurant." His tone was steady but absent of brotherly warmth.

I nodded.

"I can't believe the constant vandalism." He shook his head in disgust. "Dee took it upon herself to patrol the place."

"She's a good one," I replied, and he smiled like a proud father.

I see you, Brother.

"Do you ever think about our early years?" he wondered as we both sipped from our coffee and watched the surfers. He was referring to my "golden years" in Venice when I was initially discharged from the Marines and moved into the neighborhood just before Nico enlisted.

"Those were good times," I said. "I knew nobody, and suddenly I had Nico and you as friends."

Holden beamed and we lost several minutes exchanging ridiculous stories from that period of three unlikely friends in a crazy neighborhood by the ocean.

His face turned serious.

"Even back then, I had some questions about you..."

My body tensed up, and I wasn't sure if it was his implication or the growing itch in my chest.

"What's the fucking point?" Holden sighed and shook his head. "Can we have a moment of truce?"

"Yes, we can."

I smiled at my friend.

Will it last, though?

He looked around, eyes narrowed, before he turned to face me.

"Stay safe, and please don't get in our way. It's getting more and more dangerous here."

Cold rage coursed through my already cold, wet body.

Nobody can stop me, dear friend—just a delay.

"Moment of truce, Brother," I answered honestly, and he eventually nodded slowly, accepting the terms of our arrangement.

The rest of the day was spent with Dani and the kids until the little monsters were obliged to go to their beds and give their exhausted dad a break.

I was eager to crash until I reached the bedroom door and found Dani reclined on our bed in sexy lingerie, erasing everything but lust until we were both spent and fell asleep in each other's arms.

It felt like only a moment later when her hand shook my shoulder until my eyes opened.

"What?" I asked, seeing the alarm on her face and feeling the weird sensation in my mouth.

"Go look at the mirror."

I dragged my achy body out of bed, wobbled to our master bathroom, and turned the light on.

Oh fuck...

INFECTED

"So far, none of us got it. Just focus on your family and let us know if you need anything." Roberto's update and fatherly tone brought a little relief.

I was in my studio, looking at the mirror, my right hand on my swollen red neck.

"Good, good. I called everyone who came in contact with me, and none have gotten it so far," I replied.

Which is good, cuz I feel like shit.

"Get better," he said before we hung up the phone.

I dropped my hand and walked to the desk where there were two vials full of dark red blood next to my computer. A chuckle escaped me when I recalled Dani's face when she learned her blood was needed.

My queen hates syringes, I thought as I heard her voice and the sound of three pairs of feet scurrying around in the house above me.

My ear vibrated as Jack's call came in.

"The messenger should be there in about thirty minutes. Are the samples ready?"

Looking at the liquid in the glass, I sighed.

"Yes. Ready."

"Good..." He told me they were doing a marathon testing on everyone, including Custer, who I'd seen just a few days earlier. "Do you need anything?"

"Nah. We'll ride it out here at home and have all we need," I said.

My breathing was labored by the time I got to the top of the stairs, and I could feel the weakness spreading through my body.

Dani was looking at her phone in the kitchen while the kids were watching morning cartoons in the living room.

"Hungry, Baby?" she asked without raising her eyes to look at me.

"No. I'm fine," I replied as I slowly approached her. Her neck still looked normal, which was to be expected, as I was the family's "patient zero."

She quickly closed her phone and shoved it into her pocket.

What...?

"Did anyone else get it?" she asked.

"It will take a few days to know, but hopefully, it will remain in this house. I'm sorry it's going to keep you from working with your furry friends."

She returned my smile and surprised me with a new detail for our self-quarantine. Our neighbor had offered his yard as a great place to relax outside with the kids without infecting the rest of the neighbors.

She's fast. Already talking and arranging.

"Should we alert the health department?" she asked.

I wouldn't trust them for shit.

"No, Honey. We're taking all the steps to isolate ourselves, and you have already notified our neighbors. We're fine."

Her eyes narrowed momentarily, but she sighed, as she always did when my other world hung like a fog between us.

"Okay. Then let's talk to the kids."

Yeah, let's do it from the couch, I thought, realizing how hard it was to stand.

THE VISIT

Ari and Leelee played with their toys on the grass in the back of our complex, where our neighbor allowed us to enjoy some sunlight and air while "self-quarantining." It had been two days since my throat had swelled up.

Thank God this thing doesn't affect them, I thought as I watched my kids. *Besides the fact that their parents are in no shape to join them.*

Dani rested inside, as the Dragon had made her tired beyond what was expected.

It's okay. I have quite a time debt to make good on with these two.

The kids were without masks, but I had my gaiter covering my neck and a surgical mask over my mouth and nose. Even properly distanced, I did it out of respect for my neighbors, who probably all knew about our situation. Some came by to say hi and others just waved from afar.

"No!" exclaimed Lil to Ari when he tried to grab the toy she was holding. It was one of her first spoken words, and she wielded it like a club on everyone in the house.

The warm sun felt good on my achy body, as the Dragon had done a number on all my systems. Wild headaches and constant fatigue in addition to the discomfort of the throat swelling.

The blood results confirmed we had a new strain that had been scantily reported around the globe thus far. My infection was the most matured, confirming my suspicion that I had brought it home, most likely from Chicago.

Poor Moss.

Jack had executed a reverse investigation and ascertained that Moss was infected and so was Alfa. They were all quarantined, including some folks at the Ranch who had come in contact with them.

A new strain... riots... My mind was too sluggish as it tried to solve the riddle. *The migrants maybe, being moved around by the Travelers?*

I was about to dive into that rabbit hole when the Israeli agent sent me an urgent text. Two officials had entered the complex with a neighbor's help.

Oh boy.

"Ari, keep Lil with you and watch something she'd like as well. Daddy needs to do something."

I handed him the tablet. He grabbed it and ran back to his sister, who giggled and waited with a smile.

Two masked people approached us from the other side of the courtyard, dressed in cheap businesslike clothes.

They work for the city.

I walked toward them, planting myself just outside of our unit. They stopped about ten feet away and pulled out their identification.

"We're Department of Health inspectors. Are you Tanner Washington?" asked the woman whose entire face was hidden beneath the oversized sunglasses and wide mask.

"I am."

I used the *Sense* to override my exhaustion and irritation.

"We're following up on a lead that your family is infected, yet we've found no record for testing. So, we figured to stop by." Her tone was a gross combination of suspicion and condescension.

"A lead, huh?" I replied, glancing toward Chelsea's open window in the unit closest to the gate.

"Well, are you infected, Sir?" asked the man, whose blue eyes looked tired.

I brought down the gaiter to show them my red neck. Both of them nodded, and the woman took one step back.

"Now that you know, is there anything else you need?" I didn't try to hide my disdain for the entire conversation.

They looked at each other, and the man babbled for several minutes about the need for proper isolation and procedures, which I assured him we were taking.

When they then turned on their heels and left, the heavy feeling that had started with their arrival remained.

This isn't the end of it. They were fishing. Damn it.

Turning back to the house, I saw Dani standing by our door, eyes blazing.

She must have heard the whole thing.

"We need to stay on our toes when outside in public view. Someone is after us…"

Her face contorted with anger.

"Who? Chelsea?"

"Pray that it's her and nothing else…" I grumbled. "Come on, kids. Grab your toys. It's time to go inside."

My phone chirped as I picked up the last few toys the kids couldn't carry on their own. It was Holden.

The black and white police SUV waited in the parking lot outside our walled complex. I stopped ten feet away from the car, close enough for me to see Holden in the passenger seat and Officer Dee driving him.

I nodded at Dee.

"Hey." I kept a good distance from his window. "You'll never believe who visited me today..."

"This is fucked up," he replied after I told him about my encounter with the inspectors. "Health Department doesn't do home visits..." he added, his tone troubled. "Do you know who snitched?"

"I think so, but it doesn't matter now. Just watch and let me know if you hear anything."

Questions in his eyes, he nodded and kept them to himself.

"I'll let you know if something comes up."

PRESUMPTIONS

The special messenger picked up the new batch of blood samples, which included the children's this time, even though it had cost Dani and me a lot of grief and yelling. I wanted to ensure we were all clear of the Dragon and have it in writing.

Just in case, I thought as I watched the messenger drive away.

The late morning sun felt good on my skin, but it reminded me how isolated we'd been since the two-day health department visit. After the inspectors left, Dani and I had agreed to keep everyone inside to prevent further escalation with the local government.

Her words still echoed in my mind, "You haven't been home enough to see what's happening around here. Even the mayor went on TV to welcome snitches on those who break quarantine."

Government-sanctioned rats belong in dictatorships, not America.

I was still out by the gate, enjoying my moment of freedom, when my thoughts turned to Chelsea as the cause of everything going wrong. My father had tried to discourage me from jumping to conclusions, but it didn't work.

It's her.

I sighed loudly and turned back toward the house, determined to use some of my slowly returning energy for work before it disappeared again.

My eyes slowly took in the stats on my screen. In one day, the nation recorded over fifty thousand new reported infections, while the daily death toll increased above one thousand people.

Fucking madness. They did it without a single shot fired.

"Tanner! Ari got outside," yelled Dani from the kitchen.

Damn it.

They'd been fighting in the kitchen for the last twenty minutes. He wasn't good at being trapped within four walls for too long, but I didn't think he'd disobey his mother so blatantly.

I closed the laptop, grabbed the mask, and ran out of the studio into the courtyard. Ari had a few places he liked to hang around, and my gut told me to check the vegetable garden first in the back of one of the neighbor's units.

When I arrived, he was flushed red with anger and his fists were clenched as he looked up defiantly at Chelsea towering over him from a safe distance.

Of course!

"Ari, get over here."

I noticed the quick smirk that graced his angelic face before he ran toward me.

You little devil!

"He wasn't supposed to leave the house. I'm sorry for that," I apologized as I grabbed his hand and turned us back toward the house.

"Your son should know better than to leave the house without a mask. Also, he shouldn't be going around the complex." She spit the words like daggers at my back.

I looked up to see Dani rushing out with Lil in her arms.

Oh shit.

"Go to your mother. Now," I commanded Ari.

Eyes wide in surprise, he hurried toward Dani. My eyes locked with my queen's long enough to assure her I had this. She sighed and nodded, and I turned back to face Chelsea.

Fucking Comrade mask. Fucking woman!

Two car horns broke the tension, and I saw the police SUV stop in front of the complex.

"What? Suddenly you're *not* going to harass me. At least these assholes are good for something!" Chelsea was trying to provoke me.

"We're not done, Chelsea."

"No, we're not," she replied.

"Was that who you think ratted you out? That woman?" asked Holden.

He'd come alone this time, and we sat in his car in our spot in the parking lot outside my complex.

I nodded, and he sighed.

"Well, it was a woman, but not this one…" Holden shared that after some digging, he'd discovered that it was Victoria who had pushed the right buttons at the health department. "I wouldn't have found it if she didn't have so many enemies already," he added with a grunt.

My surprise was genuine, as I'd barely paid any attention to the councilwoman since my tense exchange with her during the funeral convoy standoff with LAPD.

"I couldn't find a shred of why she would target you. After all, you guys never tested anywhere," he continued.

"When did she report us?" I asked, sensing a growing pit in my stomach.

"Monday, August 10th," answered Holden, his eyes narrowing as his mind was probably tracking the reason for my question.

That's when it started. Nobody knew…

"Yeah, isn't that the day your throat got red?" he asked, pointing at my neck that finally looked normal again. "You called me to let me know to check myself."

He's fishing again...

I nodded, and he continued, "Where do you think you got it anyway? Didn't you just come into town? And why would Victoria target you like this?"

I don't want to break our truce so fast.

"Can you please update me if they make more efforts to harass my family?" I asked, completely deflecting all his questions.

His dark face flushed a deep red, but he nodded in resignation.

"I'll do my best, but you must be careful, Tanner. Don't break quarantine until you're cleared. They won't turn a blind eye as I do..."

"Appreciate you, Man," I said as I exited the car, already plotting my next steps.

I filed a report with the RCC about all that Holden had revealed to me and then waited for the call. The ear vibration started twenty minutes later while I was looking out through the studio's glass door, seething.

"Holden was correct. The councilwoman was the one to start everything with the health department," confirmed Jack. "We're going to keep an eye on your local government now that they've targeted you."

"Yeah. I blamed my neighbor too fast. But I still don't trust her." I used the *Sense* to calm the anger that flared every time I thought of that brainless parrot.

"Son, since Alfa is quarantined, I've got an Old Glory team ready to come and evacuate all of you back to the Ranch. Your team almost rebelled when they heard they'd been sidelined," he sighed.

"What? Why would we do that?"

"This councilwoman worries me, Tanner. Nobody should have known that you were infected in Chicago," he said.

"Not exactly nobody," I replied, feeling the noose tightening around me.

But who? Why?

"Yeah. I know. We've got a leak somewhere," he grumbled. "Anyway, I'm not keen on having my family and grandkids behind the lines, so can you convince your hotheaded wife to see reason? She can rest, and the Ranch will provide it."

Rest? She's already bossing me around.

"It's a waste of time, Dad. We're not leaving," I answered. "Definitely not like this."

"What do you mean 'not like this?'" pushed Jack.

The Beast began to stir after being dormant for days.

"First, they might consider me making this exact move and intercepting us like criminals who break quarantine," I replied.

"Weak argument, but go on," said Jack.

I pushed against my irritation.

"Second, Dani and I would never just cut and run without saying anything to our friends. Dani is practically a surrogate parent right now with Celeste's kids, not to mention my role."

"Fine. Go on." His tone was resigned.

"That's it," I responded tightly.

"Bullshit, Son. What's the other reason?"

"Tell him the truth," suggested the Beast.

"I want them to reveal themselves. To see how far they will go." Anger had seeped into my tone.

"This makes no sense, Son, and you know it. You're making the fight personal."

My fists clenched, and I resisted the urge to slam my desk.

"You don't understand, Dad. It's all personal! Millions of Americans are going through this, and their local government targets many for this or that edict. They don't have protection and support as I do. It's driving me nuts!"

"What...?" he pressed and warmed his tone. "What is driving you nuts?"

"My guilt! Okay? I'm guilty, and I know it. I was there when this abomination was first revealed, and now there's this!" I let go of the resistance and slammed my fist on my desk. "How could I be so stupid?"

"Fine! Mistakes were made. I get it. But you're back now and fighting. You can carry it from elsewhere. What's really stopping you from bailing out?"

Nico's words rang like bells of doom, "You could have stopped it, Hermano…" and my heart raced.

"I gave my word to a grieving father," I replied.

"Even if your family is the price? Are you ready for that?" His fatherly tone had been cooled by the voice of reason.

We spent a moment of silence, as he must have noticed that my vitals spiked and I needed a moment.

"Okay, Son. What are our next moves? Focus."

Thank you.

"Are the 'docs in order?'" I asked.

"Yes, Son. I spoke with Eli earlier this week, and he mentioned something about it in case it would come to that."

"I got it then. Just let me know if you hear about them coming again."

"Do you think they're coming?" he asked.

"Yes, they are," growled the Beast with satisfaction.

"Only one way to find out."

FOR YOUR SAFETY

– Venice Beach, CA –
Saturday, August 15, 2020

"**I** hate it," growled Dani, turning her head away from the sight of me pricking her finger with the small needle. She put her other hand on the desk in my studio to brace herself.

"Baby, this isn't a syringe," I pleaded with her, suppressing my laughter.

"Oh, shut up already and finish!"

She kept her eyes in the direction of the early morning light coming through the patio glass door.

"I'm done," I said, as the tiny amount of blood filled the sample plate.

Snatching back her finger like a wounded animal, she rose from her chair, blue eyes rumbling like a storm that wanted to drown me.

Yeah, I'm tired of it too, Baby.

With every day cooped inside, our nerves frayed a bit further. The combination of lingering bodily exhaustion and energy-filled children was not wearing well on either of us.

"They're coming," whispered the Beast, sensing my desires, and prickling my body with anticipation.

"What?" Her forceful tone surprised me, and I looked up into her eyes that held a question I didn't understand.

"Huh?"

"Your face... Never mind." She shook her head. "The kids will be up soon!" she grumbled her sign of departure.

"Are you good with the plan?" I asked.

Her mouth closed briefly before she rhymed back the steps I gave her. She addressed every detail, and I nodded in appreciation.

When she was done, instead of leaving, she placed her hands on her hips, an angry smirk rising as dots connected behind her narrowed eyes.

Oh shit.

"Tanner Washington... you bastard!"

Bracing myself, I stood up to face her as she advanced slowly toward me.

"You want this, don't you?"

"What?" I tried one more time to deflect, but it was hopeless.

"Don't 'what what' me! You think they're coming for us, don't you?"

My face hardened, and it took her aback for a split second when I stood my ground, fists clenched.

"Yeah, I don't think they're done with us. It can come at any time." It was my turn to growl.

Her face reddened with anger.

"You didn't answer my question. Do you *want* this to happen?"

"She sees me... Don't deny her," whispered the Beast.

I resisted the urge from taking me over, but some of it spilled out, "Yes. I do."

Shock replaced anger, but only for a moment. She launched her body forward, slapping my face at lightning speed.

Fuck.

"Are you serious? Are we your bait? How could you?" she barked at me, switching to Hebrew in the middle of her questions. "We've been living under this crap for months now. Every day is a living nightmare..." She vented, tying all the horrors of the pandemic, the riots, and Nico's death. "I'm barely holding on some days, and then you pull this stunt!"

The shackles tightened. My devotion and love for my family constricted my breath for a moment, holding my darkness at bay.

"For now..." the Beast's words echoed and faded.

My hands reached for hers, and she reluctantly reached back.

"I'm sorry."

Her eyes searched mine until she eventually nodded and mumbled about getting ready for our uninspiring morning routine.

The small plastic comb removed the old wax like a knife cutting butter. I'd cleaned most of my boards and was working on the last one when an unexpected visitor arrived.

"Rabbi!" I heard Ari's voice shout from the balcony above.

A sense of warmth filling my tired chest, I dropped the comb and reached for the mask hanging by the front door.

Opening the door, I had to raise my hand to shield my eyes from the glaring noon sunlight.

"Good eyes, Scout," I told Ari as I stepped outside.

Across the courtyard, Rabbi Shemtov was walking toward us, dressed in board shorts, an oversized Hawaiian shirt, and a straw hat, holding a nine-foot longboard. He looked wet, and his beaming face confirmed my assessment.

The power of the ocean.

"Ahoy, Captain," I called through the mask.

Shemtov laughed as he approached, dropped the board by me, and surprised me with a firm hug.

"Come on. It's been days since you got it. I'm not afraid," assured the rabbi, sensing my concern.

We bantered about surf and the neighborhood before Shemtov asked, "Would you mind if we pray quickly for your complete healing?"

I glanced up at Ari, who was watching us closely. The rabbi followed my gaze and made a face that made

Ari giggle. It helped to quell my inherent resistance to religious ceremonies.

"Of course, Rabbi," I replied, and he led the blessing, with me echoing it in Hebrew.

"Today, I prayed for you. Maybe one day you'll do me the honors," he said after we'd finished.

His words begged me to quiet my mind and reflect on them, but my phone rang and chirped at the same time.

"Holden," I called into my earbud while my eyes scanned the text from the RCC.

"They're coming for you," he started.

Quickly, I activated the "chip record" feature via the phone, which allowed a Rogue to use the phone to record all signals around the user and then store them on the chip, from which it would be uploaded to the RCC as a ping of urgent interest.

"Who's coming?" I asked, motioning for Shemtov to wait a moment.

His words confirmed my worst fear and woke the Beast from its slumber.

They were coming to take my children away.

FOLLOW TANNER'S JOURNEY

Where is Tanner leading them?

Follow his journey **@Tanneralfa on X** and
TannerWashington.com and stay tuned for...

ASSAF RAZ

Assaf Raz immigrated from the Israel to Venice Beach, CA, in his early twenties and began the journey to citizenship in a country he had long studied and revered. For more than two decades, he built his American Dream through real estate and a handful of other entrepreneurial pursuits. After a spiritual rebirth in his early thirties, he found the woman from his dreams, started a family, and began to write. First, he wrote a short memoir about his awakening *(Rite of Passage)* and then he started a novel fueled by his love of Roman history and the alternative history genre. He quickly set aside that project for the Old Glory series when his concerns about America piqued in 2020 during the lockdown and riots that unfolded in the streets where he lived and worked. Assaf and his family have been on the road since 2022.

www.ingramcontent.com/pod-product-compliance
Lightning Source LLC
Chambersburg PA
CBHW060557300726
48975CB00005B/1357